ASCENDANT

AN AGRIPUNK THRILLER

THE MARTINIERE LEGACY BOOK TWO

JOYCE REYNOLDS-WARD

CHAPTER 1

"Mr. Martiniere, Ms. Barkley, we're on final approach," the pilot of the small corporate jet announced. "Going to be some turbulence."

Ruby looked up from her computer projections and glanced out the window as they entered a cloud bank. She shivered, dismissed the display, and tucked the comp chip back into the fist-sized scanner she always carried. Then she made sure her seat belt was securely fastened. Across the cabin, her business partner and ex-husband Gabriel Martiniere winced as he copied her actions.

"Thought we'd be able to avoid the early wave from Hurricane Charley," he muttered, rubbing the left shoulder where he'd been shot six months ago, just before their lives had changed and they had gotten back together. "At least that was the original forecast. Feeling the barometric pressure change though."

"You've got your meds?"

Gabe nodded. He slipped his hand into a pocket and pulled out a pill dispenser, shaking one into his hand. "Might as well take one now. Non-drowsy."

"That's good." Ruby eyed him thoughtfully, concerned.

Six months ago, Moondance, Gabe's home ranch, had burned. He had moved to her Double R ranch in Northeastern

Oregon as part of their biobot business launch. Since then, she had become more aware of the lingering side effects from Gabe's bout with the nasty G9 virus that had killed his second wife Rachel and left him impaired. Gabe could cover up a lot—but they shared a bedroom, if not a bed, due to space constraints at the Double R. He couldn't hide everything from her.

Gabe leaned back in his seat and closed his eyes, fingers tightening on the armrests until white showed under the brown on his knuckles. "I fucking *hate* small planes. Even corporate jets aren't big enough."

"At least it's not as bad as when you were hopping from rodeo to rodeo in during Cowboy Christmas in July," she said.

"Oh God, how the hell did I ever keep from getting killed during that era?" Gabe opened his eyes and freed one hand to rub his left shoulder again. "I was an idiot."

"Sheer luck and being drunk out of your skull."

Gabe snorted. "And the pills to get through it. Don't forget the pain pills. Typical dumbass saddle bronc rider. But it changed when we got together."

"At least you never rode bulls."

"I'm not *that* damn crazy. Those were the guys whose money I took when we played poker."

The plane bounced and Ruby's fingers also clenched the armrests, hiding her own fear. Gabe at least had an excuse for not liking to fly. His parents and sister had been killed in a plane crash when he was twelve, and he ended up in the care of his uncle Philip, who had always hated Gabe.

For her it was simple dislike of flight.

But it was time to meet on-site with their third partner in BMS Associates, Jeff Swait, and see what progress he had made in integrating his Swaitbot with two forms of her current RubyBot to create the RS Defender and the RS Protector. They hoped to have the prototypes on the market by next spring.

Amazing how Martiniere money manages to fast-track product approvals.

It had taken her years to earn approvals for the RubyBot. But that was before the Martinieres came into her life.

Then again, there were a lot of things that she hadn't anticipated would be smoothed out by Martiniere money, whether it was Gabe's or his cousin Justine's. Travel. Financing lab expansions. Building repair and maintenance. Not needing to worry about paying bills.

She was still getting used to this life.

"Hope it's not so stormy that we can't run the tests." Gabe dropped his hand from his shoulder, wincing.

"Not supposed to be." The plane steadied as they dropped below the cloud cover. Cloudy but at least not windy or rainy yet.

And Justine vets her pilots meticulously, Ruby reminded herself.

Gabe's cousin might appear to be an airhead on the surface, but that was just for appearances. Underneath that superficial façade Justine was as much of a detail and control freak as any of the Martinieres.

Including Brandon.

But then again, their son got that as much from her as from Gabe.

The plane delicately touched down on Swait's airstrip—one of Justine's contributions to BMS Associates as a silent fourth in the operation, along with the open use of her three planes. *Can't science like you,* she had said when they had objected to her insistence that they put in airstrips at the Double R, Gabe's Moondance, and Swait's Arkansas farm. *But I can contribute to your safety and security, and minimize the threat from Daddy-damned-dearest.*

Daddy-damned-dearest was just one of the diminutives that Justine used to mockingly refer to her father Philip. Head of the Martiniere Group, infamous not only for their agricultural technology, data gathering, and pharmaceutical operations but the slightly shady recreational body modifying business...and their heavy participation in human trafficking involving mind-controlled indentured workers with bodies modified to their contract owners' specs.

Gabe had testified against Philip and adopted a new identity as a result, before he met Ruby. Their divorce twenty-one years ago had been fueled by Gabe's fears that Philip was going to attack Ruby and Brandon—and Philip's use of mind control on Gabe kept him from telling her who he really was. But he'd not told Ruby about his worries concerning Philip—until six months ago. Sure, some of it had been shaped by the Martiniere mind control technology that kept Gabe from saying even his own name until the G9 wiped that programming from his brain. But still—

A lot had changed since then. Ruby, Gabe, and Jeff had successfully gamed the AgInnovator, the oldest of the reality shows that provided funding for new agricultural technology. The Innovator had brought Ruby and Gabe back together, and they found new allies in Jeff Swait and other farmers and ranchers deeply involved in agtech to counter the effects of climate change.

The plane taxied to a stop. The copilot came back to open the cabin door and lower the stairway. As a wave of humid heat washed into the cabin, Ruby patted the top of her head to ensure that her silver-streaked red hair was still confined in its snug bun. Then she pulled on a flat-crowned, wide-brimmed white hat and tied the long silken scarf ties under her chin. Her typical summer straw Western hat wouldn't fit over the bun and wasn't professional enough for a business trip like this. Or at least that was Justine's opinion.

Ruby stood and stretched, grateful now that Justine had insisted on wardrobe upgrades, aided and abetted by Ruby's old rodeo queen advisor Vickie. The cream-colored silk—*real silk!*—shell and slacks felt much more comfortable in this humidity than the jeans and lightweight long-sleeved snap-button cotton shirts she wore at the ranch.

Gabe smiled down at her. "You look good," he said as he

donned his own hat, a gray trilby that matched his gray slacks and shirt, and shrugged into a lightweight gray jacket that covered his shoulder holster. He grunted as he struggled to get the jacket over his stiff left shoulder. Ruby helped him get it settled.

"So do you." She made a face as she stepped back to study him. "I just don't like that shade of gray. Doesn't go with the brown skin."

He shrugged. "It's the Martiniere image. I don't want to stand out." He gestured for her to go first.

"Tan would be better," she said as she picked up her bag, automatically checking to make sure that her snub-nosed .38 was secured in the carry pocket. She still didn't like carrying all the time—an artifact of *her* past—but at least Justine knew the best solutions for concealing weapons for all different levels of dress, from business casual to white-tie formal.

"I don't *like* tan," Gabe complained as he extracted his folding cane from its holster pocket on his belt. "Philip wears that all the time."

"I need to sic Justine or Vickie on you then, because I really don't like that shade on you."

It made him appear less healthy, bringing out the paleness that was part of post-G9 syndrome. Vickie Chandler, Ruby's former rodeo queen advisor who was now one of her dress consultants, had complained about the look of that gray tone on Gabe as well.

"Like hell," he grumbled behind her as she stepped out of the plane. "You keep my cousin out of my wardrobe. And that includes Vickie, while you're at it."

God, he's grumpy. Must really be hurting today.

She chose to ignore his comment for that reason and strode toward Jeff Swait, leaving Gabe to walk more slowly behind her. Swait waited for them at the edge of the tarmac, wearing green shorts, sandals, and a colorful green and blue tropical print short sleeved shirt that looked good against his dark skin. A tan trilby sat on top of his tightly curled black hair.

"Gabe, Ruby. Hope the trip wasn't too rough. Sounds like Hurricane Charley is camping out right at landfall for a few hours. Good for us." Jeff grinned as Gabe joined them.

They bowed in greeting. She already felt sweat popping out where her hat made contact with her head.

God, it's muggy. How do people stand living in this? I couldn't do it.

"It was okay until the landing," Ruby said.

"Well, I'll do my best to get you two in and out of here before the storm hits. Should be a good test for both Defender and Protector. Plus I seem to have had a breakthrough with Pollinator."

"Now *that's* some good news," Gabe said.

They headed for the electric truck waiting a few yards away, Ruby and Jeff matching Gabe's hobbled pace.

"Three of us will fit in front," Jeff said.

Ruby nodded. She climbed in easily and settled herself in the middle—a bench seat instead of the bucket seats in the trucks she and Gabe drove. Gabe wrestled himself in. Jeff set the auto-drive and collapsed the steering wheel. Ruby fished her water bottle out of her purse and took a couple of swallows before passing it to Gabe.

"I think you'll like what you see with the Defender," Jeff said. "It really wants to go bigger, and I've tweaked those parameters." He hesitated. "I got some info from Temira Cho. The non-indentured farm labor pool seems to be much smaller than in previous years—almost nonexistent, in fact. And the indentured ones that are showing up are *different*. More mechanical."

"Really," Gabe said. "Have you seen any of them?" He pulled a handkerchief out of his pocket and dabbed at the sweat on his brow.

"The pool sent me two of them when they couldn't find me any non-indentured workers. But those indentureds are problematic around the Defender. It keys on them and not on any stray biobots left in the field. We had an incident when we tried to use them."

"That's troubling," Ruby said, biting her lower lip. The Defender had evolved from a counterbot her lab had developed last spring. Rogue killbots had showed up in various cultivated grain fields, not just at the Double R, but at her neighbors and at Moondance. Normally killbots worked to eliminate previous biobots that hadn't shut down and decomposed like their programming required. The killbots' own programming was supposed to limit them for both duration and location. But the rogues wouldn't stop, and spread aggressively.

The counterbot prototypes of the Defender had behaved well —except for one of Ruby's fields that had been tampered with by some of Philip's indentured workers. There, when that same interference had routed a drone cam over the field, the counterbots had attacked the cam and brought it down, leaving no trace once they were done with it.

"Yeah," Jeff said. "What happened with those two indentureds reminded me of that incident you had with the cam."

"How bad was it with the indentured?" Ruby asked.

"Temporary immobilization. The Defender swarmed them hard."

"That could be useful," Ruby said.

"Did you scan the indentureds to see what implants they might have?" Gabe asked.

"I didn't even get the chance," Jeff said. "They reported it immediately to their labor pool administrator once I got the bots off of them. My lease was cancelled and they were off the place before I could do anything."

Gabe sighed. He tapped his fingers on his cane. "Any idea of their origins?"

"Blotted AgI identification tattoo on the left hand," Jeff said. "A fresh trefoil tattoo on the neck. I didn't see it, Carrie did."

AgI. The parent company of the AgInnovator competition,

also involved in agtech development and specialty ag indentured labor pools as well as loan operations for farmers and ranchers.

This is not good. Ruby's gut tightened.

"What color was the trefoil?" Gabe asked.

"Red and black."

Gabe's lips tightened. "Martiniere Group, then. Spying on us."

"I thought so," Jeff sighed. "It's taking longer to get workers on site as a result. That's why I talked to Temira. To see if it was a Midwestern thing."

"How's she doing?" Ruby asked.

Temira Cho had been one of their competitors in the Superhero, the first one cut from competition. She had gone on to place two levels down in the competition, in the Star Innovator level which granted five years of funding at $100,000 per year, as long as she could show consistent progress with her program. But it was a far cry from the $3.75 million for five years with no check-ins that was a part of the Superhero, or even the three million for five years that Ruby, Gabe, and Jeff had earned by filing a collaboration agreement to end the competition.

"She's making progress," Jeff said. "But she's noticed the same thing with the labor pools in Illinois. Minimal non-indentureds. And of the indentured, not many options besides the more mechanistic, body-modded ones."

Gabe shook his head. "Is she using them?"

"No. Higher expense but she's going with non-indentured, non-implanted support workers. She has more labor resources available there than I do. It's always been tough here to find non-indentured labor, and when we do use indentureds, I try to find ways to buy them free. I hate using indentured workers. And these new ones—no. I don't want them anywhere near my place."

"I imagine so." Gabe tightened his lips. "Were you able to get any pictures of the indentureds in question?"

"Now *that* I can give you," Jeff said. He extracted his scanner and popped out the computer chip, calling up a projection. "Here's their full-body ID shots."

Gabe and Ruby peered at the projection. Gabe reached into it and rotated the picture. "We need to send copies of this to Kris and Brandon. They'll know more about these body-mod versions." His lips tightened. "The second one resembles one of my kidnappers. But that person didn't have a Martiniere trefoil or an AgI diamond on them. Then." He zoomed in on the left hand that showed a blue-green blur.

"Go ahead," Jeff said.

Gabe nodded. His fingers danced in the projection. "Copies sent to Kris, Brandon, Justine, and us."

"Might want to send copies to Charlie and Tim," Ruby said. Charlie was the ranch manager for the Double R and Tim for Moondance. "See if any indentured like that starts sniffing around the ranches."

"Good idea." Gabe repeated the action. Then he leaned back into the seat with a heavy sigh. Jeff closed the projection.

The truck swung around to halt by a grain field where several people waited by bot growboxes. Ruby squinted at the field, not quite recognizing the grain.

Swaitrice? Must be.

Jeff had originally been developing biobots to improve the drought tolerance of dryland rice, breeding a complimentary strain that required less diagnostic work from the bots while increasing carbon and water uptakes.

"Here we are. Looks like Carrie has everything ready to roll," Jeff said.

"Is that some of your Swaitrice?" she asked.

Jeff grimaced. "Yeah. This field didn't work well with the Swaitbots. It's really frustrating because this substrain has some desirable characteristics I'd like to use. But the RNA in this version doesn't respond to bot manipulation, so—" he shrugged. "Might as well kill off the Swaitbots and see if I can still recover some rice for the harvest. It'll produce something, at least."

Ruby waited while Gabe eased out, then joined him. They followed Jeff over to the people by the rectangular growboxes that resembled beehives, only twice the size. A dark-skinned woman with hair wrapped in a colorful red, blue, and yellow cloth headed for them.

"Ruby, Gabe, this is my farm manager and sister, Carrie Swait," Jeff said. "Carrie, this is Ruby Barkley and Gabe Martiniere."

"Pleased to meet you," Carrie said, shaking hands with both Ruby and Gabe. "I've been really enjoying working with the RubyBot, especially the counterbot. It's really responsive."

"Oh, the counterbot isn't my work," Ruby said quickly. "My lab staff threw that one together last spring. Martin Thompson and Julie Paprivides. I'll pass your complements on to them."

"Please tell them it's solid work," Carrie said. "I think you'll like what we did with it."

Ruby walked alongside Carrie as Gabe and Jeff followed them to the boxes. She felt like she was walking through a wave of sweltering hot air that sucked at her legs and arms and weighed her down.

If it's hitting me this bad, what about Gabe?

She glanced back at him. Other than sweat beading on his forehead, he seemed to be all right as he talked to Jeff.

"Jeff said you had an incident with the Defender and indentureds," she said quietly, returning her focus to Carrie. "Gabe suspects that they were Martiniere Group spies."

"It wouldn't surprise me," Carrie said, tightening her lips. "They didn't act like typical indentureds."

"How so?"

"Their focus was wrong," Carrie said. "Most of the time the indentureds I've seen on other peoples' places are pretty much *tell me what to do, no questions asked*. No curiosity until they're on task. No distractions. These guys? Looking around. Almost like they had ADHD. I had to yell at them, and that's one of the things you *don't* normally need to do with indentureds. In fact, it's one of those things you *shouldn't* have to do with ag indentureds. At least that's what I was told when training."

"I wouldn't know. No labor pools where I am."

Carrie side-eyed Ruby. "No labor pools—not even with indentureds?"

"Not a big enough population where I am to justify the expense except for very specialized labor needs. Nearest ag labor pools are in Hood River, Ontario, and Hermiston, and those are three-to-five hour drives away. Plenty of people in Thunder County either do contract work or are looking for side jobs. Plus I have interns from the local high school. I had to go to Portland and Hood River to find the two labor pool workers I have on site."

"Ah. Got it. Well, we have a lot of indentureds here but no independent contractors and darn few side hustle workers," Carrie sighed. "Looks like I'm going to need to find a different option. There's almost nothing in the labor pool this year other than ones like these two. Definitely no non-indentured. When I'm looking for indentureds, I'm trying to get them toward the end of their contract period so that we can free them, but—not many of those left. Mostly lifetimers anymore."

"You've been buying up contracts?"

Carrie nodded. "And giving them a bonus to get the hell out of town before they get shoved into indenture again. That happens a *lot* around here. Especially for nonwhites."

"Geez. I can send you the pitch proposal I sent my local high school for interns to give you some ideas. Or is that a problem here?"

"Hadn't thought of that option before," Carrie said. "But yeah, I'd love to develop interns."

"Maybe your state ag school as well."

Carrie pursed her lips thoughtfully. "Yeah. Thanks."

Ruby shrugged. "I've had to be creative over the years. Not a lot of money, and obviously not a lot of options."

"Your suggestions are helpful. Until now our labor pools have been the best choice for finding workers, so I've not needed to think about other options. So here we are." Carrie stopped by the boxes. She introduced the two men and one woman, all Swait relatives.

"Pleased to meet you." Gabe stood by Ruby, smiling at them, suddenly seeming to be bigger than usual as he put on his social face. Ruby murmured a response, muffling the desire to laugh at his posturing. After all, self-promotion and projection *was* part of deposing Philip as the Martiniere. Gabe had to play the role.

"Okay, let's get this show rolling," Jeff said, rubbing his hands together. "As I told Ruby and Gabe, this field isn't working well with the Swaitbot. So we're going to kill it."

"How tightly programmed to targets are these Defender bots?" Gabe asked.

"This was the field that we started to clear with the new indentureds," Sara, a Swait cousin, said. "After the first batch of counterbots swarmed the indentureds but didn't touch the Swaitbots in the field, I kept the algorithm pretty broad. I had no idea at all what they might have planted in the field or tampered with, and I didn't want to take a chance. I'm wiping everything out."

"Good idea," Gabe said. "Can I look at the algorithm?"

"Of course."

Gabe and Sara stepped aside as Sara brought up a projection. Gabe focused on it, poking at several lines of programming, a smile spreading across his face as he became more immersed in studying it. Ruby turned to Jeff.

"Should we wait for them to finish sciencing or go ahead with the test?"

Carrie chuckled. "Sara will be pissed if we *don't* wait for her. She's our head lab tech and she's been itching to see how this program works."

Sara and Gabe rejoined them.

"Sorry to hold things up," Gabe said. "That's a robust algorithm. Let's see it in action."

Ruby held her breath as Nick and Michael carried the first beehive-looking growbox to the edge of the field and tipped it slightly, forgetting the heat, the mugginess, the sweat trickling down her back between her shoulder blades. She never tired of watching a bot release, especially the colorful forms based on the RubyBot framework that looked like tiny ladybugs. The wave of bots spilling out of the box was an iridescent dark teal at first, fading in intensity as the bots spread to cover the nearby section of the field. A yellow glow caught her eye and she turned her head to see Gabe and Sara poring over a projection—feedback from the Defenders as they activated.

Gabe chuckled. "I *like* this. I really, really *like* this. Damn. Martin is going to be itching to get his fingers on this one, Sara. You folks have done well with it."

"We've got a box of samples to send back with you," Sara said.

"Good."

"Onward to the next sector, then," Jeff said. Ruby watched as he flipped a switch on the remaining boxes. A faint roar, and then, one-by-one, the boxes levitated, tiny flames pushing them up. The punch of another button, and the boxes slowly processed along the edge of the field.

"Now that's some sweet tech," she said. "We're still using trailers, forklifts, and scooters to move our boxes."

Jeff grinned. "Propane-powered platforms with programmed stops. Works great during the rainy season. Not so great for long distances, but moving growboxes to the fields? Oh yeah."

"You selling them?"

"Mmm, they're not in production. I just kludged them up to meet the need. But I can get you some by next spring."

"Gabe," Ruby said. "Take a look at this."

"Huh?" He looked away from Sara. "What?"

She jerked her head toward the slowly moving growboxes. "Take a look at that," she repeated. "Self-propelled growboxes. Think that might make things easier during mud season?"

Gabe pursed his lips thoughtfully. "Should be useful. We can only use it during snow and mud, though. Those flames look like they could start fires once the vegetation dries out."

"That's when we use the crawler trailers. But something like this would sure save us a world of hassle during snow and mud seasons."

"Oh yeah, I agree. How many are you going to order for the Double R? Moondance could use half that amount."

"Jeff and I are still talking. Not in regular production."

"Hey, if both of you are interested, then we'll get to work on it over the winter," Carrie said. "Two of you—probably even more folks will be interested."

"Damn, looks like I've got to get this production up and rolling too," Jeff said. "But you said this wouldn't work once things dry off in your area?"

"Too much of a fire hazard," Ruby said. "We are limited in what equipment we can use from—oh, about late June to November. And I could see some issues with ice formation when there's snow on the ground."

"Tell you what," Jeff said. "Once we're done with harvest I'll come up and see what I can figure out for your climate. You think this might be a good Barkley-Martiniere-Swait product?"

Ruby and Gabe exchanged glances.

"Don't see why not," he said. "We can market transport mechanisms to go with the growboxes. It's a logical side market."

"Sounds good."

The second and third releases were much the same as the first. At last they approached the final corner. Ruby noted that Gabe was gimping more and leaning on his cane heavier, sweating harder than ever.

"You holding up okay?" she whispered to him as they hung

back while Nick and Michael prepared to tip the final box. She noticed that Jeff, Carrie, and Sara seemed to be tenser and edgy with this release.

"I'll be all right," Gabe said. He brought out his handkerchief and wiped his brow. "It'll be better once we're back in the plane and have AC. I need to take more meds, but I can hold out until we get back to the Double R."

"Don't work yourself sick," she cautioned. While she'd not experienced Gabe in the depths of a bad post-G9 syndrome flare, what she'd seen so far of his mild occasional ones were bad enough. He *hurt* when he had an attack.

"Not a problem." Gabe straightened up, lips pressed together tightly.

"Hey, you might want to watch this one," Jeff said. "This section is where those indentured workers came under attack."

"Right there." Gabe moved his cane to his other hand and took Ruby's arm. "Changing angles will probably help," he said softly to her.

She nodded, matching her strides to his as he leaned slightly on her. As they reached the box and stood, he rested his right arm around her shoulders and put more weight on her. Ruby braced against the additional pressure, wrapping her left arm around his waist so that it looked like they were being affectionate rather than it being a necessity. Over the past six months they had worked out this discreet means of giving Gabe a rest break after long periods standing. But she didn't like how much more frequently it was happening as time progressed. Still, it was clear he needed the support. Especially in this heat and humidity.

And the close contact kept feeding the number of social media followers who had become entranced by the Ruby and Gabe reunion storyline during the Superhero competition. *Keep that going,* Brandon had advised just a month ago during one of his whirlwind stops at the Double R. *Especially since Philip is playing around with politics and hinting that he'll run for President.*

We need to keep Dad front and center as much as possible, and your relationship is a good means to humanize him.

Nick and Michael carefully tipped this final box. The first thing Ruby noticed was a phenomenon similar to what she had observed earlier with the cam drone six months ago. Instead of flowing smoothly out of the box in a bunched wave and dispersing evenly at ground level into the field as the other releases had done, the bots scattered widely the minute the lid popped up, soaring six inches over the top of the rice plants.

"You have interference!" she snapped. "That's exactly what happened in my Homestead field."

"The readouts are wrong," Sara muttered, reaching into her projection. "And they're not responding to my input, just like it was when we had the indentureds here."

"Let me see." Gabe straightened up and joined Sara. Ruby went to the edge of the field. The bots had stopped their scattering and were circling around an area about twenty feet from the edge of the field, the circle tightening up more and more. As more bots left the grow box, they started streaming toward their compatriots, forming a dark teal vortex.

"Something's out there," Jeff muttered. He started toward it.

Ruby grabbed him. "No. Don't."

"I had to knock the Defenders off of the indentureds. I may need to get whatever that is."

"Don't," Ruby repeated as a low hum began to emanate from the swirling bots. "That's nothing living. They'll destroy it, and I don't think you want to be in the middle of whatever they're doing."

"How are we going to know what it is—Nick! Michael! Stop the release."

The box lid dropped with a clunk.

"I think I can model whatever they're after," Gabe said. "But I agree with Ruby. *Don't* get in the middle of that vortex. With those numbers they could hurt you."

"I'll slap you silly if you try to go out there, bro," Carrie added. "And tell Kinsey."

"Shit," Jeff muttered at the mention of his wife. But he stayed put.

The hum grew louder and more ominous, turning into a growl. The bots drew tighter together into a funnel cloud, iridescent flashes of light reflecting off of their shells, a miniature tornado that looked odd without a storm around it.

Then, suddenly, the funnel formation descended into the stalks and out of sight. The plants shuddered. A wisp of black smoke smoldered from the area for a few moments, then snuffed out.

"Whatever it is, it's gone," Sara said, staring at her display. "Boom! Just like that."

"Get me a place to sit down and pull up my big comp screen, and I can whip up a model for whatever it is from your data, Sara," Gabe said tersely. He hobbled back to Ruby, leaning on her again. "Shouldn't take me more than half an hour, if that, to come up with something."

"I guess we should go back to the house and do that," Jeff said. "Kinsey and David are fixing a light supper for us."

"Let's finish the release," Ruby said. "See if there's any change in behavior with that thing gone—or if there's any more out there to trigger them. Hey, at least this is promising. We know the Defender has even more potential than we thought. I see what you meant about it wanting to go bigger, Jeff."

"Yeah," Jeff said slowly, watching as Nick and Michael tipped the box yet again. "But I'm not sure I like what that implies."

"We won't know for certain until I've got us a model of whatever it was that the bots destroyed," Gabe said, an edge in his voice.

They watched as the remainder of the bots behaved as they should. A handful at the end of the release buzzed above the plants toward the spot where the bots had swirled before, but they traveled in a straight line and dropped immediately.

"Okay," Jeff said. "We've got a light meal back at the house, and workspace for you to whip up that model, Gabe. Sounds good?"

"Sure. Just going to take me a little bit longer to get back to the rig."

"I'll fetch it." Jeff quickened his steps even as he summoned the truck to him. The others remained with the boxes.

Once they were out of earshot, Ruby whispered to Gabe. "Any idea what the Defender went after?"

"I'll know better when I see the model," Gabe murmured back, leaning heavy on her, heat throbbing into her from him. "But I'll lay odds that it's a surveillance device of some sort. One way or another those indentureds managed to get it planted."

"I know better than to bet against you in this area," she said, as the truck stopped in front of Jeff. He climbed into the truck and headed for them. "And we should let Brandon and Kris know about this latest indentured development."

"I'll be very interested in their input," Gabe said. "Maybe we should make an appearance at that Biobot Producers Alliance conference that Bran's putting together after all."

"Maybe." She had argued that they should hold back from being too visible as Brandon had started putting the Alliance together, hoping not to attract any more attention to the BPA from the Martiniere Group than necessary. Brandon and Kris had concurred. "I'd sure like a good excuse to talk to Temira Cho."

"I think that's a very good idea," Gabe agreed. He exhaled. "And I will be glad to get out of this godforsaken humidity."

"Me too," she said.

CHAPTER 2

THE WIND BLEW HARDER AS GABE AND RUBY CLIMBED BACK INTO the plane at dusk, whipping the brim of her hat and forcing Gabe to use his free hand to hold his on. After they entered the cabin, Gabe hesitated by his chair. He shrugged out of his suit jacket and tossed it on an empty seat, followed by the hat. He slowly removed his holster and gun, securing it in a lockbox, then continued back to the couch.

"Tired?" Ruby asked, untying her hat and stashing it in a closet, along with her purse.

They had stayed later at Swait's than they intended, in part because modeling the device that the Defenders had attacked had been more of a challenge than Gabe had expected. But then there was socializing with Jeff's extended family and staff. One effect of Jeff's winning the Superhero and participating in BMS Associates, the official entity that had risen out of their alliance, was that he had been able to employ all of his sisters' families in some form or another. This was the first time she and Gabe been able to meet them, along with his wife Kinsey.

Gabe exhaled, wiping his brow. "Yeah. And we still have to talk to Bran." He cast her a pleading look. "Sit with me, please? I'm hurting and it really helps when you're there."

God, I'm a sucker for that look.

Ruby drew herself up and headed for the bathroom, doing her best to push back the irritation rising in her. Here she was, falling into that caretaker role that her friends had warned her about six months ago. She was hot and tired herself, and wanted to do nothing other than vegetate on the flight back to the Double R.

But it's worse for him because of post-G9 syndrome, she reminded herself.

"Wipe down first," she said as she pulled a couple of washcloths out of the cabinet over the sink and dampened them with cool water, tossing one to Gabe. "We're both going to be sweaty and stinky and this'll cool both of us off faster." Ruby stared at her reflection in the mirror. Small red and silver tendrils of hair hung around her face. Her usual moisturizer and mineral powder regime had managed to keep the sun at bay and resisted sweat. But she looked tired. Dark circles under her eyes to match those under Gabe's. The sharp chin and prominent cheekbones that showed more when she had a long day. Even her freckles were paler than usual.

The engines powered up and Ruby realized she needed to get seated. She ran the water and splashed her face, patting it dry with the washcloth, then wet it and wiped face, arms, anything that wasn't comfortable. But she was still hot and sticky, would be until the AC kicked in. Ruby dropped the washcloth in the laundry compartment. Gabe chucked his cloth at her so she could dispose of his as well. It smacked her in the face.

"Hey!" she snapped. "Watch what you're doing!" Irritation surged again.

"Sorry. My aim's off. I was hoping to hit your hands. Didn't mean to hit you in the face."

She stretched before joining Gabe on the couch and fastening her seat belt. Gabe's hand slipped over to hers and clamped down tightly as the jet whispered down the airstrip and climbed sharply. Once they stopped climbing, he sighed, releasing her hand, and rested one arm across her shoulders, pulling her close.

She resisted the temptation to stiffen up, reminding herself that he had a reason to look for reassurance as a nervous flyer. Plus, Gabe still felt hotter than he should be.

"Thanks. God, that heat just takes it out of me. The AC feels good." He leaned his head back.

"It's not fun, that's for sure. Even with my hair up."

"I like the wispy tendrils though." His hand moved off of her shoulder to finger the strands of wayward, mostly silver hair for a moment before dropping back.

"Yeah, even *my* straight hair gets a frizz in this humidity."

Gabe yawned. "Let's call Bran. Shouldn't share everything over an open line but maybe get him prepped for tomorrow's meeting."

"Did you send any explanation with those pix?"

"No, just that we needed to add this to the GMR Group agenda."

"Okay." She straightened up and called Brandon.

Their son blinked at them as his projection appeared, showing him seated at a desk in Justine's Chicago condo with multiple virtual screens around him. "Mom. Dad. How did the Defender test go?"

"There were some—interesting results," Gabe said. "Somewhat like the Homestead field last spring."

"Homestead—oh. *Oh.* Have anything to do with those pix you sent?"

"Possibly." Gabe choked back a second yawn. "Sorry. Long day today and it's damn humid."

"Understand. Kris is checking those pix out using her *particular* connections."

Particular connections with that emphasis and the sour look on Brandon's face—Kris must have gone underground amongst the Chicago labor pool indentureds.

"How's the Biobot Producers Alliance conference prep going?" Gabe asked.

Brandon scowled. "It would be a lot smoother if we didn't

keep running into roadblocks with contracting outside support staff. Dad, I keep telling you that we absolutely need to expand hiring at all levels for security's sake. Contracting out stupid little things like catering staff is proving to be a problem. We're not big enough to keep from being outbid."

"Then don't serve food," Gabe said.

"For a two-day conference? You've got to be kidding. No one will take us seriously."

"It's a launch, not a party."

"Dad. We're trying to convince these people to join the Alliance instead of AgI. Otherwise they're going to stick with AgI. I know how this works. I can get us some high-level industry people as BPA members but things have to be done right." An irritated note crept into Brandon's voice. "No, we don't need to provide high-end champagne service, even if I could get my hands on something decent. That's not what you do with something like this conference. I'm having problems with basics, down to sourcing real coffee and packaged pastries that don't taste bitter for the morning sessions. I'd just as soon not serve slurry for lunch."

"Save the slurry for dinner," Ruby advised. "And bring in lots of synthwhisky to make it taste good."

"I'm not going to go so far as to serve dinner," Brandon said. "Not at this point in time. Beyond our reach. But I'd like to have a decent lunch service."

"Kid, I'm not made of money. Until BMS starts bringing in money from the Defender and Protector releases next spring, cash's going to be tight," Gabe said.

"Dad, I'm not talking about big bucks for an AgI level promotion. I'm talking about hiring the right people for the job. Pay a bit more to get good folks in place so that we can run conferences like this a lot more smoothly without worrying that the Martiniere Group is going to tamper with our supplies. Judicious investment. We want this first conference to be a success, don't we? Then while we don't go with the full AgI lavish treatment, we *need* to look like we're not a two-buck outfit."

"Brandon—" Gabe's voice sharpened.

"Hey, hey, hey," Ruby elbowed Gabe. "Let's talk about this tomorrow. Justine might have some sourcing ideas. It's been a long day for everyone."

"All right," Gabe conceded grumpily.

"Yes, Ma." Brandon slumped back in his chair, rubbing his forehead. "Part of the problem is that we keep getting staff sent to us from the labor pool who somewhat resemble the pix you sent. And even though I've said no indentured when placing my orders, that's what the local labor pool has available." He ran his hand through his dark hair. "Kris is tracing other options. But I've also heard a concerning rumor. About Philip."

Gabe tensed against Ruby. "What?"

Brandon raised his hands. "A whisper from one of the local politicos to Kris during a conversation about finding decent food service. Philip is in Chicago tonight making a speech to the Real Truthers at the opening of their nominating convention. He's the keynote speaker. But that's another reason why I'm having issues pulling reliable staff and supplies together. The Reals are outbidding everyone and running the prices sky high."

"You have contracts with the staffing agencies, right?"

"Dad. That's not enough. I keep telling you, we're being outbid." His voice became sharper. "And I no longer have the weight of AgI behind me. That makes a huge difference when I'm up against the money the Reals can pull down. I've been told that to my face by several people. Folks I've worked with in the past."

Gabe growled. "All right. Do what you need to do *this time*. Just don't go too far over budget. We'll talk more tomorrow. Your mother's right. Justine may have some ideas."

"I'll do my best." A chirp sounded from his end. "That's Kris. I've got to go. See you tomorrow."

"Tomorrow," Ruby said. Brandon's image faded as Gabe growled again and threw his right forearm over his eyes.

"Rubes, I swear that kid of ours is going to give me a heart attack one of these days. We don't have as much funding as he seems to think we have. Even with Justine's help."

"He *does* have experience running these sorts of events after working for AgI for nearly seven years," Ruby said. "And so does Kris."

"And just how much fucking money does Georgy Batineau throw away on bullshit at AgI? How much of that crap did Brandon learn while working for him?" Gabe exhaled through his teeth. "I suppose he's right, damn it. But god, it makes me crazy. We're still playing catch up with Philip and I just. Don't. Want to spend any more than I have to until we get a better income stream coming in. I don't have the resources of Philip plus Georgy."

"We're in a development phase and that requires being bold about spending money," she reminded him. "And we do have Justine."

"Who has her own agenda."

"But Brandon is right about contending with AgI. Georgy's going to pull more money out of Philip to counter us, because the Biobot Producers Alliance will be yet another serious competitor to AgI. We need to be convincing when it comes to courting those other biobot producers away from AgI, especially if Philip's making a serious play for the Presidency. There's more than enough old Republicans in the Reals with money to burn, who bounce back between them and the Honest Republicans, and many of them have ties to ag."

Gabe slapped his hands down hard on the couch and made her jump, for a moment bringing back childhood memories when a slapping sound like that meant bad things were about to happen.

"God *damn* it, Ruby, that's exactly why we have to be careful with our cash flow! Sooner or later we'll need to provide legal support for some of those producers to break contracts with AgI. A virtual conference would have been better. Spending money on frivolities like a live gathering—"

"The conference isn't a frivolity, damn it, Gabe! You know as well as I do that more things get done in face-to-face schmoozing when you're building up a new organization like this, especially when we're up against AgI and the Martiniere Group! A virtual conference is not going to raise confidence in our potential allies about the Alliance's eventual effectiveness. Furthermore, it's an investment. We need their membership money, and going live is how you start this stuff," Ruby said, biting back her own irritation. Not time to let it show. Not if she could shake Gabe out of his current focus. "And odds are that Philip is running his appearances at the Real Truthers convention to coincide with our conference. We're going to need to take that consideration into account for the future."

"Shit, he's going to run us out of money!"

Her voice sharpened as her frustration with Gabe's focus on the costs grew. "There's more to it than just money. Stop being so bullheaded and second-guessing what Brandon's doing, damn it, Gabe! This is his area of expertise. God *damn* you stubborn Martiniere men!"

She exhaled, realizing suddenly how angry and hot and tired and aggravated she was, and it had been a *long* day. Ruby got up from the couch and went to her seat, spinning it away from Gabe and dropping her head into her hands.

God damn this Martiniere bullshit.

She needed a break. She needed to do something away from endless politicking and spreadsheet calculations and strategizing. She needed to get away from hours of working with Gabe, with Brandon, with their bull-headed Martiniere stubbornness. Ruby gulped and raised her head, still not looking at Gabe. How long had it been since she'd been able to ride out alone on the land and recharge, to build up her tolerance for coping with this craziness?

For that matter, how long had it been since she'd been able to swing up on one of her horses, even in the arena? That answer came quickly. At least two weeks. Four-year-old Legacy needed work. Her yearling brother Dancer should be getting ponied and handled. Three-year-old Flash needed to be prepped for next year's sales. There hadn't been time for any of the young horses, much less the finished horses for casual rides.

It didn't help that riding alone outside of the arena was just plain impossible since Gabe Ramirez had become *Gabriel Martiniere*, rebel heir-apparent to the Martiniere Group empire. As his current business partner and mother of Gabe's son she was too much of a target. Whatever this relationship was that they had going didn't help either. Too damn many memories of how Gabe had treated her during the divorce. Sure, he'd been panicked at the time but—when he acted like this it reminded her too much of that era. She wanted to rip hard into him, and she shouldn't. Not when it was most likely fueled in part by his own frustration with post-G9 syndrome.

Tomorrow. I'm giving myself some time away from damn men. Maybe I can talk Justine and Beck into riding out for target practice.

It had been a month or so since they had a Ladies Practice Shoot.

Gabe coughed. "Ruby. Please. Fuck. I'm sorry," he groaned. "I'm being stupid."

"I'm sorry, too. But you don't need to be getting pissy about what Brandon's doing." She swung her seat back to glare at him.

Gabe shook his head. "All of this is happening so damn fast. Six months ago, you weren't even talking to me, and the Super-hero was starting up."

Ruby stared down at her hands. "Yeah, well, learning why you left me made a big difference. And if I hadn't stepped up to help you out after the kidnapping and fire, Brandon would have."

"And he was in too big of a mess himself to do that, anyway." Gabe slumped lower on the couch. "How the hell do you do it,

Ruby? You and Brandon both. I was raised to this life. I should have a better tolerance for all of this baloney, including security considerations. Yeah, the mentality comes back after thirty years away from all of this damn Martiniere crap. It's still damn hard for me. Brandon seems to have just glided into it." He raised his hands in frustration. "How the hell do you two pull off dealing with this much change, this fast? God damn it, *I'm* the one who should find this commonplace. Shit!"

Ruby tightened her lips and looked away from Gabe, not wanting to meet his eyes. "You forget. I killed my meth-head father after he killed my mother, when I was six." Her voice sharpened as she continued, to keep the memories from choking her voice. Anger was safer than tears. "Dealing with that damn near broke my grandparents. And then the divorce. Branny and I did a lot of scrounging and wheeling and dealing after you left. Coping with sudden change is *what my life has been.* Brandon's learned to handle a lot of weird shit because he's had to do that!" She sighed, the brief flare of anger subsiding. She *had* to let go of the past, but sometimes it crept up on her. "Damn it, Gabe, *trust* our son. He's good at organizing and always has been."

"He gets that from you."

"From both of us. You're no slouch at organizing when you put your mind to it."

"Not like you two. And you trained him to be a decent shot."

"Thank you." Begrudgingly said, her lips tight. He *meant* that compliment.

"Rubes. I'm sorry for being an ass. I'm real good at that." Gabe pursed his lips. "When I was sick and thought I was dying, I kept reliving how I treated you during the divorce. I was a prime ass then. And now I feel like shit and I don't dare take the good meds until we get back to the Double R so I'm taking it out on you. I'm sorry."

"Not an excuse." She still didn't want to cut him too much slack.

"You're right, though. It's been a long day. And all of this—"

he waved his hands. "That's part of my problem right now. It was good to get back into the field today and work with the algorithms. That's what I really want. That's what I'm really pissed about. I want to be Gabe Ramirez, crack bot wrangler and microbial specialist, not *Gabriel Martiniere*, not take on Philip. I want to be that young smartass saddle bronc rider who could ride a good horse for hours in the mountains and stay in the field until I couldn't see in the darkness. I hate being weak. I hate being tied down to his business crap. But I don't seem to have one hell of a bit of choice in how things unfold. Not unless I want to hand a gun to Philip and watch him kill you two before he shoots me, because sooner or later, that's the alternative if I *don't* do the Martiniere dance. That's what really frustrates me."

"And then there's this bullshit with the indentureds," Ruby said in a low voice. She couldn't argue with Gabe about Philip's intent. Nor did she want to face Philip without Gabe at her side.

"Yeah. That." Gabe leaned his head against the back of the couch. "The situation with the Martiniere Group is no fucking better than it was thirty years ago. If anything, that trafficking in mind controlled indentured is worse now that they've got those recreational body mods in production." His voice cracked. "God damn Philip. If I'd had you at my back when I testified about that mind control programming back then, maybe I wouldn't have run. Not worried about what he would have had Joseph and his goons do to anyone in the Family that I cared about. Faced him head on when I was young and strong and could have *stopped* this shit, instead of trying to do it now as a middle-aged G9 cripple. Fuck. Fuck. Fuck."

"Fat chance of that, Gabe. I wasn't twenty-one when you testified, and you wouldn't have risked me then."

"I know. And he would have swatted me like a fly then if I hadn't run, whether I had you with me or not." Gabe slapped his hands against the couch again, softer than before, not hard enough this time to make her jump. "I didn't know enough, Justine couldn't help, not like she can now, and Serg was just as marginalized as I was even though he was learning to be a sneaky little shit around the Group. I saw what Joseph was doing with those sex-modded, mind-controlled indentureds. Heard Philip's plans to extend indenture to provide ready-made pharmaceutical research subjects, because," he signed air quotes, *"if the working classes can't stay out of debt they might as well work off their liabilities doing something useful."*

"He said stuff like that?"

"And worse. As you can imagine, dinner table conversation around Philip is not pleasant." Gabe's lips tightened. "But. I couldn't have united the family factions against Philip as a young man with no experience other than my degree. My only possible ally was my grandmother, the Matriarch, but she was sick and I sure as hell didn't want Philip focusing on her."

"The Matriarch?" Another piece of Martiniere family lore she didn't know much about.

Gabe nodded. "A title for my grandmother Donna. Donnagran. Who is a power in her own right when she's healthy." He sighed. "Maybe I should have reached out to her. At the very least she might have helped me twenty-one years ago. But I didn't know what shape she was in. I should have checked, but I was stupid. Just like I shouldn't have let Philip stampede me into divorce."

"Yeah."

Ruby stared at her hands again, remembering how she'd come across Gabe and Mariah Meyers making out in public during their divorce. *More shit memories.* And Mariah wasn't just a competitor in the old Superstar, and then again in the Superhero. Her affair with Gabe had brought about the divorce. Yeah, mind control had been involved, but it still didn't make sense to Ruby. Mariah had also been involved with Georgy Batineau with AgI, was still in a relationship with him now. Why had she gone after Gabe? Just because she could?

"Rubes. I'm sorry. I'm really sorry. Hey. Marry me?"

She snorted. "No. How many times do I need to say it? We're

friends. Business partners. That's enough. Do we really want to go down that path again?"

"I'll keep asking until you say yes," he said softly. "I mean it. Would you say yes if I was still just Gabe Ramirez, not Gabriel Martiniere?"

"It doesn't make a difference," she said. "The answer would be the same."

But that wasn't exactly true. It would be easier to say yes again to Gabe Ramirez than Gabriel Martiniere. And she wasn't certain just how much he still mourned his late second wife Rachel.

"Justine Martiniere," her com chimed.

What now? she wondered as she accepted the call. At least the call gave her and Gabe an excuse to stop wrangling and bringing up things she didn't want to remember. Like Mariah.

Justine's projection appeared between them, the cubicles behind her revealing that she was in a bathroom. Gabe's cousin wore a low-cut bright red formal dress tightly fitted to her lanky form and her brunette hair was carefully styled in a bouffant, reminiscent of the old pictures of Great-gramma from the 1970s that Ruby had on the bedroom wall.

"I don't have long but the two of you need to know this," Justine said without preamble. "I'm at the Reals opening reception." She glanced around furtively, lowering her voice. "Gabe with you?"

"On the couch. We're still flying back." Ruby got up and sat near Gabe so that Justine could see him as well, her projection following Ruby.

"Good." Justine frowned. "Cuz. You've gotta up your game now. Daddy dearest has just announced his candidacy for the Presidency at tonight's opening dinner, and asked for the Reals' nomination. Interdicted so it won't hit the news until tomorrow morning." She looked around. "I've got to go. Need to play the game a little bit longer. But thought I'd better tell you before you hear it from other sources. More tomorrow." She winked out.

Gabe covered his face with one hand. His other hand fumbled for Ruby's. She let him take it, swallowing hard, ice shards roiling her gut. This news was expected, but to actually hear it was different.

Gabe rubbed his face and dropped his free hand on the couch.

"And there it is," he said, his voice dead and emotionless. "Fuck. Oh god, Rubes...." His voice trailed away as he stared at the window opposite from him.

"We have to stop him," she said hoarsely, joining him in staring straight ahead.

"No other choice," he agreed. He released her hand and rested his arm on the couch. "And I'm being stupid tonight to you and Bran. Can't do that. Lashing out is what Philip or my father would have done. I've *got* to get past that behavior. I know better."

"We're both tired," she said. "It's been a long day."

Will you live up to this resolution?

"And there's more days like this ahead." Gabe exhaled. "I don't need to be making things worse by being an ass. I'm sorry. Really sorry."

"I'm not much better. Letting the past haunt me when I should let it go. It's not like you haven't apologized enough. It's just—we sometimes slip back into those patterns. That's why I'm going to keep saying no to your proposals. We fall back into old habits."

Gabe winced. "Then I guess I'm going to have to show you I mean what I say." He dropped his right hand on her neck, gently massaging it. "We are a piece of work, aren't we, Ruby Barkley?"

She gulped and fought against leaning into his hand. It felt so good, but was it wise? "For sure, Gabriel Martiniere."

He groaned. "That still sounds so strange coming from you. Yeah. Gabriel Martiniere. That's who I am now. Fuck."

She gave him a sideways look and her resistance started to crumple as she saw his sad face. "All right, Gabriel Marcus

Martiniere Ramirez," she said, using the Spanish surname protocol he preferred. The pleading expression on his face and those soft brown eyes had always been her weakness. He was so damn good at making up after a fight. If only sex was still on the plate. But that was another thing the G9 had taken away from him, and her interest in sex with anyone, not just Gabe, was—minimal. Had been for twenty-one years.

No one but Gabe for me these days—and I'm not sure about him.

"That's better. Sort of." He gently tugged at her. "Come back over and cuddle—please? After this news I'm feeling—oh hell, I don't know exactly what I feel now."

Ruby relented. Arguing was tiring, and those icy splinters stabbing into her gut that were caused by nerves would make her sick if she kept up the battle.

"I need it too," she said in a low voice as she scooted over to him.

Truth.

He slid his arm around her, pulling her tight against his side. She relaxed against Gabe as his lips brushed against her hair. The tight lock on her gut eased.

Why can't I just settle into this? Why isn't this relationship enough?

Trust. When she got to the bottom of her feelings about Gabe, trust was the issue she couldn't resolve. At one time Ruby had thought she understood *Gabe Ramirez*. Gabe Ramirez would put her and Brandon first, even if he had the occasional roving eye. Until Mariah it hadn't gone beyond looking.

But *Gabriel Martiniere*…as he moved more and more back into his Martiniere self, she had to wonder just how ruthless Gabe could be in pursuit of his goal. At what point would he decide that he needed a polished woman more familiar with the ways of politics, high finance, and corporate deals to realize his objectives? Someone who was more like his cousin Justine, instead of a rancher ex-rodeo queen?

Silence hung between them. Gabe's fingers traced a trefoil shape on her arm. The Martiniere trefoil. Marking his territory?

Gabe squeezed her close, both arms around her now, as if he were reading her thoughts. He kissed her forehead. "Part of me wishes that I could scoop up you and Bran and his Kris and run."

"Where?"

"That's it. There *is* no safe place. Especially if Philip manages to get elected on a Real Truthers ticket and has the resources of the Feds as well as the Martiniere Group to come after us."

"We'll find a way to beat him," she said, even though her voice quavered.

Gabe leaned his head against hers. "Oh Ruby. Ruby. Thank you for your confidence. Yes. With you and Bran at my side, we'll find a way to beat him."

But his arms around her trembled and she quivered against him. They huddled together as if to shelter themselves from the growing darkness outside the plane, finding a temporary refuge in each other.

If it could stay like this.... She didn't finish that thought.

CHAPTER 3

EVEN UNDER THE INFLUENCE OF HEAVY SEDATING MEDICATION, GABE still woke Ruby with nightmare-fueled yelling twice that night. She had to sit on the side of her bed and reach over to him in his recliner, shaking his shoulder, before he stopped. At some point early in the morning, noises from the bathroom connecting their room to the one Brandon and Kris used when they were at the ranch told her that they had arrived. They were clearly trying to be quiet, but Ruby would rouse at the slightest whisper, always had from earliest childhood, when a strange sound might mean trouble.

After each awakening Ruby stared up at the ceiling, but not long enough to justify switching on her reading light and picking up her book. She forced herself to think about riding horses and nothing about business, remembering favorite gallops. Each time the memory of Legacy running under her, so much like her great-grandmother Sunshine, eased her back into sleep.

Ruby rose at her usual hour, right at daylight during August. Normally she'd wake Gabe as well, but as she looked over at him sleeping peacefully on his side in the recliner, she decided against it.

God, he looked *old* with his face sagged in slumber, aged and exhausted as he burrowed into the soft fabric of the afghan rescued from the ruins of his Moondance house. She supposed that Rachel had crocheted it, and her lips tightened. Another ghost, and this one wasn't his fault. Rachel had smoothed out Gabe's hard edges, perhaps even brought him to the point that he could admit when he was wrong, helped him become the man that Ruby could let back into her life.

It should have been me.

But it was silly being jealous of a dead woman she had never met. And who knew how things would have turned out if she and Gabe had stayed together?

Ruby quietly gathered up her clothes and tiptoed into the bathroom to dress. Maternal instinct stirred and she paused by the connecting door. One of the kids was snoring—it sounded like Brandon. Ruby smiled as she caught herself listening closely to the rhythm of his breathing, a habit that had arisen after they'd both been so sick with that mutated flu when he was a toddler.

Yes. Definitely Brandon. Same breathing rate and pitch that he used to have during the late summer allergy season. Well, he could wake Gabe when he got up. She slipped back into her room to gather notepad and pen and scribbled a quick note asking Brandon to do that, then stuck it to the mirror.

She pulled on her slippers in the hallway and went downstairs, turning left to go into the kitchen, following the sound of voices. The coffeemaker gurgled and Ruby's nose twitched. Was that *real* coffee she smelled, not the synthetic substitute which was the only coffee she could usually find at the Lakeside market these days? That meant—

Justine sat at the 50s-era green Formica and chrome table that had been Granma's pride, two screens shimmering in front of her as she talked to someone, voice only, typing on the virtual keyboard hovering over the table. She waved as Ruby entered the kitchen and pointed toward the coffeepot with a grin.

Real coffee, then. Ruby fumbled in the cupboard for an

ancient Painted Ponies cup, last of the set she had cherished for years, and carefully extracted the carafe from the coffeemaker. For once the mechanism that stopped the flow of water worked. She filled her cup, replaced the pot in the coffeemaker, and sat across the table from Justine, inhaling the heady scent of *real* coffee, and *good* to boot. She took a sip as Justine dismissed screens and keyboard.

"You're grinning ear to ear," Justine said.

"Mmm," Ruby said. "This is damn fine coffee, Justine." She took another deep breath. "It's wonderful. Thank you."

Justine shrugged and leaned back in her chair, pinching the top of her nose. This morning Ruby couldn't help but note Justine's strong resemblance to Gabe, in spite of the cosmetic surgery he'd had while in witness protection. His brows and nose were slightly different, but they shared the same brown eyes, high forehead and cheekbones. Justine then ran her fingers through her shoulder-length brunette hair, a habit shared by both Gabe and Brandon, and picked up her own cup.

"I got lucky and came across a good shipment. Thought you and Gabe should have a treat, especially after yesterday's news." She sighed. "God damn Daddy-fucking-dearest. He was on a roll last night."

"How on earth did you manage to get into the Real Truthers?" *Was that the safe thing to do?* was what she really wanted to ask but didn't dare.

"Donald had an invite. He needed an escort and we thought it would be amusing. We've both been keeping an eye on the Reals just in case something like this happened. Daddy-poo has been courting them for years, ever since the Honest Republicans booted him out early in his political aspirations. Don got a hint of this and invited me along."

Justine's mouth quirked in a half-smile at the mention of her ex-husband Donald. Ruby didn't understand *their* relationship any more than she could figure out what was going on with her and Gabe. Donald apparently lived on an island with several girlfriends as part of his divorce settlement with Justine.

Still, not only did he continue to manage Justine's finances—he was a former banker—but he was her tech advisor. One thing he had done for her was to install a dead man's switch worm in the Martiniere databases, called *Donald's Little Divorce Present to the Martinieres*. As long as Justine responded to specific prompts at random intervals, the worm remained inactive. If she didn't respond within a set period, the worm activated to trash the databases. Apparently it had partially activated at least once in the past before Justine stopped it—which was now sufficient motivation for Philip and Joseph to leave her alone.

"Amusing?" Ruby sipped her coffee again. "How so?"

"Just a reminder to Joey and Daddy-poo not to fuck with me, above and beyond Serg's security protocols," Justine said as her mouth curved into a sly grin. Serg Vygotsky was a cousin who managed security for the dissident Martiniere factions. "Some of Joey's goons have been sniffing around my supply operations and causing problems. I told my people not to put up with it any more, up to and including extreme force." Her face hardened. "Watching Daddy dearest's eyes pop out when I showed up with Donald on my arm was the best part of the whole damn evening. Somehow, he never got the memo that despite being divorced, we're still very good friends."

"How bad were things at the Reals?"

Justine shook her head. "I'd sooner save the report for the Group meeting, Ruby. It's ugly. Shades of the teens and '20s."

"Yeah, we got news like that yesterday ourselves," Ruby said.

Justine's brows lifted. "Tests didn't go well?"

"They went well enough. No. Other information."

"Oh."

Ruby set her cup down as Beck O'Toole came into the kitchen, clad in plain white tee shirt and black cropped jeans with black suspenders, her short bleached white-blond hair standing straight up and slightly tousled, as it always was. Beck and her partner Rick Keysing had moved their stem cell stemline business to the Double R after their labs in the Portland area had been firebombed. While the perpetrators had been tied to a section of the Martiniere Group directly controlled by Philip, they had never been caught. Since Rick and Beck's stemlines were key for Ruby's bots, it had been an easy decision for her to offer them refuge on the Double R.

"Is that real coffee?" Beck asked, staring at the coffeemaker.

"Help yourself," Justine said, grinning. "Courtesy of JSM Corp."

"I love you," Beck purred. She poured herself coffee and peered at the meal schedule posted on the refrigerator before pulling out the creamer. "Oh crud. Brandon and Kris in charge of breakfast for the meeting today? Are they even here yet?"

"They got in late last night," Ruby said. "I heard them."

Beck opened the refrigerator door. "Ah. New trays in here. Cold cuts, cheese, and fruit." She retrieved the creamer, poured some into her coffee, and replaced it in the fridge.

"I wonder where they got the food. Brandon was complaining about sourcing to me and Gabe last night," Ruby said. "Apparently the Real Truthers are hogging up the resources in Chicago."

"You mean *Daddy-damned-dearest* is hoarding resources," Justine said, wrinkling her nose as if she'd smelled something bad. "That's who's doing all the buying for the Real Truthers. Daddy darling wants that nomination bad. I brought pastries beside the coffee. With the GMR meeting happening this morning I figured we'd need all the sweets we can get."

"Yeah. Hey. Either of you want to go shooting afterwards? I'll ask Kris too."

"I can't," Beck said. "Got a grow that needs tweaking this afternoon. It's one of the fussy ones and while Rick can do it, we're getting paid enough for this batch that I don't want to take chances. This stemline likes me better than him."

"Shooting?" Justine perked up. "Oh good. I can find a use for those damn posters Joey pushed on me. I brought them thinking you might want to use the damn things for target practice."

"Posters?" Ruby savored her coffee before putting it back down. Lovely, lovely real coffee.

Justine scowled. "Campaign posters to wave during Daddy-poo's speech. His minions were handing them out to everyone at the dinner last night. But Joey made sure I got a whole pile of them, and then one of his goons followed me to make sure I didn't trash them."

"Guess we know who to thank for our targets today," Ruby said.

A grin twitched Justine's lips. "I might just take pictures after we're done and send them to Joey. I'm feeling just that damn bloody right now."

"What's got you feeling that bloody, Tine?" Gabe shuffled into the kitchen. A smile spread across his face as he focused on the coffeepot. "Did you or Brandon bring the coffee?"

"Brandon's not had the time," Justine said. "That's a gift to the GMR Group directly from JSM Corp." Her smile faded. "I need to give him a hand with the Alliance conference organization. Not for any lack of ability on his part. Brandon just doesn't have the pull to outbid Daddy-damn-dearest now that he doesn't have AgI behind him."

"He said something about that earlier." Gabe joined them at the table. "He and Kris will be down soon. Showering." He reached out and rested his hand on Ruby's. "A good thing we got that out of the way last night."

"Too damn sweaty from Arkansas to go to bed without showering first," Ruby said, slipping her hand out from under Gabe's as she picked up her cup with both hands to inhale the fragrance again—*precious precious real coffee.* "I don't know how people handle that humidity."

"They manage." Gabe gave her a puppy-dog look, brown eyes pleading. "But I agree. I liked the warmth but not the humidity."

Ruby sipped a couple of mouthfuls of coffee and put her cup back down. She eased her hand next to Gabe's so that their fingertips brushed. He slid his hand forward and curled his index finger around her little one.

"Maybe we ought to set up and have the rest of the crew join us. One of our offices or the dining room?"

Justine wrinkled her nose. "How about dining room? More comfortable if we're going to combine breakfast and meeting."

"We're going to meet over breakfast?" Brandon entered the kitchen and homed in on the coffee. He poured the last of it into his mug.

"Yes," Ruby said. "And you'd better be fixing a new pot, or else we will all kill you."

"I have my priorities straight. *Kris* will kill me if I don't make a new pot." Brandon dumped the cloth filter and rinsed it before situating it carefully. "Especially since it's real coffee. Ma, where did you get your hands on this stuff? Smells really good."

"Hi," Justine said, waving her hand. "Me. Over here. That's who you thank."

Brandon saluted her with his mug. "Working late and rising on farmer time. My sleep-lagged body thanks you, Justine. Where's the beans?"

"You know your way around this kitchen," Ruby chided.

"Yeah, but with all the new folks in the household over the past six months things do get changed." He fished the beans out of the freezer, then retrieved the coffee grinder from the cupboard.

Ruby rose. "We'd better set up. Beck, can you holler at the lab and barn crew that we're going to be ready soon?"

"Got it." Beck ambled out onto the porch. A moment while she slipped on her clogs, and then the screen slammed shut behind her.

"Be there in a minute to set up tech," Brandon said. "Do we need much?"

"A few projections, nothing more unless we have someone linking in," Gabe said. "Tine, what's Serg's status?"

Justine groaned, rubbing her forehead. "He's in Europe right now tracking down some sourcing supply issues I'm having that are a little—suspicious, shall we say, and I don't want to call attention to him. Donald stumbled across something weird and warned me last night. I just got off the comm with Serg to tell him more. I don't think what we're seeing is tied to family business, more an issue of local corruption. But I want to shut that bullshit down pronto nonetheless."

"Damn, I wish Serg could link in. I'd appreciate his input, but if he's not available, he's not available." Gabe shrugged.

"Let's get started. Gabe, get plates and serving ware," Ruby said as she pulled out a serving platter. The sooner they got this meeting over with, the sooner she could be outside. "Justine, can you put your pastries on this platter and bring it out? I'll take the cold cut plate."

Justine took the platter from Ruby and moved pastries from a box to the plate. Ruby eyed one maple bar, then decided against grabbing it right away. She carried the cold cut plate into the dining room and set it on the old sideboard. The big oak table needed a couple more leaves to accommodate everyone. She flipped the tablecloth to one side and began to wrestle the table apart. Gabe came to help, setting plates and silverware on the sideboard. As she pulled the leaves out of the storage underneath the table, he inserted them into the middle.

"Big enough?" she asked.

"Looks good to me."

They pushed the table together and Ruby eyed the table again. Probably all right with the current tablecloth.

"Never thought we'd have business meetings around this table," Gabe said in a low voice as she straightened out the tablecloth.

Just barely fits.

She chuckled as she crawled underneath the table to slide the center leg in place so it would support the added leaves. "Oh, Granma and Gramps had all sorts of meetings here, and Great-Gran and Great-Gramps before them. Irrigation district, organizing the health district, Quilt Guild sew days, all sorts of stuff. This table has seen a lot of decisions made."

"Let's hope that it's a good omen for the Group," Gabe said in a low voice. "I've a gut feeling that things are going to get bad soon. Especially with Philip announcing his candidacy for the Reals nomination. What kind of crap is he going to be promoting as part of his platform?" He moved chairs around the table.

"Maybe what you're feeling is just bad dreams from last night."

"Maybe." He didn't sound convinced. "Right now I feel like I did while waiting to testify."

"It'll be all right," she said, not wanting to admit her own uneasiness. She moved the food to the center of the table as Justine came in with one tray of pastries.

"Ruby, I need another platter."

"Okay." They went back into the kitchen together, passing Brandon as he carried a projection display into the dining room, five floating cams following him. Ruby retrieved another platter and handed it to Justine. For the moment they were alone in the kitchen.

"So here we are," Justine said softly. "The Reals and Daddy dearest are living it up big, and meanwhile we're having an opposition breakfast meeting in an old farmhouse." She chuckled softly. "Daddy-poo would find it appalling. Contradicts all of his elitist instincts."

"How many more Family members would feel the same way?" Ruby asked.

Justine shrugged. "We won't know for sure until Gabie makes his declaration to become the Martiniere and starts asking for support."

Ruby joined Justine in laying out pastries. "Gabe nearly lost it with Brandon last night over cash flow."

"He has to get over money worries." Justine frowned and glanced toward the dining room. "For one, Donald can come up with cash with minimal hassles. Let's talk more while riding."

"Agreed." Ruby fetched the remaining trays from the refrigerator as Beck clomped back into the kitchen, followed by Charlie. "Charlie, can you put the coffee in the pitcher and make more?"

"Real coffee?" Charlie asked, easily retrieving the insulated carafe. "You'll be lucky if any of it makes it into the meeting."

"Yes, it's real, and you'll be in trouble if you drink it all."

Charlie laughed.

"Let me help you." Beck grabbed one of the trays and headed for the dining room.

"Hey honey, give me a hand with the coffee," Charlie said to his husband Martin as the lab crew entered the kitchen. The remainder of the crew—Rick and Julie, along with Charlie's assistant Terri, followed Ruby.

Once everyone had loaded plates and assured themselves of enough coffee to get them through the first part of the meeting, they settled around the table. Gabe stood up.

"Everything set, Brandon?" he asked.

"Go ahead."

"I'm calling this August meeting of the GMR Group to order." He sat back down. "So. We've a lot on the agenda. Let's start with the big piece. Philip announced his candidacy for the Real Truthers nomination for president that's going to be awarded at the end of their convention. Justine. Can you tell us anything about his platform, or did he say anything of note?"

Justine waved her hand to indicate her mouth was full as she took a gulp of coffee, then set her cup down. "Oh, he said a fucking lot of bullshit that's downright dangerous if even half of it gets adopted and implemented. In a nutshell, Daddy dearest pitched a return to the economic and social policies of 2017, which, as you can imagine, played well to the Reals. A rollback of the reforms of the '20s that got eviscerated in the late '30s, with a hefty dose of *if people can't manage their finances then they deserve to be made into servants for those who can.* But there's more. He wants to lift the Climate Emergency Act of 2032 that was the impetus for the first AgInnovator competition."

Gabe scowled. "Wait a minute. That's not going to sit well with Georgy and AgI."

"AgI was losing money when Kris and I left, thanks to the number of reality show project financing competitors that keep springing up," Brandon said flatly. "This could be good news for the Alliance. Might make a few producers sitting on the fence between us and AgI to swing our way."

"Well, Georgy and Mariah were there and they didn't seem to be too damn upset by Daddy's plans," Justine said. "Now it might be playacting on their part but I don't think so."

"Higher investment percentages into labor pool and indentured management beyond agtech," Brandon said sharply. "Kris can tell us about that."

"Kris?" Gabe raised his brows at her.

Kris finished chewing and sipped coffee. "I unmasked my tat and slipped into the Chicago catering labor pool to talk to the indentureds. It's scary. Very few of them are regular indentureds, and they all carry new Martiniere tats, transfers from AgI. Most of them have body mods and mind control links. When they're not working catering jobs, they're sex workers. No choice in the matter."

"*What*?" Gabe snapped. "Since when has that been legal? I know that the mind control option was being discussed from what you told us after leaving AgI, but I thought the Indentured Act of 2032 ruled that out. And the sex worker piece? With new Martiniere tats?"

"They're—conditioned to accept that," Kris said. "Which has never been the norm, at least when I was in the labor pool. I've got a call out to Pat." Kris's sister Pat was still part of the AgI indentureds, feeding Kris information about the body modifications and developments within the company.

"It's part of Daddy-poo's big plan," Justine said sourly. "And there's more to it. He wants to expand the Indentured Act to include possible recall of *all* persons subject to indentured status in a state of crisis, like, say if another pandemic hits, even if their options have been paid off." She looked at Rick and Beck, then Kris and Brandon. "The way he described that nasty little darling, *all* persons who've ever come under Indentured Act provisions are subject to recall. That includes you, Brandon. As Daddy-fucking-dearest was *so* careful to tell me afterward. While gloating. And mentioning Brandon and Kris specifically."

Gabe's "Fuck no!" echoed Ruby's as Brandon's lips tightened while Kris looked down.

Justine nodded slowly. "Fuck, yes. There's been some sneaker legislation that opens up what indentured owners can do to their lifetime indentures. The callback was too far even for the New Democrats and the Honest Republicans, so it didn't pass the last congressional session. But that's on the table as part of the Real Truthers platform."

"What about free workers in labor pools?" Julie asked tensely as Terri next to her paled.

"If you've ever come under the control of a labor pool, free or indentured, Daddy darling's proposals apply to you."

Terri pressed her lips together and shook her head. Julie took her hand. "We'll fight it. There has to be a way to fight it."

"Not if Philip gets elected and activates emergency clauses," Gabe said tightly. "Okay. This ties into what Ruby and I learned yesterday at Swait's. The ag labor pools in Arkansas are pretty much indentured only. Furthermore, Jeff says you can't get any indentureds that aren't significantly body modded. And they're mechanical in their behavior."

"Carrie Swait also told me that most indentureds have good focus, while these didn't." Ruby repeated what Carrie had told her yesterday.

"Were they possible spies?" Martin asked. "That's a new behavior for the Defender."

"And this is another agenda item," Gabe said. "What happened at the Defender tests. It all fits together. Go ahead, Ruby."

"We saw an interesting phenomenon in the section of the field where the indentureds had been," Ruby said. "I didn't risk running cams of it because I was afraid that the Defenders would be diverted to them. The Defenders focused on something and destroyed it. Very similar to what we had happen in the Homestead field last spring with those older versions."

"I was able to model it finally from the Defender datafeed," Gabe said, clicking up a projection. Martin and Julie immediately linked in and called up copies, both poring over it.

Martin looked up. "Data recorder was their target, from what I see, but there's something more I can't figure out. The Defenders shouldn't have responded aggressively to a simple recorder. Julie?"

She nodded, biting her lip as she focused. "I'm trying to improve resolution to see it better, but it's definitely a spying device of some sort." Julie reached into the projection and twisted it slightly. "I saw something like this while working on a military project in PDX—shit! Are you sure it was completely destroyed?"

"We halted the release when we realized what was happening," Gabe said. "When we released the rest of the Defenders, only a few reacted to what was left. I'm pretty confident that whatever they were after is gone. What's up?"

"That device also has the ability for timed releases of toxins," Julie said.

"*What*?" Ruby said.

Julie nodded. "Just what I said. I can't tell if it actually released toxins, but whatever that device was, it had that capability."

"Wonderful," Ruby sighed. "So there's a potential for sabotage usage."

"Yes," Julie said. "I'll look closer at the indentured stats. It's supposed to be tied to a cyborg prototype, not a standard indentured." She frowned. "But that's the other thing. This is *military* tech. Not civilian."

"The Martiniere Group has military contracts," Gabe said.

"But how did it get into the labor pool? And how many farmers and ranchers are using this type of indentured right now?" Kris frowned. "Pat has been warning me about some ultra-secret indentured work going on at AgI over the last month or so. She was going to try to dig out more details, but so far it's been hard."

"Temira Cho told Jeff that she's not using indentured workers at all," Ruby said.

"What about these two indentured that Jeff had problems with?" Gabe asked. "Can we get some idea of what variety of indentured they are, and how much of a threat they pose?" He snapped his fingers and the shots of the two indentureds from Swait came up.

Brandon, Kris, and Justine brought these images up on their individual comps for closer study. Kris and Brandon murmured together as Brandon manipulated the image.

"I need to send these pix to Pat," Kris said finally. "I saw a few of those versions around AgI last spring but they weren't in the general indentured population. They're from the research compounds in Los Angeles, where she is. She will know more. But that's definitely an AgI tattoo on both of them."

"Carrie said they had fresh Martiniere Group trefoils tattooed on their necks," Ruby said.

Kris raised her brows. "Now that's weird. You can't run two unblotted tats like that on any indentureds. They conflict with the nanoprogramming. Even if one is masked and inactive."

"But what if they're owned by a subsidiary company?" Gabe asked.

"Subsidiaries don't mark. That's a primary owner thing." Kris thrust out her left hand. "See my tat?"

At first it appeared as if there was nothing there on the pale brown webbing between Kris's thumb and index finger. She tapped on it. A blue and green diamond appeared where she had tapped, with a red slash floating above it, bright against her dark skin.

"The red slash inactivates the nanos in my tat that identify me as an indentured," Kris said. "What most call blotting. Brandon and I have come up with a means to unmask the tat without the slash so that I can talk to indentureds and appear like one of them, without risking someone in AgI activating it."

Justine stirred. "You're certain that's a reliable tech?"

"No," Brandon said curtly. "I want that AgI tat removed because the inactivation code can be hacked. But Kris thinks it's too valuable to remove yet."

"Bran. With this tat masked I can slip into indentured space and spy. No one can use a scan to pick me out. Who else do we have with that ability? We *need* me to be able to collect this information." Kris frowned at Brandon.

Exasperation sharpened Brandon's voice. "I don't think it's safe. I scan it nightly to make sure AgI doesn't get its hooks in you. But I don't think that's enough protection."

"We still need me to be able to talk to the indentureds," Kris said firmly.

"Hey." Gabe raised his hand to stop them. "Not helping things. How does Kris's tat differ from those on these two workers?"

"There's no red slash on them," Brandon said. He enlarged the picture and pointed to the blue-green blur on the left hand of one of the indentureds. "I ran a probe. It's not inactivated. So either the Martiniere Group tat is fake, or the AgI tat is."

"Or they've formed an alliance," Gabe said harshly.

Brandon shook his head. "Not possible, not the way that implant tats work. But this requires analysis work to dig into it further. I've got to get back to Chicago to finish off the Alliance conference prep. Can anyone else do the research in the labs here?"

"I'm on it," Julie said tensely. "Kris?"

Kris and Brandon exchanged a glance. "Bran has to be back in Chicago right away," Kris said. "I need to be there tomorrow morning."

"I can get you there tonight if he doesn't need you before then," Justine said. "Going shooting with Ruby after this meeting, but I plan to be back in Chicago this evening. Want to join us?"

Kris shook her head. "Much as I'd like to go for a cathartic shootfest, I want to get right on the analysis. You okay with me coming back later?" she asked Brandon. "I wouldn't think you need me for the tech run through."

"Compared to the Innovator it's a piece of cake," he said, smiling at Kris. "No. You need to run the analysis with Julie. That's more important."

"Okay," Gabe said. "We'll talk about results of your analysis this afternoon before you leave, Kris. Now. What about this political proposal of Philip's?"

"That's my evening meeting," Justine said. "I've got my legal team working on the implications. They should have a report for me by then. Serg will be back from Europe, and I'll send him here with what I have tomorrow. I need to be in Chicago for both the Alliance and the Reals to stay on top of things there. I can't get into platform meetings today, but there's more going on tomorrow that I can attend."

"Okay. We have those pieces dealt with for the moment. Tine, can your legal team start devising defenses against Philip's indentured proposals, just in case?" Gabe waved at the others. "We have too many vulnerable people in our operation besides Brandon. I don't want to sacrifice any of them."

"That was my plan, Gabie." Justine smirked at him. It faded quickly. "And the vulnerability isn't just in the GMR Group. I have too many employees at risk in my JSM company as well. I plan to lurk around the edges at both the Alliance and the Reals to see who I can influence. Some of those Reals last night did not look happy. They won't bolt to the New Dems or Honest Repubs, much less the Classic Democrats…but they might sit out the election. Of course, we're over a year out. Things can change and fast."

"Can we trust them, though?"

Justine spread her hands. "I wouldn't bring them into the inner circle. But we could sure use their income in the Alliance."

"Agreed." Gabe pursed his lips. "So we have Julie and Kris investigating what information we can strip from the data Swait gave us about his indentureds. Martin, are you working with them on that?"

Martin shook his head. "Getting the Defenders you brought back from Swait ready for the test release here tomorrow. I want to sow some nasties on the Homestead field this afternoon as prep."

"Okay. Julie, do you two need a third? I can jump in if you need my support—unless Martin needs me," Gabe said.

"If you could rove between us that would help, Gabe," Martin said. "It's pretty simple but there will be moments where I could use an extra hand in the lab. Terri can help me with the field, and if someone else can jump in out there—"

"I can help with the field part," Ruby said.

Gabe squinted at her. "You and Justine are going shooting."

"I'm taking just a little bit of down time. Not the whole rest of the day. There's always paperwork that needs to be done."

"You need some down time."

"You do too. When are you taking it?" The words came out sharper than she intended. Gabe's lips tightened.

"I'm going to rest before going to the lab," he said. "You clearly need some time out riding."

"All right. See that you do it." She glanced at Julie and Kris. "If he shows up at the lab in sooner than two hours, chase him back to the house, okay?"

"*Ruby*," Gabe growled.

Brandon chuckled. "You just got called out by Mom, Dad. I

would not push your luck." He stretched. "What else do we have? I need to head out as soon as I can."

"I need to talk to Martin and Rick for lab planning," Gabe said. "The rest of you don't need to be here for that."

"All right!" Justine said. "Next meeting?"

"Given what we're dealing with, I think we should have a full Group meeting after the Alliance conference, next Monday," Gabe said. "Then we'll know more about a lot of things."

"Sounds good." Justine nodded. "Ruby, I'm going to change and will be ready to ride out soon."

"Good." Ruby took her plate to the kitchen. Brandon followed her.

"Last night was a bad one for him, wasn't it?" he said softly to Ruby. "It shows."

She nodded. "Rougher than usual. The nightmares had quieted down for a while but they were back worse than ever. I don't know if it was the flight, or learning about Philip running for the Presidency, or what."

"I'm worried about him holding up. We need him to counter Philip. I am not ready to become *the* Martiniere. There's a lot of work that needs to happen before then."

"I know, but," Ruby sighed. "I'm worried, too."

"Ma, I *know* you can kick him in the butt and make him take care of himself. You did it for me after all, and that was one Martiniere man." Brandon grinned at her. "He's older and at a disadvantage."

"And he's set in his ways," Ruby said. "We were apart for twenty-one years. Some habits are hard to break."

Brandon eyed her. "You need to take care of yourself too, Ma. Dad's not the only one I worry about. You look tired."

"We're all tired. There's a lot going on."

"Yeah. And this latest news speeds up the pace." He took a deep breath and leaned against the sink, staring down at the gray-flecked white vinyl tile. "I really am worried about Kris keeping that tat. It's not as benign as she makes it sound. There are a couple of pieces of the implant that I wasn't able to inactivate to my satisfaction. Phenerome and hormone generators that are only inserted into women's tats. The only thing that gets rid of those pieces is complete removal."

"What purpose would those serve?" Ruby thought she knew but—no. No one had mentioned this prospect. And how would it work, anyway, in freed former indentureds like Kris? She leaned against the sink next to Brandon, sipping the rest of her cup. As good as the coffee tasted, this had to be her last cup. She was already feeling jittery from the buzz.

Brandon glanced at her and grimaced. "Birth control overrides."

Ruby scowled into her cup. Exactly what she thought. "So how does it work?"

"Overrides, kidnapping, artificial insemination, keeping the former indentured confined until she bears the child." Ruby gasped. Before she could say anything, Brandon held up a hand to stop her. "No, it hasn't happened so far among former indentureds in the US. I know that Beck says otherwise from her links with European indentureds. But Kris has heard rumors from her networks that former Martiniere indentured women are experiencing unanticipated changes in their menstrual cycles, and Pat says it *is* being attempted with the current indentured in the research compounds. She's still trying to find out more about it. At least there doesn't appear to be forced sex on a large scale involved. So far. Nothing bigger than the stuff Dad testified about thirty years ago."

"Have you told your father about this yet?"

"And add to everything else he's juggling? Not until we have more solid information. We're hearing a lot of weird stuff that doesn't play out. But." He paused, looking out the window. "The other piece is that Kris and I are talking about getting married. Having kids. I *do not* want AgI or anyone else mucking around with her body."

"She's not willing?"

"Oh, she's willing. It's a matter of timing." Brandon sighed. "And she's right. We have to get Dad placed in charge of the Martiniere Group before we dare make any sort of commitment to each other. I am *not* going to create a potential defenseless hostage if I can help it. At least she knows who I am, when you didn't know who Dad was. I just hope…." His voice trailed off.

She reached out and took his hand. "Good luck, Bran. Seriously. I approve."

"Do me a favor. Please don't tell Dad that Kris and I are discussing marriage and kids. Not yet."

"Why?"

He shook his head. "I can't explain why you can't tell him because of promises I've made to him. Promises I've made to Kris—that we've made to each other."

"I don't understand."

"Forget I've said this then, Ma. Okay?" He gave her a pleading look so much like Gabe's. "It's not that it's a bad secret that he's hiding from you or anything like that. It's just that it involves issues he has to work out for himself about becoming the Martiniere. If you tell him about me and Kris, he might rush through things that shouldn't be hurried for my sake. Squabble as we do, I'm nonetheless getting a feel for how he operates as a Martiniere as opposed to Gabe Ramirez, plus learning from him and Justine just how this family works. Dad does better when he can work the long game, and his focus needs to be on Philip. Not on me."

"Martiniere Family issues then."

Relief spread across his face. "Exactly."

"Damn it." She finished her coffee and set the cup in the sink, then went to the refrigerator to check the schedule. Beck and Rick's day to clean up the kitchen.

"Yeah." Brandon crossed the kitchen and hugged her. "And with that, I'm going to drop in on Dad, then head back to Chicago. You stay safe, okay?"

"I will," she promised.

CHAPTER 4

RUBY RUBBED HER RIGHT SHOULDER AS SHE LEANED AGAINST Legacy, holding Casey's halter rope. It ached after all the shooting they'd done, not just her saddle rifle but trying out new weapons. Justine had produced a modified new semiautomatic rifle, the SPA7, that Serg had come across in his European travels. It was a lovely, balanced weapon that broke down easily for concealment, and was oh-so-seductive to shoot as well. And oh-so-potentially-dangerous in the wrong hands.

Which might even be ours.

But she had to admire the skill with which Justine broke down the rifle and placed it into the compact gun case in front of Casey. Ruby had never probed very deeply into the businesses that made up Justine's JSM Corp, but she had the strong impression that weapons dealing and design was one facet of them.

"I'm going to message Serg when we get back to the house," Justine said, as she disassembled the SPA7 and carefully put away the pieces. "We take delivery of two hundred of these little beauties next week to be split between here and Gabie's Moondance, with five hundred more in two weeks pending my approval. I approve. What do you think?"

"It certainly performed well. But do we need that many rifles?"

Justine shrugged as she stood and put the case in one of her saddlebags.

"Contingencies. I prefer to figure out how many of these little darlings we need to get rid of *after* Gabie dumps Daddy-fucking-dearest from the Group leadership. Better than to not have enough and need them."

"There is that."

Justine pulled a bioplast bag out of the other saddlebag and marched up the narrow draw toward the various logs and stumps that served as backstops for the impromptu Double R shooting range. She stopped at the closest one and took pictures before sticking the remnants of the hole-ridden Philip Martiniere campaign poster into the bioplast.

Ruby checked over the mares while Justine cleaned up. Neither Casey nor Legacy showed signs of washy, nervous sweat.

Good.

There hadn't been any time to desensitize Legacy to gunfire after they had been shot at in the spring. It was a relief to see that the golden mare was not bothered. And Casey was familiar with gunshots, after all, as she had been used for hunting in past years.

Justine trudged back with the bag of shot-up posters. "That was good," she sighed. "I'm ready for lunch now."

"I'll get it." Ruby turned to her own saddlebags and pulled out the lunch sack, handling Justice a sandwich. "Now that we're done shooting, we can hobble the girls and let them graze."

"You sure you trust me after last time?" While Justine knew how to ride at a fairly high level, she had never learned practicalities such as how to put hobbles on a horse. The last time they went shooting and hobbled the horses, somehow the hobbles on Justine's mount had come loose.

"Casey won't run off from Legacy, not like Red. Besides, practice is always good."

"All right," Justine said reluctantly.

Ruby quickly hobbled Legacy and dropped her lead rope on the ground to drag. She checked Justine's hobble job.

"What looks good for a place to sit?" she asked Justine. "Log, ground, shade, sun?"

"You pick," Justine said. "Are we getting dirty or is there a blanket?"

"No room for a blanket with guns, ammo, and lunch."

Justine laughed. "Priorities! All right, as long as there aren't a lot of bugs."

Ruby glanced around, then headed uphill toward a small patch of bunchgrass under a big Ponderosa pine. The ground had enough of a slant that getting up shouldn't be much of a problem. She was feeling the stiffness from the hours of flying yesterday. And there was sufficient shade to blunt the rising heat of the day. At least the dry heat of mountain desert country was much more pleasant than the muggy Arkansas heat of yesterday.

"What is it that you wanted to talk about? Something you didn't want Gabe to hear, I assume," Ruby said.

"Yeah. It's an additional complication that I just learned about," Justine said, frowning at the last bite of her sandwich.

Ruby tightened her lips and shook her head. "God damn, it's like everyone has something going on that they don't want me to tell Gabe about. What's *your* secret?"

"It's nothing tangible—yet." Justine finished her sandwich. "But it's something that Serg came across in Europe, along with that sweet little rifle."

"Go on."

"Pictures of Angelica, Gabie's mom. With Philip. Before Gabe's birth. Nine months before."

"Oh. But maybe there's a reason."

"*That* kind of pictures, Ruby. Compromising. And the timing would be such that...." Justine's voice trailed off as she poked at the ground with a twig. "And you know what is the funnier complication? The same source has pictures of Saul, Gabie's dad, with Renate, my mother. Before Joey was born. Same timing."

Ruby's eyebrows shot up. "That *is* a complicating factor."

"Yeah. Nothing that would change things for me, or Gabe's sister Louisa. But the boys. There always *has* been some speculation about Joey's father being someone other than Daddy-damned-dearest, but until two weeks ago there was nothing to support it. Both Saul and Daddy-poo went extremely private when us kids were little. For a few years we even lived together in the same huge European estate. I was too young to remember much going on except there were a lot of guards and a *lot* of shouting between the adults at the end, and Donna-gran was *pissed*. Which you don't want to see with our grandmother. But before his cosmetic surgery Gabie always looked more like Daddy dearest than Joey does, while Joey is the image of Saul." She sighed. "Long story short, an old family connection contacted Serg with these pictures. Supposedly reliable. It would explain a lot—like why Daddy *didn't* kill Gabie but chose to attack those close to him. I've wondered about that for some time, *really* started thinking about it six months ago."

"Photos can be faked."

"I know. That's why I've had Serg looking into records and searching for anything more tangible before resorting to DNA testing. We're limited there. If we find some evidence that Gabie is Daddy-poo's son instead of Saul's, and vice versa with Joey, short of making them all take DNA tests, that really blows things up. Serg's also been feeling out the Old Country relatives. Joey is not popular with them at all. Gabie? And Brandon? They're cautious but intrigued by them."

"It still seems like a big pile of a sexist hot mess to me," Ruby said. "You're more than capable of running the Group. More so than your brother, from what I've seen of Joseph. Why haven't you stepped up?"

"Because the Martiniere Group *is* a sexist hot mess, especially at the higher, older leadership levels. The younger members—

Brandon's age—are different. But none of them are at the Board level to influence decisions about who is and isn't eligible yet. Tradition says that the Group is always led by someone from the Board families. And it's likely that Brandon will have kids, unless something happens to him. That is a huge factor for the older and more traditional family members. Gabie has an heir young enough to have his own kids eventually. They have to pass over Joey and Gabie to find the next child of Louis and Donna who has kids and grandkids. That would be our uncle Gerard, and his son David. And David only has a daughter, Juliette."

Ruby frowned. "Does a child have to be legitimate?"

"Oh no. But Joey's never had much interest in anything more than one night stands, and as far as I know none of them have resulted in a kid. I had a hysterectomy when I was young—and had no desire after that to become a mother."

Ruby traced a circle in the dirt with her index finger, thinking it over. Brandon hadn't said anything about not telling Justine.

"Someone may be taking action to change Gabe's unique status," she said reluctantly.

"What do you mean?" Justine sat up.

"Brandon told me that Kris just heard that any former female indentured who still carries a tat can have birth control overridden. He mentioned artificial insemination."

"Oh fuck. I heard the rumors about Europe, but here?"

"They're not sure about the US. I know Beck left Ireland so that even as a former indentured she wouldn't be forced into having some bigwig's baby."

Justine sighed. "Shit. I knew about Beck. Have heard the same rumors and just haven't had time to talk to Kris about it yet. You don't think...oh yes. It wouldn't just be Joey seeking an heir that way. Daddy-damned-dearest would definitely try it. Ooh. What happens to Joey if our dear father gets a batch of heirs that Daddy-poo likes better than him? Or if he acknowledges Gabie as his son?" She paused. "Although. Who's going to raise a kid of Daddy-dearest? He's not going to live forever. Even though he keeps trying to find an anti-aging serum."

"For that matter, who else in the Group would benefit from A.I. babies? Or other powerful men? How many of those damn Reals would jump at the opportunity to spawn a horde of their own?"

"It wouldn't be just the Reals," Justine said. "God, Ruby. Um. Would clones be possible?"

"Human clones, no. As far as I know. Not yet." Ruby tapped her chin thoughtfully. "I'd have to do a more thorough lit search to be certain. There's been some problems with the process in humans, last time I looked."

Justine chewed on her lower lip. "They have to make provisions for raising babies in any case. Either for the women to raise their babies or for a crèche-like situation. Easy enough to trace through supply movements if it is a big enough operation. They'll want the best for their broodmares and then their spawn so they'll take them out of indentured space. And then there would be a need for support staff. It would require...." She stared out at the draw, tapping her fingers on the ground, then started tracing numbers into a dust patch.

"It's as yet unconfirmed," Ruby said while Justine worked, as much for her own reassurance as for Justine's.

"But oh, yes now this all makes sense," Justine said finally. "Last night's rhetoric at the Reals. If they can call back former indentureds because they like their gene scans enough to have them carry babies for them...then they will. Don't kid yourself, *anyone* who comes under indenture gets a gene scan. Some of those men in the Reals would be quite happy to have a harem of forced indentured sex slaves, especially gene-selected women." She gestured toward the ground, then scuffed it up to obscure what she had been tracing. "I need to look at some more specific data, *but* when I think about it, off the top of my head there's a supply trend that would indicate such plans are in the works. Just from movement of materials."

"What does that mean? And how far along do you think they are?"

"Early stages. Otherwise I would know more about it from my connections." Justine looked at Ruby. "Which means it's a lot easier to disrupt their plans."

"Brandon didn't want me to tell Gabe about this possibility just yet. Not until we know more from Kris's investigation."

"We need Gabie to focus on the Group and on Daddy *dearest*." Justine spat out the last word. "We don't know enough to tell him more. Yet."

"More secrets." Ruby sighed. She drew her knees up to her chest and buried her head. "I hate keeping secrets."

"What can I say? We're a secretive bunch." Justine paused. "Well, here's one I bet Gabie hasn't shared with you. Has he asked you to marry him yet?"

Ruby raised her head. "Several times. And I've told him no."

"Huh."

"I'm just not ready yet. Still figuring out all this Martiniere stuff."

"Understandable." Justine rolled over onto her stomach, focusing on fiddling with a dried grass stem, twisting it into a form. "But here's the deal. Gabie probably *can't* tell you about this piece, but I can."

"What do you mean?"

"Early mind manipulation by the family would block him from saying anything. Gabie's a high-level heir, so this would have been programmed into him at a very young age. Ooh. Brandon hasn't had that conditioning—that's something else to consider. Anyway. Priorities." Justine's mouth tightened. "Do you really want to gain power within the Martinieres, Ruby?" She looked up from the twists she was making in the grass stem.

"I have the distinct impression that I may need to do so for my own protection," Ruby said slowly.

"Exactly. This is how you do it. *When*—not *if*—you remarry Gabie. There is a ceremony performed by certain heirs within the

Martiniere Family after they marry. Not all—it's done by the choice of the Martiniere spouse. The Martiniere Ritual is what it's called. And it is based upon that conditioning I just mentioned. You see, every Martiniere heir at the Board Family level goes through programming from an early age. Women too, even though we're not eligible to inherit. Trigger words that stop them for a moment. Remember when I took the gun from Joey at the end of the AgInnovator?"

"First time I met him and Philip. It's not something I'm going to easily forget."

"I have certain trigger words for Joey, and he the same for me. We're *limited* in what we can do to each other. Unfortunately, I have no words for Daddy. Serg does for certain things, Gabie may still have one as well. The only one who has all the words would be Donna-gran—and she had a hand in creating the most recent version of the programming."

"This Martiniere Ritual does—what? Gives me control over certain people?"

"In most cases, yes. It would give you the words for people Gabie already has them for. But. There's more. Gabie is not the acknowledged Martiniere heir yet. Bring the factions together behind him, especially the old country Board member Families, and he becomes *the* Martiniere-in-waiting." Justine sat up, brushing off her front and dropping the twisted grass into the dust beside her. "With all the privileges of *the* Martiniere, including limited access to everyone's words, with only the Martiniere having his words. Unless Donna-gran gives Gabie more power than that. But she's the Matriarch. Doesn't give her everything, but...."

"Then Joseph has that much power now." Ruby noticed that Justine had twisted the stem into something close to a Martiniere trefoil.

Justine shook her head. "There isn't a Martiniere-in-waiting right now. Not Joey. Not Gabie—yet. The Board can't agree on anyone, hasn't since Gabie disappeared. There's a couple of other prospects out there, but Gabie's in the lead simply because he's the only one with a son. And there's a growing sentiment that he did the right thing thirty years ago when he testified against the company."

"Oh God, this *is* a sexist hot mess. Except for—Donna-gran? Your grandmother—the Matriarch?"

"Donna-gran is a law unto herself, and even she doesn't have that much power over Daddy dearest, alas," Justine said sharply, reaching for another grass stem. "Otherwise things would be a lot better for women in this damn family. All the same, it's a sexist hot mess in transition, *finally*. Here's the deal. You remarry Gabie. Then immediately afterward you go through the Martiniere Ritual. That gives you an independent status within the Family. Your voice carries the same mind control authority as Gabie's does in Family matters, as long as he lives, but not the Group, alas. When he dies—*poof!* It's all gone, unless you're the Matriarch. And even that is limited."

"But Philip and Joseph—"

Justine waved dismissively. "They have no influence in this situation. In fact, if they did act, they would immediately lose all credibility within the Family, especially amongst the oldest and most traditional members."

"But—how is this sort of mind control even possible?"

"The Martinieres have been in the body and brain mod business for years, Ruby. Use of psychotropic meds combined with mindfulness training and biofeedback, for starters. Conditioning and coding to very specific triggers. It's gotten more sophisticated over the years." She held her hand out to Ruby, pointing to a ring with a dark blue stone on her right hand. "Words coupled with activating a program in this ring. There are wedding rings passed down within the family for this exact purpose. It's tied to marriage for us women."

"Wow. I—I don't know what to say." Ruby stared down at her hands. "Do *you* think I should say yes to Gabe the next time he proposes?"

"It's up to you, lady. Marrying the lead candidate to be *the* Martiniere is going to be a big thing to take on, and I don't advise you to be casual about it. Especially given the history that you and Gabie have." Justine dropped the second stem twisted into a trefoil next to the first.

Ruby sighed. "And if I don't do it then I'd better get the hell out of the way for someone else who can."

"Pfft!" Justine snorted. "Fat chance of that happening. No. Gabie's head-over-heels about you. It shows big time. It's you or no one. He can get away without looking around because of Brandon."

"I wish I could believe that he's that much in love with me," Ruby said softly. "What happens if I don't marry him?"

"Nothing except that's one less tool we can use against Philip. You'd still have some authority. But the old ones don't necessarily have to receive you or listen to what you have to say." Justine shrugged, snapping off a third stem. "It's not a big deal at this stage of the process. Gabie isn't ready to approach the Board, either himself or through Brandon—and you."

"I just don't know." Ruby sank her head in her hands. "I'm worried about Brandon. About Gabe. But where do *I* fit in? What about what *I* want? What *I* feel?"

"What *do* you want? Forget all this other stuff. What does Ruby Barkley want to do with herself from now on?"

Ruby raised her head. "I want…to see the RubyBot line do well. Not just the variations we're developing with Jeff Swait, but the mods Gabe and I have come up with in the past six months. I want to see Brandon settled down and successful. I want to keep riding good horses in beautiful country, maybe even someday be able to have a breeding operation. I want…." Her voice trailed off, then picked up, more firm. "I want to be respected in my own right and not as any man's shadow. I suppose that rules out any role I might have as a Martiniere wife."

"You might be surprised," Justine said. "After all, the last wife of a Board member to swear to the Ritual? Angelica. And she was hardly Saul's shadow." She dropped the third trefoil twist by the others.

"Gabe's mother?"

"Yes. She was anything but a pushover, from what little I remember. And you know what? My father never offered my mother the opportunity for the Ritual." Bitterness crept into Justine's voice. "He was such an ass to her. Cruel. She drank herself to death."

"I'm sorry."

"Thanks. I know you understand what that's like."

Ruby nodded. "And I had grandparents to take me in." She shuddered. "Doesn't make it any easier. Not with what I remember."

"At least you got to shoot your damn father."

"As a six-year-old," Bitterness matching Justine's earlier tone crept into Ruby's voice. "After hours of being terrified when they kidnapped me from Granma and Gramps that last time. Escalating fights, crazy meth stuff. *She* went looking for the gun first but I hid it from her, because by then I'd figured out if one of them killed the other, I'd be next. Then *she* jumped *him*. After *he* beat her to death, he turned on me. That's when I shot him. Gramps—he thought such a thing would happen. That's why he brought me out here to practice shooting, even though I was a little kid. That's how I knew what to do."

"God, Ruby."

Ruby shook her head. "It was fast and violent, and it was over and done. Not like what you went through."

Justine bit her lip and looked down. "I got lucky with Donald. We were organizing—what we do. And—Daddy-poo was playing games with us. Don and I make good business partners and occasional lovers, but nothing more than that. Mismatched sex drives. He likes to play more than I do. I'm an adrenaline addict and workaholic. I want to dance on the edge and take risks. Not so much him. The intrigues he gets into through me are enough, or so he says."

"I don't know about me and Gabe," Ruby said slowly, playing with a pair of pine needles, delicately trying to weave them together as she spoke. "Working with him again as a colleague and partner…it makes me regret the twenty-one years we spent apart. Some of what changes things is the Martiniere money, but the last breakthroughs that earned the RubyBot its distribution license? Gabe helped solve those problems. And the improved delivery system for his latest microbial brew? I worked that out."

"But—?" Justine prompted.

"Personally, I don't know. The last few weeks we've started to snipe at each other like we did during our last year together. It's stress. I know that's what it is. It doesn't help that the house is full and we share a room if not a bed. I sleep in my office for a couple of hours some nights just to get some space." The pine needles snapped. Ruby sighed and picked up another two, this time with more green along their two-inch length.

"Sex doesn't help?"

Ruby snorted. "What sex? I haven't been interested in years and Gabe is—well…."

"Oh shit, he got *that* G9 side effect."

"Yeah. And that raises another issue. I am absolute *shit* as a caregiver. It makes me nervous. I do what I'm supposed to do but I could be a hell of a lot better. As a girlfriend I can detach. I don't know if I can do that as a wife, and from what I've read of post-G9 syndrome, the condition only gets worse."

"Those are all factors to consider," Justine stretched.

"I also don't want to be swallowed up by the Martinieres more than I am already."

"Trust me, you're not the first or only Martiniere-adjacent woman who's expressed that sentiment to me," Justine said. "You're being smart. Though if anyone can step into the role of Gabie's wife without losing herself, you can." She laughed bitterly. "You're of more use to me as your own woman. Yeah. I admit that I exploit everyone around me. That's what I do. I'm my father's daughter in that respect. All the same, I *like* you, Ruby Barkley, just as you are, as a friend. There are damn few women I can say that about."

"Thanks."

"I hope this talk helped."

"It does," Ruby said. "Learning about the Ritual and a bit more about family structures. No matter what Gabe and I end up doing, it looks like I have a role to play, for Brandon's sake if nothing else." She stood up and brushed off her seat. "Gives me a lot to think about. And if Gabe is Philip's son, then that throws another twist into the whole game."

"It does, doesn't it?" Justine stood. They ambled down to the grazing mares. "I admit, an involvement with Daddy-poo doesn't match what I know about Angelica. Unless she had an ulterior motive, I just don't see it happening. And Mother never talked much about Saul—although come to think of it, she seemed to go into more of a decline after he died. Joey *is* six months younger than Gabie, so if monkey business was going on, it was nearly simultaneous. But without any more documentation, who knows what was going on?"

"Another thing to figure out."

They bridled the mares and unhobbled them. Ruby did a last check to ensure that cinches and saddlebags were secured before she swung up on Legacy.

Their return trip took them by the lower fields that had been treated using the RubyBots in the spring. Ruby paused Legacy to eye each field, pleased with the height and the color of the different grain crops. Justine rode ahead, calling up her comm once they were back in connectivity range. From the bits and pieces that drifted back to her Ruby surmised that Justine was reporting the morning's shoot to Serg. She held Legacy back to give Justine some privacy, even though she hadn't activated a shield to block her conversation.

At last Justine turned Casey and rejoined Ruby. "Sounds like I approved that next SPA7 shipment just in time. Serg says that new orders have quadrupled since Philip's speech last night."

"Other Martinieres or someone else?"

"He doesn't know for sure right now and that's what bothers me. He says two-thirds of the destinations are here in the US. That may or may not be Martinieres. The European orders—yes. He's certain those branches of the Family are arming up." Justine was quiet for a moment. "That doesn't mean anything too drastic right now, Ruby. The old country Family members maintain hefty weapons stockpiles and add to them whenever they sense changes coming. Philip's speech last night may have been enough to set some of them off."

"That's not good."

"I would not get excited about it just yet. We'll see what happens once they get their hands on those weapons." A world-weary, cynical note came into Justine's voice. "It is also just as likely to blow over in a few weeks. Then they'll sell off the excess to whatever band of revolutionaries is out there shopping at the moment. The old country likes to play in those areas when openings arise."

"God." Ruby took up a firmer contact as Legacy spotted the barns and quickened her step, checking the golden mare before she broke into a trot.

"They can be nasty bastards," Justine said as they passed through the gate and into the barnyard.

Beck met them in the barn, paler than usual.

"It's starting," she said, her voice harsh with fear. She pulled up the long sleeve of her lightweight shirt to show Ruby and Justine her old indentured tattoo. "My tat's been activated, and my period is two weeks early."

The red slash that had obscured the old tattoo of Beck's former indentured owner, Biosystems AG, was gone.

"What am I gonna do?" Beck asked, her voice turning frantic.

"They can't take you off the ranch," Ruby said. "We can surround you with security."

"They've overridden Kris's cancel too," Beck said. "She's in the house trying not to freak out. I mean—god. Another six months and I would have made it to my scheduled hysterectomy date—if it didn't get stretched out again. And maybe been able to get those hormone tags neutralized in my tats." She burst into tears. "But now what? Now what?"

Justine and Ruby's eyes met. Justine nodded, lips tightening. Ruby nodded back.

"I can fix this," Justine said to Beck as Ruby took Casey's reins. "We can't do it in Lakeside, but let's sit down with Kris and figure this out. One way or another we'll get this taken care of. I know someone who can do it. I do this all the time for women in need." She turned to Ruby. "I hate to dump the horses on you but I'd better deal with this."

"Don't worry about leaving me with the horses. I don't know squat about—dealing with this—and I probably don't want to know." Though she desperately wanted to ask.

A brief grin tightened Justine's lips. "You're right. It's need-to-know only. All right, Beck. Let's get this process rolling."

After caring for the mares and putting them in a large pen, Ruby checked in with Martin in the lab. He was poring over a small mechanical figure.

"Couple of hours before I'll need you," he said. "No need to go through decontam again, just meet me outside. I'm preparing a few nasties that these darlings will release, plus copies of the behavior I extrapolated from what we could get from those indentured at Swait's to see if that's a trigger. It won't be a perfect simulation of that situation Swait described but it will give me data on the Defender response. That way if we need to expand its role, we can."

Ruby shuddered at the thought of what those expanded roles might include and glanced around. "Where's Gabe?"

"Went up to the house for lunch and hasn't come back yet. Probably just as well with the latest developments—you heard?"

"Beck met me and Justine at the barn."

Martin nodded. "Luckily she'd finished her work on the grow—which was why Gabe went back to the house before it happened." He jerked his head toward the isolated section of the lab that was Beck and Rick's domain for cultivating their stem seeds. "Rick's locked down, finishing it off. He still doesn't know. I'll tell him when he's done."

"How are Julie and Terri taking the news?"

"Scared. But they didn't get implants. You hired them the day before they went indentured, so they're feeling pretty damn lucky right now." Martin gave her a tight grin. "I've got the lab under control. So, say about four-ish."

"Okay. Thanks."

There was no sign of Justine or the others when Ruby came into the house, kicking off her boots on the back porch. Nor were they in her office. Ruby went down to Gabe's office. No sign of him there, or in the living room. Maybe he was actually resting?

She went upstairs. Their bedroom door was firmly shut and she heard the faint whir of the window air conditioner, as well as voices coming from Brandon and Kris's room. So that was where they had gone. For a moment Ruby considered joining the other women. But fatigue pulled at her. Taking a lie-down sounded very good after the restless night.

They don't need me in the middle of it, she decided. *If they want something from me, they'll call.*

Justine's comment that this was need-to-know only nagged at Ruby—who was she, the Rescue Angel who helped women with reproductive issues?

Probably not, Ruby decided. That would require even more resources than she thought Justine had available. But that didn't mean that Justine wasn't tied to the Rescue Angel somehow.

Instead she went into her bedroom. Gabe lay in his recliner, curtains pulled over the windows so that the room was dark as well as cool. While his eyes had been closed, they popped back open and he lowered the recliner footrest as she quietly shut the door.

"The mess is getting more complicated," he said quietly. "I can't hear everything but I heard enough to know something's going on with Beck and Kris."

"Yeah." Ruby sighed. Now that she was up here, the coolness of the room and the darkness felt good. Standing here made her realize how tired she was.

"What's up?"

She shook her head. "I'm letting Justine handle it. Connections." She decided not to share her sudden suspicion about Justine being connected with the Rescue Angel.

"Makes sense."

"And I was checking on you." She tensed, in case he snapped at her like he had earlier.

He chuckled. A good sign. He'd gotten some rest, then. "I think you need to take your own advice."

"Lying down looks good," she admitted. "But I'm not enthusiastic about changing my clothes to do it. I'm going to help Martin with distributing the test nasties in Homestead when he's done. He'll be ready in two hours. I should work in the office, but...I'm tired."

Gabe shifted his position and patted the recliner seat. "I'm not so big that I take up this whole monster. Come join me." When she hesitated, he added, "You're not so big, either. I may be getting old and decrepit, but I can still have a pretty lady sitting on my lap. Especially one wearing eau de horse and gunpowder." He raised a brow at her. "Specifically, a pretty lady who just yelled at me this morning about resting but who clearly needs it herself. Come on. I don't bite."

"Flatterer." But he *was* persuasive. She emptied her pockets on the dresser and pulled off her socks before approaching the chair. Despite Gabe's confident words, sharing the seat looked cramped. And she wasn't sure about sitting on his lap.

"Here. You aren't going to break me." He opened his arms. She eased herself down. His arms tightened around her and held her firmly. "I'm not made of porcelain, Rubes. Even with the post-G9 syndrome."

"You're sure this is okay?"

"Relax. Rest." He pushed them back and shifted sideways so that the majority of her weight was on the chair and not him. "Better?"

"Yeah," she sighed. "Oh. I should set a timer." She reached up and wiggled her fingers to set the alarm.

"Did you see Martin's robots?" Gabe chuckled when she was done. "I think he's letting his inner mad scientist out."

"Oh God yes. Tomorrow's test is going to be interesting."

They fell silent, the faint whir of the air conditioning blurring out all but the most high-pitched voices next door, still sounding worried.

Ruby tensed. "Maybe I'd better go see what's going on."

"Relax," Gabe said. "Tine can handle it." He sighed. "I stuck my head in just to check when I first came upstairs. Tine told me to butt out and rest. That you knew what was going on. That I needed to delegate because I had enough other things to worry about." He stroked her cheek. "Is she right?"

"Yeah. She's the expert. You and I need to stay out of it."

"Delegating is hard. I want to know everything. But I can't." He sighed. "So you two had a good shoot fest, ride, and chat? You're not as edgy as you were."

"Yeah. New rifle that Serg found, the SPA7. Very portable, accurate, decent recoil, just a darling to shoot and will easily convert to auto."

"I see." Once again, he traced the Martiniere trefoil on her cheek. "Good thing you two hit it off so well. She's a good source for learning about the Family. I'm not sure I want to know even half of what she and Serg are up to with her JSM Corp."

"We talked a bit about the Family."

"Oh." His forefinger stilled for a moment, then resumed tracing the trefoil. "Scary prospect, isn't it?"

"More like a sexist hot mess, even though your grandmother sounds like she's not part of it," Ruby said sourly. "And you know me, Gabe. I don't go stomping around spouting feminist platitudes. But really? Your family's business setup is medieval as hell."

"It was set up by some very controlling and very powerful men of their time, several centuries ago. And changing it is going to take a lot of work."

Ruby took a deep breath. "She also told me about the Martiniere Ritual."

His finger stopped again. "She did." His voice was emotionless now. "I don't want you to feel forced into this, Ruby. Not for my sake. Not even for Bran. I—" he choked and gulped, swallowing hard, eyes widening.

"Is a mind control compulsion interfering with what you want to say?" she asked.

Relief softened his face. "Yes, damn it!"

"I always thought those things were science-fictiony."

"They are very real. And apparently the G9 didn't get rid of *all* my programming." His finger started moving again on her cheek. "But I meant what I said. I don't want you to think that you're being forced into this. Or that you have to marry me because of—" He gestured with his hand. "Things I can't say. Right now."

"Do you think I would really do that?"

"If you thought it would make things better for me—or Bran—yes. I know you would. But I don't want you to say yes because it would make a difference in fighting Philip. That's not what I want. I want you saying yes because you want to be married to *me*. I'm getting old. I'm sick. I'm selfish, and I don't want to be married to someone who feels compelled to do it for political reasons. Doesn't mean I won't stop asking until you reach a point where you can say yes whole-heartedly, because

I'm hoping sooner or later that will happen. I just know it's going to take time."

Ruby sighed and moved slightly so that her head was on Gabe's chest.

"I'm not ready yet," she said in a small voice.

"I understand," he said, his voice matching hers.

The voices in the other room seemed to steady and calm in pitch.

—*Ruby*, Justine texted. —*Where are you?*

She sighed and turned away from Gabe to subvocal her response.

—*Resting. With Gabe.*

—*Won't disturb then. It's settled. Leaving now. Back tomorrow with details.*

—*Thanks.*

She settled back down.

"Urgent?" Gabe asked.

"Justine. The situation is managed. I'll know more tomorrow."

"The slightest hint of what this is about?"

"Indentureds. Connected to Philip's proposals."

"And affecting Beck and Kris—no." Gabe moaned. "I'm going to trust you and Justine on this one, but I think I have a pretty good idea of what's coming down." He sighed, tensing a little under her. "I should probably get up and get back to work."

"No," Ruby said firmly. "*We* are going to rest here for a couple of hours. Even if I have to hold you down to do it. You just gave me that lecture. Listen to it for yourself."

"That's my Ruby." Gabe murmured. His comm chimed and it was his turn to shift to subvocal. It didn't take long.

"Well that's good news," he said. "Tim. The house at Moondance is finished. Not the labs—I told him not to prioritize them. But the house at least is done."

"Oh." Disappointment washed over her. "What does that mean?"

Are you moving back there?

Just thinking about Gabe moving out made her heart sink, in spite of her speech to Justine about wanting space. To not have him here….

"Want to come with me tomorrow to inspect it? After the Defender trials, of course. I'd sure appreciate the company. I—really don't want to look at it alone. Memories. And I want your input on several things about what to do there."

"Sure," she said.

"Thank you." He kissed the top of her head. Ruby snuggled close to him. But even though she was tired, sleep evaded her, her thoughts roiling and keeping her awake.

Gabe certainly *sounded* like he loved her. But he'd been loving and concerned like this before, then bolted when the threat from his family became too great. What would stop him from running again if he thought it would keep her safe? Did she dare trust him?

CHAPTER 5

"What kind of nasties did you plant out here last night, besides those robots?" Gabe asked Martin as the big crawler pulled the trailer full of rectangular, beehive-like growboxes along the narrow track leading to the Homestead field. Ruby sat between them, half-listening to their conversation as she programmed her scanner to track the data that the Defenders would—hopefully—be sending back to them. But there was one glitch tied into Martin's robots that kept resisting her best efforts. Eventually she'd defeat it. She just had to find the bug in the programming.

"A little bit of everything I have on hand," Martin said. "I decided to focus on how the Defender performs against deliberate sabotage by mechanical or biological means instead of the typical pest and weed issues. I want to see if we can push Defender to work against field saboteurs. I've got four robots out there programmed with the data you brought back, each with slightly different emphases."

"Can the Defender be pushed to work away from fields?" Gabe's voice tightened.

Ruby tuned Gabe and Martin out as she focused on the programming. They were just brainstorming, and she honestly didn't want to be part of this security discussion. Getting this tracker to function properly was more important. There it was—ah. The monitoring program popped up above her scanner, and she ran her test self-check. Working as it should, *finally*.

"There." She closed the program and settled back. "That's ready to roll."

"Looked like you had to fight the algorithm," Gabe said.

Ruby shrugged. "Not bad. I left out a bracket in the coding and had to nitpick my way through to find it. It's a little bit different from what we've done before, and a finger just slipped to input the wrong thing."

"What do *you* think? Would it be possible to modify the Defender for security monitoring that isn't ag-related?" Gabe asked, a hopeful note in his voice. "We've been talking about it."

She considered the question. "It's possible," she said finally. "But I'd have to compare algorithms with either Justine or Serg —or one of their people, to be certain. Someone with more of a security programming background than I have. I'd be inclined to hand this project off to one of our associates with greater experience in security applications. That way we aren't repeating mistakes they've made and recreating structures they've already designed."

"But it's possible?"

"Depends on what kind of bot you're wanting to produce. Cams, sensors, that sort of thing, no doubt about the ability of the Defender to go that far. More than those applications, though, and I'd have questions."

"We'll see how the bots as they are now do against my robots," Martin said. "But those robots are hardly state-of-the-art. More just cobbling together a semi-credible watered-down version of potential non-human or extremely modified human threats to a field. That isn't as great a deviation from the Defender's original purpose to *eliminate all threats to the crop*. But mechanical? Extreme body mods or cyborgs? That's something I'm not sure of."

"You're thinking cyborgs are a possibility now?" Ruby raised her brows.

"Yeah, I texted that concern to Martin late last night," Gabe said grimly. "One of my nightmare thoughts, and extrapolating what another of the purposes for calling released indentureds back into service could be. I don't know how feasible it is. *Yet*. I suspect Serg can tell me. I keep thinking about those indentureds who showed up at Swait's. What has been done to them? Not completely cyborged, not so far. But how close do they come? And how can we defend ourselves against that possibility?"

Ruby shivered, remembering what she had already learned about Martiniere mind and body modifications.

"We need to create a firmer fail-safe for the hard stop mechanisms in the Defender before we go much further in our research," Martin said. "Otherwise we're at risk for the Defender interpreting normal equipment operating in the field as being a *threat to the crop*. What you're talking about will require good on-off switches."

"Have to develop bigger stem seeds, for one thing," Ruby mused.

"That's one aspect," Martin said. "And the other piece is that Ruby is right. This should be done by security experts, not ag experts branching out into security. For security purposes I'd want to go more toward a bio-based, cyborged design than I did for those robots. Even then we run into problems with energy consumption. Keep them small. Robots—with some modifications—will work fine for field saboteur defense because they won't have to be that big. They won't be continuously active except for regular scans, and those aren't big power draws. I would think that a non-ag security app would require more continuous movement."

They stopped at a gate, and Ruby slipped past Gabe to open the wire and post structure, then close it behind them. She scrambled onto the trailer with Charlie, clambering on top of one of the sturdy growboxes. It was easier for Gabe to sit on the outside seat because of his bad leg, but damn, it made things hard for getting in and out to open gates. Maybe she'd rejoin them after opening the next gate. For now it felt good to sit in the sun as the day warmed up. And it got her away from that security conversation that she felt was doing nothing except allowing Gabe to work through his paranoia.

Charlie grinned at her. "Getting cramped up there?"

"A little. They're sciencing at each other, too. Security applications—extrapolations from those robots we set up yesterday. Cyborgs."

"That's a little out of our expertise, isn't it?"

"Oh hell, yes. I think that if the data shows that the Defender has possible security expansions beyond crop protection, then we should hand the concept over to Justine and Serg to play around with. Of course with appropriate licensing agreements and so on, but let them deal with it. They're the security experts. Not us."

"Eh, Martin and Gabe like to play the mad scientist game, and Gabe has always veered toward that side of things. Martin was all excited about robots last night after he got that text from Gabe." Charlie grimaced. "Boy, did I ever get an earful. He's thinking about how they could be applied for more monitoring uses."

"It would be a useful extension. Meanwhile, Gabe is running paranoid and protective," Ruby said. "It's justified, but I'm not sure it's a good idea to push the Defender that far."

Charlie snorted. "He's always had security on the brain. Granted, it's understandable now that we know he's a Martiniere. It explains a hell of a lot about the way he left the Double R twenty-one years ago."

"Oh? If you told me the details back then I don't remember." She scowled. Too much of that era was a blur in her memories. Self-defense, she supposed. Her mind screening out too much that was painful to recall.

"I did, but you were in pretty bad shape when you and

Brandon got released from the hospital. I told you when you asked where Gabe was, and neither of us said any more. But I think it was a full year before you were back to yourself."

"Yeah. I don't remember anything in detail about it, except that I seemed to have a brain fog that lasted forever."

Charlie sighed. "Short version. When Gabe showed up to pack his stuff and leave, he was distraught. Frantic. I tried to tell him that you and Brandon were doing poorly at the hospital and he screamed at me that he already knew that." Charlie shook his head. "What he said, I can't remember in detail now either. Been a lot of years, and Martin and I had our hands too full with running the ranch while you were sick to think about the specifics of what he said."

"I thought you had told him what had happened." Ruby cocked her head, confused. "That he came in drunk and had been partying while Bran and I were in the hospital. I remember that much."

"Drunk?" Charlie considered for a moment. "No. I don't know why you would have had that impression from what I said. The Gabe I saw was stone-cold sober and scared shitless. He *sounded* deluded and drunk, but the fist he laid on my chin was not thrown by a drunk man."

"He *hit* you?" No wonder Charlie had been so negative about Gabe for years.

"I was trying to stop him from leaving. Trying to tell him that you needed him more than ever. He took a swing at me. Connected. Left me flat on the kitchen floor. By the time I got up he was gone."

"Oh Charlie. I'm sorry. I didn't know."

"I didn't tell you the details because first it slipped my mind, and then I thought he'd gone nuts and you were better off without him. He just wasn't making sense. He thought you were dying and Brandon not much better, even though I tried to tell him otherwise. Things were bad but not *that* bad. And he was crazy about what things he was taking. He was much more focused on loading up every damn weapon he owned and as much ammo as he could get his hands on than anything else except his comp and his data."

"He told me that he thought Philip and Joseph were the cause of me and Bran getting sick," Ruby said. "And that was why he left, to draw their attention away from us."

"You know, he did mention something about Joseph. But it was so outlandish and discombobulated that I didn't know what to think. And then, well, the divorce got pretty ugly. I thought he'd flipped and gone asshole on you."

"That's the part that I still can't figure," Ruby said. "Why did he go asshole? He claims he had to go over the top to make the separation believable. But he also claims that mind control forced him into it."

Charlie shook his head. "He was young and freaked out, Ruby. Not a real excuse, in the long run, but the man I saw? He was honestly convinced you two were dying and that it was his fault." He paused. "Guilt can sure warp a brain. Or maybe what he says about mind control is true. Maybe that was it. I don't see that man in how he's behaving now."

"I just don't know if he can flip his behavior on me again," Ruby said in a low voice as they approached the last gate. "Or if he can be influenced into doing that."

"People do change, Ruby," Charlie said as she hopped off to open the gate. "He's different now. And now that you know about the mind control—"

She didn't answer Charlie but opened the gate. Gabe grinned at her as they drove by.

"You can come back up here," he called. "No more gates."

She stopped to consider it. "All right," she said finally. It would get her away from another conversation she wanted to avoid.

Charlie mock-winced. "And leave me all alone back here?"

"Don't want me getting jealous now, do you?" Gabe winked

at Ruby as he pulled his legs back to make it easier for her to scramble over him.

"As if!" Charlie yelled back while they started up. "You've been doing science flirtation with my man!"

Gabe laughed and put his left arm around Ruby's shoulders as the crawler climbed the last stretch to the Homestead field. She chuckled. This closeness reminded her of their early years on the ranch together.

"This feels good," he said. "Getting out first thing in the morning to do trials. Hey. I don't think it will take us that long to deal with things at Moondance. Want to do lunch in Pendleton?"

She glanced down at her jeans and shirt. "I ought to change first."

"Nah, why? Only the tourists are gonna be dressed up. I wasn't thinking anything super fancy because I don't want to mess with changing, myself."

She thought about it. Wherever they went, it would have to accommodate their bodyguards. "You have a place where you don't have to worry about our guards?"

"Several. Sushi. Diner. Steakhouse. Just not the brewpubs or the distillery. They're busier and not as secure."

"Surprise me," she said.

He grinned at her. "You drive to Moondance, I'll make the reservations."

"It's a date," she said as they pulled up to the Homestead field. "And besides, I'm going to be crunching data from this test on the way over. You may want to see the results. Our bodyguards can do the driving."

Gabe shrugged. "Works for me." He slowly extracted himself from the crawler. "I'm still getting used to having them around when we go off the place, especially when we're not visiting restricted access sites like Swait's."

They waited by the crawler while Martin and Charlie hauled the first box to the field's edge, then joined them.

"I did something different with these," Martin said. "Controlled activation. One problem we had both with last spring's incident and with what Swait experienced is that the bots detected a threat upon release and went out in attack mode without spreading. That's all well and good, but...I want to see what happens when we have Defenders in place and then have them counter an attack. Until I can reliably switch them on and off, I'd just as soon not offload anything that might be considered a threat into a live Defender-seeded field, even for testing purposes."

"Doesn't controlled activation serve that purpose?" Ruby asked.

"It's new to the algorithm. The on switch works fine. I'm not as confident about the off switch performance—and whether it can be done more than once."

"An on-off switch would be useful," Gabe mused.

"And I'm working on it," Martin said. "Today's data will be useful."

He and Charlie tipped the box to release the bots. These bots were a purplish-blue, darker in hue than the previous teal-colored versions of the Defender. They moved in a sluggish wave out of the box, spreading more slowly than usual.

"One of the problems with my current algorithm," Martin said, brushing a gray-brown chunk of hair out of his eyes. "Controlled activation slows down the dispersal."

Once the bots were out of the box he and Charlie replaced it on the trailer. Then they jumped into the crawler.

"Coming?" Martin called.

Gabe shook his head and waved them on. "Hope you're okay with that," he said to Ruby. "I don't think they need our help and we won't be in their way." He unfolded his cane and leaned on it. "Besides, the less I have to climb in and out of the crawler, the better."

"Gives me time to get the monitors running." Ruby pulled out her scanner and activated the scanning program. It showed the dispersal of the Defenders but their activity was strangely quiet. Gabe pressed close, surveying the numbers with her.

Charlie and Martin returned with the crawler.

"Activation time." Martin pulled out his scanner and punched in a code. Ruby glanced at the field. So far there was no activity out of the norm to be seen as the Defenders woke.

"Are there any passive threats in the field?" Gabe asked.

"No," Martin said. "We know how the Defender reacts to them so I set up threats that I can trigger one at a time. Now. Activating toxin release. Botulism. Four sites."

Four hotspots lit up on Ruby's projection. Visual inspection didn't show anything happening at first, though the projection showed the Defenders moving toward the hotspots. Suddenly purplish-red swarms lifted from within a five foot diameter circle around each hotspot to an altitude of about two feet above the top of the stalks of wheat, converging with the same swirling formation that she and Gabe had seen the day before yesterday at Swait's. Then they descended.

"Good knockdown," Gabe said. "Sixty percent elimination, rising."

Martin nodded. "Let's see what happens when we throw more at it. E-coli."

Four more hotspots popped up on the display. The reaction was similar—first the closest bots on the ground started moving toward the new threat. Then from about five feet out, swarms took to the air to congregate over each hotspot.

"Botulism response slowing," Gabe reported. "But still proceeding. Eighty percent knockdown. Fifty percent on e-coli."

"Let's throw a little more at them," Martin said. "Salmonella."

I didn't know Martin had access to that stuff. What else does he have tucked away in that lab? Ruby bit her lip as four more hotspots lit up, watching as bots broke away from the first sites to meet the new response.

"Responses to previous threats slowing and the current

threat is taking longer to resolve," Gabe said. "Botulism eighty-five percent elimination. E-coli sixty-seven percent. Salmonella forty-two percent. But presence is still declining. Just slower."

Martin nodded. "Let's see how long it takes for those to die down before I launch my last one. I'd just as soon make sure we've got those three things eliminated."

"I'll take up my station," Charlie said. He climbed in the crawler and drove away, not stopping until he was on the other side of the field. After he climbed out, he pulled on a biosuit, then hauled out the firefighting foam canister and sprayer that was standard ranch equipment during the summer.

"What *is* the last one?" Ruby asked. "And why is Charlie suiting up?"

"Fire," Martin said, voice tight and hard. "From the robots."

"Shit," Gabe said. "If it gets out of control—Jesus, Martin, this is fire season!"

"That's why we're doing it this early in the morning, before the afternoon breezes start up," Martin said. "And why Charlie's suiting up. The targets are close to our nasties but Charlie's wearing a suit just in case he has to throw foam and the Defenders haven't gotten rid of the bugs. Plus the foam has biosuppressant nasties of its own. *Not* going to risk anything getting away."

"All right," Gabe said.

The three of them watched the readout as the numbers declined to near-zero presence of a threat.

"Here goes," Martin said. He waved at Charlie. Charlie acknowledged, moving stiff-legged to the edge of the field.

The robots started moving, each toward a hotspot. Small Defender swarms converged on them. Two of the robots seemed to attract more attention than others.

"What are those?" Gabe asked, gesturing toward the data on the screen.

"They carry codes simulating the presence of more nasties,"

Martin said. "Hmm. Not responding as robustly to the comm packages. That's different from Swait."

"Overwhelmed or prioritizing?"

Martin shrugged. "Depends on what we see in analysis. Here goes with the fire."

Nozzles extruded from the lurching robots. More swarms descended on the two robots that attracted the most bots. Flame drizzled out of the nozzles on those two devices, never getting a full release. Wisps of smoke rose around the robots as they collapsed, then faded.

The other two robots shot out more robust plumes of flame. Other Defenders converged on them as strips of wheat caught on fire. One robot started spinning, spewing fire, before it collapsed. Flames rose around it. The other one halted, sparks emitting from it before it, too, collapsed at the end of a line of fire. Ruby couldn't see what was happening as smoke rose from the field so she concentrated on the results.

"Not as strong as the other responses," she said.

"Fire needs work, then," Martin muttered. "Charlie! Go for it!"

Charlie moved into the field, spraying magenta-colored foam on the flames. Ruby, Gabe, and Martin studied the activity report on her projection.

"Fifty percent of the Defenders are still viable after everything's done," Martin said finally, as Charlie finished extinguishing the flames. "Not as good as I'd like."

"All things considered, not too bad," Gabe said.

"You'll run the performance analysis?" Martin asked Ruby.

"Might as well be doing something on the way to and from Moondance," she said.

Charlie returned to the field with a collector. He started scooping up bots.

"Good. That'll give me time to dissect Defender samples," Martin said. "And what's left of my robots and the diffusers. If anything. I'm going to suit up and collect samples." He headed around the field to the crawler.

"How are you holding up?" Ruby asked Gabe. "Looks like another long day ahead."

"Took a quarter dose of Activate this time, before we left the house," he said. "So far, so good."

"You sure you want to mess with lunch after Moondance? Or will that be too much?"

Gabe took her hand. "Ruby. We've got a two hour ride to and from Moondance. That gives me *two hours* each way to rest. I know you're concerned, but I *need* to get these meds figured out. One way or another."

"Just don't want you relapsing."

"I've got it. Nor do I want to be snapping and irritable, either. Message received." But he squeezed her hand to soften his words.

At last Charlie and Martin finished in the field. They carefully placed several items in biosecurity bags, then did the same with their suits. Ruby and Gabe watched as they took turns spraying each other down before climbing back into the crawler.

"I think we want to ride back in the trailer," Gabe said softly to her. "That decontaminant isn't something I want to smell."

"Me neither," she agreed.

When Charlie and Martin pulled up, she waved and pointed back to the trailer.

"We're riding in back!" she called.

"Don't blame you one bit," Charlie said. "It stinks in here. Don't do it if you don't have to!"

They headed for the trailer. Ruby helped Gabe clamber up on a box, then hopped up herself, giving Martin the high sign to start up.

There was something satisfying about sitting together on top of the growboxes on a bright sunny late summer mountain morning after completing a test. She wished that developing and testing new biobots was the only thing they had to think about.

But that part of their lives was long gone.

"Wow," Ruby said as she eyed the completed Moondance house. "It looks just like it did the one time I saw it."

Gabe squinted. "There's some slight differences in the finish, but this side looks fine." He hobbled toward the front door. Tim Vanhorn, his ranch manager, opened one of the double doors. Tim's wife Kathleen waved hello as she carried a box inside.

"Contractor sends his regards, but he can't be here for the walkthrough," Tim said. "You okay with that?"

"Yeah," Gabe said. "You can pass on any changes I see necessary." His hand tightened on Ruby's before they went inside. She caught her breath as they went through the foyer and entered the great room. The window-studded west-facing wall rose to a sharp peak two stories above the main floor, just like before. However, the huge model spaceships from several different TV and movie series that had hung along the roofline were gone, as were the beautiful large, stellar-themed quilts that had been on the walls. Their footsteps on the polished pine floor echoed in the cavernous space.

Gabe closed his eyes tightly for a moment, wincing. Then he opened them and strode over to the windows. "Looks like the autotint in the windows is working better than the original," he said to Tim.

"Newer tech," Tim said.

Ruby followed Gabe, only now realizing just how big this great room was.

"It's huge without furniture," she said.

Gabe turned sharply away from the window. "Yes. Rachel liked to throw parties. She invited her gaming friends to visit, and they had some mini-conventions here."

That's right. Gabe had said she liked to go to science fiction conventions, and they took Brandon to them.

Somehow, she had a hard time picturing Gabe at a science fiction convention.

He went through a hallway to their right and she followed. "This is one of the residential wings," he said to her, opening the first door on their left. "And this was our suite." He hesitated in the doorway, nostrils flaring. Ruby peeked past him. Another big room, with two large walk-in closets and a half-open door revealing a bathroom counter. A sliding door opened onto a balcony and she could see the wide expanse of the valley below the house through the glass.

Once again, Gabe closed his eyes for a moment, shivering. He walked halfway into the room, stopping dead.

"You might want to look at the bathroom, Ruby," he said. "If they replicated it like they should, it's pretty impressive."

"They followed Rachel's original blueprints," Tim said behind them.

"You're not coming?" she asked.

Gabe shook his head. "That was—that was where—that was where Rachel collapsed. I—I can't do it. But please, Ruby. Look at it, make sure the finish job looks good. I trust your judgment."

"All right." She walked into the bathroom. The west wall was solid glass, tinted not only for privacy but to minimize heat loss while adding natural light to the room. She turned around. A long vanity held two sinks. She flicked on the light switch by the mirror. Lights set into the mirror illuminated it—a dimmer switch allowed her to adjust the light levels. Then she noticed another dimmer at the other end of the mirror. She tried it out, to discover that it managed the light for that section.

"*Nice*," she said to herself.

"Everything all right?" Gabe asked. It sounded like he had retreated closer to the door.

"Just admiring the mirror setup."

There was a long low-threshold shower next to the counter that was big enough for two people. Next to it was a jetted tub. Across from the tub were both a toilet and a bidet, and a closet.

She opened the closet doors. One half held what appeared to be an instant hot water system while the other had shelves, some on rollers. She closed them and looked around. Blond wood on the cabinetry.

"It's nice," she said. "Not my style, but nice."

Gabe exhaled. "There's more rooms."

The next door to the left opened into a smaller room, also with its own bathroom and walk-in closets.

"Brandon had this suite in the original house," Gabe said. He checked the closets and the bathroom. Ruby followed him. This bathroom was less elaborate, though it had a smaller shower and tub. Gabe nodded to himself and left the room. A third door revealed another bedroom. Then the hallway opened into a wide space with a pocket door that made the area a separate room.

"Video and gaming room," Gabe said. He turned and walked back down the hallway, gesturing at the one door across from the rooms they had inspected. "Tim and Kathleen's apartment. All okay there, Tim?"

"Kathleen's busy unpacking. So far, so good. She's happy with how it came out."

They crossed back through the great room to inspect kitchen, pantry, and the other wing, designated for guests, which held four bedrooms, two on each side of the hallway.

"This place is huge," Ruby said. "I didn't realize how much so when I was here before."

"Rachel liked to entertain. Her family often came to visit us before she got cancer again," Gabe said, voice tight.

They returned to the great room to go downstairs to where his office had been before, along with furnace room and another office. Then they went back to the great room. Gabe headed for the sliding glass door that Ruby hadn't noticed before. She followed him onto the large balcony. He sighed and leaned on the railing.

"What are you planning to do with this place?" she asked,

steeling herself for the answer as she joined him. "It's awfully big."

Gabe clasped his hands together, staring out over the valley below the ridge point that the house sat on.

"I had it rebuilt to the original plans for a purpose. This needs to be the formal Martiniere headquarters."

Her heart sank. "Does that mean you are planning to leave the Double R?"

"What? No, no, no. I want to separate the Martiniere functions from the Double R." He turned and leaned sideways against the railing to face Ruby. "I have no intention of leaving the Double R unless you make me." He looked down at his clasped hands, then back up. "It's just that I really don't want any of the Martinieres other than Justine and Serg to set foot where we live unless we specifically invite them. The Double R needs to be our personal, private space. I do not trust many of the other members of my family as far as I can throw them."

"So, a meeting space."

"Meetings. Entertainment functions—this location is better than Thunder County for those things, anyway. Ruby, what the hell? I was thinking of this as a place for Brandon and hopefully Kris to live. Not us. Not me. Too many ghosts."

"Oh." She took a deep breath and turned her back to the railing, staring at the house and not at him.

"Shit. You really thought I was planning to move back here?"

She nodded.

"No. Unequivocally no, unless you throw me out. You're not planning to do that any time soon, I hope?"

She shook her head, unable to speak past the knot in her throat.

"Ruby." Gabe stepped forward and started to reach for her chin, then stopped as she flinched back, dark memories rising from when her father used to do that. "Sorry. I forgot." He put his hand on her back instead. "I can't come back here to live. I really can't. But restored, it's the kind of place that has its uses in my role as *Gabriel Martiniere*." He stressed the name. "But that's all it is. It will make an excellent headquarters for Bran. I think he likes the place better than me, anyway."

"Okay," she choked out.

"Ruby. Hell. What is going on?"

"I—" She turned to stare out over the valley again. "It's just that this place is reminding me more and more that I'm *not* the kind of woman to make a Martiniere wife. I—I wouldn't know what to do." She blinked hard to fight back tears. "It's beautiful. But formal parties? Dressing up? Geez, if it wasn't for Vickie and Justine helping me with my wardrobe, I'd still look like what I am—a hick hayseed rancher."

"Ruby." He gently turned her to face him. "You are not just a hick hayseed rancher, and besides, I *had* that sort of trophy wife with Rachel. It's not what I want now."

"But you still love her." Her voice quavered more than she wanted it to.

"I'd be a shit if I didn't still have some feelings for my dead wife, wouldn't I?" His voice roughened. "Yes. I lived that life for a while with her. But I still loved you even back then, while loving her—despite everything that happened during the divorce. I love you while still acknowledging that I once loved her."

Ruby sniffled and closed her eyes hard, shaking her head, overwhelmed by the sudden flood of emotion. Too much today. The talk with Charlie, and now this….

"Ruby. Look at me. Please." His voice cracked and she slowly opened her eyes. "Rachel fit my life as it was after I left you. But this life you and I are living, this move to depose Philip, would tear her apart. I couldn't do what I'm doing now if she were still alive."

"How do you know?"

"She was tender. Soft, compared to you. And yet…." His voice trailed off and he was silent for a few moments before he spoke again. "She did have her tough side. Just not in the right way to deal with the Martinieres. But her toughness—" He blinked hard and shook his head. "I was a scaredy-cat shit unwilling to face the consequences of making that kind of attachment with my family background. And who had a bad habit of running away from the result of my choices, both good and bad."

He drew a shaky breath. "I went to hell because I couldn't live with what I'd done to you in the divorce. Rachel took that Gabe Ramirez, smacked me into shape and put me back together. She changed me into a better person. But this life that we're living now?" He gestured with his right hand. "Yeah, she would have been a Martiniere wife of the sort that Philip and Joseph were talking about as ideal. Submissive, compliant—and self-destructive. Like Renate was. I watched Renate fall apart under Philip's bullying during my teen years. Managed to help Justine avoid the same sort of bullshit."

"She's hinted at that."

Gabe brushed away a tear trickling down Ruby's cheek that had escaped her control. "But really? Everything we're doing today. The field testing. Looking at performance analyses together. Even coming here—that's what I want from a woman. The Martinieres would have eaten Rachel alive." A smile briefly twitched his lips. "Not you. When you slapped Philip back in February? God, I loved it. I was *so* proud of you. Do you know how few people would have had the guts to do that, especially on their first face-to-face meeting with Philip Martiniere?"

She stared at him, mute, unable to form words.

He loved me doing that. He likes what we're doing.

Gabe cupped her cheek.

"Another thing. Rachel wanted to meet you, Ruby. The last six months of her life she kept pressing for me to reconcile with you." He swallowed hard. "Now I know what was going on, why she wanted it to happen. She was fading. She knew it. And her family had abandoned her, except for her brother Rafe—" He swallowed hard again. "I think she was so damn desperate for a family connection, and you, as Bran's mother—" He shook his head.

"Oh Gabe." She was able to force those words out, aching with him.

She wanted to meet me.

"Thunder County locking down to isolate because of the G9 ended that talk of getting together. But she wanted me to reach out all the same, to mend things between us. I was too chicken-shit to try it then, and even when the County opened up after things calmed down and there was a vaccine, I was too afraid of your reaction." He gulped. "You want to know the major reason why I don't want to live here, besides the fact that it doesn't fit the life I want now?"

"Why?"

"Officially Rachel died during medevac." He shook his head again. "She actually died in my arms. In that bathroom. G9 hit us both hard and fast, flattened us within two hours. She collapsed and started seizing after puking all over the bathroom, didn't even make it to the toilet. I was hallucinating like hell and barely able to hold it together. Tim and Kathleen were still living off site, so it was just us here. I called 911, took her in my arms when the seizure was done. She was gasping for breath. Then she stopped breathing. I screamed. I yelled. I begged her to keep breathing, *but she didn't respond.*"

Gabe's voice broke and he blinked hard. Tears ran down his cheeks. "I started giving her CPR. I don't know how long it was until the paramedics got here, but she never breathed on her own after that seizure. They pronounced her dead as the heli-copter lifted during medevac. And I kept hallucinating. Some-times I was doing CPR on her. Sometimes it was you. You were both dying and I couldn't keep track of whether I was here or at the Double R twenty-one years ago."

He shook his head a third time and pulled her to him, trem-bling as he gulped. "Oh God, Ruby. Oh God. And I have had nightmares about it ever since."

"Oh Gabe." She could picture the scene now, after seeing the bathroom.

He choked. "For the last six months, ever since I've been back at the Double R, it's been you dying in my arms instead of her. Every. Damn. Time. The dying body in my arms changes from Rachel to you. Just like it was when I was hallucinating during her death. *I'm losing both of you.*"

Oh God. Oh God. Oh God.

He pressed his head against hers, his body shaking harder, sagging against her. Ruby held him tight, stroking his back, shaken, unable to say anything that wouldn't sound facile and banal.

Oh God. To lose someone like that. Oh God. And then to dream about it happening to me—no wonder he grabs at me when he wakes up from one of those nightmares. No wonder he wants me in the bed next to his chair. Oh God.

She gently reached up and stroked the back of his head, murmuring softly like she used to do with Brandon to comfort him.

At last Gabe raised his head and wiped his eyes. She reached up to cup his cheek. He closed his eyes and leaned into her palm for a moment. Then he kissed it, straightening up and shakily exhaling.

"Thank you for coming with me. This—was harder than I thought it would be."

"Yeah," she said unsteadily. "I get it now."

"I think we've seen enough," he sighed. "I'm done with those memories. Let's get out of this damn place and get some lunch. I need to go over a couple of things real quick with Tim, and then I'll be ready to go. Can you let David and Janet know that I'll drive to the restaurant?"

"Sure."

He kept his arm around her as they went back inside, halting in the foyer before he slipped his arm away.

Ruby walked out to the truck, feeling shaky and uncertain.

But a niggling doubt still clung to her. Would Gabe leave her again if he thought it would keep her safe? Especially if he was having nightmares about her dying? She still thought he might, if he thought it might protect her.

Ruby's lips tightened.

Got to break him of that notion. Somehow.

FOR THE FIRST TIME IN AGES RUBY LET HERSELF GET MILDLY DRUNK over lunch. The restaurant turned out to be in an old hotel that overlooked the valley and provided a mountain view as well. A bottle of Albertan Pinot Gris appeared with the menus and by the time they had finished the first bottle a second one appeared. They drank about half of that bottle.

As if Gabe had read her mind, they avoided touchy subjects, and they walked back to the truck with arms around each other's waists. Janet took the wheel as they settled in the back. Gabe still held on to Ruby as he leaned his head against the seat's headrest.

"Well, that's done," he said. He exhaled. "But on the positive side, The View is as good as ever."

"I wouldn't have thought a hotel restaurant would be that good," Ruby said, settling back. She was *stuffed.* Granted, it was August, and the height of the produce season, so that fresh food was available. It would be difficult for any restaurant to have problems serving their full menu. Hard to avoid pigging out when she knew things would be different later on during the winter. "How did you find out about it? They clearly know your tastes."

"I went there a couple of times a week after I'd recovered enough from the G9 to go home. Brandon actually found it, and took me there to cheer me up, get me out of the house while in recovery mode. I liked it well enough to keep it up after he left. It was different from—different from every other place else I'd gone in town. You know he spent several weeks with me once I was released from the hospital, right?"

Ruby shook her head. "He didn't say anything about it. I had wondered how it worked out that he was able to pop in for a regular visit for about three weeks. But he just told me he was in the area researching for the next Innovator production."

"He was doing that as well. But yeah. Rachel's family would have nothing to do with me after she died." A shadow crossed his face. "They took her body back to LA and buried her there. I didn't even know where it was for the longest time."

"That's awful."

"Oh, they didn't like me that much to begin with. My involvement with Rafe's Alvarez Armory really annoyed them. And her father knew who I really was. In any case, while Tim and Kathleen had moved into the house after—everything, Bran managed me. He helped with my meds, my PT, and kept me from diving right back in that self-destructive hole I'd been in before Rachel. I kept going to the View after he left. Just for something different."

"It's a good find."

"It's a nice place to eat, even when supplies got short over the winter. And no memories of anyone other than Bran." He exhaled. "I needed that. Though he was pushing for me to reconcile with you the whole time I was in recovery."

"He kept bringing that up constantly until I told him to shut up—about eighteen months ago?" Ruby said.

"Yeah, that would be the time frame." Gabe snorted. "I was scared shitless when Bran managed to get us both into the Superhero. I didn't know what to expect. And then you walked into the Green Room wearing your old Round-Up princess outfit and hat. Except for some gray in your hair it was as if you hadn't changed at all. Suddenly my world went right again. Even though fucking Philip showed up."

"Thanks—I guess."

He yawned. "And now the Activate is wearing off—helped

out by all that wine. Damn, it was nice. We need to do that again. Napping now. I don't think I'll be good for much of anything else today."

"Me neither."

His arm snaked out to pull her close and they snuggled, both drowsing.

Gabe didn't wake her with his nightmares that night.

CHAPTER 6

It was Ruby's turn to take care of garden chores the next morning. After she ran her final analysis of yesterday's test in preparation for this morning's meeting, she went out to gather produce. She picked a big bucket of green beans, summer squash, and searched through the cucumbers, searching for small ones to make into pickles. There were enough to justify hauling out the big crock to ferment them for old-fashioned dills.

She continued to sort through the rows. High summer meant lots of fresh food bounty, not just for eating but storage. And given the bigger numbers of people staying at the Double R these days, Ruby had planned a full-sized garden this year, including peppers and tomatoes in the greenhouse.

Once Ruby finished her harvest, she turned on the drip irrigation system, checking the connectors to ensure they hadn't blown out. All that done, she sighed with satisfaction, eying the produce. It was going to take several trips to haul it all.

Gotta love summer harvest.

Justine came out of the house.

"Hey! Justine! Give me a hand here!" Ruby called.

Justine came over. "I was looking for you anyway. I want to talk to you before the meeting." She eyed the pile of produce. "Are we eating all *that*?"

"Some of it. It goes faster than you think, especially since it's fresh. But I'm going to freeze about half the beans. The cukes are going into brine for pickles and I'll dehydrate some of the tomatoes as well. But we'll have fresh salad makings for lunch."

"Damn," Justine said. "I didn't realize you were this much of a gardener, too."

"The garden filled a lot of holes in the budget when Brandon was little, both before and after the divorce." Ruby shrugged. "And with up and down food shortages over the past thirty-some years, I got into a habit of keeping up with the garden. When things got really desperate, I grew a patch of wheat for our own use. I haven't ground my own flour for a few years, but I still could if I want."

"I wouldn't have the first idea of where to start."

"I grew up doing this." Ruby gathered up several buckets and handed them to Justine. "It becomes second nature."

They carried the produce into the kitchen.

"So now what?" Justine looked at the buckets. "I'm assuming you just don't stick stuff straight in the fridge and freezer. Might as well learn a little bit about this process. It's a nice break from business."

"I feel better about uncertain times when I have full shelves and freezers."

"You're not worried about power outages?"

"That's why we have the solar panels and battery storage backups."

Ruby coached Justine through prepping the vegetables to go into the refrigerator. She sorted out the veggies to go to Julie, Terri, and the security staff cooking their own meals in the bunkhouse, and put them back in the buckets.

"If you'll take these buckets down to the bunkhouse, they'll deal with this stuff."

"Sure." Justine picked up the buckets. By the time she returned, Ruby was fixing the cukes for brining. Justine leaned against the counter next to the sink, watching.

"What can I do to help?"

Ruby gestured toward the green beans. "Wash them up."

"What's the process?"

Ruby pointed to the colander she'd used to rinse the greens that was now sitting in the drying rack. "Pinch off the top and bottom and put the beans in there, then rinse them when the colander is full. Just leave the tips in the sink. I'll clean them up."

"Got it."

They worked side by side at the double sink.

"So, everything's set up for Kris and Beck," Justine said. "Beck's going back to Chicago with me tonight, and the procedures happen tomorrow. There's just one thing."

"What's that?" Ruby put the washed cucumbers in the crock.

Justine grimaced. "The Biobot Producers Alliance conference. Tomorrow afternoon is when it starts. Kris is determined to go ahead and work it like she and Brandon planned once she's done with her surgery, but I don't think that's a good idea. I'm obviously not a good choice to fill in. No logical connection between JSM Corps and the BPA, and it'll look like the Martinieres are moving in on it. It's one thing for Brandon and even you or Gabie to be there because you have industry ties. I don't."

Ruby dropped the dill into the crock and started to mix the brine. "I can make room in my schedule to take care of that. How many days will it be?"

"Take care of what?" Gabe came through the kitchen. "Mmm. Fresh cherry tomatoes. And I see you've put Tine to work." He put his arms around Ruby and hugged her.

"Covering for Kris at the BPA conference," Ruby said.

"Kris thinks she can march out of the procedure and be on her feet all the rest of the day. On the day the conference opens, when things are the busiest," Justine said, scowling. "Ruby, at the minimum you need to be there for two days. Oh, and this colander's full."

"Spread a towel on the counter first. Then rinse, and dump

the beans on that. Then do the rest." Ruby poured the brine into the crock.

"You're pickling, Rubes? I haven't had good homemade pickles for years."

"Yep." Ruby checked to make sure she'd prepared enough lime and salt water to adequately cover the cucumbers, then put a plate over them. "Gabe, please grab three quart jars from the pantry."

"All right." He went into the pantry and returned with the jars, setting them on the counter and rubbing Ruby's shoulders. "So you're talking about going to the conference after all? I thought we were staying away to avoid drawing unwanted attention."

Justine dumped the rinsed beans on the towel. "The situation's changed slightly, enough that it makes sense for Ruby to go. It's not a good idea for Kris to be on her feet for at least twenty-four hours after the procedure, preferably longer." she said. "It's not like what Beck's going through, but the side effects of pulling those hormonal tags in the tats isn't pretty, either. It can end up being more difficult."

"I guess I can work from Chicago," Gabe said.

"What do you mean, you *guess* you can work from Chicago?" Ruby grunted as she lifted the crock. "If you're going to stay here talking, then *help*. Put this in the pantry. You know where it goes."

"Yes ma'am," Gabe said, grinning as he took the crock from Ruby. "Weren't you doing this to me years ago, every time I walked through the kitchen?"

"You know the routine if you're gonna poke your nose in here during the harvest," she retorted as she followed him with the quart jars. After checking to ensure that the brine covered all the cucumbers, and placing the water-filled jars on top to keep the plate submerged, Ruby covered the crock with a towel. "There! First batch of dills set to do their fermenting thing."

"You work too hard," Gabe said, shaking his head and resting his hand on her back.

"Grab me about—" She paused, eying the pile of beans on the towel. "Six freezer containers. Quarts."

As she left the pantry, she picked up a bioplast bag and put about half the pile of beans into it before sticking it into the refrigerator.

"Where do you want the containers?" Gabe asked.

"Kitchen table. Then if you could get the blancher started that would be great."

Gabe set the containers down and went back into the pantry, coming back with the big two-piece Graniteware blancher. He left the strainer portion with Ruby and filled the pot partway with tap water, then set it on the stove to heat. Ruby snapped the beans into thirds and dropped them into the strainer.

"So. Chicago. How are we handling it?" Gabe asked.

"How we're handling it is that *you* are staying here and taking care of things," Ruby said. "How long will I be gone, Justine?"

"Two nights, maybe three, depending on how Beck pulls through the surgery. Having another woman around will really help, especially with the BPA conference keeping all of us hopping."

"Ruby, I don't like this idea of me staying here." Gabe joined her in snapping the beans.

"Damn it, Gabe, it's not necessary for both of us to be there."

"Ruby, I—I'm worried about you being there alone. And being away for two or three nights."

"I'm not going to be there alone. Justine will be there. Brandon will be there. We'll have security."

"But Joseph and Philip are in Chicago," he protested. "That's too close to you for my liking. *I want to be there.*"

"And what exactly are you going to do in Chicago besides be underfoot and fret about Ruby when she's out and about?" Justine said. "She'll be *fine*, Gabie. She'll be in my condo, along with Brandon. Serg is staying in his own place across the hall from my condo. Ruby's a big girl who does just fine taking care of herself." Justine finished rinsing the rest of the beans. "Go ahead and dump them on the towel?"

"Yes, please."

"I'd *be* there. Just in case you need me," Gabe insisted.

"And you'll attract Daddy dearest's attention not just to Ruby but to Beck and Kris as well as Brandon and the BPA, more than they're watching already. It's a fucking security nightmare to have *both* of you in Chicago right now, Gabie, especially you," Justine said sharply. "Bad enough to have Ruby there. But one of us has to keep an eye on Beck and Kris after the procedures, and someone has to step into Kris's role to help Brandon. I can't do it all. We need one more leadership person, and Ruby's the best possibility available who will also attract the least attention."

"I don't like it. Don't like being away from you, Ruby. Not overnight."

"We have to do a lot of things we don't like, Gabe! Now. Don't you have a meeting to prepare for? We'll talk about this later," Ruby said.

"Ruby—"

"*Later,*" she snapped. "Get ready for that meeting!"

"You're damn right we're going to talk about this later," he growled before striding out of the kitchen.

Justine sidled next to Ruby. "Break these into thirds?"

"Pretty much."

Justine shook her head. "Wow. You've got his number but good, Ruby."

"What do you mean?" Ruby stretched, then went back to work.

"I know that look. That tone of voice. Unless he's changed a hell of a lot, that's Gabie digging in for a battle. Saw him and Daddy-damned-dearest go into their worst fights just like that. But you just sent him off, and he *listened* without too much of a fuss."

"Oh, that fight will come later," Ruby said grimly, finishing off the beans. She checked the water. Not quite boiling yet. She filled one of the sinks with cold water. "Trust me. He and I will have a big knockdown, drag-out argument before you and I leave. We had fights like this when we were still married. That behavior is nothing new."

"But still. I'm amazed that he listens to you like that." Justine shook her head. "And boy, does he ever seem clingy today. I haven't seen him like that with you before."

"Moondance yesterday was pretty emotional for both of us." She paused. "He told me how Rachel died. After I'd been in the room where it happened. He—he couldn't even stand to see it. There's—lots of issues involved right now. For both of us."

"Serg told me that Gabie wants a crew on site ASAP for security installations. Top of the line, independent power sources, add in fencing and gates. Something about it being a Martiniere headquarters, for GMR at least."

"Yeah." The water was boiling. Ruby eased the strainer in, put the lid back on, and set the timer. "He wants to split off the Martiniere ops to Moondance, keep that stuff away from the Double R."

"Well, that does make sense. From the descriptions it sounds more defensible, especially if Serg and his crew give it the treatment Gabie wants. But for practicality, how will it work for that purpose? What kind of eye appeal will it have? If it's going to be a headquarters it needs to look the part."

Ruby reached into the freezer and emptied ice trays into the sink full of water. She refilled the trays and put them back. As the timer buzzed, she grabbed potholders and pulled the strainer out, letting the hot water drain back into the pot.

"If you could turn off the stove that would help," she said to Justine as she dumped the strainer into the ice water, then set the strainer on the towel. "I think Moondance will work as a headquarters. By my standards the place is pretty nice. Cedar shake siding and roof—might be faux cedar but looked pretty real to me and Gabe has the money now to do that right. Great room rises two stories, west wall of windows that looks out on the valley. Big room that could easily hold up to fifty people if the furniture is configured right, big balcony off of the great room." She stirred the cooling beans. Not quite ready. "And seven ensuite bedrooms."

"That would work," Justine said. "It *is* closer to the interstate."

"Yeah. It's a pretty striking location, out on a point."

"I'm liking this the more I hear about it. Is anyone going to be living there?"

"He said something about it being a residence for Brandon."

"Yeah. That needs to be happening pretty soon."

She fished out a slotted spoon from the utility drawer. "Grab the containers from the table. Let's get these darlings into the freezer."

Justine brought the containers over and Ruby ladled the beans into them. "I will be very interested in your take on the situation in Chicago," she said, lowering her voice. "There's more than the BPA that we need help with. I need backup for the last night with the Reals. Donald went back home. I have an extra banquet ticket because I will not go to this event alone, and Brandon's not the best choice. If he'll even leave Kris's side at that point."

"Really." Ruby finished filling the last container. She grabbed a grease pen from the junk drawer and wrote *Green Beans, August 2059* on each lid before placing it on the container. She handed three of them to Justine and picked up the remaining three. "Let's take this to the basement. We can talk better down there."

They walked through the pantry and down the basement stairs. Ruby put the containers into the upright freezer that she used to freeze vegetables and fruit. Justine glanced around at the big chest freezer, the boxes for the root vegetables, the strings of already-harvested garlic, and the shelves with food that had already been processed this year.

"Wow. You really are a prepper."

Ruby shrugged. "Dealing with food shortages ever since the '20s. So. What's happening?"

Justine leaned against the chest freezer. "One." She tapped her left index finger with her right. "Brandon thinks we have some ringers in the BPA. Serg and I figured that would happen, but you know the terminology and the jargon better than us. I've got the list of suspects. If you can go over them tonight that would be great to see if we are right or not."

"I can do that. Wait." Ruby raised her hand. Had she heard footsteps in the kitchen above? She cocked her head. "Thought I heard someone upstairs, and Gabe's the only other person in the house right now."

Justine nodded, waiting until Ruby lowered her hand. "All okay?"

"Didn't hear anything else. But this is an old house, and sometimes it makes noise."

"Okay." She tapped her middle finger. "Two. Tomorrow afternoon is registration and workshop signup, plus the keynote and one breaking session. If you're there working the table you can help keep the ringers from co-opting any one workshop."

"The process?"

"Brandon can go over it with you tonight. There's some preliminary requests and again, if you could vet those...."

"No problem." Ruby looked up. Was that just the house or was someone up there? Gabe *could* be pretty light on his feet, even with the limitations of post-G9 syndrome. No. Probably not. "Go ahead."

"Three." Ring finger. "The Reals. I need you there for a couple of purposes. We won't be hiding who you are, but Daddy dear and his buddies think all women are stupid. Daddy-poo and Joey will not say anything important around you at the banquet, but maybe some of the other attendees will." Justine stopped as the screen door slammed and someone's quick footsteps echoed across the kitchen floor. Then she continued. "Especially because you're Gabie's woman. You'll get hit on, especially if you play up your naiveté about gatherings like this. Get a few drinks into these guys, flutter your eyelashes, and who knows what they'll tell you."

More footsteps overhead, but Ruby chose to ignore them. "Are you *sure* I'm the right person to be doing this?" She frowned at Justine. "I'm not all that great at schmoozing. It was the toughest part of the rodeo queen world for me. I tend to geek out about the tech stuff."

Justine laughed. "Ruby, that's *exactly* why you're the perfect person to do this. Look. They know you're significant to Gabie, that you have his ear. But you aren't slick and super-polished, so they'll underestimate you. A little awkwardness is good in this case. Plus you're an attractive older woman who clearly hasn't had body mod work done, you're in shape, and if things get weird, you can handle yourself. I'd be reluctant to take Kris into this setting even if she was one hundred percent because she doesn't have the combination of experience and lack of exposure that you do."

"I'm in," Ruby said. She glanced up, wondering about the noises she'd heard earlier. On the other hand, if that *had* been Gabe and another person, wouldn't whoever it was have said something to him? "But god, if Gabe finds out beforehand…."

"Given the way he's gone all clingy, yeah. This is important. You're really the only one who can do this."

"You said that Philip and Joseph are jumpy about Brandon?"

Justine nodded. "Bits and pieces that I've heard at the Reals. There's been a lot more interest in Brandon because of the BPA. That has caught some attention in certain circles." She grinned. "I mentioned something about Brandon around Daddy dear and the flinching was epic. They clearly see him as a threat."

"I hope he's being careful."

Justine looked around and lowered her voice. "Joey and his

heavies tried to jump Brandon the other day when he was out and about doing BPA business. He and his bodyguards beat the crap out of them—Brandon knocked Joey flat."

Ruby closed her eyes tight for a moment, shuddering. "Oh God. I don't know that I wanted to know that. I guess I'm glad he can hold his own."

"I wouldn't get too worried about your son. Brandon trains with his guards daily, and I've seen him practice. He's quicker than Gabie was at that age and he's a better fighter, in Serg's estimation. There's already buzz going around the Reals about that fight. Joey is not popular, even amongst that collection of bizarros. So when the Reals get a look at Brandon's mother, especially the Family members there, and see what a badass you are *without* a ring and control words, that's going to give him more credibility. Another reason for you to be there."

"Am I really that badass?"

"More than you realize. The other piece is that this is not a setting for Gabie to be in right now, given his current condition," Justine said grimly. "I've seen how much he struggles at times."

"We're still trying to find the right dosage of the new meds," Ruby said, also keeping her voice low.

"It shows. He has to get stable before he does something like this. Worst case, you and Brandon will need to represent him to the Family. Taking you to the final banquet for the Reals is a good first exposure for you."

Ruby swallowed hard. "It has to happen, but boy, I'm finding the whole prospect intimidating."

A sympathetic expression softened Justine's face. "That's why I think this is the perfect opportunity to introduce you to the big players. Let them get a look at you. They're going to be wondering what role you play when it comes to Gabie's goals. And it will give you the chance to learn some faces and make alliances. Still up for it?"

"Now more than ever." Ruby sighed. Her comm chimed with

the meeting reminder. "We'd better get back upstairs. Time for today's meeting. When do we leave?"

"As soon after that as we can. Give Beck time to settle in and prep."

"Sounds good." Ruby headed up the stairs. There was no sign of anyone in the kitchen now. Maybe it *was* just the floorboards creaking for no reason.

CHAPTER 7

As the meeting wrapped up in Gabe's office, Ruby headed for the door, hoping to avoid an argument about going to Chicago. But the others except for Justine reached the doorway first.

Gabe's voice halted her.

"Ruby. We need to talk about you going to Chicago."

She turned to face him, crossing her arms. "What's there to talk about? Brandon and the girls need me there." She noticed that Justine slipped into a corner and sat down, making herself small so she wouldn't be noticed. Support or entertainment? Hopefully a little bit of both.

"Then I want to come along."

"You heard Justine when we talked about it earlier. It's not a very good idea. You'll attract too much attention from the wrong people to what we're doing."

"Damn it, Ruby, it's dangerous!"

"So are a lot of things I do here on the ranch every day."

Gabe exhaled and came around to the front of his desk, leaning on it and crossing his arms, mirroring her. "This is different."

"How?" She threw her arms wide. "Tractors and crawlers flip over on steep hillsides, even with experienced and careful drivers. Horses can hurt the most skilled of handlers, same for the cattle. Lab accidents. Thunderstorms. Breakdowns."

"You're experienced with all those things! But you are *not* experienced with the risks you're going to be taking at the BPA. Especially with Philip and Joseph there. You need backup."

"And I *have* backup. Justine. Brandon. Serg. I'll be *fine*, Gabe."

"Yeah? Brandon got jumped the other day!" He glared at her.

"Justine said he beat the crap out of Joseph and gave as good as he got." She wondered how he'd heard about that.

His nostrils flared. "She told you about that incident."

"Yes. She also says he's faster than you were at the same age." Ruby drew a deep, steadying breath and walked toward him. *Defuse*, her instincts whispered. And yet a part of her wanted to engage and have this out now, not later. She was *not* going to have him hovering over her protectively all the time. Even if he *was* having nightmares about her dying. "Damn it, Gabe, what purpose does your going with me serve?"

"I'd be there to protect you!"

"And you risk the safety of both Beck and Kris as well! God damn it, Gabe, stop reacting. Think about the legal strictures on removing those damn hormonal implants from both of them, as well as Beck's hysterectomy. It's a damn good idea not to alert anyone to their presence—or at least Beck's."

"The procedures are legal."

"Not if you look at the details of the law!" Ruby snapped back. "They're both former indentureds and are restricted from interfering from the implants by copyright law. The last thing we need to have happen is for Philip and his people to find out that we're supporting two former indentureds who are getting their implants removed. That might just give the Reals and their lackeys an excuse to harass the girls when they're in recovery!"

"That's why I need to be there. To help you manage the situation."

"That's exactly why you *can't* be there! Shit, Gabe, don't you get it? Just yesterday you were telling me that you thought it was a good idea for Brandon to establish a separate residence. Now you want to draw more attention to one of his projects while we have this tricky situation playing out? Does. Not. Make. Sense."

Gabe shook his head and ran his fingers through his thinning gray and black hair. "God damn it, why do those procedures have to happen *now* and in *the same damn place* as both the BPA and the Real Truthers convention? Why can't they just go to Portland to have it done?"

"Because Chicago is where Justine has the connections for them to be done safely and secretly." Ruby drew a deep breath. "They don't just hand those surgeries out any more, Gabe. Especially for former indentureds."

"Why can't it wait for several weeks?"

"How long will it be until some corporate asshole holding their papers demands that we turn them over? Or kidnaps them? Sure, Beck can stay safe locked down here until someone comes onto the place with papers asserting their control over her—but what about Kris? What the hell do you think it's going to do to Branny if his love is yanked away from him to breed brats for Philip or Joseph?"

"That's fucking unfair and unrealistic!"

"Is it?" She lowered her voice to a deeply cold register. "And you are fucking deluding yourself if you don't think that's exactly what they have planned. What better way to demoralize one of their biggest threats?"

"The same argument applies to me if something happens to you. And you're deliberately choosing to walk right into it!"

"It's a calculated fucking risk, Gabe. No, it's not the best choice in the world, but the other options are even less desirable. Do you want Kris going out to work at a public conference where she *could* get snatched, when she's recovering from a difficult procedure? Or how distracted Bran will be if he's having to protect Kris, when his entire focus should be on making that conference work?"

Gabe slammed his hands against his desk and stood. "All well and good for that piece of this trip, but what about you going to the closing banquet for the Reals? I heard bits and pieces of you and Justine talking about it in the basement. Now that's just walking right into fucking trouble, Ruby, and *I won't have it!*"

"Did you hear her rationales for it as well?"

"That. Doesn't. Fucking. Matter. It's unsafe and *I don't want you doing it!*" He grabbed her upper arms.

"Let go of me."

He gave her a little shake. "Not until you promise me you won't set foot in that banquet. Promise me, Ruby. *Promise me.*" His eyes widened as his trembling voice rose.

"Bullshit!" She yanked away from his grasp and slapped him.

They glared at each other, breathing hard.

Ruby continued, her voice low and flat. "You do *not* lay hands on me like that, *ever again.* You've *never* had the right to lay hands on me like that. I. Am. Going." Her tone slipped into horse trainer disciplinary harshness as she prodded him in the chest with a forefinger. "Sit the fuck down. Shut the fuck up. And *listen.*"

Gabe seized her wrist. "Stop poking me."

"Let me go." She raised a fist in threat instead of an open hand. They glowered at each other. Stalemate.

Finally, Gabe released her wrist. He threw his hands up and went around the desk to drop into his chair with a sigh. "All right. I'm sitting the fuck down. I'm shutting the fuck up. Explain to me just exactly why this God damned bad idea is the best choice."

Ruby put her hands on the desk and leaned toward him. "Sooner or later I have to prove myself as something other than a hick hayseed rancher chick and ex-rodeo queen if we're going to stay together. Especially to the Martinieres. But also to myself. You want me by your side. Great. But my role is more than that of being eye-candy. I am not a breakable precious little dolly, but your partner and equal. And if you can't handle that, then *get the fuck out of my life. Again.*"

Gabe reeled back in his chair. "Whoa. Ruby."

"I *mean* it, Gabe. Twenty-one years ago, you did the shit-ass thing of bailing out of my life because you thought I was in danger and that it was your fault. I am still not certain that you wouldn't do again if you decided that it was the best for me." Her voice rose. "You *do* not decide these things without talking to me first and respecting my choice as a rational adult to take these risks! Never. Ever. Again." She gulped. "God damn it, leaving me like that was the worst fucking thing you could ever have done. And now it looks like you are headed down the same fucking pathway of protecting and sheltering me without my input, and *it isn't going to work!*"

She slammed her fists on the desk in an echo of Gabe's earlier action. "We are either God damned equals and partners or we're nothing!"

The sharp sting from hitting the desk broke the intensity of the cold rage simmering inside of her. Ruby straightened up with a shudder, flexing her hands.

Gabe pressed his lips together, shaking his head and glancing down. Then he looked up, eyes narrowed and hard. "Okay, Ruby. What do you expect to accomplish by going to the Reals banquet?"

She drew a shaky breath. "It gives me a chance to present myself as something other than the rodeo queen who won the Superhero. Plus I just have to *be* there. I don't have any responsibilities. Nothing to do. A low pressure introduction to that world without you there. Without Brandon."

"Low pressure is hardly what I would call it." Gabe snorted. He turned his glare on Justine. "Tine. I saw you duck into that corner. Sufficiently entertained?"

"That wasn't my reason for staying behind but yes, it has

been entertaining." Justine rose to join Ruby. "She didn't need my support, as it turns out."

"This is your idea. How much risk is it?" he snapped in a dead, flat tone that barely masked his anger.

"It's sufficiently public that neither Daddy dearest nor Joey will do more than verbal sniping. Especially after Brandon beat the crap out of Joey." A faint smile quirked her lips. "Want to see the pix?"

"No. Is that all this is about?"

"No. There are Family fence-straddlers who might talk to Ruby. Who might reach out to you through her. Certainly, the rumors circulating after Brandon and Joey tangled have made some of those folks think. Consider this as an exercise in coalition building as well as good practice for Ruby. I think it's worth the risk."

"And what if Philip decides to make a scene?"

"Oh hell, after what I just saw with you two, she'll kick Daddy-poo's ass *hard* if he tries anything. Ruby has my vote as the top bitch of the Martiniere women, and she's the toughest Martiniere woman I've ever seen—including Donna-gran." Justine bared her teeth in a humorless grin. "If anything, we might *want* a scene to happen. I'm willing to bet that Ruby will garner even more Family support after that."

Gabe groaned and leaned his head on his hand. "I'm just— I'm afraid—" He sighed and smacked his head against the back of his chair, exhaling hard. "Tine, you know what Philip is capable of doing. What he could do to Ruby. Do I have to show you the scars on my back as a reminder?"

"Gabie. It's time. For Ruby's safety as much as anything else." Justine's voice sharpened. "She needs to be seen not only as someone valuable to you, but as someone who doesn't need you by her side to keep her safe. She needs to develop connections. And she's right. Even if you *were* married, you're acting like an overcontrolling shithead. Get your head out of your ass and think. You've got a woman here who can be a powerful ally and asset. Don't throw it away by being yet another fucking medieval Martiniere sexist!"

Gabe spun his chair away from them. Silence reigned for a few minutes. Then he turned his chair back.

"You're right, both of you," he said in a low voice. "But I don't have to like it. I'm going to be scared shitless the whole time you're gone, Ruby." He winced and buried his head in his hands, shaking it.

"Serg is going to be at the banquet," Justine said softly. "We already planned a heavy guard presence. And I'll have Serg slip Ruby some appropriate and shielded weapons. She'll have time to practice with them."

Gabe raised his head. "Okay. But." He pointed a shaking finger at them. "I want some input in what you're wearing to the banquet, Ruby. If you're going to be there as my representative, I want it to be *known*."

"That's fine," Ruby said. "I'll take any and all suggestions."

"Gabie—" Justine said, a cautious note in her voice.

"You'll know what I mean when you see it. How soon are you leaving?"

"As soon as we can get Ruby packed. Beck's wrapping things up in the lab."

"I'll be up in a little bit."

"Okay," Ruby said. "I guess we'd better get started, hmm?"

She didn't wait for further conversation but fled the room, Justine right behind her.

"Wow," Justine said when they reached the bedroom. "*Wow*. You weren't kidding about a knockdown, drag-out fight. I mean —I saw video of your argument at the Superstar after the divorce, but this—"

Ruby collapsed in Gabe's armchair, half-laughing, half-crying with emotional letdown. "That was nothing. We got into a public fistfight during our final breakup. Luckily my lawyer bailed me out of jail—we both got arrested over that one."

Justine rested a hand on Ruby's shoulder. "You gonna be okay?"

"Yeah, yeah, just give me a moment." Ruby buried her head in her hands and took several deep breaths. Then she went to the bathroom to splash water on her face and grab her medium-sized suitcase from the storage there. She dropped it on the bed. Justine was studying the clothes in Ruby's closet and rubbing her chin.

"What look should I adopt for BPA, do you think? Maybe something to suggest a bit of the rodeo queen but with more sophistication?" Ruby joined her.

"Hmm," Justine said. "Problem is that even with AC it's going to be hot and muggy in Chicago. You're going to want light clothing and a light jacket to take on and off depending on when you're inside or outside."

"More silk, then." Ruby frowned. "Maybe a dress for one day? If I'm running around doing organizational stuff tomorrow, I'm going to want slacks that day. I just don't have that many good pairs. I suppose jeans won't work?"

Justine shook her head.

They rummaged in the closet and drawers and came up with three ensembles plus a spare—a pair of black slacks coupled with a green top and a dark blue one, and a couple of sleeveless dresses, one green and black silk, the other one a purple linen. The silk dress came with a lightweight black jacket that would work for all combinations.

"Now comes the hard one," Justine frowned. "The Reals banquet. You're too tall and slim to wear any of my formal wear. But I've not seen anything I like for that event here, even amongst the new stuff, and shopping is going to be a *pain*, especially if Gabie wants approval."

Gabe hobbled into the room, carrying a garment bag and an intricately carved black box. He handed the bag to Ruby.

"Sorry. Took me a couple of minutes to pull this together. I've got the Reals banquet taken care of for you. I hope. Try this on. It may not fit but it should be close. Tine can get someone in to do alterations if it's too big. It's a little out of style, but—" he swallowed hard. "It should look good on you."

Ruby carried the bag into the bathroom. She opened it to reveal a long, high-collared sleeveless black dress with shimmering emerald green and gold quarter-inch threads woven in amongst the black background. She washed her hands before she changed into it, struggling a little with the zipper and her ponytail, then stared at the somewhat sophisticated reflection in the mirror. It was loose in the top but not bad. Side slits came halfway up her thighs. A smaller bag inside the big one held low-heeled matching sandals. She bent to pull them on, and despite the fabric's stiff look, the dress flowed with her. Definitely not confining.

She opened the door. Gabe stood there, arms crossed, appraising as she walked across the room. The sandals were surprisingly comfortable and they *fit*.

Justine choked. "Gabie. That isn't—Angelica's formal dress!"

"That is."

"I thought it was lost. Mother was looking for it years ago."

Gabe shook his head. "It had been sent ahead of Mom and Dad for that last event. No one looked in the box after the plane crash to see what it was. They just sent it to me. I hid it from Philip. Put it in storage. And then there's—this." He picked the black box off of the bed. "Ruby, these go with it." He handed it to her. "You can't wear the ring, not yet. It's a Martiniere command wedding band. But the earrings, necklace, and brooch should work."

Ruby gasped as she opened the box. In one compartment sat a pair of two-inch long emerald and pearl earrings set in gold that were worked into the shape of the Martiniere trefoil. Another section held a matching necklace with a bigger version of the trefoil at its center. Others held a gold, emerald, and pearl ring and a trefoil brooch. She remembered a long-ago promise Gabe Ramirez had made her, at—what rodeo? A big one, but it had been too many years since then, and they'd both been hyper from post-competition adrenaline mixed with too many beers and whiskey shots for her to remember much of anything except the intensity with which he'd said it.

Someday I'll put emeralds on my Ruby, he'd said. At the time she had thought it was just a joke poking fun at their dead broke status. As she looked up at him, Ruby realized that Gabe remembered it too. He smiled weakly and nodded.

"I promised you this a long time ago," he said. "And—I won't be there to do it." He glanced at Justine. "Tine. Record this please."

"All right, but why?"

"You'll see soon enough. Ruby. Have Brandon put these on you the night of the banquet, and record that process. It's significant." He gestured to her. "Give me the box and take out your studs."

She put a hand to her chest. "Should I take off my locket?"

"Not for this but the actual night, yes."

Ruby handed him the box as Justine brought out her scanner and set it on record. He put the box on the bed while she undid her pearl studs. Gabe carefully dropped them into the box's lid. Then he picked up the first earring.

"Ruby Marie Barkley. With these gems I, Gabriel Marcus Martiniere, pronounce you in partnership with me, and that you speak with my voice." He deftly inserted it into her right earring hole.

Justine gulped, eyes wide, her free hand covering her open mouth. Ruby held still as Gabe put the other earring in, repeating the statement. As he fastened the necklace around her neck and pinned the brooch on her right shoulder, he said it again.

"*The Martiniere emeralds,*" Justine breathed, lowering her scanner when Gabe stepped back. "Gabriel. I thought—Philip thought—Mother thought—how did you find them? They've been lost for years!"

"They've never been lost," Gabe said, a curious half-smile playing on his lips. "Well, perhaps until I was eighteen. Dad had suspicions that something wasn't right before the plane crash happened. On my eighteenth birthday I got a registered letter from an attorney I'd never heard of. Dad had parked the emeralds with her for safekeeping." He circled Ruby, his smile spreading. "Ruby, they look perfect on you."

"It sounds like there's a history with the dress and jewelry," she said.

"The dress belonged to my mother, and the emeralds are an heirloom that belongs to the Martiniere or his heir," he said softly, taking her hands. "I remember the last event that I saw this outfit on her, a late Christmas dinner in Paris with the French family members, before I went back to military school." His voice cracked and went lower. "You look splendid. If anything, the dress and emeralds look better on you with your red hair, Ruby, than they did on my mother."

"The Martiniere emeralds," Justine repeated. "Oh God, Gabriel. You really *do* want to make an impression on Daddy dearest, don't you?"

Gabe wheeled to face her, brows rising. "I want no doubts about Ruby's status, especially since we haven't remarried. If you're going to launch her as a Martiniere and my partner, then *do it*."

"Oh, that'll *do it* all right." Justine nodded. "I can hardly wait to see Daddy-poo's expression when he sees Ruby. And it'll jog some fond memories in some of those older Reals. Oh God, Gabie, this is *perfect*."

"I'd better figure out something with my hair and nails," Ruby said.

"Nails we can take care of today when we get to Chicago. Hair the night of the banquet." Justine shook her head. "Oh Gabie. This is amazing."

Gabe didn't look away from Ruby. "Like I said, I want no question about who Ruby's tied to." His voice lowered, and there was a quaver in it. "Ruby. Does this answer the question about whether you're my equal or not? Because your wearing those emeralds announces that I place the highest level of trust in you. The only thing missing is the ring, and that can only be worn after we're married. Remarried."

"Yes," she said, her voice faltering. "And now…I'd better get these things off and put away. Thank you, Gabe. Can you—can you help me take them off properly?"

"I'll go check on Beck," Justine said quickly. "Meet you downstairs, Ruby."

She stood still while Gabe carefully took off the jewelry.

"Can you undo the zipper?" She turned to him.

"Of course."

He carefully unzipped the dress as she lifted her ponytail. "I used to watch my father put the emeralds on my mother before formal functions," he said in that same quiet voice. "He used to say, *Someday you will do this for a woman you love, Gabie. Be very careful about who you give your heart to.* And then my mother would laugh and kiss him. They loved each other very much."

"I'm surprised the jewels and dress survived the fire at Moondance." Ruby carefully walked to the bathroom, half-closing the door so they could keep talking but give herself some privacy. But she had to wonder. If Saul wasn't Gabe's father, but the father of Joseph—what did that mean?

Or did Angelica and Saul cut a devil's deal of some sort? Why?

"I didn't keep them at Moondance. I gave them back to the attorney just before I testified, along with the dress, and asked her to keep them safe. Not to turn them over to anyone but my designated heir or me. I—I went back to her office and brought them here two months ago. I knew that sooner or later I would want you to wear them."

Ruby bagged the sandals and the dress, not sure of what to say.

"And—well—someday I hope to put that ring on your finger," he said awkwardly as she came out and put the garment bag on the bed. "Ruby. I'm sorry about earlier. It's just—I mean it. I'm scared about you encountering Philip and Joseph without me there." He handed Ruby her pearl studs and she carefully put them back in her ears. She noticed that he had put the box in her open suitcase.

"Sooner or later that meeting will have to happen, Gabe. I meant what I said about needing to prove myself. And, honestly, I'm still afraid you'll run off again if you think it will keep me safe."

"I'm sorry, Ruby." He spread his hands. "Forgive me. Please? I was stupid. Again. Please. I'll even kneel to beg your forgiveness. Like I should have done years ago at Southfork instead of fighting with you." He lurched to his knees.

Ruby sighed, swallowing hard past a sudden lump in her throat, almost in tears herself as she looked down at him. Gabe didn't do things like this. Never. Ever. Even when he was wrong. She had never seen him kneel to beg forgiveness for anything after an argument. Not until now.

This has to be real. He means it.

She would think about what that meant for her stance about marriage later.

"Oh Gabe. How can I not forgive a man who finally fulfilled a promise to put emeralds on me? Even if they are just a loan for a special event." She reached for his hands. "Get up, you big silly. I forgive you."

He grunted and groaned, using the bed as well as her hands to help himself rise. After he stood, he held her hands, a solemn expression on his face.

"One thing. The brooch used to be able to tie into comms. Have Serg look at it when you get to Chicago. It's possible he may be able to resurrect and update the programming, even though it's been unused for forty-some years. I might be able to listen in to the conversations you have. And if he can tie it into your comm—I can talk to you privately, tell you about the people you meet so you understand how they tie into the

Martinieres. It was new technology when Dad had it implanted into the brooch. He and Mother used it to compare notes privately when they circulated at formal functions."

"I will."

"The ring—at one time it was like Tine's. Only it gives you control over every Martiniere, not just a few. Something happened and it failed my mother. It needs to be reprogrammed before you can use it." His hands tightened on hers. "Philip will challenge your right to wear the emeralds without the ring. Make sure that Tine has copies of both me and Brandon putting them on you to play back for him."

"They *are* that important, then. I thought so. Justine's reaction when you put them on me gave me that impression."

"Yes. By bringing them out, by putting them on the woman that I openly acknowledge as my partner—even though we're not married right now—I'm not just giving you legitimacy to speak for me. It's my declaration that I am the Martiniere-in-waiting. Unconfirmed by the Board, of course, but possession of the emeralds will go a long way toward making it happen. Are you ready for this? I'm marking you as a player."

"Yes," she breathed, trembling. "Yes. It scares the shit out of me, but—yes."

His hands closed tightly on hers and he raised them to his lips. "Ruby, I'm fucking terrified. Not just for you but for what this means for all of us. You think we've been living under tight security before? After this banquet, after this demonstration of my intent, it will be even more so. All of us will be targets. No more quiet meals out like at The View—though we weren't doing much of that anyway."

"I understand," she said softly.

"Bran should plan to relocate to Moondance immediately— one thing I'll be working on while you're gone will be to get it ready for him and Kris. I'll have Serg speed up the security setup. I'll talk to him while you're traveling." He sighed. "You sure you don't want to drop everything and run?"

"Where would we go? And how could I leave the horses?"

He laughed bitterly. "That's the truth of it. There's no way out of this but forward."

"Gabriel Marcus Martiniere. How different is this from sitting on the back of a nasty-tempered saddle bronc in the second between the gate swinging open and that first big buck? No way out but through the ride. Only this ride is gonna be more than eight seconds long."

His laugh this time was less bitter. "Oh God, Rubes, you say just the right thing."

Then he took her in his arms, holding her tight.

"Just be careful," he whispered into her ear. "Come safely back to me. And those emeralds—they're yours to wear by right as my partner and hopefully someday my wife. Brandon will inherit them for Kris, but not until your death, unless you choose to pass them on to her." He kissed her. "And they are my promise not to run out on you. I'll wait until I feel you're ready to ask you to marry me again. Just—be safe. Be careful. Please. If something happens to you, I don't think I could stand it."

"I will be careful," she said. "I'll call every night at bedtime. And—if you're having a rough night, call me."

"I'll try not to. You're going to need your rest."

"Don't worry about that. I'm probably not going to sleep well either."

They stood there for a few moments, holding each other tight.

"Ruby? Gabe?" Justine called from downstairs. "It's time."

"Be right down," she answered. She pulled away from Gabe and put some last items into her bag, then zipped it up. Gabe took the garment bag and would have picked up the suitcase, but she thwarted that by taking his free hand. They descended the stairs hand-in-hand to join Beck, Rick, and Justine. Beck's face was tight and solemn as Rick clutched her hand just like Gabe did Ruby's.

The five of them walked silently past the barns and labs to

the airstrip, the other three moving faster than Gabe and Ruby. She took the five-minute walk to look at her beloved mountains, the edge of prairie country that spilled right to their base, and her ranch.

Her life would be different when she returned, but these things would remain the same. She had to remember that. Had to stay grounded.

Rick passed them on his way back to the lab, his face grim and worried. He didn't say anything, but Ruby understood how he felt. They stopped at the bottom of the stairway where one of the guards waited. The others had already gone inside. The guard took the garment bag and Ruby's suitcase.

She turned to face Gabe. "Well. This is it. Here we go."

He gently placed his hands on her face and bent to kiss her, soft at first, then harder. His hands slipped from her face to pull her closer to him and he held her tight, breaking away from the kiss to bury his head where her neck and shoulder met. At last he gulped, raised his head, and kissed her a second time.

"I hope this gets easier," he said, his voice shaky. "Because the path we're taking means that this is the first of a number of times one of us has to stay behind. God, I hate this, Ruby. I so want to be on the plane with you. Please be careful. Please stay safe."

She reached up and stroked his cheek. "We'll talk tonight. I promise." She drew a deep breath and blew it out slowly.

He kissed her forehead and stepped back. Ruby climbed into the plane. One of the front seats was empty, Justine in the other one, looking out the window. Beck sat in the seat behind it, head buried in her hands, body shaking with repressed sobs. Ruby went to the empty seat and settled herself in. The plane taxied to the end of the airstrip and turned. As it raced down the strip she saw Gabe still standing there, watching them leave. She half-raised her hand to wave goodbye, even though she knew he probably couldn't see it.

Then she leaned her head against the seat. Silence hung

among the three women as the plane climbed. When it leveled out Justine sighed. She got up and sat by Beck.

"It will be all right," she said quietly. "Dr. Caruthers does a lot of these procedures. Not just the hysterectomy but the tag removal. I've taken many indentured women to her. She's the best surgeon for these procedures that money can buy."

Ruby swiveled her chair to face Beck and Justine as Beck raised her head, eyes red, cheeks wet from her tears.

"I'm scared," Beck said in a low voice. "I've heard too many stories about tag removal complications."

"Frankly, it's going to be easier for you than Kris," Justine said in a softer voice than Ruby had ever heard her use before. "Tag removal plays hormonal havoc with women who keep their uterus and ovaries." She sighed and patted Beck's hand. "I don't blame you for being scared. But I can assure you, I've gone through this routine with many former indentured women. You'll do just fine." She glanced at Ruby before refocusing on Beck. "If you want, I can give you an anxiety med and have you lie down in the bedroom in back. Will that help, or would you prefer to stay up front with us?"

"I—I think I want to lie down," Beck whispered. "I want to be out of it. I don't want to be brooding about what could happen. Do you know the Rescue Angel? I've only heard rumors of her from my networks. She sounds—a lot like you."

Justine smiled sadly as she reached out to brush away Beck's tears. "Honey, you're talking to her right now. I'm not kidding when I say I've done this for over two hundred indentured women, worldwide. And—other things, for non-indentured women in trouble as well."

"You're—you're—you're *her*? Oh God, if you only knew the many times I prayed for your help, for your intervention... you're the best...." A fresh outburst of tears broke free from Beck.

"Come on." Justine helped Beck up. "Take a pill and lie

down. It will help. You're scared and worried. I understand." She glanced over at Ruby. "I'll be back in a little bit."

"Okay."

Ruby exhaled as Justine guided Beck toward the bedroom in the back of the plane.

Justine is the fabled Rescue Angel.

The Rescue Angel was a mysterious woman who aided women in trouble, not just indentured women, but women in difficult reproductive situations. The Rescue Angel arranged adoptions. Abortions. Surrogate pregnancies, and more.

On the one hand, it was surprising. On the other…it wasn't. This explained a *lot* about how Justine did things.

After a while Justine returned. "Poor kid. She's scared to death. The hyperhormonal tweaking from her tags doesn't help things either. She's asleep now. But dealing with this type of reaction is one reason why I needed you to fill in for Kris and me at the BPA." She shook her head. "Beck and Kris will require psychological support for the first forty-eight hours due to the hormonal aftereffects of the tag removal. Luckily this isn't an abuse situation. That's—more complicated." She poured herself a drink from the kitchenette at the front of the cabin. "Want something?"

"Just water. I'm glad you're here and were able to help," Ruby said in a low voice. "It also clears up some things I'd wondered about. How long have you been doing this?"

Justine pursed her lips thoughtfully as she handed Ruby a glass of water before sitting down. "Probably about twenty years. Donald and I started doing it together. He coordinates communications and scheduling. The whole playboy thing of his is a cover, of sorts. We divorced when things got too weird to juggle and explain, and we needed some deniability. Plus—other issues that I can't disclose without getting his permission to speak. And the pressure from Daddy-fucking-dearest and Joey. With the work he does, he doesn't need me to be calling attention to him. That was more valuable than what our relationship was becoming."

"I'm glad you're there. Not just for Kris and Beck but for all the other women."

"Thank you." Justine tossed back the drink, shuddering. "But it makes for some unquiet nights when I think about what these women are experiencing."

Ruby almost said *I can imagine* but didn't. "I—I would never have known."

"It's a tribute to my mother. What she suffered. I couldn't help her. But I can help other women." Her tone changed. "You know what all this means with the emeralds, right? Gabie told you more, I hope."

"He said that this is basically the announcement that he is the Martiniere-in-waiting. Oh. I'm also to tell you that you should have both recordings available *when*—not if—your father challenges my right to wear them."

"Already thinking ahead to that." Justine exhaled. "He's been open with you about the implications of wearing the emeralds. *Good.* He has been too damn secretive. You should have known about all this years ago."

"Yeah." Ruby raised her chin. "If I'd known about him being a Martiniere and what was at stake then, there never would have been a divorce. But he's also too damn protective. I *hope* this means he'll open up more."

"You'll probably have to knock some sense into him every once in a while. But from what I've seen—you should have no problem doing that." Justine slumped in her chair. "And damn. I mean it when I say you are the toughest Martiniere woman of the batch. I was impressed by how you handled Gabie. I honestly didn't know if you needed support, and I've seen enough of the Family men in action to know that things could get rough." She snorted. "Shit, Brandon's not the only one who could beat the crap out of Joey. You could kick his butt, too. Big brother is slipping in his conditioning, but even more importantly, I think I'm the only woman he's met to date that he can't intimidate. Until you."

"I'm more than a little nervous about that banquet. Is it stupid to say that I'm most worried about making conversation? I get butterflies in my gut when I think about schmoozing."

Justine waved dismissively. "You will do just fine in conversation. Besides, you've got that public presentation experience. It seems to me that riding a galloping horse full tilt around an outdoor arena with loud music blaring and people yelling takes a lot more nerve than talking to people. Not to speak of barrel racing."

Ruby laughed. "I still feel awkward about talking. Riding is easy-peasy." She stroked the locket at her throat. "I'd just like to find a way to still wear this since it sounds like I can't with this dress. A good luck charm."

"Mmm, it can be in your hair. My stylist Timothy will find a way to make it work. It's pretty."

"It also has a picture of my grandparents in it. I wore it to every event I was in. Even AgI. Superstar and Superhero both. Didn't always mean I won, but I never got hurt."

"Let's hope that luck holds." Justine pulled down the window shade next to her seat and leaned back in her chair. "Going to be a lot going on when we get to Chicago. I'm going to nap. You might want to as well."

"I'll try." Ruby closed her window shade.

But her drowsing was fitful. The image of Gabe standing there alone by the airstrip kept popping back up. She wondered how he was doing.

This is your life now, Ruby. Get used to it. He has to as well.

CHAPTER 8

JUSTINE'S PENTHOUSE SUITE IN CHICAGO WAS ANOTHER NEW experience. Ruby helped Justine steer a groggy Beck out of the elevator while spare bodyguards carried their luggage. Other guards not only stood outside the entrances of the two condos on that level, but also flanked the elevator and the stairwell doors. On the one hand, it made Ruby nervous to have that many guards around them. That just spoke to how risky this situation was.

On the other, this *was* the life she was saying yes to. Would be getting into deeper once she showed up at that banquet wearing the Martiniere emeralds. Having this much protection was a reassurance.

Ride the buck, she told herself. *Ride the buck. You can do this.*

As one guard opened the door for them, Justine gestured to the opposite door.

"That's Serg's condo," she said. "A little smaller, but otherwise the mirror image of this one."

They walked into a big space with windows all around. There was a wet bar to their left, and a pillar divided the living room space from a dining area partially hidden by tall, dark cabinets. Brandon sat at the big dining table, three screens projected around him as he scribbled notes on a pad.

"Hey Mom. Tine." His voice softened, though he kept his focus on the projections. "Beck. Good to see you here. Tine, Kris is in the office. She says she's working, but I think she's having meltdowns and doesn't want me sucked into them. She kicked me out of that space."

"How bad is it?" Justine asked.

"She's not getting any work done on our shared files." Brandon gestured at his projections. "That's fine. I told her we've got everything covered. As for severity—she's trying to hide it from me. She's seen enough of these activated tags in her indentured past to worry her. I tried to get her to medicate and rest to prepare for tomorrow. She's not listening."

"That's fine," Justine said. "I'll get Beck and Ruby settled, then deal with Kris."

"Thanks, Tine." He shook his head. "I know better than to push at this point." He looked away from his projections. "Ma, Dad said you were stepping in for Kris this weekend. Thanks. And that you might be able to spot some of our ringers. Think you could do that soon?"

Ruby winced as she saw the bruises on his face. "Let me drop my stuff wherever I'm staying and then I'll be back."

"Just keep in mind that the nail stylist will be here in an hour," Justine said.

"I will. Mom, I'm letting Serg know you're here. He wants to look at a brooch?"

"I'll explain when I come back," Ruby said.

They continued down the hallway and past several doors. Justine stopped at one. "Here you are, Ruby."

Ruby entered the room, followed by the guard carrying her suitcase and garment bag. Once she was gone, Ruby closed the door and looked around. The room was stark, even more so than the hotel rooms she'd stayed in during the AgInnovator recordings in LA. White walls, white carpet, white bedding, white armless chair, white dresser and mirrored vanity, white closet doors. The only things that broke up the snow-like whiteness were gray metal light fixtures by the bed and the chair and a panel outlined in gray on the wall by the door.

Tinted windows made up the outer wall and she wondered just how secure that was. She saw a balcony railing and went to check the door opening onto it—and spotted yet another guard on the balcony. More secure than she thought, then. Experimenting with the buttons by the door revealed blinds—white, of course—that raised from the bottom up. She ran the blinds halfway up the window, not particularly interested in looking at the cityscape right now.

Then she surveyed the room in more detail. A half-open door led to the bathroom. A big king bed took up most of the space. Ruby opened the wall panel to find a row of buttons marked *TV, Silencer, Safe, Lockdown, Security, Respirators/Hazmat, Fan, Air Scrubbers, Weapons.* She closed the panel and turned to her luggage, pulling the dress out of the garment bag and hanging it, then placing the slippers underneath it. She noted the locked cabinets inside the closet and wondered which ones were *Safe, Respirators/Hazmat,* and *Weapons.* Ruby supposed that if she pushed the relevant button in the panel, something would light up to indicate which was which.

She quickly unpacked her suitcase, transferring clothing to the closet or dresser, then putting her cosmetics and personal care items in the bathroom—more gray against white there. After that, she picked up the carved black jewelry box and returned to the dining room. Serg and Brandon were at the table, bantering easily, as if they were old friends.

"What's the story with the brooch?" Brandon broke away from the conversation.

"In a minute." Ruby set the box on the table and came over to Brandon. She delicately placed a finger under his chin to raise it so she could take a closer look at Brandon's injuries. "I want to look at this. You're going to be a sight at your event tomorrow."

"Easily covered up with makeup," Serg said.

"I'm *okay*, Ma," Brandon said as she studied him, letting her move his head with her fingertips. "Nothing's broken, not even my nose."

"Can't say as much for Joey," Serg chuckled.

"I'm still going to check," Ruby said. "I *am* your mother, after all." A fading bruise on his left cheekbone. Another on his jaw, the same side. The skin around his left eye was still a little puffy but it was clear and only the slightest bit of color was under that eye. She dropped her hand. "I've seen your father with worse."

I've given your father worse.

"That fight was a piece of beauty," Serg said. "Joey did not know what he was getting into. Brandon could go pro as a fighter if he wasn't Gabe's son and in line to become the Martiniere."

"Eh, it was nothing," Brandon said.

Serg raised his brows. "Dude. I've seen trained mixed martial arts pros less quick and agile than you. And you don't have any qualms about dirty fighting, which is big."

Brandon shrugged. "Thank our ranch managers for that. Martin and Charlie took me out behind the barn and taught me the basics when I was ten, and we kept on practicing. They said it was just in case I took after Mom and Dad and wanted to hit the rodeo circuit—and Dad thought it was a good idea when he learned about it. He put me through martial arts classes when I stayed with him, and I continued training into college and after."

"*Really,*" Ruby said, crossing her arms. "That's news to me. All of it."

What else did Gabe do with Brandon while he was growing up that I don't know about?

This piece made sense, though she wished she'd known about it. Gabe had clearly been thinking ahead about a potential threat from the Martinieres.

"It made my life easier on several occasions, long before I knew I was a Martiniere."

"What do you mean?" Ruby asked.

Brandon sighed. "Mom. Do you really want to know? Now, of all times?"

"Yes."

He looked down for a few moments, then back up. "All right. I was being bullied. During the water rights fight. Remember when I didn't want to go to school?"

"Yes."

Oh, she certainly recalled that time. Brandon had begged to go to online instruction only. While he'd formerly been in Little League and soccer, he hadn't wanted to do any sports—surprising for a kid who was athletic. He refused to explain why. She'd finally given up at that point because she couldn't see reasons for it, and couldn't afford the *good* online instruction. Things were so bad with the ranch that she couldn't dedicate the time that Brandon clearly needed from her. Gabe and Rachel had recently married, and she sent Brandon to them to finish the rest of the school year in Blue Bucket as a desperate attempt to keep the moody spiral he was descending into from getting worse. She had been terrified that he was going the route of the Barkleys.

It had been an excruciating and painful time in her life, almost as bad as the divorce. Fights at meetings. Slurs and whispers because Gabe had left her and she wouldn't date anyone new. Demands that she sell the Double R to *some man who knows what he's doing*, preferably one of the Barkleys, from Aunt Grace's shiftless family. Threats, to the degree that she took Charlie or Martin with her when she went to town for a while because while she could defend herself, what might happen if she failed was something she didn't want to face. Then coming home to a broody, sulky kid who wouldn't talk about what was bothering him. And then he was skipping school.

"I was getting beat up regularly until Charlie and Martin started coaching me."

"Why didn't you tell me then?"

Brandon's lips tightened. "Because you had enough to deal

with and it would have been *just one more thing*. Even at that age, I knew you were juggling a lot. That's all I want to say about it. Now. The brooch?"

Ruby sat down. She wanted to know more but forcing Brandon to talk clearly wasn't going to work. Maybe Gabe could tell her later. Serg leaned close, dark eyes keenly focused on her as she opened the box. She turned it so they could both see the contents.

"The Martiniere emeralds," Serg breathed, awe in his voice. "I thought they were lost. I've only seen them in pictures. They're a lot more impressive up close."

"Gabe's had control of them for over forty years," Ruby said. She glanced at Brandon. "Your father wants you to put them on me for the Reals banquet. It's a gesture which has meaning."

Serg slipped a jeweler's loupe into his left eye before he stretched out his left hand. "May I look at the brooch?"

Ruby placed it on his palm. Serg tapped on his loupe and delicately fingered it, a pale blue beam from the loupe darting around the center stone and then the pearls and diamonds surrounding it.

"What meaning do these emeralds hold?" Brandon asked. "I recognize the trefoil. A Family thing?"

"They're the property of the Martiniere and his heir and are usually wore by their women," Serg said without looking up from his examination of the brooch. "One reason the Family has been so strife-ridden is that these jewels have been missing for a long time. It's one mark of the succession within the Family. An authentication of power." He handed the brooch back to Ruby. "The ring?"

She handed it to him. "Gabe said I can't wear this yet."

Serg nodded as he studied it. "It's a wedding command ring. The controlling ring of the set." Once again, he tapped his loupe and activated the blue light, biting his lip as he examined the ring. Then he sighed and took out the loupe. "The ring is going to take more time and work than we have right now to fix it. The programming that it's supposed to reinforce has been wiped. I—don't want to try working with it. Not here. Not with everything else I need to do right now." He gave it back to Ruby. "But the brooch looks like it should operate just fine. I'll need your commset to align it. Give me a moment to get my tools, and I'll update it while you and Brandon talk. I—don't feel right taking it even out of this room. Not away from you."

"That's fine," Ruby said. "Brandon. What do I need to do to help you?"

Brandon lifted a finger. He spoke after Serg left. "Couple of things first. The big one. Dad and I had words about Moondance."

"He's pretty committed to his plans for that place."

"I know, and I agree with him about making it the center of our Martiniere operations. Eventually." Brandon started to lean his head on his left hand and winced away, straightening up. "But Kris and I aren't going to be living there for a while. That's what he had problems with. Serg is negotiating the purchase of a safe place here in Chicago for us."

"Why here?"

"Moondance is just too far away from things for us to use it as a base at the moment. Plus I don't think it's a good idea to have what we're doing on that front too closely tied either to Tine's work or Dad's Martiniere ops. It's going to get ugly."

"I—see. How did your father take that?"

"Not well at first." Brandon ran his fingers through his short dark hair, then leaned forward to rest his arms on his legs, interlacing his fingers. "He accepted my decision after a while, but he doesn't quite get why. I'm not walking away from the commitments Kris and I have made, especially now that I'm a Martiniere. If anything, they're more important for me to keep up now. Long term, the indentureds we liberate will be an asset to GMR, if not the Martiniere Group, as freedpeople. Another piece. What Kris and I are doing can potentially interfere with Justine's work. Besides the argument that we don't want all of our top-level people in one place, what she's doing is valuable too. Necessary. Can you help me get this through his head?"

"I'll try," Ruby sighed. "But we've got our own things to work through."

"I bet." He sat up. "Second thing. *Why* are you going to that event with Justine?" He waved at the emeralds. "I get this, but timing? Risk? He's really worried about you going without him or me with you, Mom, and I'm with him on that."

"You too?" Ruby sighed. "Justine thinks there's a very strong possibility that I will find potential allies at the banquet that won't talk to her. Or you. Or Kris, even. Especially with the emeralds that mark my status."

"Are you going to be able to handle this?"

"If I can't then we're all in big trouble," Ruby said. "Bran, we can't always pick our timing. But here's the tough piece, and one reason why I'm going for it in spite of your father's objections. He is struggling with post-G9 syndrome. It's only going to get worse, not better. *If* he's going to reclaim his position in the Martiniere Group in order to reform it, *if* he's going to lay down the foundation for you to be his heir to that position and continue the reforms, *including* the treatment of indentureds, then this has to happen sooner rather than later."

Brandon sighed and leaned forward again, rubbing his face. "I was afraid his health was one of your reasons. Okay." Serg returned to the dining room with a toolbox. "Serg. What kind of weaponry can we give Mom for that damn banquet?"

"I'll need to look at the dress," Serg said, setting the toolbox on the table and picking up the brooch. "But my father did design weapons for Angelica. I can get his documentation. I'll talk to him."

"Okay," Brandon said. "Ma. Tomorrow morning. We start with training practice at Serg's. Not just for the banquet but for the conference."

"Good idea," Serg said. "Ruby, can you pass me your comlink?"

"All right," Ruby slipped her comlink out of her ear. "Now. Brandon. What do you need me to look at?"

Brandon flipped one of his screens toward her. "I've highlighted my major suspects. After that just take a look through the rest of the preregistrations, okay?"

"Got it." She turned to the screen as Brandon turned back to his work and Serg bent over the brooch.

She finished checking the preregistrations late, between taking time out for nails, a light dinner, and Serg's periodic tests of his work on the brooch. For a moment she debated not calling Gabe—it would be eleven at the ranch.

No. You promised.

If she didn't call, Gabe would be frantic.

Ruby tentatively poked the *Silencer* button in the panel. Then she sat in the armless chair and called Gabe.

He was in the bedroom, moving about—pacing? His face was tight and worried as his projection solidified. He relaxed as he saw her, and he collapsed into his recliner.

"I was getting worried, Rubes."

"Working late," she said. "A lot of preregistrations to go through. It's a good thing I came to help, though. Justine's been tied up with the girls. They've both been stressing pretty bad."

"Things got done?"

She nodded, tapping her ear. "Serg got it set up. You should be able to hear every conversation around me once I connect with the brooch's systems. You can talk to me. I can't talk to you without being overheard, though. That blocker piece isn't working and he doesn't feel like it's a good idea to tackle it with the deadline we have." She hesitated. "I'm running a silencer program on this call. Built into the room."

"Good idea. I don't want to trust it too far, though. You're doing okay?"

"Other than being in a room that makes me think I'm in a snowbank, yeah. Every time the AC kicks in I start looking for my snowshoes."

Gabe chuckled and peered past her. "Ouch. It's pretty stark from what I can see. Surprising since Tine has always liked color. Rest of it that way?"

"Just a sec. I'll show you." She got up and slowly turned in a circle so he could see her surroundings, then sat again. "And there's a control panel with things like *Weapons* and *Respirators/Hazmat* listed."

"I'd expect nothing less from a residence under Serg and Justine's control." Gabe sighed. "Brandon and I had —discussions."

"He told me."

"What do you think?"

She chewed her lip. "The fact that Justine is supporting his actions tells me a lot. She's in this indentured situation a lot deeper than *I* realized."

"I haven't wanted to know much about her operations."

"Ever heard of the Rescue Angel?"

Gabe's face tightened. "Bits and pieces. You mean—?"

Ruby nodded. "Uh-huh. If you're thinking what I'm thinking...." She let her voice trail off, unwilling even here to speak details over the comm.

"Oh shit. But that explains a lot."

"It's a damn good reason for Brandon and Kris to have a separate and secure base."

Gabe sighed. "God. I'm just worried about you. All of you."

"I'm worried about you and the kids too," she said in a low voice. "And while this condo is nice, it's not home. My nose is drying out from recirc and scrubbed air. I miss being able to have my windows open. I miss not hearing the animals. Even the damn wolf howls." She hesitated. *Oh hell. You're in this deep enough now. Say it.* "I miss you," she said even more quietly.

Gabe reached toward her, then halted. "I miss you too. But I feel better just seeing you. Everything on track?"

She nodded and held her hands up, turning so he could see her nails. "This is step one for the nails. Gold base for the BPA. Part of my banquet prep for the Reals includes the nail artist painting the Martiniere trefoil on each nail, fingers and big toes both. Justine's idea."

"Oh my God, Tine is really going over the top with this." He laughed.

"Hey, might as well go all in, right?" She giggled, then grew solemn. "The girls and Justine leave early tomorrow morning and will be back sometime during the day. She's supposed to keep me posted on progress. It's a good thing that Branny has opening day tasks to keep him occupied, because he's nervous as a cat."

"I would be too, in his place." Gabe was quiet for a moment. "It's probably good for him that you're there. I just wish I could be too."

"I know." She yawned. "I'd better go to sleep. Serg wants me in his gym along with Bran bright and early for training. By the way, why didn't you ever tell me you were putting him through martial arts and fighting classes when he lived with you?"

"I didn't think you'd approve."

"I probably wouldn't have," she admitted. "But I wasn't aware of the bullying. He wouldn't tell me."

"He was getting beat black and blue, and his opponents were skilled enough to hurt him in places that wouldn't show unless you made him strip down—not something you would do as a single mother once he was ten. Charlie and Martin taught him basic dirty fighting, but he needed to know more."

"God, Gabe. Why didn't someone tell me?" It made sense. She had thought Brandon was just being lazy at times and trying to dodge the chores she desperately needed him to do. But now —she understood he just didn't want to show her he was hurting, because she *would* have pried until she knew what was going on.

"Branny pitched a fit every time Rachel or I brought up telling you. He didn't want anyone to say anything about it. You were fighting everyone for survival. He wanted to protect his mama because he knew you'd add battling for him to the load you were carrying and it could create more problems for you. It broke my heart, Rubes. It really did. He was—I understood why. So, I ran him through as many martial arts classes as we could cram in, because *I* wanted him to be able to face those fuckers down and kick the shit out of them. I didn't want him to be running like me. He was so proud when he won a big fight with them."

Ruby sighed. "Now *that* I remember. He got suspended from school."

"But it didn't happen any more, did it? And he went back to regular school after that, didn't he?"

"No. And yes."

"I wanted him to be safe. Just like I do you. And that's why you didn't know." Gabe sighed. "God, Ruby. I miss the hell out of you already. I've gotten used to sleeping in the same room."

"I'll be home soon." She yawned again. "I need to go to sleep."

"Stay safe and be careful."

"I will."

She rested her head against the back of the chair, staring up at the ceiling. *Conference tomorrow and the day after. Then the banquet. Then I can go home.*

It seemed like forever.

UP EARLY TO WORK OUT WITH SERG AND BRANDON AS JUSTINE, Beck, and Kris left. Serg's living room was his gym space. While Brandon warmed up and lifted weights, Serg took Ruby through a self-defense assessment including knife work, ending with them donning boxing gear. Brandon stood on the sideline, cheering Ruby on.

"All right," Serg said finally. "Bran, I know where that right hook comes from now. Your mother, not Gabe. Ruby, that's a darn impressive swing you've got."

"Thanks," Ruby said, puffing slightly and picking up a towel to wipe her face. "I used to spar with Gabe when we were first together. He taught me a few tricks as well."

"You're in good shape for someone in her fifties."

"Ranch woman. Lots of physical work."

"Well, there's people who could take a few tips from you, especially when it comes to fitness," Serg continued. "I talked to my father and read his notes last night. That dress has a pocket to hold a palm stunner, and there's room to accommodate a small knife or derringer on your thigh about—excuse me for this." He knelt and delicately placed his hands near but not quite touching her upper thigh. "Here. Which would you prefer?"

"Derringer. I'm not that good with knives."

"You're not that bad, either. With a little practice you'd be really good. Okay." Serg got back to his feet. "There's a pattern in Dad's notes for a practice outfit that matches the dress. I'll print it out today. I don't think I'll give you the poison option because for one thing, Dad didn't specify what she was carrying. I suspect curare or fentanyl myself, but if I don't know…."

"What?" She shouldn't be shocked by this but she was.

Serg shrugged. "Angelica carried poison vials in that dress to use on knife blades as well as—other uses."

"Whoa. You're saying that my grandmother was that kind of badass?" Brandon said.

"Angelica grew up in a tough family," Serg said. "The Ramirezes have drug cartel connections. The Saldivars. Her upbringing was very similar to what Gabe, Tine, and Joey received when it came to self-defense. Anyway. Other options include smaller knives, and electronic gadgets of various types depending on the situation. I think that giving you a palm stunner, and a couple of small knives to have just in case is a good start. Oh. The dress's material is lightly armored and there's some fine electronic wiring in it—probably the missing part of the brooch's functionality. I'm amazed at its capabilities, one of Dad's best creations. Brandon, there's a specific place to pin the brooch on it. I'll show you tomorrow evening."

"Okay," Ruby said.

"You can go on back to Tine's," Serg said. "Wait. What are you carrying today?"

"Chest holster, my .38," she said.

"Treated for security?"

"Should pass any scanner."

"Good. Anything else?"

"Nothing."

"What kind of footwear?"

"Boots under slacks today." She'd chosen her comfortable dress Lucchese boots to wear with slacks. They'd cost her a fortune years ago but they'd also lasted a long time.

"Will they hold a sheath of some sort?"

"I've carried a stunner in the past, as well as a derringer."

"Just a minute." Serg went over to the tall cabinets separating the kitchen area from the foyer. He came back with a small derringer in a clip holster and handed it to Ruby. "Two shots. Need any more?"

"I hope not."

"She should be okay," Brandon said. "It's all very public and we've got good security. Depends on what we end up doing for dinner. I may want to come back instead of going out just to check on Kris."

"Okay. I'll be at the Reals today, but not for the whole thing," Serg said. "If you change for dinner, Ruby, check in with me, okay? You're done now. Bran, it's your turn."

She lingered for a few minutes to watch as Brandon and Serg went to work. This bout appeared to be no holds barred. It was a mix of kick-boxing, martial arts, and just plain street fighting from what she could identify. Brandon was quick and lithe, reminding her of how Gabe moved at that age. Even to her untrained eye it looked like Brandon was getting more blows in than Serg, pushing his defenses hard.

At last the rumble in her stomach drove Ruby back over to the kitchen to pull together a quick breakfast, then shower and dress.

AT THE CONFERENCE, RUBY FELL QUICKLY INTO THE ROUTINE OF checking registrations, confirming work sessions, and screening last-minute attendees. Brandon placed her with a screen at the end of the main registration table to deal with problems. Occasionally she needed to call him over to deal with complications, but that wasn't often. It was straightforward work, and she relaxed as it became clear that today, at least, lacked no more issues than one would expect at an event like this. She was also impressed by the organization that Brandon and Kris had pulled together.

I suppose after all those years at AgI he's figured out event systems, she told herself.

At last they were in the final five minutes before the keynote. Most of the crowd had drifted away into the main auditorium for the opening presentation. Ruby scanned through the system to winnow out any possible glitches in Brandon's visuals. Justine had texted her a few minutes earlier that they were back at the condo. Kris and Beck were all right, and sleeping. She'd relayed that message to Brandon.

A cough jerked her attention away from the screen. "Well, well, well. Ruby Barkley. If you aren't the last person *I* expected to see here," Georgy Batineau, head of AgI, drawled.

Ruby tensed. She quickly typed a message to Brandon.

Complication. Come quickly. Get Bonnie to handle the kickoff.

She swiveled her chair to face Georgy. "That makes two of us, then. Coming to check out the competition?"

"Perhaps." Georgy eyed her appraisingly. "You've certainly cleaned up nice since you've started hanging out with the Martinieres. If I didn't know better, I wouldn't realize you were the ex-rodeo queen."

"I've always been more than just a rodeo queen," she said, biting back the sharp tone she wanted to use. She quickly scanned her list of non-arrivals. "Are you pre-registered under a different name or did we miss you somehow? I didn't see your name or Mariah's on the list."

"I'm not pre-registered," Georgy said. "And Mariah isn't here. She's at the Real Truthers conference." He rolled his eyes. "I got sick of politics, so I thought I would see if you have any day passes."

Brandon strode out of the auditorium. He slowed his pace, at first startled. Then he put on a big smile Ruby recognized from the Superhero as his *smoothing things out* face.

"Georgy!" he called. "What a surprise. Come to see if we're a threat to AgI?"

Georgy chuckled. "I suppose there's a little of that aspect involved. No, I got bored with the Real Truthers—that's more Mariah's thing than mine. I wanted to see what you had going with this Biobot Producers Alliance. Or am I persona non grata?"

"Not at all, not at all," Brandon said smoothly. "Though you might make some of my people nervous—after all, the BPA could be viewed as potential competition to your non-Innovator financing and production. But right now we just have a keynote. You're welcome to attend my presentation in—" he paused to check the quick overlay on his wrist. "—two minutes. On the house. See what we're doing."

"No, no, no, that won't be necessary," Georgy said. "Actually, I was hoping to have a chat with you and Markey."

"*Kris* is down with a bug," Ruby said. "That's why I'm here, to help Brandon."

"Ah. Well, perhaps I'll have that chat now with your mother instead, Brandon," Georgy said smoothly. "You do have a presentation to get to."

Brandon tensed. "I'm not sure about that—Mother?"

"Do you need my assistance?" She pressed the button to alert the bodyguards that were lingering around the catering table. "I can cover this."

Brandon relaxed slightly as two of the bodyguards, Diane and Jack, drifted toward them. "I'd appreciate it if you would. Let me check one last thing on the screen." He came around the desk. *"Do not leave the premises,"* he snarled into her ear on the side away from Georgy.

"Got it," she said out loud as she shut down the screen and slid her chair back. Brandon moved away to talk to the guards. "Georgy, I probably should stay close just in case Brandon does need me. But we have drinks and I don't think the food selection has been too picked over yet—there'll be more demand after the opening session. Will that work for you?"

Georgy's eyes flicked toward the guards. "Don't worry, I'm not about to get your guards fussed. On site works for me, especially if we can be somewhat private."

"That can be arranged." She got up and joined Brandon and the guards. "He wants to talk," she said in a low voice. "I've got it, Bran. Go to your presentation."

"Thanks, Ma. You be careful."

"Part of my job these days," she said to him, then turned to the guards. "Can you set us up an isolated table where you can watch us but not overhear? Just a two-seater." She hesitated, instinct making her add, "Out of easy sight lines from outside."

"How about over there?" Diane pointed to an out-of-the-way corner. "We can move a divider so you won't be spotted from outside."

"That would be perfect. Thanks." She smiled at them and joined Georgy. "They're setting it up now."

Georgy glanced down and half-grinned as he spotted her

cowboy boots. "So the rodeo queen is still there under the surface."

"Always has been." She waved toward the bar and the food. "Honestly, I could use a little drink and nibbles right now. Shall we?"

"I can *definitely* use a drink." He moved closer to her than she liked and she extended her stride so that he had to scramble to keep up. Good. Maybe she wouldn't have to stomp on his instep to get him to move away.

"Manhattan, please," she told the bartender. "His drink is on my account. Georgy?"

"Same for me. I'm surprised. I thought you were the girl for straight shots?"

"I'm working right now."

"Kind of surprised to see you here. Isn't this your big production season?"

"Not quite yet. And Gabe's managing things back at the ranch."

"Ga-bri-el," Georgy said slowly, drawing out his name. "That's quite the thing, him turning out to not just be a Martiniere but the missing Martiniere heir. Did you know all along?"

She shook her head. "No, I had no idea until the end of the Superhero." She took her drink and picked up a pre-packaged small plate with cheese, crackers, and some fruit that didn't look too bruised. Despite all of Brandon's fussing, the food service selection appeared to be decent. And unlike the Superhero, the cheese was in small amounts but still real. Probably Justine's doing.

By the time Georgy had chosen a plate—she noticed he also went for the small fruit, cheese, and cracker plate—the table was ready. She walked over, waiting for Georgy to sit before she settled as far across the table from him as she could, noticing that he chose a chair facing the wall with his back to any observers. That action made the hair tingle on the back of her neck in warning. She'd never seen Georgy be this cautious in all her years dealing with AgI. Mariah, yes. Georgy, no.

"So," she said. "What's going on?"

Georgy looked around nervously. "This is actually better than I had hoped. Though I'd also wanted to talk to Markey—"

"*Kris*," Ruby said firmly. "Her name is Kris. She's no longer indentured, and you don't need to use her last name as an identifier any more."

"Kris, then." Georgy lowered his voice. "She's got a sister who's still indentured, Markey Two—right?"

More prickles on the back of her neck. *Has Kris and Brandon's operation been discovered?*

"Yes." Ruby sipped her drink.

"She's being watched." Georgy swallowed. "And it's not a good thing." He sighed. "There's a big mess right now and it's getting worse with the rumors of a potential indentured rebellion. If Mar-*Kris*, is in communication with her, she needs to let her know. That's what I wanted to tell her."

Shit! Ruby kept her face steady and calm. *Survival, Ruby, survival.* "Surely you're joking."

"Oh come on, Ruby. Even in your isolated little corner in the middle of nowhere you've heard about issues with indentureds in the harvest sector this year. Especially since you're working with Jeff Swait."

More trouble, then. "I've been hearing about indentured supply issues, true. But what does that have to do with an indentured rebellion? And what's your purpose in talking to me about this?"

Handle this like Gabe would. You've seen him in negotiations enough times over the past six months. Make Georgy spell it out.

"It's a long story," Georgy said. "And I don't have that much time to tell it. Actually, I'm glad you're here. I need to talk to Gabriel." He glanced around nervously again. "Look. Things have changed at AgI in the past few years. A couple of our prototype projects went bad and there's getting to be a glut of reality shows operating on clicks. Not just in ag but in other sectors, like student loans and other financing. The Superstar segment of the Innovator hasn't been funneling future projects to our R and D section like it has in the past, and our revenues are down. The Superhero brought in a surge of investment, but our bread and butter has always been in the consulting and licensing of the Superstar products. You probably know that from Brandon."

"Yes." She wasn't hungry now, nerves like spikes of ice poking at her gut, but she still forced herself to take a bite of the cheese to help absorb the alcohol.

"AgI has been running into financial issues over the past few years. We went looking for investors, and, well, Philip Martiniere—not the Group, Philip as an individual—controls a thirty-five percent interest and is on the Board of Directors as a result," Georgy continued. "He's been insisting that his people take positions of power in our Indentured Workers Division. It made sense, given the Martiniere work in body mods and indentured contract management. Mariah was a persuasive advocate for allying with the Martinieres based on their experience."

"I'm not surprised," Ruby said icily. "So how many knives do you have in your back right now?"

Georgy raised his brows in surprise, then chuckled. "I forgot. She was involved in your divorce. Still some hard feelings, eh?"

Ruby shrugged. "I don't trust the woman as far as I can throw her. Never have."

Georgy took a big gulp of his drink. "Look. Gabe's cousins have been attending the Reals so I'm sure you're getting some feedback on their proposals, especially Philip's."

"Oh yes."

"Well, the Martinieres—Philip and Joseph—are not waiting for legislation," Georgy said. "They're acting. And because Mar—*Kris*—is associated with Brandon, that's brought her sister under closer scrutiny. Now maybe she's not doing anything she shouldn't, but if she is…she needs to know she's under watch.

That's the explanation for why I wanted to talk to Kris. And— part of why I want to talk to Gabe."

"I see," Ruby said, sipping her drink. "I will let Kris know."

"But there's more than that. Plans are afoot about using the indentureds in ways, that…well, I tried to veto the proposals Philip brought to our Board after the Superhero, and…." Georgy sighed. "Long story short. I'm in trouble. I can't trust Mariah because I think she's in bed with Philip—literally. And that's my other thing, besides passing on a message to M—Kris to warn her about her sister. I'm in bad trouble, I need help, and I need to talk to Gabe in person. Can you set it up?"

"Let me talk to him and get back to you. Would you have a site preference?"

"Someplace easy for me to get in and out, away from urban areas." Georgy looked around again, frowning. "The next week would be good."

"I'll check with Gabe and get back to you," Ruby repeated. "A contact?"

Georgy pushed a slip of paper across the table. "My private comm. Daytime contact only. Mariah's too close at night." He gulped the rest of his drink. "Thanks, Ruby. I'd better get going before my absence is noticed. Thanks, again. Oh. And tell Gabe he is one hell of a lucky man."

He got up and walked away, leaving his plate mostly untouched.

Ruby took her time finishing her drink.

Now this is an interesting twist.

She wondered what Gabe's reaction would be.

CHAPTER 9

"What. The. Fuck. What motivated Georgy to do this?" Gabe's projection stared at Ruby after she dropped the bombshell about Georgy's meeting request. They were with the others, in Justine's living room. Ruby had decided that this needed to be a group call once Justine returned from the Reals' last session—she and Gabe could talk privately later. Brandon sprawled in an armchair. Justine leaned against one arm of the couch, still in her evening wear, while Ruby sat in the other corner. Serg paced behind the couch.

"That's the question I have," Ruby said. "And more. Georgy was nervous as could be the whole time talking to me. That's not a behavior I associate with him."

"Bran?" Gabe asked. "You've had the most experience with Georgy."

"I don't know. He didn't seem to be acting that much out of the norm from what I've seen."

"Damn, Ruby, I wish you'd been able to record that talk."

"Didn't have the time to activate cams and I don't think he would have talked quite as freely with overt recording," she said.

"I'm worried," Brandon said. "I mean, we've assumed that Pat is being observed, but if it's significant enough for Georgy to warn us—damn! And we are so close to—no, no, I'd better not say this even on a secure line."

"It's for the best," Serg muttered.

"Did you know about the Martiniere involvement with the Indentured Workers Division, Bran?" Gabe asked.

"I knew Philip invested in AgI but not the specifics, of course, beyond him being an additional financing source once the Innovator started having financial problems due to competitors," Brandon said. "I hadn't been focusing on the Board because I had too many other things happening." He frowned. "Now I wish I had been paying attention. Management issues were coming up, even before we left, but I didn't know the leadership of that division was that closely tied to Philip. Kris might have more knowledge than I do, but…she's asleep right now."

Gabe's face softened. "The procedures go all right?"

Justine sighed. "More or less. Some complications with Kris. Even if Ruby wasn't going to the Reals banquet tomorrow night we would need to stay over until then. Beck went through it better than Kris, as I expected. But they're both going to need some recovery time. Beck and Ruby will be back at the ranch day after tomorrow. Kris?" She shrugged. "She and Brandon will make that call."

"That's good." Gabe tightened his lips thoughtfully. "Ruby, let's have Georgy meet us at Moondance on Tuesday at noon. I can have things sufficiently in order by then. Serg. Security detail, as tight as you can make it. Once we know a date and time for certain, then we can work out the rest of the mechanics."

"Should I plan to be at this meeting with Georgy?" Brandon asked. "Kris and I need to move on a few things, and I don't know how ready we'll be to meet with him by Tuesday."

"No," Gabe said firmly. "I think we'd better keep this meeting to just me and your mother. I want to keep you two away from Georgy in case this is a trap. You're the future of our reforms." He ran his fingers through his hair and shook his head. "This accelerates our timeline even more than your appearance at the Reals tomorrow night, Ruby. Okay, Tine. I'll admit it. You were right. Tomorrow night needs to happen."

"Glad you can admit it," Justine said.

Serg stopped pacing and leaned his hands on the back of the couch. "I can have my security crew at Moondance day after tomorrow to set things up, Gabe. That be soon enough?"

"It'll have to do. I'll send you specs and topo maps so you know the layout." Gabe turned his head and called up a screen. "Sending it now."

"I've some idea of what the design is like." Serg bared his teeth in a feral grin. "Looked it up six months ago. Looks reasonable for the most part."

"Rachel's designs with my influences. More of my touches in the rebuilding than in the original, though. Establishing a safe perimeter is going to be interesting—there are cliffs in some places on that ridge. It's one reason why I chose that location, but your people need to be aware of them."

"All right." Serg straightened up. "I'm off. I'm looking at those Moondance files. See you soon, Gabe." He left the condo.

"Anything else, Dad?" Brandon said, rubbing his face. "I'd like to be with Kris. Even if she's asleep. Just to make sure… bad enough I had to leave her for this call." Ever since they returned from the conference to free Justine to go to the Reals, he had been at Kris's side.

Gabe's face softened. "I understand. Look. Bran. I think we better make contingency plans to have Moondance as your place to stay when you're in this part of the world. You and Kris should only come to the Double R for meetings. Too easy and tempting a target otherwise. But the same is true for the two of you and Justine. How far along are you in getting this separate condo in Chicago?"

"Closing next week, and we take possession immediately. It will take several weeks for Serg's people to install their gadgets, reinforce windows, et cetera. It does come with some reinforcement but not up to his standards."

"Can't be helped, I guess," Gabe sighed. "Okay. Be careful. Go take care of your lady."

"Talk to you later." Brandon got up, pausing to kiss Ruby on the cheek before leaving.

Justine stretched and yawned. "And I'm going, too, Gabriel. I'm exhausted. It's been a long day on medical watch, then political games."

"Thanks for all your work," Gabe said.

"Pish. It's part of what I do when I'm not pretending to be a brainless airhead heiress." She slipped off her heels and stood up. "And don't get too worried about Kris and Brandon staying here. Once the Reals are done, I'll either be in LA or at the ranch." She frowned. "Unless you have another place in your neck of the woods that I should plan on staying at?"

"No, Tine. Bran and I are going to be the targets, I think. I'm more concerned about them drawing attention to your work."

"Understood, and don't be worried. I'm not." She yawned again as she went to the wet bar to pour herself a drink. "Night now. See you soon."

"Do you want me to call you back from my room so that you don't risk vertigo from the connection as I walk?" Ruby asked Gabe after Justine left the room.

"Nah. I'll close my eyes. The meds have been behaving lately, so less vertigo sandbagging me."

"Okay. Going now—after I pour myself a shot."

Gabe chuckled as she got up and found Justine's best Scotch. *Real* Scotch, not synthwhisky. "After a day like this I don't blame you. I have one waiting here."

"It's been a wild day for sure." She hesitated, then grabbed the bottle before heading down the hallway. Just in case she wanted more. "Gimme a moment."

She entered her room, set drink and bottle on the vanity, and turned on the *Silencer* option. Gabe's projection shimmered for a moment, then firmed up. He sat at his desk, leaning back in his chair, eyes closed as he held his drink—a straight shot almost brimful, like hers. For a moment she was tempted to undress to give him a pleasant surprise, then rejected the notion. It was unfair to him. She had been careful about exposure over the past six months of sharing a bedroom, even though the G9 had trashed his libido. He'd not said anything about it and had exhibited the same care in return. She wondered if he was still trying to hide his scars from Philip's beatings.

But she pulled the derringer out of her boot and put it on the dresser, then kicked the boots off before grabbing drink and bottle and sitting in the chair.

"I'm settled now," she said. "You still there?"

He opened his eyes and raised his glass to her before sipping from it. "We need to figure out what kind of proposal we can lay before Georgy. I'm betting that he needs us as a white knight to keep Philip from exercising a hostile takeover. I'll look at the AgI numbers. Georgy said that Philip owns a thirty-five percent share?"

"Yes, personally, not in the name of the Martiniere Group. And that he's on their board."

Gabe winced. "I'll see what we can leverage. If—and that's a big *if*—we decide to help him."

"The RubyBot preorders are looking pretty good," she said. Now she was glad she'd advocated keeping the original RubyBot separate from the daughter versions that they were developing with Swait. "We can throw our shares from the ranch income into the mix—I'm sure Bran would be willing as well. That should land us a decent loan."

"I hate risking them, especially for that ass Georgy," he said, taking another sip before setting his drink down. "I really don't want to borrow against the RubyBot."

"Don't discount your microbials, either. That's another piece we can leverage."

"They aren't as lucrative as the Ruby. Oh well. Other than Georgy, how's that conference going?"

Ruby leaned back in the chair and took a sip. "Pretty good so far. Brandon and Kris have their systems down solid. I've been promoting all of our products, especially since Jeff can't be here. There's a lot of interest in the basic RubyBot as well as the Protector. Makes sense with the drought in the Midwest this year." The Protector focused on maximizing drought tolerance, which had been one of Swait's projects. Combining it with the RubyBot had been an easy task, certainly not as complicated as developing the Defender.

"So you anticipate more preorders for next spring?"

"Yes, after harvest time this fall."

A companionable silence fell between them as they both sipped their drinks.

Gabe tossed back the rest of his drink. "Look. Ruby. Talk to Tine. See if it's okay for Beck to travel after your banquet tomorrow night. I'm even more worried now, with Georgy approaching us for help against Philip. No matter what happens, I'll feel better when you're back here. And we need to talk about —other things."

"I'll see what I can do." Ruby contemplated her drink, not wanting to inquire further about *other things.* Not yet. "One thing that I didn't mention earlier is that Georgy thinks Mariah is in bed with Philip—literally. It wasn't something I wanted to discuss in front of Justine. You know Georgy. It could be total bullshit intended to get a rise out of me." She swallowed the rest of her drink and poured herself another, less-full, glass.

Gabe furrowed his brows and tightened his lips. "It's entirely plausible that she and Philip have an arrangement. I've wondered about the timing of Mariah's attentions to me back during our divorce." He gulped half his drink. "When I think back the *coincidental* nature of her popping up in Pendleton— yeah. I have to wonder. I know she uses seduction as a tool. She admitted it to me years ago."

"Georgy made a crack about it when I asked him how it felt to be knifed in the back. Which made me wonder. A sympathy ploy?"

"Could be." Gabe finished his drink and set the glass down. "But Georgy plays the field as much as Mariah would. It will be interesting to listen in tomorrow night. Just wish I could see it. Oh well."

"I have a feeling that setting up a cam to follow me around won't be well received."

"Oh absolutely. Has Serg come up with defenses for you?"

"Better than that. His father had schematics for the dress's security setup. Apparently your mother also carried poisons."

"Now *that's* news to me."

"He's not giving me any of those. He has printed out a dress copy for me to wear during practice tomorrow morning, complete with assorted weapons. Oh. And that dress is made of light armor material. He didn't say what it was."

"Better than nothing. Now I know why Mother wore that dress frequently." Gabe shook his head, a rueful expression on his face. "Ruby, I never thought we'd be having discussions like this."

"But here we are." She finished her drink. "You sleep okay last night?" She already knew the answer to that question from how haggard he looked, but maybe he'd talk about his worries.

"No. *That* nightmare again. Repeatedly." He looked at the bottle and his glass. "I shouldn't, but I'm going to have another. Maybe I'll get some better sleep. Maybe not. Last night I ended up coming down here and working until I fell asleep with my head on the desk—and woke up choking with sinus drainage." He grimaced. "Shades of life at Moondance after Rachel died. Not a pleasant memory."

"For what it's worth, I didn't sleep well either." She didn't reach for her bottle, though. Even though it was good Scotch she didn't need to face tomorrow with a hangover.

"I'll probably do the same thing tonight after you ring off." His voice was grim. "I need time to think about how to handle these possibilities with Georgy and AgI. Run the numbers. Let it sit overnight in my brain. If I do enough of it maybe I'll have nightmares about Georgy and Mariah. Or Mariah and Philip, instead of about Rachel and you both dying. God." He shook his head. "Another *never thought I'd have to consider* thing."

"I can agree with that," she sighed.

"True. Hey. When Brandon puts the emeralds on you tomorrow night, I'd like to watch. For one thing, I can guide him through the process. I mean, Serg or Justine could also probably do it—but it's something I'd like to do. I got to do it for my mother once, with my father's guidance."

"Family tradition?"

"Yes." He sighed. "I'm grateful that you're willing to put up with all this bullshit. I should have trusted you years ago. I am very, very sorry that I didn't. I should have known that you wouldn't run away screaming but have my back. I am so, so sorry, Ruby. I was stupid."

"Gabe. There's no need to keep apologizing. I understand and I'm good with it. I forgive you. Hell. I'm a quick-tempered bitch and you know it. I hope you've forgiven me for that."

She decided that a single finger's more of Scotch wouldn't be too much. Not if they were going to talk relationships. That last one had been a half-glass, after all. She picked up the bottle and poured two fingers' worth in. Oops. Oh well. That made her consumption the equivalent of a full second drink. This had to be it. She capped the bottle and set it back down on the floor.

"What's happened has happened and all the regrets in the world won't bring those years back," Gabe said wistfully.

"I could have been less explosive, I guess." She sipped the whisky. "I almost told Branny that I'd given you a lot worse bruising in a fistfight than Joseph did him."

Gabe snorted. "You should have." He rubbed his jaw where her first blow had landed that time. "God. I still remember that last fight. You were so damn pissed and yet so vulnerable. I almost lost my nerve and begged for forgiveness, nearly told you everything—or at least as much as I could, then, because I had figured out how to get around the programming. That's why I wanted to have dinner at Southfork that night. I thought that maybe I could persuade you to come to a room with me and listen, then have the best makeup sex of our lives. I don't know. I was bouncing back and forth between terror, knowing that leaving you was the safest choice for you and Branny—and falling on my knees and pleading for you to listen to my reasons for leaving and talk me out of doing it. I almost did spill everything. Even if it meant I had a full seizure because of the mind control."

"And then I told you to shut the fuck up because you *had* started to do it," Ruby sighed. "Wouldn't let you talk because Mariah had called me up to give me shit just before I left the ranch and I didn't believe one word you were saying."

"She did that?"

Ruby nodded and took another sip. "I'd been having second thoughts myself. Running the ranch by myself. Even with Charlie and Martin's help, it was a big job. I knew I was going to have to put the RubyBot on hold for a few years until I got ranch operations on an even keel. Vacillating between cattle and grains as my primary business. Looking at Bran and thinking about single parenting. How much bookkeeping I needed to do for a side hustle to keep it all afloat. Trying to figure out why Mariah had your attention when I couldn't keep it. And then she called to gloat. Called me a hick hayseed and that I would never be good enough for you. Got me riled up and pissed off." Her voice wavered a little, and she steadied it as a distant memory stirred. "Wait a minute. She said something about your family and I don't think she was talking about the Ramirezes. Gabe, she knew your history even then."

"Fuck." He groaned.

Ruby took another sip, then summoned up her courage for the question she had wanted to ask ever since talking to Charlie the other day. "Gabe. What really happened that day Bran and I went into the hospital?"

He gave her an odd look. "What do you mean?"

"When I finally was coherent enough to think about it, I asked one of the nurses if you had been to see us. The answer was no. Vickie doesn't remember you coming by at all." She paused. "And yet the other day Charlie told me that you showed up at the ranch that same day in a frenzy, told him that Bran and I were dying, raving about seeing Joseph. He did say he told me about that, but I was still so out of it for so long that I don't remember him telling me. And afterward things were so bad between us that he thought it best not to remind me."

Gabe stared into his drink. "That's the thing, Ruby. I *don't* clearly remember what happened. I *did* see Joey in Pendleton that afternoon, after I'd picked up the nutrients. Argued with him, told him to leave me and mine alone. It wasn't—the first time I'd seen him there. He grinned and told me that I would lose that which was dearest to me. Things get blurry after that. I vaguely remember driving as fast as I dared until I reached the hospital. Argued my way into a room where you and Bran were on machines, and someone had just pulled a sheet over your head. Then I got dragged out and threatened with arrest. After that the only thing I could think to do was to run."

"Pull a sheet over my head? To my best memory I was never that bad. Sicker than hell, especially after dragging myself to Branny's side several times before they gave up and put us in the same room. But they had me on IVs and a nasal cannula of oxygen at one point. Same for Bran. No masks, no ventilators. We were very sick but it never got that bad."

Gabe shook his head. "Then what the hell could I have seen?"

"I don't know." She shook her head. "Control words to influence what you saw. Could Joseph have used them on you during that argument? Implanted a false memory?"

"It's possible," Gabe said slowly. "He shouldn't have had access to any words capable of having that strong an influence on me. I vaguely remember seeing Joey and Mariah at lunch." He stopped short, his expression tightening. "Crud. It could have been a combination of a drug plus control words. I remember thinking the coffee was pretty bitter, but the coffee in that place always did taste funny. All it would have taken would have been a moment's distraction for Mariah to slip it into my coffee." He tossed back his drink and slammed the glass on his desk. "And the next fucking clear memory I have is sitting in a cheap ass motel room staring at my .45, thinking about sticking it in my mouth and pulling the trigger because Joseph was right. I'd lost what was dearest to me."

She gulped. "Oh God, Gabe. I didn't know—God." Was there no end to the horrors she was learning about their past?

"It didn't last long because—I don't know. No wait. I do know. A horn honked in the parking lot and I jumped, because my next thought was that I was going to make Joseph pay if he had harmed you and Branny. Bastard. I swear I will *make* him pay—now."

"If Bran doesn't take him down first. Serg thinks our son could have gone pro as a fighter."

"If anyone knows it would be Serg." Gabe exhaled long and slow. "I'm glad to hear this but, damn. I am so glad we were able to keep Brandon from being indentured. They might have been tempted to use him as a fighter, and…God." His eyes widened as if he had realized something more.

"What?"

"With Philip on the AgI board and in control of that indentured program, that might have *been* the plan. Especially if they're developing…oh shit, Ruby. God damn it. I'll bet that was what they intended to do with him. They knew who Brandon was all along. Who I was. Now I wonder, especially with Mariah calling and getting you riled up before that dinner. Short-term control words are possible. It would be easy enough for someone to sneak into the hospital to influence you, especially if you were sedated. It was possible. But we'll never know for certain because those things fade." An exasperated sigh escaped him and he slammed his hand on his desk. "Damn it, Ruby. They took so fucking much from us."

"From you."

"From *us*." His lips tightened and his face hardened. "They took twenty-one years from us. Fuck them. They will pay for what they've done. Are doing."

She matched his hard gaze with one of her own. "Absolutely. And I will be right there next to you to make it happen."

"God damn. Ruby Barkley, this is why I love you. I was such a fucking fool to let you go. I am not going to let you get away from me again." One corner of his mouth twisted up in a grim smirk. "Philip can make all the noises he wants about a *proper Martiniere woman*. But I've got the real deal in you, and someday we'll make it formal. Sooner rather than later, I hope."

"Someday," she agreed. "Oh. Georgy's last words before he left were for me to tell you that you're one hell of a lucky man."

The smirk widened. "He's damn right." Gabe relaxed. "I'd better let you get some sleep. Tomorrow's going to be a long day. Just—be very fucking careful, okay?"

"I will. And don't stay up all night drinking and scheming, okay? Save some of that planning for me, all right? I'm going to need it after tomorrow night."

Gabe laughed. "It'll take me a while to unwind, but all right. I'll save some of the plotting and conspiring to share with you. Just—try to come home tomorrow night if you can?"

"I will," she promised. "Good night, dear."

"Good night."

After Ruby hung up, she stared into the dregs of that last shot, thinking.

CHAPTER 10

THE NEXT MORNING'S PRACTICE WAS JUST RUBY AND SERG. Brandon had begged off to spend time with Kris before the conference started. She and Serg now sat on a bench, taking a break after she had practiced fighting in the dress copy.

"Serg," she said. "I want to learn how to use the poison option for this dress."

She bit back a smile as the usually unflappable Serg startled, tensing away and eying her with furrowed brows.

"That's not something I'd expect from you, Ruby," he said. "It's not easy to pick up, either. Why would you want it? I wouldn't figure you for someone into poisons."

"I'm thinking not so much about poisons as hypnotics and sedatives."

His brows shot up. "Still difficult and in some ways even more complicated. Surely you don't think tonight's banquet is going to require these tools?"

"Not tonight, no. But for future uses. Gabe and I compared notes about some past events, and we think that a combination of hypnotics and sedatives *might* have been used on us—him at least, but possibly me too—at some point. Turnabout is fair play. I want to not only have those tools but possible antidotes on hand."

"I see." His face relaxed. "You'll need to study the properties of the drugs you want to use. As well as safe handling. It'll take several months of training."

Ruby shrugged. "Can't be that different from what I've had to do for the horses and cattle over the years. Look up Regumate and other medications for managing equine reproduction. Careful handling, don't get it on your skin, especially if you're a woman. Plus short-term sedatives and tranqs."

"That experience will make it easier. I thought veterinarians did all that."

"Oh no," Ruby said, shaking her head. "Too damn expensive to have a vet out for every large animal shot. I've given lots of shots and oral meds."

"Let's talk after we get past the next week or so. Unless you think you'll need it sooner than that?"

"If I do then we're in major trouble. No, this is for the future."

"It will work better once you're wearing the ring," Serg said. "As will more of the electronics built into that dress."

"Which means marriage. I know."

"You're thinking about it, then."

"Yes. I'll know more about what path I'm going to take after tonight. But it's very likely. There's just—so much going on."

"Got it." Serg rose. "One more round, and then I think you're good to go for tonight."

"All right."

One item off of the preparation list.

"I SUPPOSE WE COULD GO BACK TO THE DOUBLE R AFTER THE banquet," Justine said slowly as they ate breakfast. "Beck's recovering faster than I thought. If she rests today then she'd be ready tonight. But it's going to be very late when we get there. What's driving this? Gabe getting fretful?"

"That's part of it," Ruby said. "The other piece is that this morning, I started getting a feeling that leaving tonight was a good idea. You know what I mean? It just started about an hour ago. I don't even want to come back here. I want to bug out right after the banquet."

"I know what you mean. Exactly—and you aren't the only one with that edgy feeling." Justine pursed her lips thoughtfully as she tapped her fingers on the table. "We'll need to be packed and ready. Would you want to change before leaving or go directly from the banquet?"

"Honestly? I think a quick getaway is best."

"The more I think about it the more I like that idea, too." Justine stopped tapping and picked up her coffee cup. "Even though Gabe's skittish about him and Brandon being in the same location, I think it might not hurt for all of us to clear out of here tonight. I'll talk to Brandon. The three of them can meet us at the airport. We'll take our bags with us."

"Thanks. I'll let Gabe know."

She texted Gabe with the news, not wanting to get into another conversation just yet. It would be a distraction and today she needed to be focused.

Another item checked off.

SHE COULDN'T GET AWAY FROM THE CONFERENCE TO CALL GEORGY until late morning, ducking into an alcove under Diane-the-guard's watchful eye, and kept it audio only.

"Batineau," Georgy snapped.

"Barkley. Meeting site. Gabe's Moondance Ranch. Next Tuesday at noon. That work?"

"I'll need directions or someone to meet me."

"We'll send someone to pick you up at the Pendleton airport."

"No. Mariah has too many people in Pendleton."

Ruby thought for a moment. "Walla Walla, then. We'll have someone meet you there. Plan to arrive at 11:30."

"All right. It's a date." Georgy hung up.

She texted Gabe. *Meeting arranged. Tell you details tonight.*

That item taken care of.

RUBY STILL WAS TYPING NOTES AS THE TRANSPORT VAN HAULED HER and Brandon, plus equipment, back to Justine's condo. They would leave most of the items secured in the van to load onto the plane back to the Double R. Her nerves jangled. Almost time.

"What's the rush to get back to the ranch about?" Brandon asked.

Ruby hit *save* on her last entry before answering. "Just a hunch your dad has—and a matching one on my part. Plus Justine started thinking the same thing."

"She said as much. But I thought Dad didn't want the two of us in the same place. Has he changed his thinking?"

"I haven't talked to him about this yet. Call this one of Justine's hunches that it's a good idea. You don't have to go to the ranch if there's a different location that's secure."

"Serg's place in LA might be good," Brandon said thoughtfully. "I'll talk to Kris and Serg both. It will place us closer to Pat if we need to do an extraction, and it will make contact with her easier. We can drop you and Beck off, then continue on to LA. A late night but tomorrow's wide open."

"Don't be doing anything crazy," she cautioned.

Brandon snorted. "Crazy? Ma, you're a fine one to talk. You and Dad both. Don't worry. We'll consult if it's necessary to extract Pat, because it won't be something that we can pull off alone."

The van paused to go through the security check in the basement parking structure. After Diane parked it and handed the keys over to the guards watching their vehicles, they took the private elevator to the penthouse suites. Ruby checked the time. Just enough to pack, shower, and sit down for hair, makeup, and nails before putting on the jewels.

She stopped to grab a quick bite from the refrigerator. After last night's discussion with Gabe, she wasn't so sure that she wanted to trust any food or drink that was prepared out of her sight, especially in a large venue. Paranoid? Possibly. But an event like this one was not one where she should take such risks.

Justine joined her. "Eating ahead of time?" She pulled out some cheese and started nibbling. "Wise. The other option is to go to the bathroom and puke it all up during the event before much of anything bad gets absorbed. I'm pretty good at doing that."

"I'd just as soon eat before and after," Ruby said. "After Gabe and I talked last night—yeah."

"I can't say as I blame you. I've gotten tired of puking in strange bathrooms at banquets, and risking God-knows-what viruses lurk there. Getting older and wiser."

"You do this all the time?"

Justine nodded. "How do you think I keep my figure? More to the point, in spite of the preventatives I take, it reduces exposure to substances I don't want." She grabbed more cheese. "Everyone's here. Come on back to the salon once you're dressed."

"I will." Ruby finished eating her crackers, then went to her room.

After she showered, she contemplated how best to simplify her packing. There was enough room to put the empty garment bag in her suitcase if she compacted it hard. After she did that, Ruby put on the thigh holster and slipped on the dress, checking how it lay on her after she loaded the palm stunner and small knives in the hem sheaves. The dress actually hung and moved better with a little weight. Then she pulled on the sandals, set her bag in the living area, and headed back to the small salon in the condo, carrying the box that held the Martiniere emeralds, her locket sitting on the lid.

Justine's hair stylist Timothy was working on her as Ruby came in. He grinned at Ruby and tossed her a styling cape. Ruby put it on and sat to have her nails done. A predictable order. Nails. Hair. Makeup. Whether it was prepping for a rodeo, an AgI show, or—this, the order of preparation was the same.

And then it would be time for the jewels.

Timothy completed blowing out Justine's freshly-cut and styled hair as the nail stylist finished painting the last trefoil on Ruby's nails. "All right there, Ms. Tine. You're good to go. Ruby, you have a locket you want placed in your hair?"

"Yes." Ruby nodded toward the silver locket on top of the black emerald box. "This is it."

Timothy looked at the locket, then gestured for Ruby to sit in the salon chair while he swept up the trimmings from Justine's hair.

"And what are you thinking for your style? Cut? Up-do?"

"No cutting," she said. "I normally wear it down and styled, but I don't think that's right for this event. Some sort of up-do that will hold the locket. Doesn't need to be visible."

"I can do a French twist and pin the locket to the inside, then have some additional curls with the ends. Does that work?"

"Sure."

She worked on steady, deep breathing with her eyes closed to settle her nerves as Timothy worked on her hair, finishing off with a curling iron to give her delicate tendrils by her face and on top of her head.

Just another rodeo run in. Just another rodeo run in, she kept telling herself.

"There you are, Ms. Ruby." Timothy handed her a mirror and spun her so that she could see the style in back reflected from the big mirror beside the chair.

"It looks lovely," she said, before moving to the makeup chair. "Thank you."

Timothy grinned and finished his cleanup before leaving. Justine had already gone, probably to do her own packing. Once her makeup was done, Ruby studied herself in the mirror again. She almost didn't recognize the sophisticated reflection. Timothy's French twist and artfully styled curls were not her usual styling. But she liked it.

The makeup wasn't as heavy as studio makeup. The combination of hair and makeup made her look easily ten to fifteen years younger. Ruby smiled at herself in the mirror. Now it was time for the jewels.

Taking a deep breath, she picked up the jewelry box and went to the living room. Gabe's projection faced away from Ruby as she entered, talking to Brandon.

"Wow," Brandon breathed as Serg checked her ear implant. "Mom, you look really good."

Gabe turned to look at her. His eyes widened and he smiled. "Wish I was there to see you in person."

"You'll see me later on tonight." She crossed the room and handed the box to Brandon.

"Don't muss it up too much if you can avoid it," he said, still smiling. "I want to admire you. Brandon. As we discussed. Serg will tell you the final sequence. Tine. Ready for recording?"

"Here we are," Justine said, activating the cam in her scanner.

Ruby stood tall, raising her chin, waiting. Brandon picked up the right earring.

"I, Brandon Edward Martiniere, natural and acknowledged son of Gabriel Marcus Martiniere and Ruby Marie Barkley, act in the name of Gabriel Marcus Martiniere." His voice quavered at first but steadied as he inserted the right earring. "With these gems I pronounce my mother, Ruby Marie Barkley, as being in partnership with my father, Gabriel Marcus Martiniere." He inserted the left earring. "With these gems I attest that Ruby Marie Barkley speaks with the voice and the authority of Gabriel Marcus Martiniere." He fastened the necklace around her throat and Ruby swallowed hard as the dress began to tingle.

Brandon picked up the brooch and glanced at Serg.

"Pin it on her, and say 'with these gems I confirm that Ruby Marie Barkley speaks with the voice and the authority of Gabriel Marcus Martiniere,' and place your palm over the emerald. Ruby, you should be feeling a tingle by now."

"Yes," she said.

"You will feel a sharper prick as Brandon pins the brooch on and says the words."

She nodded and met Brandon's eyes. "I'm ready," she said softly.

Brandon carefully pinned the brooch to her right shoulder and repeated the phrase Serg had told him, resting his palm against the stone. One sharp shock radiated out from the brooch along with a blinding green flash, and then the tingles muted to a soft vibration.

"I remotely witness and testify that I approve these actions by Brandon Edward Martiniere in my name," Gabe said.

Justine lowered her scanner. "Got it."

"Good." Serg eyed Ruby. "Go into another room and see if you have comms with Gabe. You should just be able to speak and hear without doing anything special."

"Is there an on-off switch?" she asked.

"No. Not yet. Just an off switch. Power charge fades after four hours. I need to do more work to get you the ability to switch it on and off."

"Understood." She walked to her now-empty room.

"Can you hear me?" Gabe asked.

"Loud and clear."

He sighed. "That's a relief. Old tech and everything. You doing okay?"

"Other than icicles from nerves poking into my gut, yeah."

"Good luck," he said softly. "I'm not going to talk much. Unless you want me to. It'll be too distracting. Say my name first if you want me to respond."

"I will. And if you can brief me as I talk to people, that will help."

"I'll do the best I can. Good luck. I love you. I'm here."

"I love you too," she whispered back, not missing his sudden sharp inhale.

"Ruby…."

"We'll talk about it when I get home, okay?"

"I'll be waiting. Go kick ass."

She returned to the living room. "Everything works," she said.

Justine rose and handed Ruby a gold lamé purse on a short chain that she could wrap around her wrist, a twin to the one that Justine now slid her scanner into. "Then let's go. Your purse has a second derringer should you need it."

"Thanks, Justine." She turned to Brandon. "We'll meet you at the plane?"

Brandon nodded. "We'll leave about nine."

"Good," Justine said. "All right. Let's go."

Into the fray.

Time to prove herself capable of becoming a Martiniere.

CHAPTER 11

A LIMOUSINE WAITED FOR THEM IN THE SECURE AREA OF THE basement parking. Ruby stepped into it, facing Justine and Serg. Suddenly everything felt unreal—the warmth of the dress softly pulsing against her skin, the expensive jewelry, Serg in formal black tie across from her, the limousine itself.

Who am I trying to fool? I can't do this. I can't.

She swallowed hard, her breath suddenly coming shallow and quick. Justine looked at her.

"Ruby," she said softly. "It's okay. You'll do fine. Take a deep breath." She raised her voice. "Gabe. Talk to Ruby. She needs it right now. She's got a panic face on."

"Hey." His voice was a lifeline in her ear, rich and full, steadying and comforting. "This is just a different version of Miss Rodeo America. It should have been yours, Rubes."

"Are you sure?" Her voice cracked.

"You were the prettiest cowgirl and the best horsewoman. This is the same kind of thing, just a different setting. You'll do fine. I'm here. I'm with you, lady." He took a deep breath. "This time you will come out on top. Don't doubt yourself, Rubes. You've got it."

She drew a deep breath and exhaled slowly and shakily.

"I heard that. Do it again. Think of riding Sunshine into the Round-Up. You got your good-luck locket?"

"In my hair."

"Then you'll be just fine."

They pulled up at the end of a line of limousines, stopping and going. "I think we're here."

"You'll do fine," he repeated. "I trust you. I believe in you. Go kick ass, Ruby, as only you can do."

"Thanks."

"I'll be here. Just quiet."

She took another deep breath.

"Better?" Justine asked.

Ruby nodded. "What happens now?"

Justine made a face. "Oh, these pretentious asses decided that we don't just need a red carpet, but we get let out limo by limo and announced. There'll be photographers and fashion coverage. Don't worry. I've taken care of your bio."

"How do we walk down the carpet?" She could handle this. She *had* to handle this. It was probably a good thing she didn't know about this part of the evening until now. She suspected that Justine hadn't told her for just that reason.

"We're all singles so we go out individually. I'll go first so you see what to do. We wait for the coordinator to say go. As you walk, you get announced. There's two marks on the carpet. Walk to the furthest one. Turn. Pause. Walk to the nearest mark. Pause, turn, pause, then continue. I'll be waiting for you."

Deceptively simple, but thank God she wasn't wearing high heels like Justine.

"I should be able to do that."

"You *will* get attention because once the Martiniere emeralds get recognized, there's going to be a lot of photos." Justine grinned. "I *might* have leaked a few hints that there would be a surprise tonight tied to the lost emeralds and Gabriel. You will be photographed, but I'm assuming you've been through that gauntlet."

"It's just a different form of Miss Rodeo America," Ruby said. "That's what I'm telling myself."

"There you go."

The limousine halted. A doorman in elaborate uniform opened the side door. Justine gracefully rose and stepped out.

"Your group?" another man in a gray suit asked Justine.

"Justine Martiniere. Ruby Barkley. Serg Vygotsky. All singles." She flicked a file to him. "Here's our bios."

Justine set off down the red carpet, smiling and making eye contact as an announcer spoke. Ruby focused on Justine—ah. The farthest mark from the limo. Justine turned, paused, then elegantly minced to the second mark close to the limo, stopping with her right foot ahead of left before turning. Ruby noted that Justine turned slowly, pausing halfway through, before pausing again, then sauntering down the length of carpet to the door.

Just like any other fashion catwalk, including 4H Style Revue.

"Next!"

Head high. Smile. Make eye contact.

Justine hadn't waved so she wouldn't either.

Gasps. Camera flashes as she walked.

"Ms. Ruby Barkley. Co-Winner of the 2059 Agriculture Innovator Superhero, along with Gabriel Martiniere and Jeffrey Swait. Managing Partner of Barkley-Martiniere Associates, along with Gabriel Martiniere."

First mark. Smile bigger. Pose. Turn. Pose. Now. Walk back toward the limo. Keep it slow.

"Partner in Barkley-Martiniere-Swait Associates, with Gabriel Martiniere and Jeffrey Swait."

Second mark. Eye contact, eye contact, eye contact. Turn. Hold. Turn. Hold.

"Former Miss Rodeo Oregon. Third runner-up and Horsemanship winner, Miss Rodeo America."

Slow walk now, with a swagger like Justine's. Don't forget the eye contact. Oh hell. Time for the Queen's wave.

As she walked to the door, she turned on the full Miss Rodeo Oregon treatment with the full wave and smile.

And then she was at the door and Justine.

"Damn you're *good*," Justine breathed as they went inside and into a reception area that had video running of the red carpet. "Stick with me now. I see the hordes approaching."

Despite everything Ruby giggled. "Hordes?" she asked as several older men broke free from their groups to hurry toward them.

"Cousin Artie, Cousin Kenny, Cousin Paul, and wannabe Cousin Zack," Justine muttered. "Starting out with the big tough ones. I'm betting you caught their eyes from the moment you walked onto the carpet. They'll know the dress and the emeralds. Gabie? You're able to tell her more."

"Board members except for Zack," Gabe whispered into her ear. *"Ken always called me a little shit. Avoid him unless he says something friendly. Which he might do if he decides the winds are blowing in my favor. Zack will kiss up to you if he thinks it will benefit him. He'll knife you in the back. Paul hates Philip's guts and will side with us by default. Artie is the one I'm not sure of. Talk to him if you can. He'll be impressed by the RubyBot."*

Before she could say anything, the men gathered around them.

"My, Justine, you've certainly sprung a surprise on us here," one of the men said, eying Ruby's jewelry and casting a suspicious look at her left hand. "Those can't be real."

"Oh, Kenny dear, they most certainly are," Justine said in her most poisonous, sweet tone. "As it turns out, they've been in Gabie's possession the entire time."

"She's not wearing the ring."

"That's because she hasn't remarried Gabie—yet. Ruby is Gabie's first wife, and they're in negotiations about remarriage."

"Well, I think you are a quite delightful sight for these old eyes, Ms. Ruby Barkley," one of the other men said, smiling at Ruby. "Miss Rodeo Oregon? That's different."

"Zack, you need to give me a chance to introduce her. You know who she is from the announcement and the video, but how would she know who you are?"

"Ms. Barkley, I'm Paul Martiniere," the third one said, bowing slightly. "It is a pleasure to meet you. I hope we get the opportunity to know each other better."

"And I am Arthur Martiniere," the fourth man said, like Paul giving her a shallow bow. "But Justine and Gabriel always have called me Artie. Please feel free to do so as well. That Superhero finale with you and Gabriel was very interesting. So you're interested in biobots?"

"I've been working to get one to market for years, and we just got our patent approvals this summer."

"We?" Artie raised his brows.

"Barkley-Martiniere Associates," Ruby said smoothly. "Gabe and me. We're marketing the RubyBot and Moondance Microbials, and specialized versions of the RubyBot in connection with Jeff Swait and his Swaitbots, through Barkley-Martiniere-Swait Associates."

"Now that is fascinating. Would you like to sit down and tell me more about these products? I'm in charge of the Martiniere Labs in France, and they sound promising. I remember your name from one of your designs from years ago. Your college advisor had said good things about you—and then you dropped out of sight."

"*Do it,*" Gabe hissed. "*I want to hear what Artie has to say.*"

"Why certainly," Ruby said. "That is, if Justine doesn't mind."

"Oh not at all, darling. I need to catch up with Kenny and Paul and Zack. You run right along and talk to Artie."

Ruby didn't miss the fleeting stormy expressions across Kenny and Zack's faces.

"May I take your arm?" Artie asked. "You are C-19 and G9 vaccine-safe, I assume."

"Absolutely."

"The emeralds look quite lovely on you, as a redhead, of course," Artie said as he led her to an unoccupied table. In a lower voice, he continued. "I assume that the brooch is still functional and that Gabriel is listening in?"

"*Whoa. I didn't know he was aware of the brooch's function. Confirm.*"

"He is listening," she said quietly.

"Wonderful. Young lady—" Ruby wanted to snort at that but didn't. Compared to Artie she *was* a young lady. "—you are quite the breath of fresh air." They reached the table and Artie pulled a chair out for Ruby to sit. He seated himself close to her, resting one hand on the back of her chair. She would have objected but she noticed that this placed him in a position where he could talk to her without his lips being seen.

Lipreaders here? Entirely possible.

"Thank you," she said.

"Forgive me for a moment. I'm going to speak directly to Gabriel."

"Go ahead," she said. "I'll answer for him."

"Perfect. Gabriel. I'm delighted to see that you are back in the game. I'm assuming this is your way of announcing your claim to being the Martiniere-in-waiting?"

"*Yes. And mention Brandon.*"

"Both Gabe and our son make that claim," Ruby said. "Gabe first, then Brandon."

"Per-fect. A clear line of succession." Artie beamed. "And what a delightful means of making your claim known." He glanced around. "Not much time as Zack and Ken are oozing away from Justine. Listen. Gabriel. We need to speak. But until then—my son Charles and I support you. Philip has to go."

"*We'll be in touch,*" Gabe said as the other two men arrived.

"We'll be in touch," she said softly to Artie even as Ken and Zack joined them.

"Artie, you can't just steal this pretty girl off on your own!" Zack said. He tried to take Ruby's hand but she slid it out of his reach. "I'm Zack Worthing, a cousin of Gabriel's. This is quite the surprise."

Ruby stood up, not wanting to be pinned down at the table. "Justine offered me a ticket, and I've always wanted to see what the Real Truthers are about."

Ken rolled his eyes. "Ah, most of this is hot air. If Philip weren't contending for their nomination, *I* wouldn't be here. Most of the Family wouldn't be here. It's a command performance, unfortunately."

"*Is* he getting the nomination?" Ruby asked archly.

"Bought and paid for." Paul joined them. "Thanks, of course, to the leverage he has over various attendees."

"Oh Paul, you're so tiresome," Artie said. "So Philip wants to play in politics. What's the big deal about that?"

"He could be spending more attention on developments within the Group," Ken muttered.

"*Hmm,*" Gabe said in her ear. "*If you can get Ken alone, see if he'll say more. Fascinated by what he's said already. But he may not talk to you.*"

"Now come on you guys. You don't need to keep Ruby all to yourself," Justine said, slipping in and taking Ruby's arm. "There are other people she needs to meet." As they walked away, she said softly, "Those four will monopolize you all night if allowed. But there's someone I really want you to meet. I didn't expect her to show up because she hates Daddy-poo's guts even more than I do. She will want to talk to Gabie."

She led Ruby into the main banquet area. Like the reception area, a large screen projected the red-carpet walks against the back wall, complete with announcements. An elegant white-haired woman wearing a shimmering red and black dress sat in a wheelchair near the head table, glowering at the three middle-aged men at the table with her. Her expression sharpened and she pointed a middle finger at one of them. Ruby couldn't hear what she said, but the man blanched and got up so quickly he knocked his chair over. It took him several tries to set it back up and he scurried off.

The elder woman turned her focus on the other two men. Whatever she said had them rising almost as quickly as the first one. Justine paused, waiting. The woman's face softened as she spotted Justine and Ruby. She imperiously gestured for the two of them to join her.

"Donna-gran." Justine curtseyed, then air-kissed the woman on both cheeks, before stepping back to wave Ruby forward. "This is Ruby Barkley, Gabriel's partner and ex-wife. Ruby, this is Donna Martiniere. Mother to Philip, Saul, Gerard, and Peter. Grandmother to me, Joseph, and Gabriel, amongst others."

Ruby curtseyed but didn't copy Justine further. She sensed that it would not be accepted—yet.

Donna-gran's sharp blue eyes measured Ruby from head to toe. "You are the mother of Gabriel's son? Legitimately born?"

"Yes to both, during our first marriage," Ruby said.

"But not currently his wife?"

"Not now. We're—talking. Negotiating."

Another head-to-toe assessment. "And Gabriel has put the emeralds on you. That speaks of his intent."

"Their son Brandon has put them on her tonight, in Gabriel's name," Justine said. "But Gabriel put them on her first, earlier. I have recordings of both."

A thin smile tightened Donna's lips. "I see that Gabriel knows better than to put the ring on your hand without a current marriage, Ruby Barkley." She pointed to the chair nearest her. "Come. Sit. Justine, I want to speak to Ruby privately. Please keep others away. Especially your father and brother."

"I will." Justine moved away as Ruby sat.

"So, you and Gabriel are divorced?"

"*Be straightforward,*" Gabe said. "*Go ahead and tell Donna-gran our suspicions.*"

"Things happened between us twenty-one years ago that we now see in a different light, and we are working toward reuniting," Ruby said slowly. "Gabriel has told me to tell you our suspicions, Donna-gran."

Donna's face softened even more at the nickname. "Ah, Gabie. I hope to see you in the flesh once again. I have missed you over these many years." She leaned forward. "What is it that you suspect?"

"That both Gabe and I were manipulated by the use of drugs and control words to separate, possibly by Philip and Joseph, and that Gabe was being pushed to suicide as a result of our divorce."

Donna pressed her lips together, nodding. "I see. Gabriel. I'm not surprised. It is a fit for Philip's methodology. Do you intend to have this woman back in your life again?"

"I already do, and I hope to remarry her. If she'll have me."

Ruby repeated the words.

"She knows about the Ritual? And will you do it with her?"

"I do," Ruby said, before Gabe could respond.

"Tell her yes to both parts," Gabe said.

Ruby did.

"Good. I want to be there when that happens," Donna said. "There are things that have not been observed for many years that I hope you will reinstate when you become the Martiniere. Your father has been most negligent, especially of late."

"Has been? But he's been dead for years. Is she losing her mind?"

Donna shook her head as Ruby repeated Gabe's comment, omitting the last sentence. "Saul wasn't your father, Gabie. Philip is."

Sharply indrawn breath in Ruby's ear as she froze, staring at Donna. Then, *"Fuck. Fuck, fuck, fuck."* More spluttering and cursing.

"He's not taking this well," Ruby said softly.

"But you are not surprised. I see that in your face."

"Justine has—suspicions, but no proof."

"And you and Justine are friends. I see. That is a good thing."

Donna raised her voice. "Gabriel. Knock it off. Ruby. Let me know when he shuts up."

"*I don't believe it.*"

"He doesn't believe it."

"Shut up, Gabriel, and listen! Is he quiet?" Ruby nodded. Donna continued. "It was part of a calculated agreement between Saul and Philip. A negotiated truce to keep them from tearing the Group apart, and I was the one who managed the negotiations." Donna sighed. "Don't talk yet. Listen. The deal was that each would sire the other one's first son through in-vitro fertilization. This knowledge was to be disclosed to you and Joseph at age eighteen. At that point you were both to be raised as successors to the Martiniere Group leadership, and allowed to prove your fitness for that role. In return, neither Philip nor Saul were supposed to attack each other. As we now know, Philip broke that agreement. You should have assumed the leadership of the Group upon the age of majority as a consequence."

"*Fuck. Fuck, fuck, fuck.*"

"He's swearing again," Ruby said, her heart breaking over what he must be experiencing. She pressed her lips together and tightened her fists to keep from joining him in swearing at *this god damned manipulative family*. "How could such a thing be agreed to? Allowed to happen?" In spite of her best control, she snapped out the words, rage simmering deep inside. This wasn't right. It couldn't be right.

"You breed livestock," Donna said. "Well, we have also bred stock in this family, girl. Human stock, and the choices we made were not always correct or moral. That has to change." She shrugged. "Philip didn't touch Angelica and Saul didn't touch Renate. That made it acceptable to all involved. I suspect Philip has destroyed all records of this agreement, except that...." She bared her teeth in what was most definitely *not* a smile. "Not all records are under Philip's control."

Gabe exhaled a deep breath in Ruby's ear. *"All right. I'm ready to listen. What did she last say?"*

"No physical contact between your mother and Philip. IVF was used." *That explains some things. Angelica and Saul truly did make a devil's deal.* "And while Philip may have destroyed most of the records, not all are under his control."

"What does she want from me?" Cold. Hard. Sharp.

Donna raised her hand before Ruby could speak. "I can guess what he is saying, if he's half the strategist I think he is. Gabriel. I want you to put things right with this family. I want you to get past your urges toward self-destruction, especially after this news—oh, I'm more aware of that tendency than you think! I want you to marry this lovely woman who is sitting in front of me, filled with her own righteous anger at this discovery. It is time."

A commotion rose behind them. "Joey! Donna-gran is speaking to Ruby!"

"She has no right to be there, no right to talk to Donna-gran! Father sent me to get her away—"

A hand clamped down on Ruby's left shoulder and pulled. She went with the motion, whirling with her clenched right fist to land it squarely on Joseph's chin. He staggered back and she noted with grim approval that his face was still swollen from Brandon's fists. Yes, Joseph had definitely gotten the worst of *that* fight.

"What the fuck is going on?" Gabe yelled in her ear.

She ignored Gabe, facing Joseph with hands clenched tight.

"Get. Away. From. Me. Joseph," she growled. "Or I'll finish the job that Brandon started, and I can do it. Understand?"

Joseph held his jaw. "You have no right to wear those emeralds!"

"Gabriel thinks otherwise," she said. "He has put them on me. So has Brandon." She advanced a step and raised her fists. "Go," she said, projecting as much menace into her voice as she could. "And leave me the fuck alone. Don't you even *think* of ever putting a hand on me again."

"You heard her." Justine joined Ruby. "Get the fuck away from her, Joey. *Now.*" She noticed that Justine held a palm stunner ready.

Ruby eased hers out of its sheath and held it where Joseph could see it. "I'm pretty damned good with using a hotshot on a stubborn cow. Want to see how well I can use a stunner?"

"You fucking bitch," Joseph blustered. "You'll pay for this. You too, Justine! Now that I know what side you're *really* on. Just wait and see! You'll pay!"

"Not if I get to you first," Justine said icily.

"Holy crap. You okay, Rubes?"

"Yes," she whispered as Joseph flushed bright red with anger and stomped off. Behind them, Donna started a slow clap. Ruby and Justine turned to face her.

"Oh, Gabie. I heartily approve of your taste in *this* woman," Donna said. "Did he hear that?"

"Yes."

Ruby nodded, not trusting herself to speak just yet.

"Alas, ladies, I fear I must dismiss you before Joseph comes back with reinforcements and we have an even bigger scene. Gabriel. Remember what I have told you. Put things right and marry this woman."

"I understand. I will remember. But I still have to convince her of my motives."

Donna nodded as Ruby relayed Gabe's words. "Ruby. One last thing."

She returned to her seat. Donna pointed to the floor in front of her.

"Please kneel. I see Philip approaching. I will formally extend my blessing to you. Justine, please stop your father from interfering."

Ruby slid to her knees in front of this formidable elder. She bowed her head as Donna placed soft hands on her head.

"It will be a privilege to see you, Ruby Barkley, become the new Martiniere Matriarch," Donna said loudly. "I give you my blessing and approval of your marriage to Gabriel. You are my choice to become the Matriarch." She leaned forward and kissed Ruby's forehead. "Now go forth, girl, and take care of Gabriel, for all of our sakes," she added in a quieter voice.

"I will," Ruby said. As she rose, she instinctively air-kissed Donna's cheeks, just as Justine had. "Will you be all right? Do you need protection?"

Donna smiled at Ruby and patted her hand. "Oh, honey. Don't worry about me. You take care of your own. I have high hopes for you and Gabie."

Ruby curtseyed and joined Justine. She was running the recording of Brandon putting the emeralds on Ruby. Philip watched it without comment. He glared at Ruby but did not say anything before stomping away.

"Come on," Justine said, her voice a little shaky. "There's a decent ladies' lounge in this joint. I need to catch my breath and I think you do as well."

"Did I muss anything up?" Ruby asked as they hurried to the ladies' room.

"No."

They slipped into the lounge, pulling two chairs close together before collapsing into them.

"You should have seen Daddy-damn-dearest's face when Donna-gran gave you her blessing. He demanded proof that Gabie and Brandon had put the emeralds on you. So I showed him." Justine shook her head. "For that matter, you should have seen Donna-gran when you decked Joey. I swear she would have gotten up and danced with glee if she had the strength to do it."

Ruby blew hard, taking slow, deep breaths to settle herself. She opened and closed her hands. No marks on her right hand, though her fingers ached.

I'll feel that later.

"You doing okay?" Gabe asked. *"I hear that breathing again."*

"In the ladies lounge with Justine. Taking a quick break."

The door opened.

"Well, well, well, look who's here," Mariah Meyers drawled as she entered the lounge. "The airhead and the pretender."

Ruby started to get up. Justine placed a hand on her wrist.

"I'll deal with this piece of junk, Ruby."

Mariah laughed, a harsh, raucous noise that seemed out of place with her platinum blond hair and metallic silver dress. "Oh my. How amusing to see you buddying up with this hick hayseed, Justine. Your taste has certainly declined."

"Better than hanging out with a betrayer and con woman," Ruby snapped.

"At least my men can still get it up," Mariah sneered. "I hear Gabe can't."

Ruby drew in a furious breath. "I'm not whoring myself to liars and thieves!"

Justine's grip tightened on Ruby's wrist before she could get up. "Look, *bitch*, why don't you just go ahead, puke and get the hell out of here," she said. "I've heard you sticking your fingers down your throat enough times at these functions in the past to know why you're in here. Concerned about what might be in the food?"

"As if I'm the only one," Mariah retorted, backing away. "I can say the same damn thing about you."

"Keep on talking, Mariah," Justine taunted. "Keep it up and whatever it is that you're afraid of will start taking effect. Then we'll have some real interesting times, won't we?"

"I don't have time for this." Mariah whirled and stormed into the bathroom section. A few moments later they heard gagging.

"It's real, then?" Ruby formed the words with her lips but didn't vocalize.

Justine nodded grimly. They sat silently until Mariah stormed out.

"Bulimia is my specialty," Justine said in a shaky voice. "And I wouldn't trust any food or drink here tonight. Especially after seeing—this. Not that I do at these events, anyway. It's a damn good thing we both ate beforehand."

"*Fuck,*" Gabe growled.

"You okay, Ruby?"

"Yeah. I'll be fine. I want to have a moment with Gabe."

Justine got up and patted Ruby's cheek. "I'll be back at the table. Things are about to get *really* lively."

Ruby leaned back in her chair as Justine left. "Wow. Just wow," she said shakily. "You doing okay after all that, Gabe?"

"*It's taking some getting used to. What did you mean when you told Donna-gran that Justine already suspects that I'm Philip's son?*"

"Serg encountered some suspicious pictures in Europe. He wasn't certain of the provenance. They were apparently explicit —which doesn't match what your grandmother said. Justine didn't want to bother you about it until she had better confirmation. But she gave me a heads up, just in case."

"*I'd trust Donna-gran before pictures. Especially since she was part of the negotiations. We all lived in the same damn mansion. All sorts of paparazzi around, and it would be easy enough to manipulate photos from that era.*"

"No matter what the mechanism, it's apparently true." Ruby sighed.

"*God. Revealing this is going to be huge.*"

"I can tell Justine on our way back to the ranch tonight."

And Serg and Brandon too.

"*That would be a help.*"

"And I'd better get back out there."

"*Keep it up. You're doing a great job. Love you.*"

"Love you too." Ruby rose. She checked her makeup and hair in the mirror, then raised her chin high, pulling her shoulders back as she went out to face the crowd.

She had gone partway down the hall toward the main banquet area when Philip Martiniere stepped out from behind an artificial plant.

"Ms. Barkley."

"What the hell do you want?" She eyed Philip, assessing possible threats. She didn't think he would attack her, not here. He didn't impress her as being as much of a hands-on brute like Joseph, in spite of what he had done to Gabe. Not to an adult, especially a woman who had already demonstrated the ability to strike back.

But caution was still advised.

"I have a proposition for you."

"I'm not certain I want to listen to any proposition you would make."

"I'd advise you to listen. Especially when it comes to Gabriel and your son."

"I hope you don't intend that to be a threat."

"Ruby. Get away from him." Panic radiated from Gabe's voice.

She ignored him.

"Take it as you want," Philip said. "If I wanted, I could get rid of all three of you like that." He snapped his fingers in her face.

"Like you tried and failed to do with Gabriel twenty-one years ago?" she said coldly.

Philip shrugged. "Here's the deal. Either leave Gabriel or get him to abandon his hare-brained campaign to take over the Martiniere Group. And give me the emeralds. Otherwise there will be consequences."

Ruby stared at him for a moment, then burst out laughing. "You think I'm going to jump to your tune just like that? What kind of fool do you think I am?"

"A fool who understands dollar signs," Philip said smoothly. "I'm prepared to sign a check to you for the equivalent of winning the Superhero. In return you influence Gabriel to either leave you or drop his campaign to take over the Martiniere Group. And you hand over the emeralds at the end of the evening. Do we have a deal?"

"I repeat, what kind of fool do you think I am? Besides, I

think the emeralds look better on me than on Mariah Meyers. She *is* your mistress, isn't she?"

"You're playing with fire, little girl." A slow flush crept over Philip's face. "And you're in way over your head."

"I think you have no idea what I'm capable of doing. And I don't need to be here listening to you." She started to walk away but Philip grabbed at her wrist. She twisted it free and stepped back.

"Listen to me, bitch." A vein pulsed in his temple.

"No. *You* listen to *me!*" Ruby stepped forward and poked him in the chest, knocking away his hands when he tried to stop her, fighting back the urge to beat him bloody like he had done to Gabe as a teen. Not the time. Not the place. "I told you once before that you don't grab me. I've slapped you for that. I will again, *ex-father-in-law.*"

"*How do you know?*" The angry flush faded from Philip's face. He almost looked frightened.

"It's none of your damned business." She took a deep breath. "Now. I am not abandoning Gabriel. You had better look to your own business because, buddy, you have totally pissed me off. No matter what happens to Gabriel or Brandon, you still will have to contend with *me.*" She stalked off.

Philip's voice followed her. "Then be prepared to reap the consequences of your choice."

"I already have," she shot back, just before entering the main hall. "Twenty-one years ago. And you will pay for your role in that tragedy, as well."

No sooner had she taken ten steps into the hall, looking for Justine, when Serg glided up to her.

"Ruby. We're leaving. *Now.*"

"What's happened?" she asked as Serg escorted her past Philip.

Philip smirked at both of them. "I warned you about *consequences*, Ruby Barkley."

"Shut up, you old windbag," she snapped back as Serg guided her out. "Serg, *what's wrong?*"

He glanced around before speaking. "Alarms at the condos. All three—mine, Tine's, and the one Brandon was closing on next week. Fires."

"Oh my God. Are the kids all right?" she asked, before Gabe could do more than inhale sharply.

"Brandon got them out. They were already headed for the airport when it happened—all three locations blew as the van left the parking structure. They'll be waiting for us. Tine's taking care of some last minute business. She should be at the limo."

"What's the timing on the alarms?" she asked as they hurried out.

"Five minutes ago."

"That fucking bastard Philip," Ruby hissed. "He just threatened me with consequences if I didn't get Gabe to stop. But this was already happening!" She took a deep breath. "Gabe. What's the security status at Moondance and the Double R?"

"*Already taken care of,*" Gabe responded. "*Went to highest level once you left for the banquet.*"

"It's good?" Serg asked.

Ruby repeated what Gabe had told her.

"Good." Serg pulled a weapon as they left the building and they broke into a run. His hand rested on her upper back as he glanced around.

Justine opened the limousine door as they reached it. Serg pushed Ruby into the limo and jumped in, slamming the door shut.

"Gabe," Serg said. "I'm switching off the brooch. Ruby can be traced when it's active. I didn't have time to activate those shielding profiles because they need more time to fix than I had."

"*Understood. Rubes. Call me with an ETA once you're in the air.*"

"I will."

Serg reached over and tapped a sequence on the brooch's main gem. Once again a sharp tingle vibrated through the dress.

"Shit," Justine said, voice trembling slightly. "I *liked* that condo."

"So did I," Serg said. "But it's clearly not safe now."

"What does that mean for our LA residences?"

"They're houses, not condos. Easier to control accesses. I'll know more when our people report back. I'm thinking you and Brandon go to the gated one. I'm getting off at the Double R unless you feel you need reinforcement. Moondance is now highest priority for my *personal* attention, especially with that upcoming meeting with Georgy."

"We should be fine," Justine said.

"Ruby, what did Philip mean by *consequences*?" Serg asked.

"He offered me three point seven five million—the payout for a solo Superhero—to get Gabe to either leave me or pull out of contention for leadership of the Martiniere Group. And give him the emeralds. I turned him down. Of course."

Serg shook his head. "Is Philip fucking stupid or what? This isn't his usual style."

"He's rattled," Justine said. "Ruby is a lever on Gabie, but she also reinforces him and gives him a lot of support. Add in the reappearance of the emeralds, plus Donna-gran giving Ruby her blessing. And they talked about something that sure seems to have Ruby on edge. Plus Ruby nailed Joey, right smack on the chin, when he tried to drag her away from Donna-gran."

Serg whistled. "Now that would have been a sight to see. I'm sorry I was focusing on Philip and not Joseph. Ruby, what did Donna-gran tell you?"

"I'd sooner wait until we're on the plane," Ruby said. "Brandon needs to know too."

Serg raised his hand. "What's that, Diane?" He listened for a moment, then nodded curtly. "Understood." He dropped his hand. "Both of you get down. We're being followed by a suspicious vehicle. Our backup has them spotted and will try to take them out."

Justine sighed, but lay down on the seat as Serg crawled forward to speak to their driver. Ruby copied Justine.

I hope we get out of this all right.

This trip was proving to be more exciting than she had anticipated.

CHAPTER 12

Once they'd reached cruising altitude and Ruby had called Gabe with their arrival time, she poured herself a big tumbler of Scotch and settled into her seat. Serg raised his brows at that as Justine and Brandon came from the back.

"Post-event reaction, what Donna-gran told you, or both?"

"Both," Ruby admitted.

Justine popped a container into the small bar refrigerator. "This goes to the labs. After that little confrontation with Mariah I thought we might want to analyze what was in the food just for funsies."

"In the food?" Serg sat up.

"She was doing the bulimia dance while Ruby and I were talking in the ladies lounge," Justine said tiredly. "And when I got the alarm alert, I grabbed a napkin, took some food, found a box, and headed out. Perfect opportunity to investigate what we've always suspected."

Brandon sank into a seat, leaning his forehead on one hand. "What the hell set them off?"

"I suspect it was Donna-gran's blessing of your mother," Justine said. "Or else the fist Ruby laid on Joey's chin, letting them know that it's not just the son who can fight. Or somehow they heard what Donna-gran was saying to Ruby—a surprise if that's the case. Donna-gran always carries a blocker. Then again, Donna-gran wanted to speak to Gabie through the brooch, and the blocker would have interfered with that."

"That's probably it," Serg said. "Ruby? What on earth could have triggered all this?"

"Donna-gran?" Brandon asked, his brow furrowing.

"Your great-grandmother," Justine said. "Donna Martiniere. The Matriarch of the Martiniere family. Donna-gran, we call her. She's now in her what—nineties? Approaching one hundred?"

"Something like that," Serg said.

Ruby took a big swallow of her Scotch, savoring the smoky burn. "What happened is that she confirmed what you discovered, Serg. Gabe is not Saul's son. He's Philip's son."

"What?" Brandon snapped, sitting up sharply. "I'm the grandson of that asshat?"

Serg winced.

Justine's eyes widened.

"It isn't what you found, Serg." Ruby took another big swallow to get her through the rest of it. "Joseph is not Philip's son, but Saul's. Part of a negotiated truce between them in an attempt to keep them from killing each other and tearing the family apart. In-vitro fertilization. She has the records." She took a third big gulp as they stared at her. "Gabe is—he wasn't taking it very well."

"Is Philip aware that you know?" Serg asked.

"If he wasn't listening in when Donna-gran and I were talking, he knows it now," Ruby said bitterly. "I called him ex-father-in-law. Fucker didn't even blink but kept trying to buy me off. Then he threatened me."

"Fuck." Brandon sank back in his chair, shaking his head.

"Oh, there's more. Joseph and Gabe were supposed to be informed at age eighteen and compete for the leadership. Donna said that Philip's involvement in the death of Saul makes Gabe the rightful heir. Gabe should have become the Martiniere when he reached the age of majority."

"Well, that certainly shakes things up," Serg sighed. "All right. I'm going in back because this latest bit of information significantly affects security and I need to talk to people. No need to bother everyone else with the comms right now." He left.

Brandon stared at his hands. "So that means I'm even closer to the title than we thought."

"Yes," Ruby said.

"Bad enough that he was my great-uncle. To know that he's my grandfather—" Brandon shook his head.

"On the other hand, I've just been promoted from cousin to aunt," Justine said. "Look at it that way. You're my nephew."

Brandon kept shaking his head. At last he sighed and stood. "I've got to take this in. But I also want to be with Kris. I'll talk to you and Dad later, Mom."

He left.

Justine eyed Ruby as she drained the rest of her glass. "You doing okay?"

"I want to rest for a while." Ruby blew out a long, slow breath. "Gabe and I have a lot to talk about when I get back to the ranch."

"I bet you do," Justine said. "I'll keep an eye on Beck and Kris. And talk to Brandon about what we're doing in LA." As she walked by Ruby, she patted Ruby's shoulder. "I guess this makes us sisters-in-law, at least once you two remarry. I like that."

"So do I," Ruby said.

After Justine left the front cabin, Ruby took off her sandals with a sigh, wiggling her sore feet. She went to where her suitcase had been tossed, and pulled out socks and her boots, putting the sandals inside the bag and closing it, but not pulling the boots on just yet. Then she poured herself another drink, dimmed the lights and stared out of the window into the darkness, her mind racing.

At some point after finishing her drink, she fell asleep.

THEIR DESCENT TO THE AIRSTRIP AT THE DOUBLE R WOKE HER. RUBY pulled on socks and boots before settling back into her seat. She noted with some pleasure that the green of the Lucchese boots matched the dress. Serg and Justine were already up front.

"You get some rest?" Justine asked.

"Yeah," Ruby said. "How are Beck and Kris?"

"Groggy, but okay."

The plane touched down, then circled toward the taxiway. Ruby saw Gabe, Rick, and Charlie standing by the hangar with a couple of crawlers. Armed security stood back from them, at least ten people—more than she had seen at once on the ranch before now. Once the plane stopped and the stairs let down, Brandon and Serg helped Beck out, followed by Justine. Kris still slept on the plane. Ruby picked up her bag and headed for the door. Gabe waited for her at the bottom of the stairs.

He took her suitcase from her and slid his arm around her waist. "You still look gorgeous," he said softly. "Did you want to walk back or ride back to the house?"

"Walk back," she said. "I need the fresh air and movement."

"Thought so, especially when I saw you had on your boots." He tossed her suitcase into the back of one of the crawlers. "Charlie, can you make sure that Ruby's bag gets up to the room? We're walking back."

"Figured." Charlie hopped into his crawler, Serg joining him. They took off. Security remained in place.

Brandon and Justine returned from settling Beck with Rick, pausing by Gabe and Ruby.

"Dad." Brandon sighed. "Mom told me."

"I thought she would." Gabe studied his son. "You doing okay?"

Brandon grimaced. "It takes some getting used to. But we'll be fine. Going on to LA. Mom, you're going to work on the conference data?"

"I'll get that pulled together," Ruby said. "But not very early in the morning tomorrow."

"None of us are going to be moving fast then," Brandon said.

"Be careful, son," Gabe said. "Things are going to happen quickly. Look to your security. We'll talk tomorrow."

"Yep," Brandon said, popping the p in the word. "And we are going to make this happen. You stay safe, too."

"We will."

Brandon gave them a wave and trudged back to the airplane.

Justine watched him go, half-smiling, before she turned back to Gabe and Ruby. "He's a good kid. Both of them are. If they survive, the Group will be in good hands for the long term. *Finally*." She took Gabe's free hand. "Before we leave, Gabie. I'm just so glad that I have a *decent* brother." She hugged both Gabe and Ruby. When she straightened up tears glimmered in her eyes. "You two be careful. Everything depends on you right now." She quickly kissed Gabe on the cheek, then turned and ran to the plane.

They watched the jet taxi to the airstrip, then take off.

"I guess we'd better head back to the house," Gabe said quietly. "Security's watching, but we're targets. Might as well not make them any more nervous than necessary." He turned and flashed a signal with his free hand. "We're walking back," he called. "Give us safe private space, please."

He nodded as one of the guards signaled back.

"Okay. We're good."

"Just one thing first." She turned to face Gabe, sliding her other arm around him. "I'm ready to answer. And the answer is yes."

He smiled. "You're sure? You're doing it for me and not because of the circumstances?"

"A little bit of both, to be honest. But mostly because I want to get something back that was taken from us twenty-one years ago. Philip pissed me off enough to make clear what I really want." She blinked back unexpected tears and gulped. "We can't redo those years. I would like to have even a tiny bit of happiness that is ours, for whatever time we have left to us. And, yeah. I want to rub it in your biological father's face if I can. There is that factor. Nonetheless, I do love you, Gabriel Marcus Martiniere, even when you are being a cranky, stubborn, buttheaded Martiniere ass. After meeting your biological father, I guess you come by it honestly."

His smile broadened. "I love that you're not afraid to take on my scary relatives. I love your passion and dedication to the RubyBot after all these years. And you're still damn good looking on horseback, good enough to give current rodeo queens a run for their money." He took a deep breath. "You've carried my children. You did a damn good job of raising our son when I wussed out. I don't deserve you, but I give thanks that you're here in my arms and are ready to resume taking on my bullshit. I love every single passionate, profane, gorgeous bit of you, especially since you're not afraid to call me out when necessary. Ruby Marie Barkley, can you stand to remarry my sorry ass?"

She slid a hand down to pinch his butt. "Doesn't feel that sorry to me. Getting you back on the Double R and off your behind has done you good. And yes, I will remarry you."

He took her head gently in his hands and kissed her, his hands sliding down to pull her close against him. When they finally broke apart, the biggest grin she had seen in years was on his face. Gabe pulled away from her to fold up his cane and stick it back in its holster.

"Can I lean on you?"

She laughed. "Only if I can lean on you, too."

They walked back in silence, arms wrapped around each other's waists, the pathway marked by the faint glow of solar lights. Ruby breathed deep, savoring the crisp, dry mountain air. Crickets faintly chirped. In the distance—probably from the Chandler ranch next door—a dog barked, disturbed from its sleep but not a defensive bark. A big blue-green meteor flamed out just before they reached the house.

Gabe let his arm slip from her but she took his hand as they went upstairs. As she pulled off her boots, he retrieved the jewelry box from her suitcase. Then he slowly took the emeralds off of her and put them away. After that he unpinned her hair, retrieving her locket and putting it on the dresser next to the box. Ruby would have gone to the bathroom to change after he undid her zipper, but he took her hand.

"Stay. Please."

"I've not wanted to be a tease," she said softly.

"You aren't being one. I want to see you. Admire you. Even if I can't do anything about it except give you pleasure. That makes me happy."

"If I can see you as well."

He smiled. "But of course."

He helped her slip off the dress, then carefully laid it on her rocking chair before undoing her bra. She went to the bathroom and returned to find him undressed and waiting. They stood there for a moment, eying each other. He had a little paunch, and his left leg was noticeably less muscled than his right as a result of the G9, but otherwise he was still the Gabe she had known. She winced at the scars on his chest, delicately touching her fingers to them.

"Did you want to see the ones on my back?"

She shook her head. "I know what they look like. From —before."

He opened his arms wide, and Ruby went to him. They kissed for a few moments, and then Gabe picked her up. She yelped with surprise.

"I may not be able to carry you up the stairs anymore, but I can at least lug you a couple of steps to the bed," he said gruffly.

He fell with her on the bed. And then his lips were on her, lips and hands moving over her body as she gasped and moaned softly.

When she was finished and she had caught her breath, Gabe held Ruby close, giving her little feathery kisses along her temples and cheekbones as they lay in each other's arms. Her eyes drooped and she sagged with satisfaction and exhaustion against him. Gabe stirred.

"We have to do something different about sleeping arrangements for the long term. But for tonight, will you join me in the chair? I put fresh sheets on it."

"Of course," she said.

FOR A MOMENT WHEN RUBY WOKE, SHE THOUGHT THE PAST TWENTY-one years had all been a bad dream. Gabe curled around her, catlike, his hand on her breast, holding her close, just like he had liked to do. Then she realized they were in his big recliner, and memory flooded back. The banquet. Saying yes to him. Everything leading up to that.

Gabe mumbled and wrapped himself tighter around her. Ruby snuggled in nearer, enjoying the familiar but long-absent contact. He stirred again, and kissed her ear.

"Morning. God, this feels good."

She turned in his arms to face Gabe, heart pounding as he gave her that slow, steady smile that had caught her eye all those years ago. "I agree."

He kissed her, little feathery caresses that deepened into a longer one before he pulled back. "But this is not going to work for long term sleeping. And I want to share a bed with you."

She laughed and leaned her forehead against him. "I think we can afford an option that works for both of us."

"I sure hope so." He stroked her cheek. "You're good with remarrying? You really are? Not just the politics, but—me?"

"Absolutely you. Fuck the politics. That's not why I said yes. But I think we need to make it formal pretty darn quickly. I'm worried about the condo attacks."

"Yeah. I'll have Serg look at the ring, once he has the Moondance needs in hand. I expect he'll have Moondance figured out today. The ring needs to be at least partially working." Gabe sighed. "It may never be fully functional." He kissed her again. "But to hear Donna-gran give you her blessing—Ruby, that is huge. That is a major endorsement of both you and me. I spent a lot of time thinking last night while waiting for you to get here. I agree with you. We need to consolidate our support, *now*. Our marriage will be a big step toward helping that happen."

"There's a lot we have to consider. But yes, I got that impression loud and clear last night."

"And it's not a factor in your choice?"

"I won't admit that it isn't." She chuckled. "But standing up to Philip and Joseph—and yes, Donna-gran's acceptance—helped me realize that yes, I can handle the big leagues. I may have panic moments, though."

"Don't we all? You aren't alone."

"But I now know I can work through them. Going through it was a big help."

"That's good. I'm having a few moments of my own. Finding out that I'm Philip's son is a big game-changer." He grimaced. "I suppose that's why I didn't die in the plane crash with my family. He thought he could influence me. But Mother and Saul raised me with their mores and ethos, not in line with Philip." He paused. "My mother hated Philip with a passion I never quite understood. Now I do. At least she didn't seem to hold being *his* son against me."

"Oh, Gabe." She stroked his cheek. "I wish I'd had more time at the banquet to help you collect information about alliances."

"Hon, between setting up that meeting with Georgy and the contacts with Artie and Donna-gran, you did plenty." He paused. "The ceremony should be at Moondance. I think it's safer to do it there."

"We could do a courthouse legal marriage first and then the ceremonial part a few days later. We should also sign pre-nuptial agreements. This is Sunday. I wonder if we can get it all pulled together before we meet with Georgy on Tuesday?"

"That's a tight timeline. Especially with prenups involved."

"Remy Trask could pull it off," she said, mentioning her lawyer and long-time friend. "I asked her to draw one up for me two months ago. Just in case."

"Yeah. I had my lawyer do that too. Same timing. I have a copy handy." He grinned. "Another reason I love you. We think along the same lines."

"We could see Remy today. Get the process rolling. She might be able to get us an expedited license—she's capable of pulling strings that you wouldn't expect. All the same, it might be a case of get the license on Monday, marry at the courthouse Tuesday morning. Ceremony on Friday at Moondance if we can pull security together."

He chuckled. "An elopement?"

"Simpler and safer than going to Vegas. Besides, I want to be married in Thunder County, and I don't think we should delay. From what Donna-gran said, us being married is a big deal within your family. They *will* have to take us seriously. And to do this so quickly after everything at the banquet—well, wouldn't that be taken as a message?"

"It certainly would." His eyes took on that faraway look that meant he was thinking through something. "All right," he said finally. "Let's make this happen. The formal ceremony should be small, with Family, but you need to have friends there too. We'll need to find a priest. That could be a challenge. I haven't been to Mass for years—and have you ever gone to church?"

"No. I haven't." She sighed. "Just how Catholic is the family?"

"It won't be a Nuptial Mass. But having a priest—even an Episcopalian—there will be acceptable. I'm betting that Justine could find one. Maybe we should put her in charge of managing that event."

"Okay. We need to see Remy. We need to call Bran and Justine. Jeff Swait and his family should know and be invited as well." Ruby tapped her lips with her index fingers, thinking.

"Vickie Chandler—she'll kill me if I don't invite her. Charlie and Martin, Terri and Julie from the ranch staff. Rick and Beck. Remy and Shannon. Bran and Kris, plus Justine, of course. The leaders of the Thunder Home Guard—they've done us a lot of favors watching the place."

"None of your family?"

"I do *not* want a repeat of our first wedding's drunken brawl, thank you very much. Besides, I haven't heard from any of them since I told Aunt Grace to go to hell. I don't want to encourage contact now."

"Okay. Let's see on my side. I need to have some Family heads present. That means Artie, Paul, and Ken, since they're already in the States. Donna-gran, of course. Others you haven't met, including Serg's father Piotr." His lips tightened. "Perhaps even Philip. That would give us some protection."

"Not Joseph, though."

"No. Joseph wouldn't come anyway if Philip's here. And even if he does, well, that's still cover against potential attacks, as long as they're present." His brow furrowed. "I'll put Kathleen in charge of catering. Her family does a mean BBQ, and she'll understand biosecurity. Especially if Justine is working with her."

"Sounds good." She stretched. "Do you want to shower first or shall I?"

"How about together?" He smirked at her.

She shook her head, grinning. "Gabriel. If I didn't know...."

"Hey. Just because that part of my body isn't responding, doesn't mean I can't appreciate your beauty." He started with the feathery kisses on her chin, nose, eyes, and lips again, then pulled away. "It makes me happy to look at you, to touch you, to give you pleasure. And who knows? Perhaps one of these days, things will improve." He kissed her again, more firmly. "I've grown up, Ruby," he whispered. "We've both grown up. And I like this relationship so much better than what we had before."

"So do I," she whispered back.

"One more thing," he said. "And I plan to tell your lawyer this as well." He drew a deep breath. "I know the limits that post-G9 syndrome puts on me. How taking on this role as the Martiniere will speed it up. I can't do that for very long. I need to stabilize the situation in the Martiniere Group so that Brandon can take over in a managed succession, not have it drop on him suddenly. I also want time for us. I intend to be very clear to Donna-gran and everyone else in the family that this is a transitional leadership, and that you have a very specific and powerful role now and in the future."

"But once you're out of the leadership…."

"That blessing Donna-gran gave you? Hon. She's willing to call you the Matriarch of the family. That stays with you until you pass it on or die." He stroked her cheek. "If you choose to take on that role, you'll be that person even when I am no longer on the scene. We can marry without you becoming the Martiniere Matriarch. But you need to be aware of this possibility."

"Will it help you and Brandon?"

"Yes."

Ruby took a deep breath. "Then whatever happens, happens. I'm in it all the way, Gabe. I said it before and I will repeat it now. I will do whatever is necessary to keep us safe—you, me, Branny, and hopefully his Kris."

It still felt weird to be driving through Lakeside with bodyguards in the rig with them, even though she was at the wheel. Ruby waved at a couple of friends as they drove through town, then halfway up the hill to Remy's office overlooking Thunder Lake.

"This should be all right," she said to the guards before she and Gabe got out.

"Let's not assume anything," Gabe said. "Inside will be

clear," he said to the guards. "Stay with the truck, and keep an eye on what's happening outside."

Ruby giggled as they went inside the office portion of Remy's manufactured home. "The neighbors will talk when they see our truck with armed guards."

"Good. We want the word to be out around town that we're under protection. That way anyone new to the area will hear the gossip."

Ruby made a face, but Gabe was right about that. Gossip spread quickly around Lakeside.

Remy's partner and assistant, Shannon, wasn't at the reception desk, though Remy's office door was open.

"Come on back," Remy called. As Ruby and Gabe both came in, her brows shot up. "Well, well, well. The bad penny himself shows up. I can't say as I'm *too* surprised at seeing you, Gabe."

"Good to see you too, Remy," Gabe said stiffly.

Remy eyed them. "You're carrying a folder, Gabe. Can I assume that I was right to print off Ruby's prenup? She was a little vague about the reason for this meeting when she called me. But I thought sooner or later this would be happening."

"I think you'll find this in order." Gabe handed Remy the folder. "Ruby's already looked at it."

"Ruby?"

"It looks good to me."

"Let me check it. Oh. And Gabe. Here's Ruby's version." Remy handed a folder to Gabe. "I strongly encourage you to talk to your own attorney about it."

Gabe chuckled nervously. "Given how you handled our divorce, I'm going to assume it's tough but fair." All the same, he opened the folder at the same time that Remy opened his.

Ruby had already studied both agreements, so she watched Remy's reaction as she paged through Gabe's documents. Remy's brows shot up quickly and she kept making "hmm. hmm." noises.

Gabe finished first and set the folder on the desk. "I have no problem signing this agreement."

Remy nodded, still focused on his papers. At last she looked up. "You're being pretty damn generous here in the case of a second divorce."

Gabe spread his hands. "As far as I'm concerned, I wouldn't *have* these assets if it wasn't for Ruby—and Brandon. I'm not so worried about being stupid enough to divorce her again. My biggest concern is protecting Ruby's assets from predatory members of my family should I die or be disabled before her, as well as her share of my estate. I've changed my will, but I want this prenup to reflect my wishes as further evidence of my intent, in a worst-case scenario where she has the Martinieres trying to strip her of assets."

"Okay. How likely is it that you'll predecease Ruby?"

"Very likely. Not only am I older, but I have post-G9 syndrome. So far it is under control with medication, but—you know how these things can change."

"Yes."

"I hope to have things settled with my family and any role I have in the Martiniere Group passed on to Brandon fairly quickly. I do not want to die as the Martiniere. I want to have time with Ruby and some goddamned peace with no clouds hanging over my head for once in my life. A lot of bullshit happened twenty-one years ago, and I owe her a lot. If I do something stupid again, I *want* to pay for it."

Remy peered at Gabe over her half-frame glasses. "You bet your ass you owe her, buster. You put my client and friend through hell."

"Remy. We've recently learned that the two of us may have been unduly influenced to divorce. It's a long story," Ruby said.

"And you're convinced of the validity of that information? That Gabe isn't going to pull the same sort of shit on you in the future?" Remy sighed and pulled her glasses off. "I'm not just speaking as your attorney, Ruby. I'm speaking as your friend."

"There's a lot of crap involved with the Martinieres," Ruby

said. "I'm—I'm privy to a lot of information right now, and—well, I'm going to leave it up to Gabe just how much we disclose. For your safety, primarily. But in a nutshell, yes, I'm convinced."

"All right. Gabe," Remy said. "I know a lot about your situation. I was a prosecutor in LA when you testified against the Martiniere Group's shady activities there. Low level, but I got pulled into assessing what could be charged and what couldn't be. I saw some of the transcripts, helped process the data. I have a pretty decent idea of the sort of things that could be going on with the Martinieres. What else happened?"

Gabe took Ruby's hand, squeezing it gently. "Did you see the parts about experiments in mind control?"

"Yes."

"We now have reason to believe that both of us were subjected to those techniques prior to our divorce. There are traditions within the family where those methods are aggressively applied. They do not work perfectly but they do exist. More than that, I suspect that the goal was to push me into suiciding. Which almost happened." His thumb traced the Martiniere trefoil into Ruby's palm. "When I came to myself after leaving Ruby, I had a pistol in my hands. Seriously thought about blowing my brains out because I'd lost all I'd loved."

Remy sighed. "Shit. I believe you. All right. Similar things have happened in connection with your family. No one's ever able to prove a link to prosecute. Fits the pattern, though. You were a threat, and Philip Martiniere doesn't screw around."

"Exactly. Twenty-one years ago, I was scared shitless that Ruby and Brandon would be targets, and I had reason to believe that if I left in the worst way possible, that the threats would go away. They did. For a short period. I thought running away would solve things. In the long run, it didn't."

"Well, you certainly *did* leave in the worst way possible, I'll agree with that." Remy sighed again. "All right. What's the plan besides signing prenups today?"

"How hard is it to get an expedited marriage license?" Ruby

asked.

"As in what sort of timeline?"

"License tomorrow, civil ceremony ASAP," Ruby said. "Martiniere Group business concerns."

"Let me look at the 2047 statutory emergency marital law changes." Remy put her glasses back on, then rolled her chair to the side desk and brought up her comp. "Okay. No minor children involved?"

"No."

"No pregnancy?"

"I've been post-menopausal for five years, Remy. Ain't happening."

"These days you never know," Remy muttered. "But you're both over fifty, one of you with a diagnosed medical condition capable of changing rapidly, so you fall within the emergency provisions of the act. Financial disclosures—you will both have signed prenuptial agreements at the time you apply for the license. Let me see. That provision doesn't apply. Neither does that. But this—Gabe, how long have you been resident in Thunder County this time around?"

"Six months."

"Barely squeaks in. But it should work." Remy switched off her comp and turned to face them. "All right, kiddos. Here's the deal. We sign prenups today and I certify copies to be filed at the courthouse. You show up there tomorrow morning for the license application. You'll be billed an extra $500 for the expedited fee. *I* will do the extraordinary thing of calling Don the county clerk so that he can do the ceremony right there after filing. Will that be fast enough?"

"That works for me," Ruby said.

"Absolutely," Gabe said, his hand tightening on Ruby's.

"Just one thing. I want a time when this is happening, because I sure as hell want to be a witness."

"Will ten o'clock work?" Ruby grinned at Remy.

Remy turned back to her side desk, chewing her lip as she

scrolled through her calendar. "Got an appointment I can't move then. Make it eleven."

"Then it's a done deal," Ruby said. "We will meet you at the courthouse steps at eleven tomorrow."

"You two have rings and such? Or are you using your old ones?"

"I have a ring for Ruby," Gabe said. "It may not be fully ready, but—I've one for her."

"And the other thing is that we will have a small family ceremony at Moondance—Gabe's place over by Pendleton—on Friday afternoon. Still working out the details," Ruby said. "You and Shannon are invited to that as well."

"I'll make sure my calendar's clear," Remy said. She pulled out two pens. "And now, my darlings, let's sign prenups. That gives me what I need to fill out the expedited license form and email it to Don so he can file it bright and early tomorrow morning. I need information from both of you to do that."

When they were done, and copies made, they left. Gabe blew hard before he got into the truck.

"That was a bit easier than I thought," he said.

"I wasn't too worried about it."

"I didn't realize Remy had been a prosecutor in LA. I'm surprised she's practicing law here with those credentials. Almost seems like a step down."

"Yeah, she came back to Lakeside shortly before we married. I've never heard the details about why she left LA."

Gabe exhaled. "Well, she's being a big help to us. I expected more difficulties."

"We've—talked over the years. She knew this was a possibility six months ago. Knowing Remy, she probably had assorted scenarios charted out and prepared. I've only surprised her a few times."

"That's one thing taken care of," he said as they turned off on the gravel road leading to the ranch. "Let's hope the rest goes as well."

CHAPTER 13

Even though this was the second time around for their marriage, Ruby was still nervous as they dressed to go to the courthouse on Monday. She picked out a pale blue sleeveless summer dress that matched Gabe's suit. Her hands quivered as she tried to zip up the back.

"Let me," Gabe said.

"Thanks." She turned to face him after he'd finished, tweaking the knot of his tie so that it was straight.

"A bit different from last time, isn't it?"

"Yeah," she said, her throat dry. "I'm not pregnant this time."

Serg had checked the fit of the Martiniere ring last night and made some adjustments. He would join them as the Family's representative. She had pulled out Gramps's wedding ring, to see if it worked for Gabe, not wanting to use anything else if possible. Surprisingly, Gramps's ring slid easily onto Gabe's finger without needing adjustment. It was in a small box in her purse.

"You ready?" he asked.

She nodded.

They walked downstairs. Serg waited for them. Charlie stood with Serg.

"I get to kiss the bride for luck," he told Gabe. "Especially since I'm not going to be at this ceremony." Charlie kissed her forehead. "Better luck this time around, you two. May you do as well as me and Martin."

"I sure as hell hope so," Gabe said, sounding hoarse.

This time Ruby didn't drive, but sat in the back with Gabe and Serg, holding Gabe's hand. Remy waited for them at the courthouse steps. Ruby and Gabe walked up to her hand-in-hand, Serg on Gabe's right, their bodyguards following.

Remy made a face. "More witnesses? They'll have to leave their weapons outside."

Gabe thought for a moment. "They're our security. But I suppose...."

Remy snorted. "You think your uncle is so desperate that he'd attack you here?"

"My father, not my uncle. Just discovered that," Gabe said absently.

"Philip has cause to try something because he wants to keep that knowledge under wraps," Serg said.

Remy raised her brows. "Fa—okay. This is definitely getting even weirder. Let me call Sheriff Wilhite. If she provides protection, will that be satisfactory?"

"Yes," Serg said. "I'm their head of security. I approve this solution."

Remy stepped aside and quietly called. "On their way," she said.

They waited until Sheriff Wilhite appeared to escort them upstairs. Wilhite and Serg talked quietly. Then they went to the bodyguards and spoke with them for a few minutes.

"Problem solved," Wilhite said when they returned. "Your bodyguards are temporarily deputized."

"Thanks, Sharon," Remy said to the sheriff.

"I'd much rather not have my deputies up against the Martinieres if I can avoid it," Wilhite said. "I don't have the resources to deal with that. If you're bringing in your own security, that's great. I will also increase the courthouse security level while you're in here." She glanced at Ruby and Gabe. "You've sure been making things exciting locally for the past six months."

"Hopefully we'll calm things down soon," Gabe said. "I'd just as soon not see a lot of disturbance in Thunder County, especially since it's my home again."

"Appreciate that. Good luck, and congratulations in advance."

"Thanks," Ruby said.

"Sheriff Wilhite, I'll be in to talk to you about some concerns and suggestions for mutual aid in the upcoming weeks," Serg said. "Probably not until Wednesday, but we can definitely help out, considering the additional pressure that Gabe's presence in the county and his heightened visibility is going to put on your resources. I've already talked to your civilian group, but it's time you and I spoke. Officially."

Wilhite nodded. "I appreciate that. Thanks." She went back inside.

"Okay," Remy said. "Here we go."

They went upstairs to the county clerk's office. Don Pettigrove smiled at them. He and Ruby were distant cousins and had been high school classmates. She had always considered him a friend, even when things had been rough.

"Always a pleasure to do a wedding, especially when you're handling the paperwork and I don't have to do much, Remy," he said. "And I'm doubly thrilled to see you happy, Ruby. E-docs have been filed with the state, and Gabriel, thank you for the prompt payment. Ready?"

The ceremony passed in a daze. Gabe almost shakily put the ring on Ruby's right hand, but Serg cleared his throat and Gabe shook his head, then slipped it on her left ring finger. He grinned at her when she made the same mistake, substituting his left hand for his right.

Several cam lights flashed as they kissed at the end. Remy smirked at them.

"Should I send a pic to the *Thunder County Report*?" she asked. "Something tagged with *Superhero Winners Remarry at Courthouse? Martiniere heir and local woman tie the knot?*"

Serg laughed. "I sent pictures to Justine and Brandon. They're dealing with social media. I'll tell them to add the *Report* to their lists. You two had better prepare to be flooded with congratulations."

"Already set up the sort program for both of us," Ruby said.

"Good."

Congrats, Brandon texted. *Slipped the announcement into my old AgI contact list. You two are already going viral.*

"Oh, crud," Gabe muttered as they left Pettigrove's office. "And so it begins. Paparazzi. Can't escape 'em."

"We can have Moondance ready for you to stay by this afternoon to cut down on the disruptions," Serg said. "If you don't mind work going on around you. It's unlikely anyone will be looking for you over there, with the ceremony here."

"No, no, that's fine," Gabe said. "Ruby? Mind staying at Moondance until Friday?"

Ruby considered the prospect. What *would* require her presence at the Double R? She'd miss her familiar bedroom, the horses, and the mountains, but on the other hand, it *would* require less running back and forth. Not harvest time yet for the wheat and barley fields, and she could monitor their condition with the RubyBot's feedback. The second hay cutting was in the barn. The cattle and horses were on summer pasture, except for the horses brought in for riding. It would work.

And besides—she needed to learn and appreciate Moondance's systems. It might actually be a quieter setting to work for the next few days. While Thunder County itself was fairly isolated, once someone got to the County it was pretty easy to reach the Double R. Moondance, on the other hand, was an easier place to screen out unwanted visitors.

"The biggest challenge will be office setup," she said. "Besides, if Moondance is where we're going to hold official

Martiniere functions, we need to start getting that organized. Make it comfortable."

"This way we can bring Donna-gran in the night before," Gabe said. "It'd be a faux pas to have her staying there without us or Brandon. But she's the only guest I'd bring on site before the ceremony. Justine and Serg are different. They're not guests, they're family."

"Agreed." Ruby leaned into Gabe, thinking about what to take to Moondance. Justine had already made noises about a dress. And—she wanted to find a bed that would work for both of them.

"It sounds like a yes, until Friday, Serg," Gabe said. "Just— tell Kathleen to put us in the guest primary, not my old suite? That one properly belongs to Brandon."

Ruby squeezed his hand, guessing what he *wasn't* saying.

He glanced at her. "You okay with that?"

"We can call it a honeymoon," she said. "At least as much of one as we'll ever get this time around, I think."

Gabe laughed and threw his arm over her shoulders. "There you go. And we'll be on site and properly prepared to meet with Georgy tomorrow."

"You're not going to have—problems with staying at Moondance?" she asked softly as they approached the truck.

"I probably will." He kissed her neck. "But it's time to start making new memories."

IT WAS ACTUALLY A RELIEF TO DIVE INTO MOONDANCE SETUP. WHILE Gabe and Serg walked through the security protocols that had been installed so far, Ruby went through the rebuilt lab with Tim and his staff, then retreated to the house to go through those systems with Kathleen before she unpacked. A flurry of texts from Justine informed them of a time, the priest, and her arrival at Moondance on Tuesday afternoon to coordinate Friday's ceremony. Donna-gran was confirmed to arrive at the Moondance airstrip in the early afternoon on Thursday. Brandon and Kris planned to stay at the Double R and would be there Thursday evening, coming over for the ceremony, then returning to LA Friday night.

Soon enough Ruby was in the downstairs office, at first organizing her section of it, then poring over data from the conference. Gabe arranged his side of the office, then scowled at documents as he crafted a potential proposal for Georgy. At last he groaned and tapped off his comp, coming across the room to rub Ruby's shoulders before bending over to kiss her ear, then her cheek.

"It's our wedding day," he said softly. "Don't you think we've worked long enough? Damn workaholics, that's us. Who else works on the day they got remarried?"

"Not everyone is bucking to be the Martiniere and has everything blowing up around them at the same time they're getting married."

"True," he said, fake-scowling. "But I swear, this sort of thing is not going to be the pattern for the rest of our lives. I promise you, Rubes."

Ruby laughed, saved her work, and switched off her comp. As the screen faded she leaned back in her chair to grin up at him.

"What time is it anyway?" Mid-afternoon, she figured, from the sun's angle through the heat-reflecting shades.

"Four o'clock. Three and a half hours or so until sunset. Temp's 97. I'm thinking that it's time to play. We're not that far from the 5 o'clock zone. Change into something casual for sitting on the deck, break out that champagne I had Serg slip into the suite mini fridge to cool, and relax. I extended the shade so it should be pretty comfortable out there. It's not the yard swing at the ranch, but it can be pretty nice out on the decks with those shades if this place is anything like the original version. Sound good?"

"Sounds marvelous. I didn't bring anything casual to wear, though."

"You might be surprised," Gabe said nonchalantly. "Look on the dresser. There's also your preferred sunblock in the bathroom, though you shouldn't need it with the deck's sunshades. Oh, and a pretty sun hat on the dresser. I remember what summer was like here, and to be honest, this is my favorite time to be on the deck. As long as these new shades work as advertised."

"You planned this," Ruby accused as he spun her chair around and pulled her up.

"Absolutely," he said, kissing her. "I meant it when I said I have a lot to make up to you." He sighed. "I wanted to do things like this for you before, Ruby. But—money."

"Having money does make it easier, doesn't it?"

He pressed his forehead against hers. "Definitely. They say that scrabbling builds character but damn. It felt like we built enough character for ten couples during our first few years."

"It must have been harder coming from the background you did."

He raised his head and wrapped his arms more tightly around her. "I'd been living a pretty hardscrabble life ever since I broke from the Family. By the time you and I got together, a lot of my rich boy habits had gone by the wayside. Except the gambling. And that was stupid of me. It put me back on Philip's radar. I just—I wanted to make things easier for us, and went about it the wrong way."

"Do I need to worry about you and gambling?"

He shook his head. "I'm gambling enough with what we're doing. So no. I have plenty of risk-taking going on and, you know what? I've somewhat lost my desire for it."

"That's good to hear."

He gently pulled her away from the desk. "Come on. Let's play."

As they entered their suite, Gabe stopped short, staring at the adjustable bed with head and foot slightly raised. "What the—where did this come from?"

"Surprise," she said, grinning. "A potential bed solution. On trial. If we like it, we can get one delivered to the ranch. It's easier to test them here than there, so I decided to take advantage of our time here to trial this one—it looked the best to me."

"Oh man." He shook his head. "Makes what I did look like nothing."

"It's the thought that counts. Besides, you're not the only one who wants to do nice things for the other. And you rebuilt this house. That's huge."

"Yeah," he said. "Actually, this is a gift for both of us since I'm sure sharing a recliner cramps you up too. I'm glad you thought of it. I could never make myself get a bed like this when it became necessary. Especially just for me. It just seemed—too final to admit what G9 did. To think that I needed to be in a special bed the rest of my life."

"That's what I thought."

"Thanks, hon. It'll be nice to be able to spread out." He gave her a gentle push. "Mine's not as spectacular as yours but—go look under the hat."

Ruby went to her dresser and picked up the big, floppy, pale green sun hat, smiling because she recognized the style as one she had favored years ago. Underneath was a swimsuit set, two-piece plus a matching light cover up in a lush floral print featuring rich magenta roses. She had one like it when they were first married and had mourned when it fell apart. A pair of matching sandals and big wraparound sunglasses finished the ensemble.

"Thank you," she said. "How did you find it? And matching sandals, no less. I've been looking for another suit like this for years. Never thought I'd have sandals, too."

Gabe shrugged as he leaned against the bathroom doorframe, watching her. "Like we both said—money makes a difference. It took me a while to find it, and I had to pull Tine in to help me at the end. Go ahead. Put it on." He headed for his dresser. "I should have some shorts in here."

When she had changed, he grinned at her. "You look stunning, beautiful one. Go out on the deck. I'll bring champagne and food."

"Are there chairs and a table out there?"

"Should be. I ordered some to be delivered."

She stepped out onto the deck, noticing that not only did the awning extend out far enough to keep it shaded in summer heat, but that the screen to block the direct sun also obscured them enough to discourage photography—or perhaps even snipers. All the same, she kept to the back of the deck. There was a big table, small side tables, and several chairs.

Gabe juggled a tray with cold cuts, cheese, crackers, veggies, and fruit in one hand and a small plate with a tiny chocolate cake in the other and set it down on the big table. "Thought wedding cake of some sort would be a good idea. And I didn't know how hungry you were, but this sounded good to me." He ducked back inside and came back with plates and two champagne glasses. At last he returned with an ice bucket and the champagne.

After filling a plate, Ruby let the dry heat lull her into lassitude as Gabe opened the champagne and poured her a glass.

"To us," he said, before settling in the chair next to hers.

"To us," she echoed.

It felt good to be taking this moment just to relax. A time to catch their breath before the next flurry of activity. They sat there, sipping champagne and nibbling, for once satisfied just to be quiet.

THE NEXT MORNING, THEY WERE BACK IN THE OFFICE. RUBY scanned yesterday's reports from the RubyBot data on both the Double R and Moondance, then moved on to inquiry follow ups from the BPA conference about the RubyBot, the Defender, and the Protector. Not a lot of orders yet, but there were more inquiries than she had expected coming in.

Need to talk to Rick about stem seed capacity, she thought. They might have to expand the labs further. That could wait until they had more confirmed orders for next spring, though—so far the actual orders were well within the lab's production ability without monopolizing Beck and Rick's output for other clients. But it could turn into a concern very quickly. She did some quick calculations and sent an email to Rick and Martin about capacity.

Ruby was skimming through Martin's response when Serg alerted them that he and Georgy were turning off the highway to drive up to Moondance.

Gabe stretched and stood. "Looks like it's showtime." He shut off his comp. "Here's the deal. If we want, we can gain a controlling interest on AgI's board without too much risk. The ownership percentages aren't quite what Georgy told you. He's counting about fifteen percent of stock held by Mariah as belonging to Philip. And there's some *interesting* movement by mutual fund investors. It looks as if they are losing confidence in the company. Especially with the rise in other funding shows."

"Is it an investment we want to make?"

Gabe shrugged as they went upstairs. "That's the question. I'm leaning more toward saying no, even though it's going to hurt people who need those payouts from the AgInnovator. Those people are why I think we should listen to Georgy, but... no is where I'm headed, for various reasons."

"What are our options if we do say yes?"

"We could turn AgI into a subsidiary of Barkley-Martiniere."

"Not thrilled about that notion. Especially taking over the AgInnovator."

"Agreed. Another factor—I'm waiting for some answers to a couple of questions I posed to Brandon and Kris about indentured status before I commit to any investment. It may make sense to just step away and watch Georgy crash if the situation with the indentureds is as bad as I think it could be. It could take AgI down hard." His voice hardened. "Don't be surprised if I decide to tell him to take a walk in a rather nasty fashion. It depends on what Bran tells me about one question. I'm just pissed off enough about what I discovered five minutes ago to tell Georgy to go to hell." Gabe ran his hands through his hair. "It's only because I'm uncertain about his role in our getting fucked over twenty-one years ago that I'm willing to talk to him now."

"Agreed." She eyed Gabe, wanting to know more about what he'd learned. *Let sleeping dogs lie,* she decided. If it was important, he'd bring it up during the meeting. If not—she could ask afterwards.

Gabe held out an arm. "Shall we make our first presentation as husband and wife in high style? Keeping in mind that we may be doing some serious butt-kicking?"

"Yippie-ki-yay. You bet your ass." She grinned at Gabe as she linked her arm with his.

He groaned and rolled his eyes. "Don't make me laugh, it'll spoil my severe aura as the Martiniere-in-waiting. I need to be a hardass for this meeting."

"I'm here to keep you from taking yourself too seriously, even when you have to get tough with someone." She dropped the playfulness. "I'll follow your lead in responding to Georgy. You know the details. I don't yet. And I'm very suspicious about his continuing involvement with Mariah."

"Me as well. Thanks." Gabe patted her hand, then opened the door. Ruby made certain that her wedding ring was prominent as her hand rested on top of Gabe's. They stepped outside and waited as the truck pulled into the carport next to the house. Bodyguards emerged first, checked the area. Serg and Georgy followed.

"Gabe! Ruby!" Georgy smirked, spreading his hands wide, spinning around to take in his surroundings. "What a beautiful place. Fresh air! Blue skies! And the house isn't bad, either."

Ruby and Gabe untwined their arms to bow politely.

"Glad you like it," Gabe said. "It's corporate headquarters, and at some point this place will be my son's residence."

"Nice to have money," Georgy said, turning around again.

Ruby rolled her eyes at Gabe when Georgy couldn't see her.

"Yes, it is," Gabe said smoothly. "Come on in."

They had decided to have the meeting in the great room of the house, stark though it was at the moment. But there were chairs, and a table, brought in from the deck.

"Ni-i-ce," Georgy said as he walked in. "If a bit bare."

"We just finished construction," Gabe said. "Furnishings are coming."

"So. Congratulations are in order, I hear. I'm surprised you had such a quiet ceremony."

"We wanted the legalities to happen quickly," Ruby said. "We are having a ceremonial event here for family, close friends, and associates. I assume you got your invitation?"

"Yes, and RSVPed. Wouldn't miss it for anything. Poor Mariah's still going to be in Europe."

"Oh, that's too bad," she said, trying to sound sincere as she sat.

"I'm sure she'll be missed," Georgy said, a falsely sincere note in his voice that matched hers.

Gabe sighed. "Okay. Let's not beat around the bush. You wanted my help. I took a look at publicly available information about AgI, as well as speaking with Brandon. Philip directly holds twenty percent. Mariah holds fifteen percent. I assume that's the basis for your telling Ruby that he controls thirty-five percent of AgI?"

"Yes." Georgy frowned. "She's unpredictable, but for these purposes I consider her to be aligned with Philip."

"A safe assumption." Gabe leaned back in his chair, gazed up at the ceiling, and steepled his fingers. "Now here's where it gets interesting. I am seeing some movement amongst your mutual fund investors, especially since the Real Truthers nomination of

Philip as their candidate for President this past weekend. That can be problematic since you're also fighting off competition."

"Yesss." Georgy dragged the word out.

"And there have been problems with performance in your indentured management subsidiary. I looked at the posted quarterly statements. Since Philip's handpicked managers came on board at AgI, there have been escalating problems with the complexity of body-modded indentureds and declining quarterly revenues. And still he manages to maintain control of that subsidiary. Seems problematic to me." Gabe paused, flinching as he received a text. Anger tightened his face and he lowered his gaze from the ceiling, resting his elbows on the arms of his chair. "Things have been especially bad in the indentured worker ag sector this year. Correct?"

Georgy squirmed as Gabe glowered at him. "Yes," he finally admitted.

"Philip's proposals at the Real Truthers are leading to a certain degree of agitation amongst advocates of indentured law reform." Gabe leaned his chin on his index fingers, still steadily focused on Georgy. "As you know, my son is amongst those advocates, shaped, of course, by his involvement with a former AgI indentured and his own brush with that potential fate. So I have a certain degree of inside knowledge about this situation. Including the fact that Philip has already shoved policies through AgI that are in line with his political proposals."

"I tried to stop him, Gabe! I really did. But I'm screwed. He wants me off of the Board. He plans to drop a hostile takeover bid on me next week and kick me out of my own company! He told me that to my face Saturday night."

"You chose to take AgI public, Georgy. You knew this was a risk."

"But I didn't think—"

"No, you didn't think! Give me one good goddamned reason why I shouldn't just sit back and let the chips fall where they may as far as you are concerned." Gabe's voice grew harsher.

"The indentured situation has gone further than it ever should, and the only thing that differentiates it from the fucking chattel slavery that our country went to war over almost two hundred years ago is that it discriminates by income and debt status, not skin color. You had the opportunity to change the situation in AgI before Philip ever got involved, *and you didn't.* Give me one good fucking reason why I should take you seriously."

Georgy paled. "But Mariah said it was a good idea to expand the indentured workers management—"

"I don't *want* to hear about Mariah!" Gabe snapped. "She's a lying little bitch who has been in bed with Philip for a long time, metaphorically if not literally. *I'm waiting.*"

"I can give you information about Philip's plans if you help me. Insider long-term plans. I can help you against him, Gabe! I really can!" Georgy turned to Ruby. "Ruby. You've benefited from our programs. Tell Gabe. Tell him it's important to help me."

Ruby looked down at her nails with the Martiniere logo still painted on them from the other night. At last she looked up. "You're getting more of a hearing from Gabe than you ever would have received from me," she said coldly. "So far I'm not hearing any good reasons for supporting you."

"But Philip—"

"Who are you really representing here, Georgy?" Gabe said. "Philip has held interests in your companies for years. Not just AgI but others. All with significant ties to the indentured worker management industry."

"Gabe, I—" Georgy threw up his hands. "I'm desperate."

"The fact is, you're at risk of falling into the clutches of indenture yourself, aren't you? How long do you think you'd survive as an indentured?"

"Gabe," Georgy whimpered. "Ruby. Please. I'm begging for help. I did give Brandon a chance—and he got free. Doesn't that count for anything?"

"I looked at the contracts you and Mariah forced on our son

as a result of his debt and the balance he assumed on my behalf this morning," Gabe said harshly. "If Ruby and I hadn't been in those finals for the Superhero and joined forces with Swait, if Justine my sister hadn't been handy and willing to back my bid, he'd have been fucked."

Georgy stared at Gabe. "Justine—your sister—that means—" he choked.

"Yes," Gabe said, his voice silkily poisonous now. "I *am* Philip's son. Confirmed by a trusted relative. You tried to screw both me and my son over. Fortunate for you that Ruby wasn't included as well—at least to my knowledge. Otherwise I would be making *certain arrangements*, and since I'm Philip's son, I think you know what *that* means."

Georgy paled. "Gabe—really—is that called for?"

"When it comes to Ruby, hell yes, it's called for. She is my wife and I do not take fucking around with her lightly." Gabe sat up. "As far as I'm concerned, Georgy, whatever trouble you've gotten into by playing footsie with *my father* is entirely your doing and no concern of mine. We are not bailing you out. Period."

"I...see." Georgy rose, trembling slightly. "Are you sure? I can tell you things about Philip...."

"I wouldn't trust one damn bit of information that you give me," Gabe said. He stood. Ruby joined him.

"I'll see myself out," Georgy said.

"You do that." They watched him walk slowly to the front door.

Before Georgy opened it, Gabe spoke.

"Oh. And Georgy?"

He turned to face them, a hopeful expression softening his face. "Yes?"

"When you report to Mariah and *my father* about this meeting, you tell them that I will interpret any attack on the indentured person called Patricia Markey to be a direct assault against my family. Understand?"

Georgy nodded. He opened the door and fled, slamming it behind him.

Gabe stared at the door, then exhaled slowly. "I suppose I was a bit too hard on him. Nor do I suppose that last bit will make any difference. But they've been warned."

"I took it as payback for all the crap we've taken from him over the years. Plus what they tried to do to you and Brandon. So no, I don't think it was too hard at all."

Gabe swallowed. "That last text I got from Bran? I asked whose signatures were on his contract with AgI." He shook his head. "He knew Georgy played a role, but until Pat got them the full contract, he didn't know who signed off on within the company. Philip did. And there were emails discussing the contract that spelled out details of their plans for Brandon. Ruby, it didn't matter how many clicks we got on the Superhero. The agreement Georgy and Brandon had was not what Brandon thought. He would have been railroaded into indenture if Justine hadn't paid off his obligations. He—they—discovered this yesterday. And Georgy is in part responsible."

Ruby stared at Gabe, shocked. It took her a few moments to find her voice. "Then as far as I'm concerned, you were too damn gentle on the fucker."

He nodded. "There's more." He took a deep breath. "One of the reasons Brandon, Kris, and Justine are returning to LA immediately after the ceremony on Friday. They are going to extract Pat from the indentured facility she's in on Sunday. She's in danger. This shit is going to blow up fast, Rubes. I think I—*we*—need to be on hand when they do it."

"So it really and truly begins now," she said.

He nodded. "It's going to be one hell of a honeymoon. I'm sorry."

"I told you to stop apologizing." But she kept her voice gentle. "Gabe. In that case—we need to enjoy what time we have. Now."

"I'm afraid you're right."

She took his hands. "No regrets. None at all. We can't afford them. The only way out is to ride through it."

"Yeah. And the slightest misstep could bring it all down on our heads."

"At least we'll be together."

He smiled and pulled her to him. "You know what? I've never really given you a tour of the land, and now that it's part yours, it's time you eyeballed your new domain. Let's change and get the hell out of the house for a while. Forget about this Martiniere bullshit while we still can. Sound good?"

"Gabe, I would *love* to do that."

CHAPTER 14

Ruby and Gabe were investigating a non-functioning wheel on one of the center pivot lines in a field below Moondance's main ridge when Justine's jet glided in to land at the airstrip.

Gabe pulled off his ball cap and wiped his sweaty brow with his forearm, creating a muddy smear across his forehead. "Think we should knock off and meet Tine?"

"Serg's picking her up, and I'm sure Kathleen can get her settled in her room." Ruby focused on the cranky wheel. The problem wasn't anything as simple as a flat, of course, and the comp diagnostic was unhelpful. Fortunately, Gabe's pivots were the same model and about the same age as the ones on the Double R, so she had a pretty decent idea of how to get it running again. "Besides, she'll want to prowl around the house and figure out space logistics for Friday. She'll be happier if we don't distract her."

"Works for me."

She found the problem. *"There."* A quick test, and it was online again.

They examined the rest of the line to ensure that the cranky wheel hadn't fouled anything else up, then climbed back in the crawler to check another field. Ruby sighed with relief, leaning back against the seat as Gabe drove, feeling pleasantly tired from the work. The tire hadn't been the only small routine fix they'd done. They had been tweaking and checking boundary sensor and in-field warning sensor arrays. The level of security possible here impressed her.

If we add the Defender with a security component, this place will make a good Martiniere headquarters. Gabe's absolutely right about that.

And it would be easier to protect than the Double R.

Besides the reassurance about security, it felt good to be back on the land with Gabe, even if this was Moondance and unfamiliar. Working on the land, getting the feel of it under her feet and in her fingers, feeling the shifts in temperature and moisture even on a hot dry day—the RubyBot codified all of these impressions, but it took actually *being there* to understand the correlation between data and conditions. At least for her.

Plus she had the opportunity to look up at the main house from below.

"How did you get everything stabilized on that cliff edge?" she asked Gabe, pointing at the portion of the great room that, indeed, hung over the rocks and sheltered the sliding doors for the deck of the office located in the basement.

"That was Rachel's doing," Gabe said. "Frankly? I have no idea how it works. Contractors and inspectors seemed to think it's functional. The location does take care of some of the security issues. In spite of the fire, when the alarms are fully activated, it's pretty darn secure."

"A bit more defensible, at least."

He nodded. "Serg has been making lots of happy noises as his team works. But that's why I didn't get too excited about more than the basic sunshades for the decks. If you notice, it's awfully hard for the typical sniper to find a good place to take a shot without triggering one of the security sensor arrays when they're up and running. It'll take a lot of work and the best sight lines are in the open. They would have to take the whole house out. Not perfect—no place is. We still have to be careful, and not be stupid like I was before. I left some holes that allowed this place to get burned—but it will be a challenge for most attackers."

"Makes me feel better about being on the decks. They are nice."

"Yeah."

They found a couple of smaller things to work on in the remaining fields. Then Gabe took Ruby the long way around through the forested portion of Moondance to check on the new perimeter arrays that Serg's people had installed.

When they got back to the house, Justine was nowhere in sight. But they heard her and Kathleen talking in the family wing. They showered and changed. Gabe headed down to the office to do a final check of his messages for the day. Ruby looked around but there was no sign of Justine. Kathleen was working on a salad in the kitchen.

"Where's Justine?" she asked.

"Revising some of her plans for Friday," Kathleen said. "Small adjustments."

"You two talk about the food yet?"

"That's part of what she's working on."

"You're okay with the restrictions?"

"They sound pretty reasonable," Kathleen said. "And we've come up with ways to control access. Considering this is a fairly small gathering, it won't be too bad."

"All right. We're down in the office if she comes looking for us."

"I'll let her know."

Ruby went downstairs and pulled up her comp. She was focused on a report from the high school agronomy teacher about the new crop of interns working at the Double R when she heard steps, then Justine's voice.

"Hello…anyone around?"

"Down here," Ruby said. She finished her response and sent

it as Justine descended the stairs, several folders in her hand. "Finding what you need?"

"It's a great place for entertaining," Justine said. "I can see why you're making this place the Martiniere headquarters, Gabe. It's set up well. I've just been thinking through the flow. It's looking like the game room will be the best option for us to separate family members for the Ritual. Easily controlled access. Donna-gran can look it over and tell us what does and doesn't work."

She placed the folders on Gabe's desk. "There you go."

"What's that?"

"Hard copies of Brandon's contracts with AgI, and emails. Just like you wanted. Chips attached to the folders. All saved to an isolated server."

Gabe picked the folders up and started thumbing through them.

Justine opened the sliding door and stepped out on the concrete deck, looking over the rail. "Oh. *That's* a drop off."

Ruby joined her. "It's impressive from below. Gabe and I were working in that field when you flew in."

"Doesn't look like an easy line of sight for snipers, either."

"It's not," Gabe said, joining them. "And the sunshades that run from railing to roofline also block vision. Still, those cliffs can be climbed. I did it when I wasn't so stove up, putting in sensors for the first security system. And if someone wants to set fire to the place from below, it's still doable. This time around I used more fire-hardened materials, and I had the cash to install extra sprinkler and foam protection. Money does make a difference." He sighed. "Though after scanning those docs, Tine, I wonder if I did enough. Philip has a significant grudge against me and Brandon."

"Learning that you're his son sure explains a lot about the past," Justine said bitterly. "And looking at those documents makes me want to strangle him. How could he be this way? Forcing Brandon into indenture as a body-modded fighter prototype? Damn it, Brandon's the only grandchild he's going to have! *His own goddamned flesh and blood.*"

"Unless he manages to get a gen-modified kid off of his indentured project," Gabe snarled.

"I don't think anything would come of it. Who the fuck is going to raise that kid? Neither one of us. Joey? I wouldn't trust a dog in his hands, much less an alleged sibling who would be a rival. And our damned father is not going to live long enough to see any child grow to maturity."

"You sure about that? Because body mods and gene mods could be a game changer." Gabe shook his head. "How much of that damned project of his is about life extension? I sure as hell can see the potential in the material I've been reading. I've talked to Martin and Rick about it too. They concur." He leaned on the railing, staring out over the fields. "There's a lot more going on with that indentured research than appears on the surface." He slapped the railing with one hand and straightened up. "It's a damned programmable army that he's creating, Tine. Coupled with life extension and gene-modding for his ideal heir. Maybe even a clone, even though current science says no."

Justine nodded. "That's exactly what I am seeing, too." She shivered. "I've gone into the indentured research compounds with Kris to pick up materials from Pat, because Brandon will not allow anyone to go in there alone. What you see in there—is scary. You don't see the prototypes out and about in public, but they're all over the compounds. Our family's old mind control stuff? It's *nothing* compared to what they are playing with in those labs. I just can't get enough data to develop a good model for what that will look like yet. That's the problem with pulling Pat out now." She shuddered. "But we don't have a choice. I am not willing to lose one more person if I can at all help it."

"There will be a price. There will be a body count. It's inevitable," Gabe said bitterly.

"The price has already been too damned high," Justine said, taking a deep breath. "For a lot of us. But one good thing has come out of all this." She exhaled slowly. "I've discovered that I have more than one brother—and that I actually have a brother I *like*, not someone I want to shoot on sight. Gabie. No matter what happens. I am so, *so* happy to have you as my big brother. I wish to hell I'd known this sooner. Goddamn fucking Daddy-poo and his fucking grandiose schemes. Damn him to hell. *Damn him.* He only gives a shit about a kid he's raised who is his *nephew*, not his own son or daughter." She gulped, tears trickling down her cheeks.

"Tine." Gabe took Justine in his arms as she started sobbing. "Tine. It's all right."

"I just—he tried to drive Donald away, just like he did with you and Ruby, only then I didn't know about you two. Donald and I sat down and talked it through, looked at the options, and together decided we had to do what you and Ruby did—without knowing it at the time."

"Hey. I put Ruby through hell doing it the hard way because I wasn't smart enough to sit down and talk to her."

"But you were in hiding and locked down through mind control programming!" Justine wailed. "And if we'd known then that we were siblings, we could have worked together! Donald and I had no one but Serg to turn to for help. And Serg was having problems of his own with his father Piotr—all settled now, but then things were rocky. I can't *imagine* being in your position, with a spouse and child at risk and no friendly connections within the Family. I just can't." She pulled away from Gabe.

"Tine...."

"I hate him. I hate Joey. I want them *both* dead. It is all I can do to be in the same room with them and not—do something stupid." She gulped. "I'm afraid one of these days I'm going to lose it. *Was* close to losing it before you reappeared. Had a plan for taking them out in one last grand suicide stroke. It was the only way I could see. Donald and Serg kept talking me out of it by giving me *just one more project*. You have been a goddamn lifeline, Gabie, you, Ruby, and Brandon. Now I have hope."

Ruby darted back into the office to grab tissues and a glass of water, offering them both to Justine. She sniffled and took them with a smile, dabbing at her eyes, then guzzling the water.

"Thanks, Ruby. I am honored to be your sister-in-law. You're the sister I always wanted and never had. I just—I am so. damned. pissed. at what happened. Especially when thinking about what could have been."

Gabe sighed. "What's done is done." He placed a hand on Ruby and Justine's backs, guiding them back inside. "And on a happier note, how are the preparations going for Friday?"

Justine gulped, smiling weakly. "They're proceeding right along. Ruby, the dress fitter will be here tomorrow morning. I have two dresses for you to choose from."

"I'm looking forward to that modeling session," Gabe said.

Justine shook a finger at him. "No, no, no, big brother. You don't get to see Ruby in her wedding dress before the ceremony. It's bad luck."

"But we're already legally married," Gabe said.

"So? This is the one that is going to count in the Family's eyes. And no, you aren't going to see Ruby's outfit until the ceremony. Period. Besides, you'll scandalize Donna-gran if she finds out—and she *will* ask. You know it."

"Mustn't disappoint Donna-gran," Gabe said, smiling faintly.

"Definitely not," Justine said firmly. "Unless you want to go through one of her tongue-lashings."

Gabe shivered. "No, I'll avoid that."

Remembering the reactions of the men at the table when she first met Donna-gran, Ruby had to agree with him. The Martiniere Matriarch was not someone to be trifled with.

If only her son accorded her the same respect.

Then again, she hadn't seen Donna-gran and Philip interact.

Brandon and Kris joined them on Thursday night to meet Donna-gran and do a ceremony walk-through. They had driven over from the Double R, along with Charlie and Martin. Ruby had asked them to escort her down the aisle and Brandon was serving as Gabe's best man.

They waited in the hangar as the small jet—Justine's personal one—landed, and her staff gently helped Donna-gran off of the plane and into her waiting wheelchair. Gabe led the procession to meet her.

"Donna-gran. Welcome to Moondance Ranch." He bowed.

"Gabriel. It is wonderful to see you again." She eyed Gabe, then gestured to him. Gabe bent over and she shakily kissed his cheeks, holding onto his hands. "I mourned when you disappeared, fearing the worst, and rejoiced when you not only reappeared, but had a lovely woman and a son. This is a joyful occasion."

"Yes, it is."

"Ruby, my dear. A pleasure to see you." This time Donna-gran kissed Ruby on her cheeks, as she had Gabe. As she stepped back, Gabe waved Brandon and Kris forward.

"Donna-gran. This is your great-grandson Brandon, and his love Kris."

Donna-gran held Brandon's hands for a few moments after the greeting, looking him over. "How old are you now, Brandon?"

"Twenty-six now, twenty-seven in December."

Donna-gran nodded. "A few years older than your father was the last time I saw him. Nonetheless, you strongly resemble him at that age—and both you and your father look like my beloved Louis, your great-grandfather."

"Thank you—Donna-gran?" Brandon said tentatively.

"You are welcome." She gestured to Kris. "And this is your beloved—Kris? Short for Kristine?"

"No, Krista," Kris said. "Though I have not used that name since I was a child."

"I see. Well." Donna-gran looked around. "Gabriel, whatever possessed you to settle in this hot, dry, brown land?"

Gabe laughed. "It grows great grain crops, along with other foods, Donna-gran. And Moondance may not be as pretty as Ruby's Double R, but it has its own beauty. Come on. We'll drive up to the house and you'll see what I mean."

AFTER A TOUR DURING WHICH DONNA-GRAN CONCEDED THAT YES, Moondance was prettier than its first impression, and then a light supper on the main deck, they retreated to the great room to walk through the ceremony. Ruby and Gabe's room was where Gabe and his groomsmen got ready, while Justine's was where Ruby and her attendants prepared.

Donna-gran joined them, eyeing what could be seen of the dress in its wrap, hanging in the bathroom. "Has Gabriel seen your dress, Ruby?"

"He'd *like* to," Ruby said.

"That's why I have it stashed in here," Justine said.

"Good." Donna-gran wheeled out of the room to start the line. Brandon escorted her to her seat, then rejoined Gabe and Serg.

First were Kris and Serg. Then Justine and Brandon. And finally, Ruby, with Charlie taking one arm and Martin on the other. A simple practice, but as Ruby took Gabe's hands, she felt a slight tremor.

"We've done this before," she whispered to him.

"I know," he murmured. "It's just—this time feels more significant. Perhaps it's the Ritual."

She nodded. *That* practice was next.

They walked through the rest of the ceremony, then did another run-through before pronouncing it good.

Then it was time to retreat to the game room to discuss the Ritual. Donna-gran looked over the hallway, nodding approval.

"A good means to restrict access. Gabriel. If Philip is present, will you allow him to attend the Ritual?"

"No," Gabe said firmly. "Brandon and I are both here to represent that branch of the family."

"*Good.* There are aspects of the old Ritual that I wish to bring back, not the usual Ritual. Sergei."

"Yes, Donna-gran?" Serg said.

"To what degree have you been able to restore the old circuits in the emeralds?"

"The brooch still is limited in what it can do, compared to those old schematics you gave me. But the ring still maintains functionality, once I wakened the charging nanos in it."

"Better than I had hoped." Donna-gran rolled her chair into the game room, which had been cleared of the rudimentary furniture that had been put in there. "As is this space. Gabriel. Who is going to be present besides you and Ruby?"

"Brandon and Kris. Justine."

"And Donald, if I may have him here," Justine said.

Gabe nodded, acknowledging. "Donald with Justine. Artie and Nora…depending on her condition and how well she can travel. Otherwise just Artie. Paul and Marie. Ken and Annette. Piotr and Serg, of course. The other family heads are unable to make it for reasons of health or business."

"Brandon, Arthur, Paul, Ken, and Piotr." Donna-gran nodded, as if running through a mental checklist. "Yes. That will be sufficient." She reached out a hand. "Ruby. Give me the ring, please."

Ruby pulled the emerald ring off and handed it to Donna-gran. She already felt bare without it. She strung it on the same chain as her lucky locket when they were out working on the ranch and she didn't want to risk harming it. For some reason she didn't feel comfortable leaving the ring behind.

Donna-gran raised the ring, studying it closely. "Good. Good." Her lips tightened and she nodded, once again looking like she was marking off list items. "I still have access."

She tapped on the surface of the emerald and a palm-sized green schematic projection popped out of it. Then she lowered the ring to her lap as the green diagram remained in place. Her fingers deftly traced new lines illuminated in yellow.

Another brusque nod as Donna-gran lowered her hands. "Gabriel. Ruby. Come here."

They obeyed, exchanging nervous glances.

"Gabriel. Your left hand please."

He extended it and Donna-gran took it.

"Ruby. Now yours."

Donna-gran placed it on top of Gabe's. Then she gently guided the projection over their linked hands.

"Don't move."

"What are you doing?" Gabe asked.

"Not now!" Donna-gran snapped. "It's been many years since I last did this, and things went wrong for Angelica and Saul because of a stupid mistake. I need to focus. I'll explain afterward."

Gabe nodded curtly as Donna-gran once again began tracing lines in the schematic. Tingles swept across Ruby's hand. She bit her lip, fighting the impulse to yank her hand away. The back of Gabe's hand quivered against her palm and her fingers twitched slightly, wanting to clasp his.

"Don't fight that instinct," Donna-gran said. "Do what your fingers desire."

Gabe's fingers tightened around hers as she clutched his.

"Yes. Yes," Donna-gran murmured. "It's working."

The tingling sharpened to a sensation like hot prickles sweeping across Ruby's hand and into Gabe's, a matching wave stinging back into her palm. Ruby gasped but didn't pull away, closing her hand even tighter. Gabe pressed his hand into her palm, squeezing her fingers hard.

Then the burning went away. The yellow lines around their hands changed to green. Donna-gran dropped her hands.

"Say your full names, as you will be from now on. Ruby, you first."

"Ruby Marie Barkley," Ruby said. The projection pulsed with each syllable of her name.

"Gabriel Marcus Martiniere," Gabe said. Once again, the schematic vibrated with each syllable.

Donna-gran eased the projection away from their hands to hover over her lap. She picked up the ring again. More tapping, and the schematic faded into the ring.

"All right," she sighed. Then she gave Gabe and Ruby a sharp look. "You can let go of each other now."

"Maybe I don't want to," Gabe said, raising Ruby's hand to his lips with a smile.

"Enough of that!" Donna-gran snapped, but there was a smirk on her lips. "You'll have time later."

Gabe kissed Ruby and let go.

Donna-gran handed the ring back to Ruby. "You can put this back on."

"So. What was that all about?" Ruby asked.

"Reprogramming the ring," Donna-gran said. "You're aware that these are created and hardened emeralds, not natural ones, right?"

"I'd wondered because of the talk of programming," Ruby said.

"Once all the emeralds were natural, not created."

"What?" Gabe startled. But Justine and Serg both nodded.

"It's in the notes," Serg said. "The switch to lab-created, hardened emeralds was how the brooch was programmed to relay conversations. But I didn't know the ring was too."

Donna-gran sighed. "Yes. Louis and I needed a means to implement the refined control programs we had developed in conjunction with our research into hypnotics. So we went to the other family heads and discussed this solution for the Martiniere and his wife. The decision was to keep the earrings and necklace as they were, but to replace the gems in the ring and brooch with high-quality, hardened, created emeralds that had implanted circuitry mimicking natural inclusions. We combined these devices with the control word protocol. And then we made more for the other Martiniere women. Just not as powerful." She smirked. "Louis always liked *The Lord of the Rings*. He'd sometimes call this ring *the One Ring to rule them all*."

"But—the projection—the circuitry—there's no way that could work," Gabe objected. "Not like this. Not in that era."

"Really? Oh, Gabriel." Donna-gran shook her head ruefully. "The Martiniere Group was engaged in high-level military research throughout our many branches. Louis hoped that Philip and Saul would follow his lead to continue decoupling the military programs from our core mission. But Philip prioritized military contracts and Saul wasn't the Martiniere long enough after Louis died to change things." Donna-gran fell silent for a moment. "The control and command routines that are now common in the Family were meant to serve as a protection against co-option from outsiders. But the way Philip chose to implement them has been intended to control first the Family, and more, I fear."

"You're talking about the grounds for the indentured command and control programs in the indentured research compounds that are maintained by the Family under the cover of AgI," Brandon said quietly. "Am I correct that they could be applied in that manner?"

Donna-gran shot him a sharp look. "Are these associated with body-mods?"

"Body and gene mods," Brandon said. "They are on the brink of creating cyborgs."

Donna-gran inhaled sharply. "You are certain of this?"

"Kris was indentured. Her sister is still in the research compound and feeding us information. I almost ended up in the damn indentured ranks myself. I saw the plans they had for me. Body-modded prototype fighter, to be cyborged," Brandon said, voice hard and cold. "Donna-gran, the testimony my father gave thirty years ago only scratched the surface of what Philip is doing today. I have seen it."

Donna-gran closed her eyes and shook her head. "Oh Louis, Louis. How did we go so wrong with Philip?" She opened her eyes. "Then Gabriel, it was a very good thing that you hid the emeralds when they came to you. I trust you and your son will not choose to follow in your biological father's steps?"

"I spoke out against what Philip was doing all those years ago. My opinion of it has not changed. If I could—I'd eliminate the control words within the family. The mind control programs in research. All of it."

Their eyes met. At last Donna-gran nodded. "All right. Ruby. Gabriel. When we invoke the Ritual, one result will be that both of you are free from the control programming currently implanted in both of you, except for the control tones that Ruby will acquire as the Matriarch."

"*Both* of us?" Ruby asked. She exchanged worried looks with Gabe, dread tightening her gut.

We were right.

"In your case, Ruby dear, it's about twenty-one years old. The schematic helped me identify the programming date but not who did it. Gabriel, your programming from childhood still exists, and was not wiped out by the G9 infection."

"I thought so. I could not speak clearly when trying to tell Ruby about the Ritual," Gabe said slowly. "Could it have caused me to act against my own will?"

Donna-gran nodded. "Coupled with the administration of the right psychotropics, yes."

"And the Ritual will free us?" he asked.

"Yes. The two of you will be able to briefly compel others that have been programmed. Ruby will have more influence since she wears the ring, but that is for her own protection. Ruby. You need to rub the ring before issuing commands. Remember that."

"I will," she said.

"All right." Donna-gran took a deep breath. "Normally, the

Family head would conduct the Ritual as part of his designation of the Martiniere-in-waiting. That can't happen now. So I will stand in for him as the Matriarch. I will put the emeralds, except for the ring, on Ruby before the wedding ceremony." She wheeled to the center of the room. "Afterwards we will immediately come back to this room. I will be here. Gabriel and Ruby, you will kneel, and put your hands on my knees." She pointed to the floor in front of her. "I will place my hands on your heads. The other Family heads and members present will place their hands on you. Then I will speak the words of the Ritual. That will bind all the families who have leaders present. For the others—Ruby and either Gabriel or Brandon must go with her to them and gain their support. Not only will going through the Ritual give you control, but it will hopefully help reunite the family."

"That's different from the Ritual I was told," Justine said.

"That is because the original Ritual has been corrupted and the Family with it," Donna-gran said. She gave each of them a measured, steady gaze. "Things must change within the Family. Success is not guaranteed—but if change is to happen, it is through all of you here that it will occur." She sighed and stretched. "And now, dear ones, it has been a long day. Gabriel, at one point you said something about a nice local wine?"

"I did, Donna-gran."

"Then let us return to that delightful deck and imbibe."

"I'm ready for that," Justine said.

RUBY RELAXED IN THE STRAIGHT-BACKED CHAIR IN THEIR ROOM while Gabe unpinned her hair and brushed it gently. It had been one of their rituals when first married. She hadn't realized until now how much she had missed it during their years apart.

"Are you ready for tomorrow?" Gabe asked, leaning forward to kiss her cheek. "You've been awfully quiet."

"I—guess. I've been thinking about what Donna-gran said after the scan with the ring."

"About the influencing?"

"Yes."

"I have as well." He came around and took her hands, gently raising her. "And I am thoroughly happy that it will end."

"So am I."

But even as Gabe took Ruby in his arms, something nagged at her. A feeling of doom—or threat—or warning—that she couldn't quite put into words, but nonetheless felt very real.

She hoped everything would run smoothly tomorrow.

CHAPTER 15

Ruby took a deep breath as Brandon rolled Donna-gran out of Justine's room to take her place amongst the guests. She looked at herself in the mirror, almost not recognizing the woman looking back at her. The sea-green dress with gold trim fit her torso snugly, falling away from her hips in a full-skirted elegant flow to the floor, and the shade complemented the deeper green of the emeralds. Her nails had been redone with the Martiniere trefoil in green and gold. Her hair once again was up in the French twist with ringlets, the locket tucked away amongst the strands of hair. A pale gold shoulder-length veil finished the combination.

This is it.

"All right," Justine murmured. "It's time to line up." She and Kris wore simple floor-length green sheath dresses with golden highlights. Kris went first, then Justine. Then Ruby stepped out. Charlie and Martin stood waiting for her beside the door, both looking awkward in their black tuxedos. They took her arms.

The music started and Kris processed out, taking Serg's arm.

A few more beats. Then Justine left, walking down the aisle with Brandon.

Ruby's breaths came quick and fast.

No different from a run in, she told herself.

"Nervous? I sure am," Charlie said.

"It's worse than our own wedding," Martin added. "Don't know why."

"Bigger ceremony," Ruby said.

"I guess that's it."

But the three of them knew better. This was a huge change in all their lives.

Ruby exhaled as the music swelled. *It's time.* They stepped out. As they turned to walk down the aisle of now standing attendees, Ruby focused on Gabe. His face was tight and drawn, but suddenly relaxed as he saw her, a smile spreading his lips as their eyes locked onto each other. Her heart pounded and she clutched onto Charlie and Martin as they walked toward Gabe.

It hadn't been like this last time. She'd been happy, yes, but a different sort of joy, leaning on Gramps's arm as he glowered at Gabe, disapproving of this match, somehow aware of the secrets lurking underneath. Then, committing to Gabe had felt like freedom from the shadows of her childhood. Now she knew it meant a greater responsibility—but not alone, never alone now.

First Martin, then Charlie, kissed her on the cheek before she took Gabe's arm. As they stepped up to face the priest, she couldn't look away from Gabe's dark brown eyes and the glow on his face, unmuffled by worry. The shadow of the Martinieres had lain unspoken between them before. Not so now, with the Martiniere emeralds around her neck and in her ears—and soon on her hand.

No more secrets between us.

Was it as simple as that?

She recited her vows in a daze, not fuzzed by a hangover but by growing joy, held rapt by the matching intensity in Gabe's eyes.

The emerald ring tingled as Gabe put it on her finger and said his vows. His hands visibly trembled as he lifted the veil over her head, but steadied as he placed his hands on her waist and kissed her.

"It's real," he whispered, wonder in his voice as he pulled back. "It's really happened. I love you, Ruby, more than I can ever say."

"I love you too," she whispered back. "Don't you dare decide to leave me again."

"I know better. And my sister and grandmother will be first in line to kick my ass if I do." He kissed her again and they turned to process down the aisle.

It was then she saw Philip glowering at them from the front row, Donna-gran at his side and pointedly turned away from him. Mariah and Georgy sat on his other side, Georgy also scowling at them while Mariah's lips pressed tightly together.

No wonder Gabe looked so tense until he saw me.

She looked away from the trio, and deliberately pulled Gabe into another embrace, kissing him long and hard as the crowd whooped, especially on the bride's side of the aisle.

"Atta girl, Ruby!" one of her friends—Remy, she thought— hollered from the bride's side. "You need us to get you a piggin' string to tie him down good so he doesn't get away again?"

Gabe barely stifled a chuckle against her lips. "Now *that* I remember from our first wedding," he said. "How many of our rodeo friends are here?"

"Only a few," she whispered, and pulled him in for a third kiss. "But just enough to start a brawl if those three pains in the ass sitting next to Donna-gran cause problems. Just need to get the boys and girls more liquored up."

"Dear God, let's hope those three don't decide to be diffi- cult," he answered, straightening up. "Though I'm damn sure our old buddies could still kick their asses."

Then they swept down the aisle in big strides, arms around each other's waists instead of decorously arm-in-arm, more whoops and hollers cheering them on. Ruby was happy to see two guards on each side of the hallway entrance as they hurried back to the game room.

Would that be enough to keep Philip out? She wasn't certain.

Brandon and Justine, then Serg and Kris joined them. Raised voices at the entrance behind them made both Brandon and Serg turn.

"Philip's giving Donna-gran a hard time about the Ritual," Serg said. "Bran, we'd better go help."

Brandon nodded and they left. Gabe moved to join them but Ruby held him back.

"Not your job today," she said in a low voice. "Let them do it, hon."

He sighed, but relaxed. "You're right. Probably best I don't. It could get nastier if I do."

Brandon and Serg returned with Donna-gran, followed by Ken and Paul, each with a woman that Ruby hadn't met yet. Donald Atwood crossed the room to stand with Justine, then Artie and the older man who resembled Serg, pushing another woman in a wheelchair. The doors closed behind them.

"Your guards are set," the man who resembled Serg said.

"And Philip?" Gabe asked, nostrils flaring wide.

"I told him he had no place in the Ritual," Brandon said firmly. "It didn't go over well."

The man who resembled Serg shrugged. "You did a very good job of handling him, Brandon." He glanced at Gabe. "Arthur and I did lend a little bit of support. He is not leaving yet, just because I would like to *enjoy* this part of the ceremony without worrying about him getting notions. Some of your friends were quite enthusiastic about dragging Philip off to have a drink when I suggested it." His mouth quirked. "I believe the woman whooping about—a piggin' string, was it, whatever *that* is?—was foremost amongst them. I heard more talk of that, plus hobbles."

Ruby rolled her eyes as Gabe groaned. "Ruby, I think Remy and the boys and girls have already gotten sufficiently liquored up if they're daring to take hold of Philip. Piotr, a piggin' string is a short rope used by ropers to tie cattle feet together."

"If Remy's in charge, there's less alcohol involved than you think," Ruby said. "And I'm betting that Vickie and Mike are in the same condition as she is, playing up being boozed while being sober. There's enough of the Thunder Home Guard out there that I don't think we need to worry. Don't kid yourself, Remy knows who she's dealing with. Nothing too serious should happen unless he overreacts."

"Oh God." Now Gabe rolled his eyes. "But on the other hand, it might just do the trick to neutralize Philip for now." He shook his head.

"I'm sure that Philip is in good hands," Donna-gran said. "I believe I met a few of your friends before the ceremony. I'm certain that things will go appropriately. Philip may be an ass but he's not a complete fool. Now. Introductions.

Piotr bowed to Ruby. "Piotr Vygotsky, Sergei's father. It is a pleasure to meet you, Ruby."

Artie beamed, gazing down at the woman in the wheelchair who looked up at him. "This is my beloved Nora, who unfortunately cannot speak for herself. Nora, this is Gabie's wife, Ruby."

"Annette," the silver-haired woman with Ken said.

"Marie." Paul's wife curtseyed to Ruby.

They turned to Kris and Brandon.

"Kris," she said tentatively. "And Brandon and I are—" she hesitated.

"We're partners," Brandon said firmly.

"All right," Donna-gran said. "We are all here. Let the Ritual begin. Gabriel and Ruby."

They knelt in front of Donna-gran and she rested her hands on their heads. Then she called the others in, two at a time, to kneel and place a hand on either Ruby or Gabe's shoulders.

Donna-gran's hand lifted from Ruby's head for a moment and she felt a soft tap on her ring. Then the hand returned.

"By the ceremony conducted today, and as the Martiniere

Matriarch, I witness that Gabriel Marcus Martiniere and Ruby Marie Barkley, husband and wife, now stand as the Martiniere and his wife."

Gabe startled. Ruby felt a similar reaction from those whose hands were on her shoulder.

"I, Donna Martiniere, Matriarch and wife of Louis Martiniere, declare that my son Philip has violated the Martiniere Code. Philip has broken faith with the fundamental precepts of the Family. Philip has violated agreements with his brother Saul Martiniere. Philip brought about the deaths of Saul, his wife Angelica, and their daughter Louisa. Philip has tarnished the honor of the Martinieres and is no longer worthy of being called the Martiniere and representing the Family. So do I swear, on my oath as Louis Martiniere's wife and as the current Martiniere Matriarch." She paused. "Do all present swear and declare that what I say is true and right?"

"So do we swear," everyone murmured, Ruby a breath behind them.

"Gabriel Marcus Martiniere is the son of Philip Joseph Martiniere and Angelica Alicia Catherine Ramirez Martiniere, per a signed agreement between Philip and Saul that their wives would bear their brother's first sons via in-vitro fertilization, to stop a war between them. Do all present swear and declare that what I say is true and right?"

"So do we swear." This time Ruby knew what to say for certain.

"Brandon Edward Martiniere is the son of Gabriel Marcus Martiniere and Ruby Marie Barkley, and is now the Martiniere-in-waiting. Do all present swear and declare that what I say is true and right?"

Once more they swore.

"Gabriel Marcus Martiniere. Do you as the Martiniere swear to uphold the honor of the Martinieres, placing it above your own honor and well-being?"

"I do," Gabe said. Ruby felt his body tremble slightly as he pressed into her.

"Ruby Marie Barkley. I pass the honor and the responsibilities of being the Matriarch of the Martinieres into your capable hands. Do you as Gabriel's wife, and the Matriarch of the Martinieres, swear to uphold the honor of the Martinieres, placing it above your own honor and well-being?"

Ruby's voice quavered as she said, "I do."

"Then rise and accept the oaths of your family."

Gabe leaned on Ruby for support as the hands withdrew and they rose. Ruby saw that the gold projection hovered above her ring. *Recording?*

Donna-gran took their hands, bent her forehead to touch them, then raised her head. "I swear to honor and support you as leaders of the Martinieres." Then she rolled away.

Brandon was next, Kris at his side, kneeling together and reciting the oath before rising to stand with Ruby and Gabe. Then Justine and Donald. Serg and Piotr. Artie and Nora. Ken and Annette. Paul and Marie.

Gabe chuckled nervously when they were done. "Donna-gran, this was *not* what I expected."

"Alas, these oaths do not yet hold within the Family's official business structures, Gabriel," she said sharply. "This is the simple part. You still have to win control of the business. But it is time for you to stand forth as the true Family leader, and be acknowledged as such. It will take much work to wrest the Martiniere Group and the Family away from what Philip has done to it. I am confident that you, your wife, and your son will do so."

"Thank you, Donna-gran." Gabe looked around. "And thank all of you, for your faith in me and in Ruby." He took her hand and kissed it. "I can't change things without your help. But I vow to all of you that Brandon and I *will* once again make the name of Martiniere an honor, with the help of Ruby and Kris." He took a deep breath. "I did not expect to be pronounced the Martiniere until I actually had control of the Group. But I thank you once again for your witness." He exhaled deeply. "And now, let's go celebrate." His hand slid around Ruby's waist. "I am a lucky and blessed man."

The others milled around them for a moment, murmuring good wishes. Then Gabe took Ruby's hand.

"Let's lead everyone out," he said softly.

The guards stood aside as Gabe and Ruby marched into the great room. Immediately they were swarmed as friends and those family members not included in the Ritual came forward for their moments with them.

Then it was time to cut the wedding cake. The table holding the cake replaced the podium where the ceremony had taken place, in front of the great wall of windows at sunset. Despite his impish grin, Gabe delicately held his piece for Ruby to nibble, and she did the same for him, remembering how they'd smeared cake on each other's faces the first time. A quick toast, and then they circulated amongst the guests, arms still around each other's waists.

Philip finally evaded the polite but firm captivity of Remy, Vickie Chandler, and Carol Reed and stalked toward Ruby and Gabe. Remy and Vickie trailed in pursuit, but Philip was quicker. He crossed his arms and glared at Ruby, looking her up and down, staring at her faintly glowing ring. Then he studied Gabe.

"So she did it," he snapped finally. "But remember. Control of the Family is not control of the Group, you worth—"

Ruby rubbed her thumb across the emerald in her ring. "Stop it," she growled, like she would to a misbehaving horse, pointing her left index finger at Philip as the ring flared green.

Philip's eyes widened as his mouth slammed shut. He tried to work his jaw, then stepped back, raising a shaking hand to point at the two of them in return, backing into Remy and Vickie before they could move out of his way.

"This isn't over by any stretch of the imagination," he finally was able to say. "Just you wait!" And with that he spun and marched out.

Remy's eyes widened. "Ruby, what on earth was that?"

"Martiniere business," Gabe said, taking Ruby's hand and squeezing it. "Best not to ask—but let's just say that Ruby does not lack for defenses." He kissed her hand as someone clapped behind them.

"Marvelous," Donna-gran said. "Ruby, who are these two lovely ladies who would have mugged Philip if you hadn't shut him up?"

"Oh dear," Gabe said, shaking his head and stepping aside. "*Oh dear.* Donna-gran encounters the rodeo queens. I need another fucking drink. Now." He kissed Ruby. "I will return."

"You'd better bring me back a glass of champagne!" she called after him.

He turned and saluted her. "I hear and obey. But I'm gonna get some *decent* dance music going as well. Enough of this drama."

"Gabriel. Get drinks for *all* of us," Donna-gran ordered.

Gabe rolled his eyes and headed for the bar that had been set up near the deck.

Ruby smiled at Donna-gran. "Donna-gran, these are two of my oldest friends. Vickie Chandler, my neighbor and mentor who guided me through my rodeo queen campaigns, and who is a former Thunder County Days queen herself. Remy Trask, who was a princess in my Thunder County Days court when I was a queen—"

"*And* your attorney," Remy broke in.

"And my attorney—Remy, just how much have you had to drink already?" It wasn't like Remy to bring that connection up at social occasions.

"Not enough," Remy said. "Not enough to stop shaking now that it's over, because I've been bossing *Philip fucking Martiniere* around—which will make my old boss shit bricks—but then I see you stopping him in his tracks."

Donna-gran laughed. "The Remington Trask who was the assistant prosecutor in *United States vs. Martiniere Group*?"

Remy's eyes widened. "Um, yes, ma'am, nothing personal, I hope?"

"Not at all, my dear. I am Donna Martiniere, confidential informant—oh, I'm not sure what number I was. We spoke a few times on the phone, but were never able to meet personally due to my cardiac surgery."

Remy's hands flew to her mouth. "Oh my God. You're *her*. Louis's wife. I—ma'am, I'm so sorry we couldn't have done more. I am so, so, sorry."

"That's quite all right, my dear." Donna-gran reached for a glass as Gabe returned with a tray. "And I am so very pleased that you are a long-term friend of Ruby's. Both of you. Gabriel, did you know that Ms. Trask was the lead assistant prosecutor in the criminal case we *both* testified in?"

It was fortunate that they all held their glasses except for Gabe. Ruby snatched his as he fumbled the tray.

"*You* testified too, Donna-gran?" He picked up the tray and took his glass from Ruby.

"Of course. It didn't go beyond being a confidential informant, alas, as cardiac issues kept me from testifying at trial. But Ms. Trask was quite charming and helpful."

"I never worked with her," Gabe said. "Only her subordinates." He stared at Remy.

"One of my greatest regrets was that I was not able to participate further," Donna-gran continued. "Another was that if I had not been ill, I would have known more about what was going on, and would have offered you refuge. I regret that."

Gabe shook himself. "That's all right, Donna-gran." His eyes met Ruby's and he raised his glass. "If I had not gone into witness protection, and become Gabe Ramirez, saddle bronc rider and ranch hand, I wouldn't have met Ruby. And my life would have been greatly diminished by that."

"Hear, hear," Remy said hoarsely.

Brandon and Kris, followed by Justine and Donald, stopped by. "Mom. Dad. Congratulations." He kissed Ruby on the cheek. "Ma. We love you. You take care of Dad. And Dad." He fixed Gabe with a steady gaze. "Don't you ever, *ever* make her regret this. Or I will kick your ass, and you know I can do it."

Gabe snorted. "As if I could keep up with you, kid. Don't worry. I know what's best for me."

"We're headed for LA," Brandon continued. "Justine and Donald are with us."

"We'll be in touch," Gabe said.

Justine and Donald said their goodbyes.

"What is holding up the music?" Gabe growled. He drained his glass and marched away as Ruby finished hers, listening to Remy and Vickie explain what it took to win a rodeo queen title to Donna-gran.

Then Gabe took Ruby's hand as the opening chords of "Time of the Preacher" rang out from the speakers. As Willie Nelson started singing, he swept her into his arms and they began to dance.

"May not be the most auspicious song, but...it's a lovely waltz. I took enough meds that I can dance most of the night. Pay for it in the morning but I don't care. And for some reason I feel like dancing to Willie tonight, and to hell with what anyone else thinks. It's *our* party and I won't change it unless you object."

"There's just one thing that would make it better," Ruby said as Gabe deftly spun her before they eased back into their waltz.

"What's that?"

"I dance a hell of a lot better in my boots."

He laughed. "I'm sure that can be arranged, my dear."

At some point during the evening, she *did* get both boots and hat on. The raucous chorus from friends and family rose to levels that both of them remembered from their previous wedding.

But they kept dancing. And Willie Nelson was still playing on a continuous loop when it was just the two of them alone on the deck near midnight, swaying to "Blue Eyes Crying in The Rain" under the illumination of the full moon.

"So this is why you called this place Moondance," she said.

"Exactly." He kissed her.

It was almost perfect.

Too almost perfect to be trusted.

CHAPTER 16

THEY WERE BACK TO PRACTICALITY IN THE MORNING, RUSHING around Moondance and preparing to go to LA to back up Brandon and Kris. At the same time they needed to balance seeing Donna-gran off without too much of a fuss.

"Come see me soon," Donna-gran said to Ruby before she got onto her plane. "You still need to learn about the intricacies of manipulating that ring. You have the voice to match its capabilities, but it takes practice to be adept. I'm thinking you'll need that ability before all is said and done. Gabriel, you know where I live. It hasn't changed. Bring her to me."

"I will," Ruby promised.

"I'll make sure she does," Gabe added.

They watched her plane leave, then got on their own plane.

Brandon called shortly after their takeoff. "We need backup, just like you thought, Dad," he said ruefully, running his fingers through his hair. "Mom, Justine thinks that you might be able to manipulate the body-modded indentureds in case we run into trouble. Donna-gran's sent her enough data to suggest that there may be a back door into their command structure programming using the ring."

Gabe shot her an *I told you so look* before he spoke. "We're on our way already, figuring such was the case. Arrival in two hours."

Relief crossed Brandon's face. "I hate to impose on you two so soon after the wedding, but—"

"We expected that this would be necessary," Ruby said. "We'd planned to be there. Don't worry about it, Branny."

"Thanks." He relaxed. "Everything go all right after we left?"

"Once Philip left it became quite the party. I think one of the highlights was Remy and Shannon line dancing with Donna-gran in her wheelchair," Ruby said. She grinned at Gabe. "I think Donna-gran left with one of my straw hats. Or was it yours, hon?"

"Did you get a picture of Donna-gran in a cowboy hat?" Brandon asked.

"You know, I have no idea," Ruby said. "I was thinking about other things."

"Darn. Well, we'll see you when you get here." Brandon signed off.

Gabe sighed. "Two more hours of peace. I'm going to lie down. Join me?"

"Of course." She followed him back to the bedroom area and they snuggled together in the bed. She drowsed, the memory of dancing with Gabe on the deck in the moonlight dominating her thoughts.

No matter what happened next, they had that moment.

THEY ENDED UP AT A BIGGER HOUSE DOWN THE STREET FROM WHERE they had met Jeff Swait at the end of the Superhero, in a heavily guarded gated complex. To Ruby's surprise, Piotr and Artie were also there, poring over separate sets of schematics while Donald moved back and forth, peering over their shoulders and asking questions.

"I see you've called in more help," Gabe said to Brandon.

He shrugged. "Donna-gran recommended I bring them in. When you take a look at what we're facing you'll see why. Artie. Piotr. Are we at the point where we have something to show Mom and Dad?"

"It's complicated," Donald said, straightening up. "And much more complex than I had expected. But I think I have enough of a grip on the schematics—or *will have*, by tonight—to safely print out indentured tattoo overlays for our ladies."

"Just the women going in?" Gabe asked.

Brandon eyed Gabe. "We *might* be able to get one of you older guys in with them, which was another reason we called you and Mom in. But that's it. It's a complex with women and desexed older men only. Younger men draw attention that we don't want. I can't do it. They have my DNA on record."

"It is organized like the old Martiniere body-mod shops from the map scans Kris got us," Piotr said. "Whoever goes in with the women will need to be wearing tattoo overlays as well."

"I want to do it," Gabe said.

"Good. You're the one who makes sense, Gabriel," Artie said. "You and Ruby don't have control words programmed into you anymore, and the two of you can support each other should we need to shut down cyborged body-modded warriors."

"They've gotten that far?"

"Not full cyborgs yet. But suits and chip implants that have that same effect." Piotr snapped his fingers and brought up a projection. Ruby shuddered. The person—if it could be called that—was gray and androgynous. Its head was bald and oddly bumpy—or was that a head covering? She looked closer. It appeared that the person wore a form-fitting body suit that covered it from head to toe. The only openings she could see were at eyes, nose, and mouth.

Gabe winced. "Put some hair and clothes on it and it could be one of my kidnappers." He studied the projection. "Is this a new generation armor suit? Whenever I had contact with them it felt like plaskin, not flesh."

"It's part of the body mod, Dad," Brandon said. "Nanosuit that links into a control chip implanted here." He tapped the base of the projection's skull. "It would feel like plaskin when you touch it. Everything operates from the chip. Disable it and you've got a minute to neutralize the suit before it kills the wearer by suffocation, and you *can't* breach it. As far as we know right now."

Gabe circled the projection warily. "Does that go for any form of disabling? Any control or codes that won't trigger suffocation?"

"There is a shutdown code, but it is very specific. No overrides," Brandon said. "Mom *might* have the ability to override using her words and the ring, but I'm not certain."

"In other words, if something happens to disable the wearer while the suit is active, then they're screwed."

"They're pawns. The suit augments physical reflexes and stamina, and is programmed for its wearer to perform specific tasks, from war to…um, sexual activity," Artie said, peering at Gabe over his glasses. "I recognize the design. It is one of our old ones that I worked on years ago. At some point they either need to desuit to rest and refuel, or collapse and die. It turns humans into programmable machines. The kind of suit each subject wears is tied to the codes implanted in their tattoos."

"How do we stop them?" Ruby asked. She leaned forward to study the stats on Artie's screen. "Not my area of expertise, but those numbers make me think that those things have a high energy demand."

"And that's what saves our behinds when it comes to Philip's potential use of these indentured as a personal army," Artie said. "You're correct. The suit burns a lot of its wearers' energy. We currently estimate an operating time of ninety minutes, at best. That's why my division discarded their use for indentured workers in agricultural spray operations. The best working time we could achieve was half an hour, with three hours down time between wearings."

"And you need the implant to operate the suit?" Gabe asked.

"As far as we know, yes," Artie said.

Ruby shook her head. "How on earth would anyone agree to that? Even when indentured? Or are these only used on lifetime contracts?" She shivered.

"It's usually lifetime contracts," Kris said, coming in from the neighboring dining room. "Once you are an indentured, you're usually put through indoctrination and behavior patterning, aided by specific medications that make you more amenable to whatever your masters suggest. Such treatments tend to reduce resistance to things like these implants. What you don't hear about is the high suicide rate amongst indentureds before final implant."

She walked to the middle of the room and unwrapped the scarf she had been wearing ever since her treatment in Chicago. A fresh scar ran across the back of her neck. "This is part of the work done on me in Chicago a few days ago. Removal of the dock for a control chip. You go along with the implant process, because if you don't things become—much worse."

"So they're under mind control," Gabe said.

"Not entirely. Until a control chip is implanted and activated —which I never received because it was scheduled for after the Superhero competition—the person has some degree of free will. Fifty percent of the implantees suicide before control chip activation due to hormonal disregulation." Kris shuddered. "I learned that last week. Suspected but only now documented. Until the control chip is activated, there are ways to work around it—Pat has stayed on top of them for some time now."

"But they've moved toward putting Pat in a suit," Brandon said. "Her final fitting and activation will be tomorrow morning. She has the control chip implanted already, but not activated. Our opening to rescue her happens when they move her from quarters to the lab."

"Pretty tight window then," Gabe said.

Brandon nodded. "We'll go over the plan later. Mom. You

and Kris and Justine need to rehearse. Otherwise you'll attract attention. Dad. We can pass you as a guard—you're exactly the sort of person that they tend to recruit for these positions working around the research indentureds. What's going to take the most time is practicing your roles. So…let's spend some time doing that, and by then we should have the rest of the data we need to identify specific control channels and codes. We're almost there."

IT WAS SCARY HOW QUICKLY SHE PICKED UP ON SOME OF THE TYPICAL behaviors of a female indentured. Ruby could mimic the submissive, slumped-shoulder posture with her eyes on the ground. But what was hardest was changing her typical big-striding walk to the small mincing steps that Kris drilled into her. At last Kris pronounced it good and they rejoined the men.

"All right," Brandon said, running his hands through his hair nervously. "We have a rough plan. Tell us what flaws you see. Pat's scheduled to go into the final fitting at 7:30 am. We drop Dad, Mom, Justine, and Kris near the compound at seven, and park close to the back exit—Piotr, Serg, and I—"

"And me," Donald added.

"And Don," Brandon nodded to him. "Sorry. The four of us take up a station there. I have staggered security backup moving into the area starting at seven as well. Dad leads the other three into the front gate—you'll be transfers of new indentureds coming in from a residential screening facility two blocks away. It's routine for these transfers to happen around the clock. You'll be going into a converted movie studio lot. It's big. It will take you just about that half hour to get in place outside of the lab. You'll be carrying a couple of alert buttons and we'll wire all four of you with specific links to each one of us so we can talk in an emergency. Red button means you're in trouble. Blue button means that you've got Pat and you're ready to go. At that point

Pat should be able to open the back door to let you out. If not, Mom should be able to command one of the guards to do it."

"Just how are we getting Pat away from her guards?" Ruby asked. "And how am I commanding them?"

"I have the codes from Donald," Piotr said. "You and I will be linked. The assignments are me and Ruby, Gabriel and Sergei, Justine and Donald, and Kris and Brandon."

"Wouldn't it make more sense for Don and Ruby to be linked?" Justine said. "I appreciate the thought of pairing me with him, Piotr, but if Donald has the codes and Ruby runs into a challenge, aren't we inserting an extra step that could complicate matters?"

"Six of one and half a dozen of the other, my dear falcon," Donald said. "It's better to have someone who knows the old security protocols talking to Ruby. Near as we can figure, they've been pulling up old tech. Serg and Piotr *need* to be the ones connected to Ruby and Gabe. They know the security routines better than me or Bran."

"And what happens if we run into problems before we reach our places?" Ruby asked.

"Try to avoid problems," Brandon said. "Minor ones—you all have credentials, and we have body-mod fakes that will cover your hands and arms, including the tats, that can pass the sort of casual scans you might encounter. No one will expect you to be wearing the full suits, and we've got chipsim overlays that look like early stage chip implants. You'll all be wearing the doubled AgI/Martiniere Group tat sims."

"What if we run into major issues?"

Gabe's eyes met hers, stark and cold. "Then we're fucked."

THEY DIDN'T SLEEP WELL. THE AIR CONDITIONING WAS ALTERNATELY too cold or too hot. If Gabe didn't wake from a nightmare, then Ruby did. At last they settled into spooning naked together, back to front, Ruby in Gabe's arms, her hands entwined with his and holding them tight to her chest as he wrapped his legs around hers. That bought them a few hours of restless, fitful sleep.

At last Ruby had one last waking that she knew was it. She lay there quietly, not wanting to wake Gabe.

His breathing changed and he started to extract himself from her.

"What's up?" she asked.

He patted her gently. "Ten minutes to alarm. I'm getting up. You rest."

She turned to face him. "I can't."

"Neither can I." He pulled her close and they lay there, breathing quietly together, not wanting to speak.

At last the alarm buzzed. Gabe snapped it off. Then he took Ruby's face in his hands and kissed her.

"No matter what happens today, just remember that I love you. You've always been first in my heart. Always."

"You've been it for me," she whispered back. "Never anyone else."

He half-smiled and leaned his forehead against hers. Then, with a sigh, he pulled away.

They helped each other don their respective body mods, including facial mods. Gabe shivered when she applied the Martiniere fake tattoo to the back of his neck. She trembled when he did the same to her.

That done, they both pulled on the gray fatigues common amongst indentureds. Gabe's hands quivered slightly as he secured her lucky locket in her hair, then pulled the skullcap over her head.

I hope that's not post-G9 rearing its ugly head.

"You going to be able to hold up?" she asked him.

He nodded. "Max dose of Activate, half dose of Modulate. I took half of Activate and a quarter of Modulate yesterday so I could dance the night away with you. I'll have one hell of a crash after twelve hours—but if we're not clear by then...." His voice trailed away, a grim expression tightening his face. Ruby nodded, understanding, remembering his words from earlier.

Then we're fucked.

They held hands as they rejoined the others. Next came attaching the covert coms. Piotr deftly attached the receiver under the skullcap behind Ruby's right ear and secured the transmitter.

"Let's step outside to test," he said.

The east wind blew warmer than she expected in the sandy walled garden, even more so than at home. Alien prickly foliage surrounded them, date palm trees and a huge jade plant by the house, as well as several different varieties of what she thought might be yucca and cacti.

Piotr walked several yards away and Ruby turned her back so she wouldn't anticipate him speaking.

"Hear me?" His voice crackled in her ear and she winced.

"Loud and clear. Almost too loud."

A moment, and then, "That better?"

"Perfect."

They went back inside. Brandon passed out ration bars for a quick breakfast, and they processed out to a waiting van.

This is it.

As she slipped her hand into Gabe's, he glanced at her and smiled. She noticed that Brandon and Kris leaned into each other as well. No one spoke as Donald started the van and drove. Gabe's thumb traced the Martiniere trefoil into her palm over and over. At last they stopped.

"Remember. Walk slowly and carefully," Kris said. "Ruby. Let's put you in line between me and Justine. That'll help with pacing."

They eyed each other, and then Gabe sighed. He slipped out the back, looking around.

"All clear," he said quietly into the van. Kris was the next one in line. Ruby took a deep breath and followed her, aware of Justine's presence behind her. The van drove off and left them standing there. She felt exposed, even though they were on the edge of what looked to be a business district.

"Line up!" Gabe said sharply. "Good God, what a batch of newbies you three are." He marched down their line, straightening Kris, pushing Ruby in line, and doing something to Justine that earned a grunt. As he walked past them he shook his head, projecting his voice louder again. "I don't know what we're going to do with this pathetic bunch! All right, come on. They'll put you right."

Ruby focused on Kris's shoulders as they walked, doing her best to match her stride to Kris's shuffle. All too soon they stopped at a gate and kiosk. Gabe marched back down their line.

"Eyes down! Hands folded! Good grief, your lot is pathetic. I don't know where AgI is getting you from, but this is *sad.*"

"Hey!" An unfamiliar voice. "What's this? Who's this and what's going on? I don't have you on my list."

"*Rub the ring and whisper special authorized shipment,*" Piotr's voice whispered.

God, she hoped the ring would work through the body mod. But Artie seemed to think it would and he appeared to be the expert, so…she obeyed.

"It's a special authorized shipment," Gabe said. "On their way to the lab."

"Special authorized shipment?" The edge in the guard's voice softened. "Oh crap, I wasn't expecting one of those this early today."

"Yeah, it's a real pain in the ass," Gabe growled. "But these are some of the Boss's super special problem girls who've been resisting indoctrination—hey! Straighten up!" he snapped back at them.

The guard sniggered. "Look like real specials all right. Though that first one appears to be kinda tasty."

"Uh-uh-uh. They're all the Boss's Specials." She could *hear* the capitals in Gabe's voice. "No touching. Me, I think they're all pains, but he's got plans. If we can ever get 'em past indoc-trination."

"Well, maybe we'll get a taste of 'em later if this batch flunks out," the guard said. "Been washing out a lot of them lately."

Gabe snorted. "Not these girls. They're all coded ZP24. Highest level. If they flunk programming, they have their other uses."

"Dang. I can dream, can't I?"

"I wouldn't let the Big Boss hear you. Come on, then," Gabe said to them. They followed him inside, the gate slamming shut behind them with a heavy clang as they marched down a single-lane roadway.

As they walked, Ruby glanced from side to side as much as she dared. Not many people were moving around yet, and the ones she saw were all in the gray suits. None looked at Gabe and his procession, facing straight ahead, moving stiffly as if they were robots come to life from an old science fiction movie.

She caught a glimpse of a cafeteria, figures sitting listlessly at tables.

Screams. A naked, pale-skinned woman with a shaved head bolted out of the building on the other side of the cafeteria.

"Help me!" she shrieked. "Help me help me help me!" She grabbed at Kris, who pushed her roughly away.

The woman grabbed at Ruby's head. Ruby ducked away and fell to the pavement, stomach churning at the terrified expres-sion on the woman's face. The woman ran in the direction they'd come from, screeching even louder than before as armed people in the gray suits descended on her. Ruby stared in shock as one shot the woman.

"And that's going to be your fate if you don't get off your ass and get moving," Gabe snarled.

Kris and Justine helped Ruby up even as Gabe glowered at her, hands on his hips.

"You three! ZP24 status isn't going to help you one bit if you don't shape up! Now get in line! You're going to be late, and," his voice dropped to a quiet and poisonous tone. "The Boss doesn't like that."

They fell back into line.

A buzzer blared and suddenly there were a lot more indentureds milling around them, some moving stiff and mechanically, others more naturally.

But not a one of them spoke. No one looked up from the roadway. The only sound was the shuffle of many feet on the pavement and the slamming of doors as people went into buildings. No words. No song. Only the endless shuffling of feet and doors banging. No natural sounds, either. No birds. She'd give anything even to hear a starling's obnoxious whistle.

Then voices. Her gut tightened as she recognized Joseph speaking.

"I tell you, they're up to something! After yesterday—"

"*As he goes by, step back and bow low,*" Piotr hissed.

"Damn it, I *know* you can spare Alexander from the brothers at least. What do you mean he's on a high priority project? Aren't I high enough in priority myself? Damn it, Dad, are you just cutting me loose for some stupid fucking reason? You think that hick hayseed bitch of Gabe's has that much power? God damn it, you used me to A.I. them. As their biological father I should have some rights to them."

She knew when to move as Kris wheeled to face the center of the roadway and bowed. Ruby mimicked her, watching Kris and Justine for behavior cues as best as she could.

"Then give me Daniel or Eric if you won't send Alexander. What? Not even them? What *is* your precious project, anyway? I helped make them. I should have priority on their use. Come on, Dad!"

Joseph stomped by, glowering straight ahead and gesturing as he spoke to Philip. Ruby held position until she saw Kris straighten up.

"*Warning from Gabe,*" Piotr said. "*Nearly to the lab and extra security ahead.*"

She grunted acknowledgment. They veered off of the main roadway into an alley and behind a generator. Gabe gestured for them to gather round.

"All right. Our data shows this as a blind spot. Building behind us is where they're keeping Pat."

"Okay," Justine said. "Kris and I will go out first, separately. Kris, garbage pickup or weeding?"

"Garbage," Kris said. "Joseph's on site. We don't want to test your facial mods to a closer scrutiny, should he come back this direction."

Justine nodded. "We'll give you two a high sign through your controllers when we see Pat come out. You're best behind the generator."

"Good luck," Ruby whispered.

Justine nodded, her lips pressed tightly together. Gabe bowed sharply to them.

"Stay safe," he breathed.

Kris tapped on the side of the generator to open a hidden compartment. She pulled out an odd-shaped mechanical garbage picker and bag, and gave a case that looked suspiciously like the one for the SPA7 to Justine. As Justine popped it open and pulled out several pieces that only nominally resembled gardening tools, Kris retrieved a couple of pistols and handed them to Gabe and Ruby. Then she tucked the case back into the enclosure and tapped it shut, the edges of the door seamlessly melding into the generator housing.

She left first, then Justine. Gabe and Ruby squatted behind the generator, weapons in hand, waiting.

"*Time to move,*" Piotr said at last. "*Slowly. Act when Kris does. Any gray suit acting like an authority or opposes you is mindwiped. Shoot them. Nothing else you can do.*"

She and Gabe exchanged glances. She held the pistol along her leg as they straightened up and moved toward the alley's opening. At least now she could look up and around, be her usual self. Kris shuffled around the door of the building across the roadway, while Justine knelt in the shrubbery next to the stairway of the building on their left.

The door to that building banged open. Six people in gray suits wrestled a dark-skinned woman in blue scrubs out of the doorway. She yanked and pulled against their restraint, wailing and screaming.

"Hey you! Over by the lab! Get away from the door!" one of the gray suits bellowed.

Kris straightened up, her garbage picker now configured as a SPA7. She shot the one who yelled at her before they could react. Justine rose and shot the gray suit close to her. Ruby and Gabe charged up the steps. One guard jumped off the steps and started running, shouting for help. Ruby shot it. Gabe clubbed another that grabbed her and then shot it. Then Kris was embracing the woman—Pat—and the gray suited guards were on the ground.

"Come on!" Pat yelled, dragging Kris as they ran down the roadway. As they ran the stiff-moving indentureds ignored them. Then a line of gray suits formed in front of them.

"Piotr, line of gray suits," Ruby gasped.

"*Rub the ring. Say activate invisibility protocol. Move out of the way.*"

To her surprise, it worked, though the gray suits moved lethargically, slowing them down.

"Stop!" Joseph yelled from behind them.

Gabe halted. "Get Pat out of here, *fast*. I'll run interference."

"Staying with you." Ruby said, as Kris and Justine hurried toward the back wall.

"Rubes—"

"*Two of us together,*" she said in a low voice. "Remember?"

"I'd spare you if I could," he said softly before they turned to face Joseph.

"I'm not of the mind to be spared or to spare anyone," she said sharply. "Much less *him*."

Gabe snorted, then chuckled softly. "That's my Ruby. God, I love you and I hope to hell we survive this."

"We will."

They turned to face Joseph. He stared at them, then started laughing.

"Well I'll be damned. That scanner *was* right and not malfunctioning when it tagged you two." His voice harshened. "Throw down your weapons."

"*You* throw down *yours*," Ruby said, projecting horse trainer voice as she rubbed the ring.

Joseph shook his head, hand quivering. "What the—"

"*You* throw down *yours*," Ruby repeated.

He threw it down but lunged at her. "You bitch, you can't completely override me!"

Gabe fired, hitting Joseph in the chest, then dove between Ruby and Joseph. Joseph staggered back with apparently no injury.

Oh shit, he's wearing body armor.

She raised her pistol, looking for an opening, *any* opening for a head shot.

Gabe and Joseph grappled with each other until Gabe yelped and collapsed to his knees, bending over his gut.

Joseph laughed uncontrollably as he repeatedly kicked Gabe, distracted from Ruby. "A damn good thing I carry weaponized G9 on me *just for you*, asshole!"

Now. She bit her lip, forcing her hands steady as she raised her pistol with both hands, aiming at Joseph's nose—*just like you did with Daddy all those years ago.* One. Blood and brains flew. Two. She started sobbing as memories flashed back, for the moment six years old again. But she kept shooting, hands steady, her muzzle following Joseph as he collapsed, wanting to *make sure.* Just like she had at six. Then she dropped her empty, useless weapon and ran to Gabe, curled up on the pavement.

His eyes were wide and terrified as he gasped for breath, shaking. She quickly swiped away tears so she could see.

"C'mon. Lean on me." She pulled on Gabe but it was hard to get him out of the fetal curl, his muscles convulsing. "Gabe. Come on."

He vomited, some of it getting on her. "I—Rubes—love—can't—bad enough—you're at risk—past vaccines no good—"

She smacked him before dragging him to his feet. "Don't you dare give up on me now, goddamn it! *Piotr! Get me some fucking help fast! Joseph hit Gabe with weaponized G9!*"

Gabe leaned heavily on her, body spasming. "Rubes. Go. Leave."

"I swore to stay with you for better or worse!" she screamed at him, tears half-choking her voice. "Don't fucking give up on me!" She wrapped both arms around his torso, crab-walking sideways as she forced him along.

Marching steps coming toward her from the *wrong fucking direction and they were fucked.*

Then Brandon was there. "Mom. I've got him. Dismiss those guards."

She stepped away from Gabe, frantically rubbing her ring. *"Go away. You don't see anything. GO AWAY."*

The gray suit guards stopped at Joseph's body but didn't raise their weapons.

One kicked Joseph's body out of its way before marching four steps ahead. "What are you doing with the one called Markey Two?"

"Fuck," Brandon breathed from behind her. "We're taking her out of here to freedom," he called.

The lead guard hesitated. "Do you have the release codes?"

"Yes," Piotr said. *"Tell them yes. Brandon needs to help you."*

"Yes," she said, her voice shaking. "Branny, I need your help."

"Him. The man with the sick one. You are the one called Brandon Martiniere?" the lead guard said.

Brandon dragged Gabe to stand by her. "Yes."

The guards exchanged glances—then dropped their weapons.

"*Here are the codes,*" Piotr said. "*Five-six-four. Release times—however many guards there are. Four-six-five, AgInnovation clear. Martiniere clear. Confirm nine-nine-one-zero. Tell Brandon.*"

She quickly repeated the codes to Brandon. Then she rubbed the ring and projected them in a clear voice, along with Brandon, as Gabe sank back to the ground.

"We are yours to command," the lead guard said.

"No, you aren't," Brandon said. "You are free. You are your own people now."

Ruby knelt and tried to drag Gabe back up, but his convulsions were too strong.

"I love you," she whispered to him, tears blurring her eyes. "I love you, I love you, I love you. Hold on, damn it."

Gray suited hands reached for him. She tried to bat them away.

"Mom. It's all right. They're carrying him. We have a physician's assistant amongst the guards." Brandon pulled her back as the guards gently lifted Gabe. He held her close as she shook with repressed sobs. She broke free of Brandon, grabbing Gabe's hand, and held on as best as she could. They ran for the opening in the wall where Justine stood grimly, her SPA7 cocked and ready. Then they were at the van, easing Gabe in. Ruby scrambled to join him, along with one guard.

"The rest of you go free the others," Brandon gasped. "Here. An override." He slammed something in the lead guard's hand, then pulled the doors of the van shut as they rocketed off.

"He has a med reaction going," the remaining guard said, voice now sounding masculine as the facial portion of his suit retreated to reveal a balding head and gray hair. He checked Gabe's pulse. "What's he on?"

"Full standard dose of Activate, half dose of Modulate," she said. Gabe grabbed frantically at her and she took his hands. "I'm here, hon, I'm here."

The guard shook his head. "That's bad. No idea of the dose of weaponized G9, I suppose."

"Whatever Joseph carried," she said.

Brandon knelt next to her. "I have G9Recover here. Prescribed for him after diagnosis. He doesn't respond well to a full dose but it's what I've got."

"It'll be something but he needs full support." The guard wiped his sweating forehead. "I'm only good for another fifteen minutes before this suit takes me down."

Brandon handed an injector pen to the guard. "Here it is."

He examined it. "That's good, but it isn't going to last. Not with a reaction like this. Nonstandard administration because that might just give us an edge until you can get real help." He jammed it into Gabe's neck. "Be prepared for a nasty reaction."

Gabe spasmed and screamed, eyes bulging wide as the van sped around a sharp corner, sending all of them sprawling. Ruby steadied him, against her will remembering his description of Rachel's death. He jerked and twitched, then puked again.

"Stay with me, damn it, Gabe, *stay with me damn it!*"

He gasped for breath. She felt his heart pounding, its beat slowing.

Nonononono.

His muscles relaxed.

"God damn it, don't you die on me Gabriel!" she shrieked, gasping through sobs.

His eyes fixed on her as he struggled for breath. She didn't dare look away from Gabe for fear he would slip away into death, vaguely aware that they had careened to a stop and the back doors of the van flung wide open. Masked and gowned people climbed in, someone demanding information from the gray suit now collapsed against the wheel well.

Someone else tried to pull her away from Gabe and she resisted.

Then Justine spoke in her ear. "It's all right, Ruby, we're at a safe medical facility. We're getting him the help he needs."

She reluctantly eased her grip but scrambled out after the medical crew, trying to hang onto his hand as they eased Gabe onto a gurney, fitting a mask to his face before running with him. Abruptly but kindly someone pried her hand away as he was pushed through double doors, leaving her shaking and gulping, tears wracking her body as she stared through the clear panels in the doors.

"It's okay, Ma, we're here, he's in the hands of the doctors now," Brandon said.

"I need to be with him," she wheezed.

Another masked and gowned person took her arm. "We need to check you for G9 exposure."

"He has post-G9 and was hit with a weaponized version."

"Have you been vaccinated?"

"Only for the standard. Not—this."

"Then you need to be checked. You're showing a reaction and you've been exposed to his bodily fluids."

"I'll come with you," Justine said. "I've been vaccinated for all variations," she said to the nurse? Doctor? Ruby wasn't sure.

"I know the protocols." Brandon said something else that Ruby didn't hear because she heard Gabe screaming her name. She strained toward the doors and Brandon restrained her. "Ma. You have to be checked. You've been exposed. Come on. They're doing what they can for him. You're not doing Dad any good by fighting. Let's get you checked out and boostered before you develop a full case. A weaponized version that triggers a reaction like this has live virus. Standard vax doesn't work against it."

"Branny?" Her voice wavered. "Are you safe?"

"I got the heavy-duty vaccine covering all variants when I was working for AgI," he said. "*You* need it now."

She let Justine and the medical person guide her to another room. Justine helped her out of the body mods and the vomit-covered, bloodstained clothing and into a gown.

"Whose blood is this?" she asked Ruby softly.

"I—I shot Joseph," she gulped. "After he injected Gabe, unfortunately."

"Is he—"

"*Yes*. I blew his fucking head apart. Multiple times." She started shaking uncontrollably, her body beginning to ache. "Oh God, I hurt."

"She's had the exposure," Justine said to the medical person coming into the room. "But some of it could be post-adrenaline shakes. Body ache as well."

"We'll hit her with the full dose."

Ruby didn't feel the injection into her arm. Her muscles relaxed and fuzziness crept over her. Then everything went black.

Gabe Gabe oh God Gabe, was her final clear thought.

CHAPTER 17

RUBY WOKE WITH A START TO THE SOUND OF MEDICAL EQUIPMENT—
not on her—and sat up, gasping and gazing around her wildly,
for a moment disoriented as memories of *Branny and me in the
hospital* ruled her thoughts.

Then adult Brandon was right there. "Mom. Mom. It's all
right. You and Dad are in the same room."

Her breathing steadied and she gulped as Brandon held her
shoulders while she oriented herself and memory returned.
Gabe. Pat's extraction gone bad. Shooting Joseph.

Oh, Gabe.

Justine joined Brandon. "It's okay, Ruby."

"Gabe," she gulped, trying to see past Brandon to the
other bed.

Brandon inhaled sharply. "Not out of the woods yet, Ma. It's
bad. Really bad."

"I want to see him." She wrestled with the bed rails. Why
was it so hard?

Brandon rolled his eyes at Justine. "Told you. I *still* hear
stories in Lakeside about how Mom kept crawling to my bedside
in the hospital, sicker than hell herself, until we were put in the
same space. Ma. Let us help you. You had a bad reaction to the
booster for this variant. The stuff Joseph hit Dad with was pretty

damn virulent. Even though you're got the all-version-vax booster, it's going to take time until you're back on your feet again."

She didn't answer, straining to see Gabe.

"Justine. It'll take both of us. She's not gonna rest until she sees him."

They lowered the rails—*finally*—and she nearly fell as she tried to climb out of the bed and her legs gave way. Justine on one side and Brandon on the other helped her stagger over to Gabe's bed. No ventilator, thank God, but oxygen cannula and lines from infusion bags—several—going into him. She fumbled with the bed rail keeping her from Gabe. If she could only touch him, stroke his forehead, lend him some of her strength….

"You hold her up, I'll lower the rail." Brandon's voice was resigned. "We'll have to keep her from climbing in with him."

The rail gave way and she leaned forward. He was cool. Clammy. No response, not even a recognizing twitch to her touch when she brushed a lock of hair off of his forehead.

"No," she groaned, breaking into tears. "Gabe. Don't do this to me. You hear me? Stay."

Justine and Brandon tried to pull her away as she tried to wriggle onto the bed with him.

"Ma, you can't. There's too much equipment." Brandon repeated it several times before she finally gave in.

"Get me a chair, then!" she snapped at them through her weeping, brushing her thumb across her ring.

They froze.

Then, "goddamned compulsion," Justine muttered. "Her commands are pretty strong even when she's physically weak. We've *got* to get her to Donna-gran for training soon."

But a chair was there, and she could sink into it, resting her now-aching head on the bed, both hands on Gabe's arm as she shook with body-wracking sobs, *willing* him to respond.

I'm here. I'm here love. Please don't leave me. Please stay. Please.

Her head throbbed worse than ever. More voices. Injection in her upper arm, followed by another darkness.

———

ANOTHER WAKING. RUBY FELT LIKE SOMEONE HAD BEATEN THE CRAP out of her. But as her eyes opened, she knew where she was this time and what had happened. She turned her head, noticing that her bed was now closer to Gabe's. She pushed herself up slowly, eyes fixed on him.

No change from that last blurry memory. No new medical equipment, but nothing had been removed either. Gabe lay on his back, eyes closed, face wan and tight, somehow smaller than he had been when they had awakened before this damned disaster.

Brandon joined her, lowering the bed rail so he could sit on the bed with her. "Mom." She swung her shaky legs off of the bed. He put an arm around her and she leaned into him.

"How long?" Her voice was creaky and unsteady.

"Twelve hours." He offered her a tube. "Suck this down. It'll help. Glucose and protein."

She obeyed, handing it back to him when it was empty. He dropped it into a trash bag hanging from her rail.

"His condition?"

"Unchanged." His voice was flat.

"Prognosis?"

"He's fighting it off but—uncertain how badly damaged he is at the moment. Waiting for him to wake to see if there's further issues. We've gotta move you two soon, too. Recordings of your shooting Joseph have hit social media, and Philip's in a rage. We need you in a safe place that isn't Philip's hometown. He wants you dead."

"The feeling is mutual." Inhale. Exhale. Pain receding. "Pat safe?"

"Justine is getting both her and Kris to a secure location." He shook his head. "For better or worse, the indentured revolution has begun. After we left that whole compound erupted. It wasn't quite what we thought it was. Which is another reason to get you two the fuck out of here. Joseph's death triggered a big info-dump about what he and Philip were up to there. *His* fail-safe in case Philip betrayed him. You don't have to fear prosecution—Remy got that covered for your sake—but Philip is now hard after you two through any other channel he can use."

Gabe winced. Ruby caught her breath. "Is he—"

"Probably." Brandon slid off her bed and lowered the rail of Gabe's bed. "You're still gonna be weak, so wait for me to support you before you try to get up. Be careful touching him because he's going to wake in godawful pain. Can't be helped until the docs can assess him. It's part of the G9 and he's in the worst possible flareup mode. But if he can see you at least...."

Brandon steadied her and punched the call button as they stood by Gabe's bed. Gabe's eyelids flickered slowly, finally opening as he groaned. Ruby caught her breath as she saw how dull his eyes were.

Like Granma at the end.

"Gabe," she choked.

He focused on her. "Rubes." Barely a whisper. He winced.

"I'm here." She tentatively reached out, hesitant in case she'd hurt him. One of his fingers reached out to wrap around her index finger as two of the medical staff entered.

He grunted in response to their questions. Silent tears ran down her cheeks as he cried out while they checked his reflexes. His hand twitched and seized hers tight, squeezing hard as the examination continued. Brandon stayed with Ruby, holding her up with an arm around her shoulders, squishing them almost as hard as Gabe was mashing her hand.

She didn't mind. She just kept her eyes focused on Gabe's pain-wracked face as he stared at her, silently lending her strength as best as she could.

At last they were done.

"Give us a moment," the one—doctor? She thought she was the doctor, hadn't Brandon and Justine told her that earlier? Ruby couldn't remember.

Brandon exhaled. "All right. Ma. Can you hold yourself up? Let me get you a chair."

She nodded, leaning on the bed, careful not to jar Gabe. "I'd kiss you but I'm afraid it would hurt," she said to him.

"Worth. It."

She leaned over and delicately brushed her lips across his forehead. He winced but momentarily smiled. She kissed his lips, and fancied that for a moment she saw the pain ease out of his facial muscles.

Brandon slid a chair against Ruby's legs and helped her down. Gabe turned his head to keep his eyes on her. She slid her other hand over his.

"So, here's the deal," Brandon said, leaning against Ruby's bed, arms crossed. "Mom, you'll be okay soon. You contracted a mild case of that weaponized G9 variant from Dad, but you've been given a booster that should cover all versions. You'll need several days of rest and another booster shot later, but other than that, you'll be all right."

"And your father?" She didn't turn her gaze from Gabe.

"We won't know for certain until Dr. Chan returns."

"Chan. Protocol?" Gabe asked.

"Yes. That Dr. Chan. Luckily, they have more treatment options than they did for G9 even a year ago, especially for secondary flares like this. They aren't optimal, but none of this shit is." Brandon paused. "Whatever Chan recommends, it has to accommodate relocation. We *have* to get you two out of LA and to a safer location. Philip will find you sooner or later, Mom."

"Why?" Gabe croaked.

"She killed Joseph after he injected you. Blew his head to pieces."

"Good. Girl." He squeezed her hand, panting slightly.

"Yeah. Well, it's causing issues. Piotr and Serg are locking down Moondance. That's the closest and best location for you, and the most optimal for recovery."

"Pat and Kris?" Ruby asked.

"Need-to-know until you're at Moondance."

Before she could say more, Dr. Chan returned, standing where all three of them could see her.

"All right. Gabriel. Can you understand me?"

"Yeah," he rasped. "Hurts. Bad."

"This is as about as bad a flare of the G9 as it can be. From the records your son got me, it's worse than your initial illness. Fortunately, we do have treatment options that weren't available then. The flip side is that they are risky for a man your age."

"Recovery?"

"We won't know for certain. Your numbers look good. The recommended treatment will bring you back to between fifty to seventy-five percent of your previous capacity post-illness."

"Numbers. Not. Acceptable." Gabe closed his eyes for a moment, breathing heavily. "Others? Riskier. But. Higher? Remember. Those."

"There *are* more risky treatments. But there is one that will get you to ninety-five percent of what you could do pre-first attack. The limitation is that we estimate it only works for five years. And it may leave you dead or more disabled than before when it wears off. If it succeeds."

"Percentage. Success."

The doctor's lips tightened. "Fifty-one percent success. Forty-nine percent death."

"Your. Protocol?"

"Yes."

"I'll. Take. Those. Odds." He inhaled deeply, wincing. "Fifty. To. Seventy—five. Post. Illness. Capacity. Not. Acceptable."

The doctor eyed Ruby and Brandon. "You're his next of kin."

"Whatever he wants," she whispered. "As long as I can be with him. Before or after transport?"

"We'll infuse the treatment, and then sedate him for transport." Chan frowned at them. "What sort of medical support will you have wherever you're going?"

"Whatever is needed," Brandon said. "Just get me a list of the requirements."

Dr. Chan nodded. "All right. We need time to prepare the treatment. You'll be able to move him in two hours." She entered something into her comp. "You should have those requirements now."

Dr. Chan moved to Ruby. "Let's take a look at you."

Ruby left one hand in Gabe's as Chan checked her over.

"Good," Dr. Chan said finally. "You responded well to the inoculation, and a few days rest will have you back in shape."

"Does this convey long term G9 immunity?" Ruby asked.

"After you get that booster in a few weeks. Restricted access, but since you've been exposed, that puts you on the highest priority list."

"Thanks."

The doctor left the room. Brandon sighed. "Two hours works perfectly. Justine's back in an hour and she'll have his permanent medical staff with her for the transfer." He signed off of his comp and stood up. "Ma. Justine brought your bags from the house. You can change now, unless you need assistance."

"I shouldn't need help."

She slipped into the bathroom and slowly changed. She was weak and tired, but it still felt good to get out of the hospital gown.

When she came out Dr. Chan was setting up a new infusion.

"Good. You're back," the doctor said. "The first few minutes are going to be painful for him until the sedation kicks in. Gabriel asked for you to be here."

Ruby nodded and set her chin firmly, sitting back in the chair. Gabe now lay on his side, facing her. She took his free hand in hers, waiting. He inhaled sharply as the infusion began, groaning and squeezing her hand, panting as beads of sweat rose on his forehead.

Then his eyelids fluttered. "Ruby," he whispered. "Love." His eyes shut.

She sat there holding his hand until the infusion was finished and all the lines were pulled.

IT WAS AFTER MIDNIGHT ONCE THEY WERE SETTLED IN AT Moondance. A Dr. Caruthers had shown up with Justine to supervise Gabe's transfer and fly with them. Gabe slept through the entire trip and the transfer to their bed in their Moondance room. Caruthers checked Gabe's vitals as she set up monitoring equipment, gave him another shot, and eyed the bed.

"Are you planning to sleep in that bed with him?" she asked Ruby.

"I'd hoped to."

"He a quiet sleeper or restless? I'm just concerned about the need for rails."

"If I'm with him he'll sleep quieter. I can watch him."

Caruthers nodded. "Figured as much. Well, I'll be in and out every couple of hours. Still getting nurse support in."

"Thank you."

"Thank your—sister-in-law, isn't that what Justine is to you? She's contracted my services indefinitely, has for some years now."

"Yes. All the same, thank you. When is he going to wake up?"

"I'm going to keep him under for a couple of days." She frowned. "Should have happened the first time he was sick, for optimal recovery. But it's hard to do the sort of monitoring required in the middle of a pandemic. It's different in this situation. The two of you are my only patients at the moment. With the indentured revolt happening my clinic is coming under too much scrutiny because of the—sort of things I've been doing for Justine. This is as good a place to hide out as any."

"You've been involved with her work, then," Ruby said. "Thank you."

"Yeah." Caruthers finally smiled. "But in case you're wondering, I was also on the ER front lines in Chicago during the G9 there. I know this little bugger pretty well, and the Chan Protocol—the treatment he had—was what I expressly trained to handle."

"Thanks." Ruby felt inadequate saying any more.

After Caruthers left, Ruby changed into pajamas and crawled into bed on the other side from all the equipment. She snuggled up to Gabe as best she could. Was it her imagination that he seemed to relax once she was next to him?

No, she decided. She wasn't imagining things.

FOR THE NEXT TWO DAYS, RUBY'S EVERY MOVE FELT LIKE SHE WAS forcing her way through thick mud all the way up to her neck. Normally she'd fight it, but now it gave her an excuse to curl up with Gabe and talk with Dr. Caruthers about what to expect.

But there was also work reviewing email and RubyBot data for both the Double R and Moondance, plus talking to Charlie and Tim about the situations at both ranches.

Brandon had disappeared after telling Ruby that the Swaits had Kris and Pat, and were guarding them.

Justine also was gone, doing God-knows-what. Ruby hadn't paid attention to outside news, not wanting the distraction in her worry about Gabe.

All parameters look good, Caruthers kept saying. *But keep in mind we won't know for sure what his status is until he wakes up. And I'm keeping him under as long as I dare to help him recover. Worst case...we'll lose him quickly.*

On the third day, Ruby muted all outside inputs as Caruthers started the process of weaning Gabe off of sedation. Ruby spent that day in bed next to Gabe, unable to concentrate even on the light fluff reading Charlie had brought the day before.

How disoriented he is when he wakes up will tell us what we have to deal with, was Caruthers's verdict. *Best case, he orients himself quickly and recognizes you. Won't know the physical impact for a few days after. But if he doesn't orient...it's bad. If they're still hallucinating when they wake up, they rarely come back and they die soon after. I'm worried because he was hallucinating during his original illness. Perhaps it was just the Martiniere mind control aftereffects, but —we won't know for sure until he wakes.*

Caruthers had taken up a station by the slider to the deck, doing her own work. Gabe's slightest twitch had them both jumping to check on him. But it was taking longer for him to wake than Caruthers had anticipated. At last Ruby settled for propping herself up on pillows, lying on her side, watching him, one hand resting on his chest.

At last Gabe's eyes flickered open. He glanced up at the ceiling, face crinkling in puzzlement. Her heart sank. Was he hallucinating? Then he relaxed and seemed to realize where he was. His hand came up and rested on Ruby's as he turned his head to look at her. That beloved slow smile spread across his face.

"Rubes," he whispered. "You're still here. I'd—hug you but I can't hardly move. So tired."

"Of course I'm still here," she breathed, hugging him close.

He had made it. He knew who she was. He was going to get better. He was *going to live.*

And for that simple small grace, she was grateful.

THE END

OUTTAKE: NEW BEGINNINGS

(Timeline—Outtake from mid-Ascendant. Gabe is waiting for Ruby to return from Chicago)

Gabe exhaled a big but shaky breath as his beloved Ruby signed off her comm after giving him an estimated arrival time for Justine's private jet at the Double R ranch airstrip. He texted the information to Rick down in the ranch labs, so that Rick knew his partner Beck was safely on the jet with Ruby and would be arriving tonight.

Now he could allow himself to react to everything he'd heard tonight.

"God damn it, I should have been there," he said out loud to his empty office once he sent that text. He slammed his right hand on the desk. "I should have been there!"

He groaned and buried his head in his hands, rubbing his face.

So close. So damned close.

The *what-ifs* whispered through Gabe's thoughts. Things could have gone much, much worse tonight than they had. So close. So damned close to tragedy instead of the mixed triumph it had turned out to be.

If Ruby hadn't pushed for Brandon and the others to leave

the Chicago condo tonight while she, Justine, and Serg went to the Real Truthers banquet, avoiding the firebombing by mere minutes. If Joseph wasn't such a goddamned incompetent idiot and didn't recognize how Ruby was different from Joseph's preferred, easily abused women.

Against his will he half-smiled at that thought. He wished he could have *seen* Ruby slug Joseph like she did, instead of just hearing it happen over that scratchy connection in her brooch wired for monitoring discussions around her.

And she'd stood up to his uncle—no. His *father*. Philip Martiniere. The biggest *what-if* of all. The worst of them—and learning this?

Philip was his father, not his uncle.

Philip is my father.

Gabe shuddered as memory evoked the painful tingles that flowed through the scars on his back. Scars left by a series of Philip's beatings during Gabe's teens and early twenties, after his parents and sister were killed in a plane crash, leaving Philip as his closest surviving relative.

Gabe shook his head. He shivered. That corrupt, vicious, evil man was closer kin than he had realized.

Philip is my fucking father.

Gabe raised his head from his hands.

Motherfucker knew it the whole damned time, too. He knew I was his goddamned son and treated me like that!

He slammed his hand on the desk again, harder than ever.

"Ouch!" He shook it to ease the sharpness but he had to admit it was a distraction from his racing thoughts.

Gabe exhaled again and got to his feet, heading for the kitchen. He had the house to himself until Ruby got back. He didn't need to lock himself up in his office to process this latest bit of news in silence. No one else was around to hear if he chose to rant and scream in frustration and worry about Ruby's safety —*I should be there with her!*

And right now he needed a good stiff drink to take the edge

off of his jangled nerves.

Gabe didn't bother to flip the kitchen light switch. The big outside security light cast sufficient illumination through the windows and he knew the layout well enough that he could make his way to the cabinet that held the shot glasses and the jar with homebrew. Made by Ruby's lab manager Martin, from grains grown here on her ranch. He poured himself a generous shot, then replaced the jar on the shelf. One drink was enough for tonight. This situation demanded a clear head, not drinking himself into oblivion, much as this news made him want to do the latter.

He leaned against one of the counters, staring outside.

"Comp. Play Preacher mix," he said aloud. As the first strains of Willie Nelson singing "Time of the Preacher" began, he sipped from the glass.

Fuck. Philip's my father, not my uncle. I'm the son of that son of a bitch. Fucking goddamn hell.

Deep inside himself, pieces fell into place. When his grandmother had told Ruby that Philip was his father, all of a sudden disparate parts of his life made sense.

Not that it mattered, or that it would change anything. But it was satisfying to know how everything fit together.

He took another sip, studying the shadows outside.

So does this really change things?

He still hated Philip's guts, and there was no doubt by now that the feeling was mutual.

He was determined to depose Philip from the leadership not only of the Family but of the Martiniere Group. Did this change anything about the process?

Only my own commitment to do it.

Gabe shuddered. *Could* he effectively fight Philip? Thirty years ago he'd chosen to run. He'd testified against his unc—no, *father.* And he knew damned good and well the depths to which Philip's vengeance could descend—hell, he bore the marks of Philip's wrath on his back.

Twenty-one years ago, when he feared that Philip's vengeance would extend to his then-wife and son, he'd run again. Nearly killed himself more than once, when the pain of what he'd done to Ruby and Brandon in the divorce became too much.

His lips tightened.

Philip had won those two encounters.

Third time's the charm, father mine. I'm no longer a fucking scared kid you can bully.

And Donna-gran—god. He loved his grandmother, he really did, but why the fuck had she kept this information to herself all these years? Surely, with her silky silvery manipulation of language, she could have let him know the truth about his heritage before now. Before he'd run that first damned time. Back when he thought his only family allies were his cousins Serg Vygotsky and Justine, with Donna-gran down sick.

Justine. His back prickled again. Not his cousin but his sister. God. But that little piece felt right. He wished he'd known this sooner.

"All the same, it made everything worthwhile to get her free from our sonofabitching father," he said out loud, taking a bigger gulp of his drink. Breaking up Philip's plan to marry her off to that sleazy fucker Walter Braun, helping her elope with Donald Atwood. Beatings that had damned near killed him. And even though he was twenty-four when the last beating had happened, he'd not filed charges. Hadn't dared entertain any thoughts of vengeance or freedom from Philip's grasp until the Feds approached him to testify against the Martiniere Group.

Now he wondered if Philip had even worse notions toward Justine than he realized. Or was she truly Philip's daughter?

Don't go there, Gabriel. Just—don't.

Things were bad enough as it were. And he didn't think that Philip's late wife Renate had the guts to seek consolation elsewhere.

But now he had Justine's firm support. Serg. Donna-gran.

Brandon—Branny—Bran. His son that was more like him than either man wanted to admit. That kid was one thing he and Ruby had done right, in spite of animosity and divorce. Bran and his love, Kris, out there doing their damnedest to brew an indentured revolution, using an approach Gabe wouldn't have thought of himself. Dismantling the structures that supported Philip's twisted indenture programs.

However, taking down Philip himself wasn't Bran's job. It had to be his. Gabriel's. The unacknowledged, poorly regarded son.

And Ruby's.

Now he dared let himself think about Ruby, swigging the very last of his drink and placing the glass firmly on the counter. He gulped, rubbing his face.

Oh God, Ruby. I can't do this without you. And when you're in danger….

Her getting into a fight with Joseph was bad enough. But then when Philip tried to buy her off, then threatened her….

His brave, beautiful redheaded Ruby. Horsewoman. Rodeo queen. Inventor. Rancher. Unafraid of facing up to *Philip fucking Martiniere* and telling him to go to hell. Worthy of winning Donna-gran's approval on first meeting, hell, earning Donna-gran's *blessing*. The only woman he'd ever really loved, even more than his dead second wife Rachel. God, he'd fucked things up so bad in the divorce. In the seven months since he and Ruby had reconciled, he'd gone out of his way to try to make it up to her. If he ever could.

But she'd said *I love you* back to him tonight before ending the comm. That she wanted to talk. He'd promised not to propose remarriage again until she was ready.

Did this mean she was ready to say yes? Oh God, he surely hoped so.

"I swear, I'll do anything to win that woman back," he said aloud, hobbling across the floor. His bad leg hurt tonight, but damn it, he didn't care. "You hear me, God and anyone else who gives a shit? I love Ruby Barkley and *I'll do anything to get her back.*" He shook a defiant fist in the air as he shouted. "Fucking Philip. If you touch one hair on her head…." He choked at that thought.

They were in the air. They were on the way here. They were safe—weren't they? Philip didn't have the capacity to knock them out of the air here in the United States, right? In spite of what had happened with his parents—Justine kept security around her three jets active at all times, to prevent the type of sabotage that had killed his parents.

But Justine's condo in Chicago was also supposed to be safe. And now it was in flames.

Gabe eyed the cabinet again.

No.

Checked the time. They were still a half hour out. A half hour until he could hold Ruby in his arms again.

Just a half hour.

And then—maybe he could convince Ruby to try marriage once more. A new beginning for both of them.

"Please," he whispered, leaning against the kitchen counter again, resting his head in his hands. "Please. Whoever. Please just keep her safe. Please."

At last he raised his head. "Double R security," he said to his comm.

"*Yes, Gabe?*" A projection of David, head of this shift, shimmered in the darkness.

"I know it's early, but I'm ready to take a crawler down to the airstrip."

"*Be right there.*"

"I'll be waiting."

At least he could stand in the cool summer night. Gabe rubbed his face, then headed out the back door to wait for the crawler's arrival.

Stay safe, Ruby my love. Stay safe. Please.

Like what you've read? Want to follow Joyce either through her monthly newsletter or through an email feed of her irregular blog posts?

Sign up for Joyce's newsletter here:

https://tinyletter.com/JoyceReynolds-Ward

Sign up for blog posts through Substack here:

https://joycereynoldsward.substack.com/welcome

Interested in further serial stories in the Martiniere Multiverse? Check out Martiniere Stories on Substack.

https://joycef1d.substack.com/p/an-introduction-to-martiniere-stories

ACKNOWLEDGMENTS AND AFTERNOTES

Acknowledgments

Once again I want to thank my friend, mentor, and marvelous editor, Phyllis Irene Radford.

Tim Landerking, hairstylist and colorist extraordinare, for his advice on styling Ruby's hair for the Real Truthers' banquet.

As always, my beloved husband Lew for his support, and the ever-opinionated Miss Olena Chic (Mocha) for her equine support.

Afternotes, Influences, and Music

Unlike *Inheritance,* this book was written in the depths of the initial Covid-19 spread and the beginnings of the Black Lives Matter protests. Again, I didn't incorporate a lot of elements from what was happening in the spring of 2020, simply because we just don't know what the long-term impacts will be.

However, in this book I start poking at the potential political divisions that may be rising out of this era. We see a little bit more of that in *Realization,* but, essentially, here in August 2020, I see the likelihood of a four-way split in the major US political parties. Here we see more of the Real Truthers (the Reals), which is a quasi-offshoot of the most extreme elements of the 2020 Republican Party. Their equivalent is the New Democrats (New

Dems), which isn't quite as extreme as some of the far left wing of the Democratic Party in 2020—but I postulate that those elements spin off completely into some sort of more explicitly Socialist party that I'm just not getting into.

The centrist parties are the Honest Republicans and the Classic Democrats.

Am I fudging things a little bit? Of course. But it's the world I created. And as someone with an undergraduate degree in Political Science (and a focus on electoral politics) plus about twenty years of experience working on low-level campaigns and as a Democratic precinct committeewoman (as well as a participant in the state governing body), I have a little bit of experience with the political process.

Musical influences:

"Delicate Sound of Thunder" concert, performed by Pink Floyd

A Valid Path album, recorded by The Alan Parsons Project

"Time of the Preacher," "Blue Eyes Crying in the Rain," "Mammas Don't Let Your Babies Grow Up To Be Cowboys," and "My Heroes Have Always Been Cowboys" as recorded by Willie Nelson. I had that last song on constant repeat when writing the confrontation between Gabe and Joseph and subsequent events. In a lot of ways it's Gabe's theme song.

BOOKS AND PUBLICATIONS

The Martiniere Legacy

First Meetings: A Martiniere Legacy Short Story
Inheritance: The Martiniere Legacy Book One
Ascendant: The Martiniere Legacy Book Two
Realization: The Martiniere Legacy Book Three
A Belated Christmas Honeymoon: A Martiniere Legacy Short Story
The Enduring Legacy: The Martiniere Legacy Book Four

People of the Martiniere Legacy

The Heritage of Michael Martiniere: A Martiniere Legacy Novel
Broken Angel: The Lost Years of Gabriel Martiniere: A Martiniere Legacy Novel
Justine Fixes Everything: Reflections on Mortality

The Martiniere Multiverse

A Different Life: What If?
A Different Life: Now. Always. Forever.

Goddess's Honor titles currently available (chronological order):

The Goddess's Choice: A Goddess's Honor Short Story
Beyond Honor: A Goddess's Honor Novella

Exile's Honor: A Goddess's Honor Novelette
Birth of Sorrow: A Goddess's Honor Short Story
Pledges of Honor: Goddess's Honor Book One
Return to Wickmasa: A Goddess's Honor Short Story
Crown Anniversary: A Goddess's Honor Short Story
Challenges of Honor: Goddess's Honor Book Two
Cleaning House: A Goddess's Honor Outtake Story
Unexpected Alliances: A Goddess's Honor Rough Draft Outtake Story
Choices of Honor: Goddess's Honor Book Three
Judgment of Honor: Goddess's Honor Book Four

Netwalk Sequence Author Preferred 2022 Editions
Life in the Shadows: Book One
Netwalk: Book Two
Netwalker Uprising: Book Three
Netwalk's Children: Book Four
Learning in Space: Book Five
Netwalking Space: Book Six (**Release Date August 2022**)

Bright Star Fair Witches
Becoming Solo: A Bright Star Fair Witches Novella

Non-Series Titles currently available:
Alien Savvy: A Western SF Novella
Klone's Stronghold
Beating the Apocalypse
Bearing Witness
Becoming Solo

Vella Titles:
Falcon of the Martinieres (**part of** *Justine Fixes Everything*)
Bearing Witness
Beating the Apocalypse

A Different Life—What If? An Alternative Martiniere Legacy Novel

Becoming Solo

A Different Life—Linda's Story: An Alternative Martiniere Legacy Novel

Federation Cowboy

Audiobooks Available:

Alien Savvy: A Western SF Novella

Released from other publishers:

"Queen of the Snows," in *Once Upon A Winter: A Folk and Fairy Tale Anthology*, edited by H. L. Macfarlane

"My Man Left Me, My Dog Hates Me, and There Goes My Truck," in *Black-Eyed Peas on New Year's Day: An Anthology of Hope*, edited by Shannon Page

"Lost Loves," in *All Worlds Wayfarer*

"The Wisdom of Robins," in *Whimsical Beasts: A Campcon Anthology*, edited by Joyce Reynolds-Ward

"The Cow at the End of the World," in *Well...It's Your Cow*, edited by Frog Jones

"To Plant or Pull Up Stakes," in *Pulling Up Stakes: A Campcon Anthology*, edited by Joyce Reynolds-Ward

"The Notice," in *Children of a Different Sky*, edited by Alma Alexander

ABOUT THE AUTHOR

Joyce Reynolds-Ward has been called "the best writer I've never heard of" by one reviewer. Her work includes themes of high-stakes family and political conflict, digital sentience, personal agency and control, realistic strong women, and (whenever possible) horses. She is the author of *The Netwalk Sequence* series, the *Goddess's Honor* series, and the recently released *The Martiniere Legacy* series as well as standalones *Klone's Stronghold*, *Alien Savvy*, and *Beating the Apocalypse*. Samples of her Martiniere short stories/novel in progress and her nonfiction can be found on Substack at either Speculations from the Wide Open Spaces (general, writing) or Martiniere Stories (fiction). Joyce is a Self-Published Fantasy BlogOff Semifinalist, a Writers of the Future SemiFinalist, and an Anthology Builder Finalist. She is the Secretary of the Northwest Independent Writers Association, a member of the Science Fiction and Fantasy Writers Association, and a member of Soroptimists International.

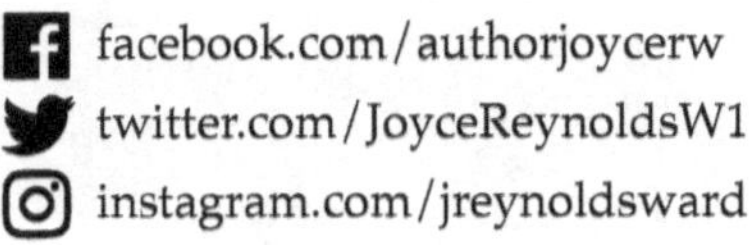